CHALLENGED

She was thirty-eight years old with an MBA
from the University of Chicago—the youngest
woman ever made an executive officer with a
corporation the size of TIE. She was articulate,
extremely competent, and gorgeous. If she
couldn't quite walk on water, it certainly
wouldn't get much above her ankles.

Somehow he doubted that his usual lines would
work on Miss Jaylene Sable . . .

Other Avon Books by
Andrea Edwards

NOW COMES THE SPRING
POWER PLAY

All Too Soon

Andrea Edwards

AVON
PUBLISHERS OF BARD, CAMELOT, DISCUS AND FLARE BOOKS

AVON BOOKS
A division of
The Hearst Corporation
1790 Broadway
New York, New York 10019

Copyright © 1985 by EAN Associates
Published by arrangement with the author
Library of Congress Catalog Card Number: 84-91208
ISBN: 0-380-89512-9

First Avon Printing, January, 1985

Printed in the U. S. A.

WFH 10 9 8 7 6 5 4 3 2 1

In loving memory of
Jane Howden Mikita,
mother and mother-in-law,
to whom loving and being
loved was the greatest success.

All Too Soon

Chapter One

Jaylene's Porsche sped along the highway, bypassing downtown Miami. It wasn't even seven A.M., but the August air coming in the window next to her was already hot and sultry. She could have turned the air conditioner on, but she liked the feel of the wind whipping through her shoulder-length brown hair. Her cheeks were glowing and her heart raced with excitement as she drove on.

She had always loved these early morning drives, but they were even better since she had gotten her new car last week. Anticipation of the day ahead kindled a blaze of freedom, power, and joy in her. Rested and refreshed, she used the time to savor the pleasures awaiting her like a gourmet about to sample a fine wine or a lover about to embrace her beloved. There were worlds ahead of her to be conquered.

Moving slightly, she felt the sumptuous leather of the car seat against her leg and smiled with satisfaction. She was thirty-eight years old and had everything anybody could ever want—certainly all that she had ever dreamed of, and more, from the silk lingerie that covered her slender body to the gorgeous machine she was driving to the fabulous condominium overlooking Biscayne Bay. And these were only the bonuses, the exterior proofs to the world that she had won.

Jaylene slowed her car and turned into a drive, stopping at the gate. Beyond it lay the offices of Trans-International Enterprises' Latin American subsidiary and her real home.

1

"Morning, Miss Sable," the guard said with a nod. He turned and beckoned another younger uniformed guard over. "This here is Bob, ma'am. He'll be escorting you to your building."

Jaylene stared at him. "But my building is right over there."

The older man just shrugged. "New security procedures, Miss Sable. All female executive officers are to be escorted until they are secured in the building proper. There's been some tension in the area."

All female executive officers. That was an interesting way of putting it, but it really only amounted to one: her. Sometimes TIE security was worse than a mother hen.

Bob spoke up. "All I have to do is walk you to the door, Miss Sable."

Jaylene reached over and unlocked the passenger door, letting the guard in. She knew what all this fuss was about. It had started when she had returned from that business trip to Brazil two weeks ago—since the publication of that photograph in the *Miami Examiner*, to be exact.

"Local Exec Charms Cuban Ambassador," the headline had read. Damaging enough, perhaps, but not as bad as the accompanying picture that had shown her smiling up at the Cuban ambassador to Brazil as they danced at a reception in São Paulo.

The paper had not been interested in her claims that it was merely a diplomatic social function and that she could not ignore another guest. No, they were only interested in telling the population of Miami, which included a large number of Cuban émigrés, how an executive vice president of TIE, Inc., had carried on, making their story as controversial as possible. The result had been a number of angry letters to TIE's Miami offices. Security was convinced that half of the population of the city now knew her face and was lying in wait for her.

The security gate was raised, and Jaylene drove to her parking space. The guard rode in silence and then walked her to the lobby of her office building in the complex.

He opened the door for her and murmured, "Have a good day, Miss Sable."

She nodded and presented her ID to another guard just inside the building. Sometimes TIE went overboard on security, she thought, but she didn't really mind. It was all part of the way TIE watched over her, and she had to admit TIE was usually a comforting presence. She certainly returned its loyalty with equal intensity.

There was nothing she wouldn't do for TIE, Jaylene thought as she rode the elevator to the third-floor executive offices. She and the company had what amounted to an ideal marriage: two partners equally devoted to the relationship and to each other. Maybe that was why she never wanted anyone else in her life. She already had perfection; there was no way things could be any better.

She stepped out of the elevator into the plush executive quarters. At seven in the morning the area was still quiet and peaceful. This was her most productive time of the day, before the majority of employees arrived and all the frenetic activity started.

She turned the corner and saw Rita Kastle, her assigned administrative assistant, sitting at her desk. Rita, a woman in her late forties whose attitudes were as outdated as her stiffly lacquered platinum-blond hair, was an adequate worker, but Jaylene would have preferred she did her adequate work for someone else. She had been with TIE for almost thirty years though, so it wasn't all that easy to accomplish.

"Good morning, Rita."

The woman's head snapped up, a tight expression on her face and a slight whine in her voice. "Oh, Miss Sable. I'm so glad you're finally here."

"What's the emergency today?" Jaylene asked as she went on into her office. Rita followed.

"Mr. Margolis has been trying to reach you."

"This morning?" Since it was around four A.M. in L.A., that seemed unbelievable.

Rita hesitated before speaking. "Well, not this morning but he called a number of times late yesterday while you were in those meetings. He's very upset about your proposal for that electronics plant in Barbados. He says TIE's electronic plants are part of his subsidiary, not yours."

That sounded like Dave, slightly irrational but always possessive of what he defined as his territory. "Anything else?"

"Mr. Whitmore's plans have changed slightly, and he will only be in town for a few hours, so your meeting will be near the airport. The car will pick you up about nine."

"Fine." Actually it wasn't. That extra time traveling to and from the meeting would have to be made up at the end of her day, but there was nothing she could do about it. Jesse Whitmore was the corporate president of TIE and she was only an executive VP in one of their subsidiaries. If either of them had to lose time, she guessed it had to be her. But it might not be altogether bad that they were meeting away from the offices. She had some delicate personnel issues to discuss and didn't want to be overheard.

"I don't know why they have to change things at the last minute," Rita said with sudden force. "I had to cancel the conference room, and Pierre is upset because Mr. Whitmore isn't eating lunch here. And—"

"Did you get us a room at the airport hotel?" Jaylene interrupted.

"Yes." Rita hesitated. "Can I write a note of apology to Pierre over your signature?" She must have clearly read the look of irritation on Jaylene's face, for she went on, "He is one of the better chefs in the area, and it wouldn't do to anger him."

If Rita had her way, TIE would be sending notes of apology to everyone in the corporation. Hadn't Rita noticed that TIE was no longer the small family business it had been when she was first hired years ago?

Jaylene sighed. It wasn't worth arguing about. Rita was already on the agenda of issues to discuss with Jesse. With any luck, she'd have Rita transferred to another position far away from this office by the end of the week.

"Do what you think best," she said, and pulled over some papers as she sat at her desk. "Just put it in my signature book."

Rita did not move. "You know, Miss Sable, it would be a lot easier if you just let me sign things for you. I always did that for Mr. Corbin."

Yes, and look at the mess I inherited when I took over from him last year, Jaylene thought. "He was free to do things as he wanted, but I prefer seeing what has my signature on it."

"Very well." Rita's voice was cold and hard, the full skirt of her pink shirt-waist dress swished disapprovingly as she left the office.

Jaylene allowed herself a frustrated sigh before she turned back to her work. Rita was a serious distraction, and although Jaylene's irritation with her was less a few hours later when she left the compound for her meeting with Jesse, she was still determined to move her. There were too many little things that Rita could not—or would not—handle on her own. Jaylene's efficiency would increase with a better AA, and that would benefit TIE. Jesse ought to be able to see that even if Frank Kareau couldn't.

As president of TIE's Latin American subsidiary and her actual boss, Frank should have been the one to go to, but he always steered clear of anything that could possibly get sticky. Especially sticky and political. And for some strange reason, that was what this whole issue of Rita Kastle seemed to be.

When it came time to broach the subject with Jesse, Jaylene remembered Frank's reluctance to get involved. Would that be the case with Jesse?

In the airport hotel's conference room, Jaylene glanced across the table at him. He was a big man, in his late fifties, who always looked as if he would be more at home in a Stetson and cowboy boots than in his pin-striped suit. That was just an image he chose to give, though, for although he did own a ranch in Texas, he and his family lived in Connecticut, and there were no cowchips clinging to his boots. He was as sharp a businessman as she had ever met, and TIE's efficiency would always come first with him.

"I want to remove Rita Kastle," she told him bluntly.

Jesse put his hand up to rub his chin. She recognized the gesture and clenched her jaw. She had been wrong; he was not going to support her.

"You want to fire her?" he asked.

"Not necessarily. I just don't want her as my administrative assistant."

He continued rubbing his chin. "Will Kareau take her?"

"Frank doesn't want her within a hundred feet of him." Kareau wasn't dumb. He didn't want to get involved in the situation in any way. What hold did that woman have over everyone? Jaylene wondered—again.

"Why don't you just give her something else?"

"Like what?" Jaylene asked impatiently. "I can't promote her. You sent me down here to clean up this operation, and I'm already hacking a lot of people who are more competent than Rita. I can't justify putting her in their place."

Jesse shook his head. "She's just a small fish, Jaylene. I'd rather not bother with her. Use the salami technique on her."

That's what she had been doing, slicing away little sections of Rita's responsibilities, but it would take a long time to get down to almost nothing—and hurt her own productivity in the meantime.

"She's a longtime employee," Jesse went on. "TIE likes to reward loyalty."

"What about the people we've already let go? And there are going to be a lot more. Why is she special?" Jaylene decided to risk the pointed question.

"She's not special. She's not important at all, and I don't know why you've zeroed in on her." Jesse's voice grew coldly accusing. "When I sent you down here last year, I thought you were just the one to clear out all the deadwood and bring this subsidiary's profits up where they belong. That doesn't mean getting rid of one AA, it means turning this place completely around. Looks to me like that's been going a little slow. What's happened? Have you lost your touch?"

That stung. "Hardly. I've only been here nine months," she pointed out defensively. "In that time I've closed three plants and relocated them in less costly areas. The staff has been trimmed by almost a hundred, and I expect to cull out another two hundred by the end of the year."

"Why that long?" He pulled a cigar from his pocket and carefully lit it.

"Personnel needs more time to develop a computer program to tell us who should go. We want to keep the tigers and worker bees without disturbing TIE's existing profile," she said. "We want to maintain TIE's present distribution of minorities and minimize our total labor cost, even taking into account severance pay and early retirement."

"Sounds good," Jesse admitted, then laughed slightly. "And here I thought you were getting soft."

"Hardly," she answered with a smile, aware that Jesse had deliberately made her angry. He couldn't really have thought she'd let herself get distracted from TIE's goals. He was the one who had recognized her determination years ago and had brought her along with him in his rise to the top. "So, what's the status of my proposal for an electronics plant in Barbados?"

"The board approved it."

"That was quick." She was surprised.

"There wasn't anything else they could do. You got us a terrific deal. Who wouldn't jump at such an opportunity?"

"Margolis was irritated with me for proposing the plant. Now he's going to be furious."

"Dave's got nothing to say about it, any more than you've got a say in his Far Eastern subsidiary." His voice was curt, and he picked up some papers, indicating that the subject was closed. Trouble was, she still had more to say on it.

"I know that," she said. "But apparently he doesn't. I've already been getting flak from him because the rest of TIE's electronics manufacturing is done in the East."

Jesse shrugged impatiently. "He'll get over it. Dave's a competitor, but he's also a professional. When the whistle blows, he just gets ready for the next play."

"Actually, he does have a point," Jaylene admitted. "Not that I think we shouldn't take advantage of this offer, but the two foreign subsidiaries do overlap in a lot of ways. We have the same kinds of plants and compete for

the same markets, and that doesn't make good business
sense."

Jesse took his cigar out of his mouth and smiled tightly.
"I read your memo on that subject, Jaylene. It was very interesting, and the corporate staff will give the whole subject a serious look-see."

Jaylene blinked rapidly. That was just like Jesse. She
didn't know whether he was pleased or irritated with her
memo detailing the areas where TIE's two subsidiaries
overlapped.

Looking at his watch, Jesse bounced from his seat
abruptly. "It's almost time for my plane," he said. "And
time you got back to earning all that money I'm throwing
at you."

Jesse picked up his briefcase and they walked down the
stairs and across the lobby. When they left the building,
a black limousine pulled up. The uniformed chauffeur
jumped out and held the door open.

"Frank must have sent his car back for me," Jaylene
murmured with surprise. It wasn't like him to be so
thoughtful.

"Oh, didn't I tell you?" Jesse had a grin on his face.
"This little baby's yours now."

"Mine?" Jaylene scarcely dared to breathe as she looked
at the elegant interior: leather seats, a bar with a stereo,
and even a phone. She tingled with excitement. This was
no ordinary gift TIE was giving her. Besides proving its devotion by surrounding her with more luxury, it meant
that, politically, she was now Kareau's equal. She had
reached another plateau.

"The chauffeur is fully trained in executive protection
techniques," Jesse pointed out.

She frowned at him.

"We got a few letters at corporate about you making
eyes at that Cuban ambassador on your last trip to Brazil.
Security has decided you need some bodyguards."

"Bodyguards?" she protested. "You mean besides the
chauffeur?"

Jesse nodded, his cigar in the corner of his mouth.

"Somebody to accompany you places and somebody at your home."

"But that's ridiculous!"

"TIE has to take care of its assets."

She smiled grimly and climbed into her limousine. That was almost what she had been thinking.

"You're getting to be pretty expensive, Jaylene. Let's see some real work from you instead of wasting time, tooling around Miami in your little Porsche." He closed the door on her protest, and the chauffeur moved the car into traffic.

Jaylene hurried down the hall toward her office. She had gone straight from her meeting with Jesse into one with personnel, and had missed her lunch again. She'd have to have Rita run down to the lunchroom and get her a salad. Her stomach protested slightly. She was hungry today; maybe a sandwich instead. She thought she had a little bit of free time now. She could read a staff report while she ate.

"Oh, Miss Sable," Rita said, stopping her before she entered her office. "Security requested a meeting with you as soon as possible, and I told them to come right up. They're in there waiting for you."

"Now?"

Rita nodded.

There went her peaceful lunch. She opened the door and found three men waiting in her office. The tall, red-haired one was Larry Bowler, vice president and chief counsel for her subsidiary, and she recognized the elegantly dressed Stuart Cavendish, TIE's corporate chief counsel. She did not know the other man.

"Gentlemen." Jaylene nodded and closed the door behind her.

"Hello, Jaylene," Larry responded. He introduced Stuart Cavendish and then the third man, Lou Hawks, the corporate director of security.

She had heard of Mr. Hawks, but she shivered slightly at the sight of him. His flat white face seemed to emphasize the lack of warmth in his blue eyes.

Jaylene forced herself to exchange greetings and then indicated the informal sitting area in the corner of her office. "Would any of you like some coffee?"

"No, thanks," Larry replied. "We just came from lunch."

"Must be nice," Jaylene joked. "Some of us peons don't have that luxury."

The men, except for Mr. Hawks, laughed with her. Then there was an awkward moment of silence as they sat down.

Larry cleared his throat. "Lou wants to cover some items with you, Jaylene."

"I know. I was escorted to the door this morning and met my chauffeur a little while ago." Jaylene laughed a little. "Jesse told me that I'm also getting someone to accompany me to work, and someone to stay in my home."

"That's all fairly routine." Hawks lit a cigarette, then took a deep drag, letting the smoke out slowly. "Actually, we came to discuss another matter with you."

Jaylene looked from one face to the other. Cavendish and Larry seemed uncomfortable, but Hawks's face stayed unchanged.

"You have a very close relationship with a Mr. Ken Bishof, don't you, Miss Sable?"

His question took her by surprise. What business was it of his? She looked into his icy blue eyes, but found no answer there.

"I know him," she admitted cautiously, her irritation growing. Surely TIE did not expect her to take a vow of chastity. "Ken and I are friends. Close friends. Why?"

"You're going to have to sever that relationship," Hawks informed her.

Jaylene's first reaction was anger. This man had no right to order her about.

"I apologize for Mr. Hawks's abrupt manner, Miss Sable," Stuart Cavendish interjected quickly. "He need not have put it so bluntly, but, unfortunately, the facts remain the same. It would be in your best interest to terminate that relationship."

She looked coldly from one man to another, angry and confused. The whole conversation was incredible. "I would like some sort of explanation for this intrusion into my personal life."

"Yes, of course," Mr. Cavendish agreed quickly. "Mr. Bishof is an attorney with a successful practice among the local Cuban population."

"I'm aware of that." She had been dating the man for six months now. How could she not know that?

Cavendish continued, "Mr. Bishof also has political ambitions in this state."

"I know that, too."

He raised his hand, asking her to let him continue. "Because of these ambitions, Mr. Bishof is courting all elements of Miami's society, and we know he has recently met with members of an extremist organization known as the Sons of Cuban Liberty."

Jaylene just shook her head. She had never heard of the group. What did it have to do with her and Ken?

"It's one of those little militia groups training in the backwaters of Florida for an invasion of Cuba," Hawks explained. "But they've also been very busy sending you nasty letters."

Jaylene blinked uncertainly. "I don't even recall the name."

"Our security people trap that kind of stuff before it gets to you," Larry replied.

"Oh." She suddenly realized that she could count on one hand the number of letters that she had received unopened in the last six months. How many threatening letters had there actually been? Her hands felt cold, and she clenched them tightly in her lap.

"I'm sure that Mr. Bishof had nothing to do with those letters," Cavendish assured her, although the thought had never crossed her mind. "But he is associating with an extremely controversial political organization, and so TIE would prefer it if you were not associating with him."

"I see," she said carefully, not certain what to say. She knew of Ken's political ambitions, but had never thought much about them one way or another. It had been foolish of her not to. She had TIE's image to uphold, and apparently she had not been doing that very well. It irritated her that she had to be told something she should have seen for herself. After all, who was more important to her: TIE or Ken? TIE won hands down.

She and Ken had had a nice, pleasant relationship, and that was all. He had been a proper date for those occasions when she had to have one, but there was never anything more involved. For either of them. Oh, he sometimes spent the night, and they had gone away for a few weekends, but he wasn't her Prince Charming, just someone to talk to. Successful executives don't cultivate close friendships within the corporation, certainly not successful female executives. So she had relied on Ken for a little bit of laughter and relaxation, but she could send him on his way without tears now. If he was a threat to TIE, he was expendable.

"We really think it would be best if you two did not see each other for a while. Surely you can see that," Mr. Cavendish said gently, apparently thinking her silence indicated pain.

Jaylene looked up and quickly nodded her head. "Of course, you're right," she assured them. She'd find a way to fill the hours that Ken used to occupy. Lord knows, she had enough work to do that she could devote twenty-four hours of each day to TIE. She rose to her feet.

"Is there anything else?" she asked.

The men stood up also.

"We know that you just recently bought a Porsche," Hawks said. "With the increased security, you won't get much use out of it. TIE is willing to buy it from you for the full price you paid."

Her beautiful little car! The anger that hadn't come over Ken came now. She didn't care who Hawks thought he was, but she was not giving up her car. "I appreciate the offer, but I think I'll keep it for the time being. Now, if that's all, I have work to attend to."

Hawks nodded, but extended his hand. "Glad you were so reasonable about all this. A lot of women would have been kicking and screaming. You can be sure it will be noted in your file."

Jaylene shook his hand for the briefest possible moment,

but said nothing as the men left the room. Once she was alone, she slowly exhaled, willing her anger to disappear. They were right about Ken, and what's more, she should have seen it herself. They were probably right about the car, too. She wouldn't get much use out of it, and the offer to buy it had been generous. How were they to know how much she loved it?

She glanced around her spacious office, feeling drained. It was a big, expensively furnished room, one of the largest in the compound, yet it suddenly seemed close and confining. A picture of herself in the Porsche flashed through her mind. Racing up the coastal highway with the top down, the wind in her hair and freedom in her blood . . .

A knock at her door made the image disappear, and Rita came in with some folders. "Miss Sable, Mr. Kareau had to fly to Caracas unexpectedly, and he asked that you attend the employee picnic Sunday in his place."

"Fine." Jaylene ignored the sinking of her stomach and took the folders from Rita, immediately paging through them. What had she been thinking of—the wind in her hair and freedom in her blood? It sounded like some overly sentimental advertisement. She had TIE in her blood, not freedom, and was quite happy with things that way.

Chapter Two

Jaylene had always hated picnics, and she woke up Sunday morning dreading the one she had to attend that day. She wouldn't be surprised if Frank had left town for the express purpose of sticking her with a task she'd hate. Except, of course, that he had no way of knowing that she felt that way.

The first picnic she could remember attending was when she had been eight years old. She had been Jane Louise Sabelski then, and growing up on the west side of South Bend, Indiana. The section of town was called Little Poland, and its Catholic residents outdid the WASPs in adhering to the work ethic. Keeping clean, going to church, and working hard were accepted as gospel. Unfortunately, her father had lived by his own set of rules, and she and her mother had been forced to pay the price for his lapses.

When she had been young, though, she had adored him. He called her his little princess and told her how beautiful she was. He was always laughing and playing wonderful music on his saxophone. She loved it when his friends came over, and she would drift to sleep listening to the sound of their music. She thought it terribly unfair when they went to play in bars and halls where she couldn't go.

Then there was that awful Fourth of July picnic when she had been eight and everything had changed. They had gone to the picnic grove the Klub Wiepszowan owned. To her it was a marvelous place, with its three flags flying: the American flag, the Polish flag, and the one for the city

of Wiepsz, the area in Poland where most of the local families originated. Under the trees was a big open-sided building where the grandmothers cooked chicken, ham, and
sausages all day and the old men handed out beer and
soda. Beyond the food building, a raised dance floor sat in
front of a small band pavilion. There would be dancing
during the late afternoon and evening.

The day always started out with gossiping and hugging
as if they weren't all neighbors who had seen each other
just that morning. The children would run off and play,
while the women would gather around the picnic tables
and talk. Later there were races for the children. Jaylene
never won any, but they all got small American flags to
wave, so she didn't really care.

Besides the softball games and volleyball for the teenagers and adults, the men always had a tug-of-war. Her
mother said it was just an excuse for the neighborhood
roughnecks to push each other around and start fights.
Her father never participated because he said his favorite
sports were making music and love.

That was why she wouldn't believe it that year when
some children told her her father was in a fight. He didn't
do that sort of thing. But at their insistence she followed
them over to the mudhole where the tug-of-war was held.

They had to push through the crowd surrounding the
men, but when she had, she saw her father lying in the
mud as the men around him punched and shoved. He
seemed to be getting the worst of it, and the children began
to laugh that he was so drunk he couldn't even stand up.

She was terrified for him and screamed at the men to
stop. Her father looked up at her as he staggered to his
feet. His shirt was torn, his trousers dirty, and his lip cut,
but he was laughing. He was thrown in the mud again and
he roared in laughter. The taunting of the children grew
worse.

Shocked and confused, Jane Louise turned and ran into
the woods. She disturbed two teenagers locked in an embrace and found a quiet spot to hide. She wiped the tears
from her eyes. Her father wouldn't fight. Those men must

have started it. He wasn't drunk, either. Those men had pushed him down.

But somewhere deep inside her, she grew afraid. She remembered that the smell of beer was always around him, and that he didn't go to work each morning like the other fathers did. Of course, being a cabinetmaker wasn't his real job, she reminded herself. He was a musician.

She squashed her doubts and went off to find her mother. The two of them would be able to help her father get away from those rough men.

When she found her mother, her father was already with her. She ran toward them happily, but suddenly slowed to a walk. Her mother was crying and her father was calling her awful names. They both saw Jane Louise at the same time. Her father's face lightened and he called gaily to her, offering to get his little princess some ice cream.

He was all dirty and bloody and Jane Louise stood rooted to the spot in shock. The smile left her father's face, and it turned mean as he walked away, cursing them both. She and her mother, with silent tears flowing, went to find somebody to drive them home.

As Jaylene grew older, her dislike of picnics did not change, and she grew adept at avoiding them. Once she was at TIE, she always had work to do at the office. Her dedication to her job, even to the extent of missing a popular event like a picnic, had impressed everyone. No one ever guessed how she hated those social outings. Or how she was dreading this afternoon.

It was Frank Kareau's job to preside over the annual employee picnic and hand out the trophies. All that one-big-happy-family talk was his specialty, not hers. Just the thought of it made her uneasy. All the backslapping and meet-the-family rituals had her cringing. She wasn't good at small talk; she never had been.

Feeling as if she were dressing for a funeral, Jaylene put on a white linen split skirt and a crisp lilac blouse. She reluctantly vetoed stockings, slipping into some sandals. Her business suits seemed a part of her, and she would feel awkward appearing before her employees in something more casual. Play clothes were for times away from TIE, for the few private moments she had. She ran a brush quickly through her dark hair, leaving it hanging loose onto her shoulders. Then she wandered back out into the living room.

"All ready for your picnic?"

Jaylene started, then smiled at Rose Locollini, her newly appointed live-in companion. She was a small woman, but solidly built. Her short hair was a no-nonsense mixture of gray and dark brown, but her blue eyes were warm and friendly. Jaylene felt herself relax under their gaze. "Yes, the car should be any time now."

Rose put down the magazine she had been reading. "Well, you certainly have a nice day for it. Back home, we were always worrying that it would rain on our picnics. But maybe your great weather is one reason so many of us midwesterners want to retire down here."

Rose laughed and Jaylene forced herself to smile. Her eyes went to the window, though, searching in vain for a few storm clouds. The sky was clear. Why couldn't all this security they forced on her decide the picnic was a risk and forbid her to go?

Rose walked into the coffee shop. She still had a few hours before Jaylene was due back from her picnic—more than enough time to get some business done and chat with an old friend. She stopped just inside the door and glanced around.

It had been more than five years since Rose had last seen Ben, but she recognized him immediately. He still looked like Sergeant Ben Wolski of the Cleveland Police Department even though he was wearing the beige uniform of the Ace Protection Service. Maybe his body was a little thinner and his hair had turned all white, but the deep blue eyes were still the same.

He rose from his table and came quickly toward her. "Rose, you're as beautiful as ever," he said, giving her a quick hug before they sat down. Each ordered orange juice and a danish. Once their waitress had left, Ben gently put his hand over Rose's.

"I heard about Jack. You have my sympathies, Rose."

She nodded her acknowledgment. "It's about a year since your Barbara passed away, isn't it?"

Ben shrugged. "Yeah, but life goes on."

After they finished eating, their talk drifted to children and grandchildren. One of Rose's sons was an engineer, the other an FBI agent. Her daughter was a teacher in Illinois. Ben's two boys were also doing well, one a salesman for IBM, the other a forest ranger.

"So how many grandchildren do you have?" Rose asked.

"Four."

"I beat you." Rose laughed. "I got five and another on the way."

"So you got more kids," he protested, then laughed heartily and ordered a cup of coffee. They were silent until it came, then Ben took a sip and sighed. "I did the checking you asked for, Rose, but I'm not sure it'll help. Our 'friend' did work for Ace, but he quit more than three years ago. He had been assigned as a security guard at a high school, and there were some complaints. Not that anyone could prove anything, but it was enough to ask him to leave."

"That sounds like him," Rose replied tightly.

"Some people heard he went to L.A.," Ben continued. "I'll try and get someone at our affiliate there check it out."

"I'd appreciate it."

They were silent again as Ben sipped his coffee. "What are you going to do if you find him now?"

"I don't know," she admitted. "Just watch him for a while, I guess. He's going to stumble again, and I plan to be there when he does."

Ben frowned at the determination in her voice. "You must have lost other cases, Rose."

"This one's different," she said. "He was a cop with me in juvenile. He was supposed to be helping those kids, not using them in his 'business.' When the judge said we didn't have probable cause to search his car and threw the case out of court, I vowed I'd get him someday.

"He disappeared after that, and Jack got sick, but I never forgot. Not a day passed that I didn't see one of those kids in my mind. When Jack died, there was nothing holding me in Cleveland. It was time to start paying back some debts."

Ben pushed his empty cup aside. "I'll see what I can do."

Rose felt a lump in her throat and did not reply. She had known Ben would help her.

He waved to the waitress for the check, and a teasing look came into his eyes. "So, I understand you're taking care of some rich, executive lady. Must be real hard living in some penthouse suite and eating caviar," he joked.

Rose shook her gray head. "It's not all that great. She's got nothing but her money. She doesn't even have a steady, so her bed must get awful cold."

"Those rich people are a little cold anyway," Ben replied. "That's why their blood is so blue." He laid some money on the table and they rose to their feet.

"Her blood's not blue," Rose told him. "She comes from the same stock as you and me. European peasants."

"She told you?"

Rose shook her head again. "No, but I can tell. Deep down she's just a lonely little girl from the old neighborhood."

"I sure am glad that you could make it, Jaylene. Frank always enjoyed our picnics. It must have been something really important to tear him away."

Jaylene smiled slightly at Dick Matthews, the picnic organizer. "I'm glad to be here, Dick. This is my first time officiating a picnic. I hope I don't mess things up."

"I've been running TIE picnics for ten years now," he told her proudly. "So don't you worry. I'll show you the ropes."

Jaylene did not reply as he led her over to a large red and white striped canopy in the center of the picnic grounds. Nancy McConnachie, her tall blond security guard, was trailing along behind her.

"All the ribbons and trophies are over here by the coolers," Dick went on. He stopped walking once they were in the shade. "Can I get you a beer?"

"No. Not right now, thank you."

There was already a group gathered around the keg.

Most of them were men, and most of them looked familiar, but not quite. They looked different in their casual clothing.

"Hi, Jaylene."

"Good to see you."

"Sure is a nice day for a picnic."

"Better stay here in the shade. It's gonna be a scorcher."

Jaylene felt her smile fade as she sought vainly for some reply. Jesse had told her that this picnic assignment would be good for her. Maybe that was his way of warning her that she had better work on the social side of her development. Balanced performance had been the main buzzword with him lately.

"I think I'll have a beer after all, Dick."

"Great, let me get it for you."

He got one for each of them, then looked awkwardly over Jaylene's shoulder to where Nancy had been. She was sitting at an empty picnic table at the edge of the canopy and looking nonchalantly around her.

Dick just shrugged and pulled a box out from under a picnic table. He showed Jaylene a gold-painted plastic trophy. "These are for the softball champs. Got them at a real good price." He pulled a packet of ribbons out. "I got these just in case we needed something extra. You know how these picnics are, there's always some games or races you didn't plan."

Jaylene nodded as if she knew what he was talking about.

"Then the kids' prizes are all over there."

Jaylene looked over in the direction he was pointing. There was a stack of boxes under another table.

"It's mostly games, dolls, stuff like that. I've got it all marked according to age and I'll hand you the right prize for each race. I thought we'd start eating soon, so we could finish by one-thirty. That way we could start the softball tournament at one end of the park at around two, and run the kids' races at the other end at the same time." He stopped and frowned. "Unless you want to play softball. Then we could put off the kids' races to a little later."

The idea of participating in the games brought a smile to

her face. She had joined a TIE softball team years ago when she had been pushing for her first promotion to management. The idea had come from an article linking management potential with participation in organized sports in childhood. Better late than never, she had thought, but fortunately for the success of the team, she broke her ankle quickly and was promoted before it had healed enough for her to play again.

No, softball was not for her, and she shook her head at Dick. "Thanks, but I hadn't planned on it."

"Well, whatever you want, Jaylene. It's your picnic, too," he pointed out. "I made out a schedule, but we don't have to stick with it."

"It would be a shame not to," she said. "You've got things so well organized."

He shrugged, but with a smile on his face, and put the trophy and ribbons back into their box. "Like I said, this is my tenth year doing it, so it gets pretty easy after a while."

"I imagine." There was an awkward moment of silence as she watched Dick put the box away. He was a short, rather stocky man in his mid-forties. She knew she had seen him around TIE, but couldn't quite place him.

"You're in accounts payable, aren't you?" she asked.

"No, traffic."

Jaylene felt her cheeks warm in embarrassment. "Sorry."

"Don't worry about it," Dick brushed away her apology. "TIE's a big company. There's no way you can know everybody who works for you. And you execs move around so much, it's hard for the rest of us to get to know you, too."

She still felt uncomfortable. "Yes, we are becoming pretty large," she agreed. "We haven't been a small company for a long time now."

"But we're still like a small company in lots of ways. We all know that TIE'll always take good care of us."

She thought of the two hundred pink slips that would go out in the next few months, and the beer soured in her stomach. She sought to change the subject. "Is your family here today?"

His smile dimmed slightly. "My twelve- and thirteen-year-olds are, but Jeannie, my wife, was feeling a bit under the weather, so my sixteen-year-old stayed home with her."

They began to walk away from the canopy toward the large barbecues. She could smell hot dogs and hamburgers burning as she took a sip of her beer.

"I hope it's nothing serious," she said politely.

He looked ahead of them. "It is and it isn't." His cheerfulness sounded forced. "Jeannie's got MS, but she was just feeling a little slow today. Otherwise she would have been here, wheelchair and all." Dick smiled at her. "She loves the picnics. Last year, we made her official timekeeper for the kids' races."

"I'm sorry she had to miss it," Jaylene said lamely, then immediately felt the remark was inadequate. She searched for something better to say, but nothing came except a guilt-ridden memory of her own reluctance to attend. She felt as stupid and tongue-tied as an adolescent. She had never handled these kinds of personal situations well. Was that what Jesse had been trying to tell her?

"Billy and Tim were kind of glad that she wasn't coming," Dick went on as if there hadn't been an awkward silence. "Without their mother keeping time in the races, they feel like they've got a chance to win."

"I certainly wish them luck," she said. She was aware that he had handled that awkwardness better than she had, and it annoyed her. Of course, he was used to his wife's illness, and those kinds of personal confidences had always embarrassed her. They stopped near the food tables.

"I'll come and find you when the games are ready to start," Dick told her. "So you can have some fun until then. Just ask if you need anything."

She nodded but had no time to speak before he was off, waving to two boys playing with a soccer ball near the parked cars. Billy and Tim, no doubt. She turned to Nancy.

"Get yourself something to eat and drink, if you like. I'm sure you don't need to hover over me when I'm surrounded by TIE employees."

"Don't worry about me," the young woman said. "I'll just be tagging along after you wherever you go."

After getting a hamburger and some salad, Jaylene skirted around some kids playing with water balloons and looked for a place to sit. At the far edge of the picnic grounds was a deserted picnic table sitting in some inviting shade, but she was here to promote good employee-manager relations. She was supposed to mingle, and went instead to an empty spot at a closer table. Two couples were sitting there, and she recognized the men as part of the legal staff.

"Mind if I join you?" she asked.

"Not at all." They introduced themselves as Jack Murphy and Mike Langdon and their wives as Tina and Darcy. Tina was very pregnant and Darcy had a toddler sitting next to her. The child was dipping the hot dog he had clutched tightly in his hand into a blob of catsup on his plate. Then he smeared it around on his face. Jaylene turned to the men.

"So how are things in legal?"

"Brief." Mike laughed.

She smiled and ate a little. "What does Dick do besides organize the picnic?" she asked. "He said he's in traffic, but that didn't help me much."

"You'd know who he was if you were in the baseball pool," Jack said.

"Or the football pool," Mike added.

She just shook her head in confusion.

"His job title is senior associate traffic specialist," Jack explained with a laugh. "But it doesn't quite cover his real value to TIE."

"He organizes the baseball, basketball, and the football pools," Mike said. "Collects for presents when someone's sick or getting married."

"He ought to be TIE's social director." Tina laughed.

"How does he manage to get his work done?" Jaylene wondered.

"His real job is president of the TIE Employees Social Club. He does that real well."

Jaylene felt a sudden blow against her back and turned around. A Frisbee had hit her. Nancy picked it up as three kids ran over to claim it.

"Go play away from all the people," Nancy told them. They gave her a sour look, but did move farther away.

"Boy, I used to be great with those things in college," Jack suddenly reminisced. "We'd spend hours on the quadrangle practicing, but I haven't touched one for years."

"I made the all-school team in my senior year," Mike said. "We could throw them backward, through our legs, and even blindfolded. God, we were good."

"I saw a dog on television that could catch one," Darcy said. "We ought to get Skipper to try it."

"Yeah, then take her on tour around the country," Mike snickered.

The only Frisbee Jaylene had ever touched was the one that had just hit her. Her college days had been filled with work. She had set her goals and hadn't let them out of her sight for a second. Aunt Sophie had taught her to avoid distractions, and she had learned her lesson well. That was why she was an executive VP and Jack and Mike were her employees.

She certainly had no regrets, but she did feel distanced from them. The only thing she seemed able to talk about was work. She rose to her feet.

"I think I'd better check with Dick and see when he needs me to start handing out prizes." She nodded to Tina and Darcy. The child now had catsup all over his shirt. "It was nice to meet you."

She dumped her half-finished food into a nearby trashcan and walked under the canopy. She could feel her arms getting sunburned and wished she had brought some kind of lotion along. She had another couple of hours before she could possibly leave; she would be a lobster by that time.

The intercom buzzed just as Jaylene was dialing the phone. Damn. It would be Ken. She had hoped to catch him at home and explain the situation to him. Now she'd have to do it face to face, and that was bound to be awkward. She told the doorman to let him up, then glanced nervously around the apartment. She hoped Rose would stay out of sight.

Jaylene had changed into a cool sundress when she had

come home from the picnic. She stuck her hands into its pockets. She didn't know why she felt slightly apprehensive about this meeting with Ken. It wasn't as though there were any deep feelings on either side. This was just another business problem, and she handled those all the time.

The doorbell rang and she started slightly. Then, taking a deep breath, she pulled open the door. Tall, blond, and tanned, Ken smiled down at her, looking like he had stepped out of an ad for an exclusive line of men's wear. Too perfect, that was how Ken always seemed, as if he was playing a part.

"Hello, darling," he said, coming into the apartment and pulling her into his arms. "I've really missed you."

His embrace and his kiss were perfect, as if he had practiced them many times before. There was no hesitation— and no spark of passion, either. She pulled out of his arms, wondering where that thought had come from. The last thing she wanted from Ken was emotion.

His hazel eyes frowned quizzically at her. "Have you been out in the sun all day?"

"I was at TIE's employee picnic."

His face registered surprise, but she spoke again before he could make any comment. "How was your trip?"

"It was all right." He followed her into the living room and sat on the sofa close to her. "What do you say we stay here this evening? I've got something I want to talk to you about."

"I need to say something, too," she admitted.

He put his arm around her shoulder and pulled her close, nuzzling her ear before his mouth found hers. His kiss was long and hard, and Jaylene felt herself relaxing against his body. She liked being held in a man's arms. She wasn't in love with Ken. She wasn't even terribly fond of him, but it was awfully nice to have someone to hold her. Those thoughts were getting too dangerous, and she pulled away from him.

"How about a drink before we get down to serious issues?"

"Sure."

He rose to his feet and took off his jacket as she went over to the built-in bar in the corner. She mixed him a highball and poured a glass of wine for herself.

Things were going to be lonely once he was gone. There'd be no one to talk to, no one to laugh with—no one to hold her. She felt a need to share this last night with him.

What difference would it make if she waited a few more hours to tell him of corporate's decision? Or would Hawks be watching her apartment with binoculars, counting the minutes since Ken came inside?

Suddenly Ken was behind her, pulling her against the length of his body. Her heart beat faster at the thought of his male love, and she forgot about Hawks and Rose. TIE wouldn't mind if she took pleasure from Ken this one last time. His mouth came down and kissed her neck below her left ear as his hands roamed over her flat stomach and up to her breasts. She felt them swell with desire.

"What do you say we sail to the Bahamas next weekend?"

Her mind's response was automatic even as her body continued to enjoy his touch. "I can't. I have to go to New York."

Ken stopped the caress of his hands and just tightened his arms around her waist. His mouth planted tickling kisses along her neck. "Good old TIE," he mocked softly. "What can it offer you that I can't?"

"Money. Power."

"But is that all there is to life?"

Coming from a man who was as ambitious as he was handsome, that was too much for Jaylene. She turned around in his arms and began to laugh. "Tell me what you want from life, then."

"Well, money and power are a nice start, of course." His hands became active again, pushing aside the narrow straps of her dress so that her shoulders were exposed for his lips. "But I'd also like to feel your body under mine."

"That sounds nice." And it would be, even if she knew it would be for the last time.

The dance of kisses along her shoulders and the touch of

his hands on her breasts awoke the passion in her. She was a loyal TIE employee, but she was also a woman. She wanted to feel a man's hands on her body, enjoying her softness as she enjoyed his strength. She needed to feel his skin pressed against hers, longed to have him enter her. She craved a man's loving to make her feel relaxed and happy and whole.

She unbuttoned Ken's shirt blindly, her hands moving in automatic response to her body's longings to touch. Their clothes were in the way, annoying barriers to the pleasures they could share. His mouth found hers and his lips became more demanding. Their pressure hardened, and she shivered in anticipation.

He lifted his mouth from hers suddenly. "Jaylene, let's get married," he said.

"Married?" She stared at him, shock dampening her ardor. "What happened on that trip of yours? Did someone tell you that a married politician wins more elections?"

"Jaylene, be serious," he protested. "Think what a great team we'd make."

"You can't mean it."

"Sure I do. We're the perfect pair." He seemed to be warming up to his idea. "We're compatible in bed. We enjoy each other's company. You've got the education, class, and poise. I've got the charm and connections. We could make it to Washington easy."

"You make it sound like a merger, not a marriage," she said.

He shrugged. "Call it what you will, it's still a great idea."

"I think it's a terrible idea," she snapped, angered by his cold, analytical proposal. She pulled away from him and walked over to the floor-to-ceiling window, straightening her dress. The lights of Miami twinkled at her from across the bay, but the sight did not cheer her as it usually did.

"What are you so upset about?" Ken asked. His voice reflected his confusion. "I thought you'd see all the advantages."

She turned to face him. "Why? Because I'm thirty-eight and still not married?"

"Because you're a businesswoman."

Didn't businesswomen like hearts and flowers, too? Didn't they need the promise of romance? He just did not understand, and that made her angrier still. "I'm a woman who happens to work in business. That doesn't mean I run my personal life the same way."

A strange look came into his hazel eyes, and something akin to a smile appeared on his lips. "Well, I'll be damned," he said softly, the look on his face making her uneasy. "Under all those modern trappings lies the heart of an old-fashioned girl. You're still waiting for your knight in shining armor to sweep you away."

"Hardly." The idea was absurd, as absurd as marrying him. "Just because I don't think of marriage as a business merger doesn't mean I check the grounds for hoofprints each morning."

"No? Then tell me why you're refusing to marry me," he demanded.

"Because I don't want to."

He smiled. "But it makes perfect business sense."

"Marriage doesn't have to make perfect business sense. It's an emotional commitment."

"You see?" He looked triumphant. "You're looking for love."

"I'm not looking for anything, but I do believe in marrying for love and no other reason."

"You aren't as modern as you pretend to be."

She was furious now. "I don't pretend to be anything."

"You'd better take a closer look at yourself then." He finished the liquor in his glass and put it down with a quiet thud. "You've got 'modern liberated lady' written all over you, in everything you say and everything you do. It's only when someone gets close enough to scratch the surface that the truth comes out. You're nothing but a scared little girl looking for someone to take care of her."

"You don't know what you're talking about," she snapped.

"No? I'm damn good at reading people, sweetheart, and I've seen a lot more of the real world than you have from TIE's fast track." He picked up his coat and flung it over his shoulder. He didn't sound angry, just so sure of himself that it scared her. "Under all that fancy education and behind the power TIE gave you, you're running scared."

She forced herself to laugh. "You've decided all this just because I don't want to marry you? Didn't you ever consider that I just don't want to spend the rest of my life with you?"

His smile grew. "See? Who talks about marriage being forever anymore? Just lovelorn little girls." He crossed to the door. "I'd better leave before we both wind up mad. There are no hard feelings; it just seemed to make sense."

She watched as he closed the door behind him, then turned to stare out the window again. Ken was wrong. She wasn't looking for love; she didn't care about that kind of nonsense. She'd had her turn at love and marriage and forever years ago, and it had failed miserably. That was when she had started listening to Aunt Sophie and realized there were other possibilities open to her.

Just because all the girls she had grown up with wanted nothing more than a home and children, that didn't mean that she couldn't reach for more. "Don't depend on anyone but yourself," her aunt had told her time and time again. So she had set her goals and made her choices. Now she took care of herself and was very happy about it. She certainly had no desire to go backward and try the dependency of marriage again. On anyone's terms.

Maybe she was old-fashioned in a way, she acknowledged. There was nothing wrong with that. She just knew that she'd never marry someone for business reasons. She was better off alone than married to someone like Ken who didn't care about her. Hell, the only thing she had ever wanted from him was his body, anyway. TIE gave her everything else she needed.

Rose appeared in the hallway. "Your gentleman friend leave already?"

Jaylene did not turn around. "Yes," she said brusquely, wondering if Rose was timing his visit for Hawks.

"What a shame." Rose sounded sincere and Jaylene felt a twinge of guilt. She did not stop Rose from going back to her room, though, and continued to stare out the window.

She played with her wineglass, twirling it slowly in her hands. She had never told Ken of TIE's decision. All her apprehension, and he was out of her life without it even coming up. It was almost funny.

What would he have said? she wondered, putting the glass down on the bar. Would he have been hurt? Angry? No, she thought, he probably would have understood. After all, it was a business decision.

She turned off the lights in the living room and walked slowly down the hall to her study. She felt more alone than she had for a long time.

Chapter Three

"It's your turn in the barrel, Jaylene."

Jaylene was reviewing some presentation material with Rita and looked up in surprise at Tom Jordan, Jesse Whitmore's administrative assistant. "It's not even nine," she protested. "I had an eleven o'clock with Jesse."

"Sorry, Jaylene, he had to change his plans."

Damn. Nothing was going right today. Neal Aldridge, her director of staff services, hadn't arrived yet with the rest of her presentation material. Then there was a financial meeting she wouldn't be able to attend if she was in with Jesse, and Neal wasn't around to sub for her. On top of everything else, she had awful cramps that would only disappear with a long, hot bath. And she was about as likely to have a half hour to relax in the tub as Neal was to walk through that door in time for the meeting.

She sighed, wishing she had made him fly up to New York with the rest of her group last night instead of letting him wait until that morning. So what if it had been the last Sunday in August? He'd have other weekends with his family before summer ended. Besides, she didn't think summer ever ended in Miami.

"I need a few minutes to straighten up here," she told Tom.

"Five."

"I need twenty."

"You've got ten."

"You're all heart, Tommy." She turned to Rita. "Rita, you're going to have to sit in for Neal in that finance committee meeting."

"But I'm not a designated alternate, Miss Sable."

"I'll make you a temporary alternate," she ordered, not in the mood to cajole. She turned aside to her security guard. "Nancy, take this material and get transparencies made for my presentation this afternoon."

"I'm not trained in finance, Miss Sable," Rita worried.

Jaylene tried not to lose her temper. It was hardly Rita's fault that things weren't going smoothly. "All you have to do is take notes. You still take shorthand, don't you?"

"Yes, I do." Rita hesitated a moment. "But I'm afraid that, lacking the proper background, I'll miss something important."

Her patience snapped. "Nancy, do you take shorthand?"

"I'm sorry, Jaylene. I don't. I do have a tape recorder, though," Nancy told her. "I could tape the whole thing, and then get it transcribed for you."

"Thanks, Nancy. I'd appreciate that." She turned to Rita. "You get the transparencies made. I need them by two this afternoon." That, at least, ought to be within her capabilities.

"That's rather short notice, Miss Sable," Rita pointed out.

"Get them done!" Even Rita could see her rage, and without another word, she began to gather the material together. Jaylene left the room before Rita could think up more excuses. Tom was waiting for her outside the office she used when she was at the New York corporate offices, with a cup of coffee and a sweet roll. It reminded her of the breakfast she hadn't had time for that morning.

"Ready?" he asked.

Jaylene nodded and reached for the roll. "Can I have a little piece of that?" Suddenly she was starving, and the piece she tore off was three-quarters of the roll.

"That was going to be my breakfast."

"You'll thank me for this when you're slim and trim," she said, eating it quickly. She felt slightly more alive with a bit of food in her, but her fingers were sticky. "Didn't you get a napkin?"

Without a word, he reached into his pocket for his handkerchief. "You want to polish your shoes on my pants?"

"Not now," Jaylene replied sweetly, and returned his handkerchief.

Jesse was ready and waiting when they reached his office. She nodded good-bye to Tom and closed the door behind her as Jesse rose to greet her.

"Jaylene, how are you doing? You look a little under the weather."

"Just my ulcer acting up," she said quickly.

He nodded sympathetically as they took their seats. "They can be a nuisance, can't they?" Then he leaned back in his chair and put his feet up on the desk. "So how are things going? How've you been?"

"Busy."

"Members of Congress are busy, Jaylene. I'm more concerned if you're accomplishing things."

"Most of the time," she said.

"Good." He carefully cut the tip off a cigar and lit it. "You'll be happy to know that the Management Review Committee thought your memo on the duplication between the two foreign subsidiaries was very good. We're going to take some action on it."

She knew better than to ask what kind of action. She would be told when Jesse thought she needed to know.

"But that's not why I called all you guys in for a one-on-one," Jesse went on. "Our computer predicts that our profits are not going to grow as fast in the next two years as they have over the past five."

Jaylene matched his direct gaze, vaguely irritated by his "all you guys" remark. So what if she was the only female vice president, she was not now and had never been a "guy." If she was, her "ulcer" would not be giving her problems once a month. She smoothed down the skirt of her somber business suit, a deep gray that was echoed in the suits of at least half the executive staff she'd seen that morning. Had she become so much a part of TIE that she was invisible? She tried to ignore her sudden touchiness and to deal with the issue at hand.

"Is that unexpected?" she asked coolly. "Our past rate of growth was above normal for the industries we're in."

Jesse's smile disappeared and his facial expression

matched the icy glint in his eye. "That's not the type of attitude that TIE expects from its financial officers."

Jaylene maintained eye contact with Jesse, but she did not reply. What was the matter with her today? Why was she letting things get to her? She'd had cramps before and they'd never interfered with her emotions or her work.

"Anyway," Jesse said, filling the void of silence between them. "I want you to reduce your head count by another hundred for next year."

Another hundred! By the time Jesse was through there'd be nobody left in the subsidiary but her and Frank. And Rita. She couldn't forget precious Rita. "I'm already cutting two hundred," she snapped angrily. "Another hundred is going to cut into muscle."

A look of surprise flashed across Jesse's face, but his reply was cool and calm. "We're all going to have to limp along a bit until business gets better."

"Corporate, too?" She could hear the bitterness in her own voice and it astonished her as well as him.

"Our rate of head count reduction is greater than in any other area of the corporation," Jesse replied, still very much in control.

"I see," Jaylene said quietly. She had to get hold of herself, or she *would* get an ulcer. Now that would be poetic justice.

"As I remember," Jesse went on, "you have a long list of 'D' performers. That gives you a lot of ballast to throw overboard."

"Some of those 'D' performers may have extenuating circumstances," Jaylene added.

"TIE doesn't meddle in the personal lives of its employees."

She said nothing.

"But that's enough serious talk," he said. "I've got a surprise for you. The Harvard Business School wants to do a case study involving TIE, and Mr. Cabot approved the idea. He even suggested your subsidiary."

Jaylene just stared at him. "A case study? Now?"

Some of the amusement leaked out of Jesse's smile. "Oh,

come now, Jaylene, surely you can handle a little thing like a Harvard professor and a few graduate students."

"Along with cutting back three hundred employees and reorganizing the subsidiary? Mr. Cabot either has total faith in me or hates my guts and sees this as a way to get rid of me."

Jesse's laugh was genuine, but then he turned serious. "Actually, it's a way to make a few points with him. He still remembers the company his grandfather founded and worries that TIE is changing too much, too fast. He likes the extra money pouring into his bank accounts, but he wishes TIE was still personal and paternal. Your subsidiary is especially upsetting to him, since you've closed some of the older plants in the States and relocated them to Latin America."

"That was domestic's decision. I didn't have anything to do with those closings."

The smile stayed on Jesse's face. "You presented a hell of a case for relocating."

"That's part of my job."

"So is keeping the chairman of the board happy. If the case study's a real problem, I'll talk him out of it, but it would go a long way toward placating him. He's part of the old boy network. A Harvard man, you know, and he'd like to feel he was helping the old alma mater out."

"In other words, do it."

"At least give it some thought. I want to close down some of TIE's original plants in New England next year, and he's going to have a coronary when I talk about it. It would be nice to have some brownie points in the bank."

"Okay." Jaylene sighed. Why did it seem that Jesse was pushing her so hard lately? "I'll take care of him."

"Good," Jesse smiled broadly, magnanimous now that he had won. "The professor is Dr. Rayburn Carroll. I'll give him your name."

He closed a folder and put it aside. Jaylene knew that her time was up. "By the way, the professor's single and reputed to be a ladies' man. I thought that since you had gotten rid of your lawyer friend, you might be in the market for a little recreation."

Jaylene couldn't stop the words. "I thought TIE didn't meddle in the personal lives of its employees," she pointed out bitterly.

Jesse just kept smiling. "Employees are consumable resources, Jaylene. As an executive, you're a capital resource. If you remember Economics 101, it's important for us to take good care of you."

Jaylene smiled automatically at Jesse's praise, but as she turned, a frown crept into her eyes. Did that mean she wasn't a person anymore?

She hurried back to her temporary office. Maybe Neal would have gotten there with the rest of her material and she could finish preparing her presentation for that afternoon. She always enjoyed them, and working on this one ought to restore her equilibrium. Especially since it appeared that Mr. Cabot would attend. It wasn't often that she got to present to the chairman of the board.

"Well, good morning, Miss Sable."

Her back stiffened. There was no mistaking that sneer. Dave Margolis, vice president of finance for the Far East subsidiary. Just what she needed to brighten her day. She turned around slowly, knowing that he would not have changed in the few months since she'd seen him last: graying hair, a bit of a paunch and cold brown eyes that would glare at her angrily. The hatred in them startled her, but she kept her voice as low and curious as she could force it to be. "Good morning, Dave."

"I see you're up to your little tricks again, sweetheart."

"I beg your pardon," she replied coldly.

"It's bad enough that you're stealing electronics plants, which belong in my territory," he hissed. "But now you're trying to take over the whole ball of wax."

"What are you talking about, Margolis?"

"Ho, ho," he mocked. "Playing the sweet little innocent, aren't we? She knows nothing about the Management Review Committee following her advice and consolidating the foreign subsidiaries."

"I didn't recommend consolidation," she snapped. "I merely pointed out some problems that exist under today's organization."

"Just presenting the facts, no doubt," he sneered.

"That's how I do it," she replied.

"I know. Just like you did in Texas." Before she could say another word, he had turned on his heel and was gone.

Jaylene sighed and continued down the hall. He was never going to forget those early days in Texas when she was the controller of a plant and he was the general manager. He had wanted to expand, and she had thought the place should be shut down. The corporate auditors had agreed with her. She had been promoted, while Dave was demoted.

Her temporary office suddenly seemed like a sanctuary, and she hurried into it. Unfortunately, her problems followed her in. She had been through consolidations before, and there was no way that they could be termed interesting, or fun. A lot of people would lose jobs, even managers and executives. Rumors would fly through all the departments. Fear would freeze the majority of the personnel, and productivity would plummet.

She sat down and wearily rubbed her eyes. When her hands came away she saw the large envelope stamped "personal/confidential" on the desk. More good news. She knew what it was and grimaced as she reluctantly opened it. "Possible Outplacement Candidates." She read the report title with a cynical smile. Good old corporate nomenclature. It could make herpes sound good.

She sat down and quickly began to review the report. What was the matter with her? She was happily married to TIE, but it was going to file for divorce if her moodiness continued. Jesse hadn't asked for anything difficult. There were five hundred and ten names on this list in her hand and they all had less than a "C" rating. Making the cuts he wanted wouldn't be hard. TIE would be healthier for the pruning.

Resting her chin in her left hand, she idly paged through the report. Her eyes skimmed over the unfamiliar employee numbers and names, their start dates, current salaries, performance ratings for each year of employment, and average rating based on the previous three years. No, it would be no problem at all for personnel to whittle this list down to three hundred. There was enough deadwood here to make a roaring bonfire.

The name Dick Matthews suddenly jumped out at her. He was forty-three years old and made twenty-two thousand dollars a year. He had been a consistent "B" performer until the last few years. Now he was rated "D." Probably since he'd found out about his wife's illness.

Jaylene sighed uneasily and slipped the report back in the envelope. TIE wasn't a charity. If Dick had time to run the picnics and other activities he ought to have time to do his job better.

At that moment Rita hurried in. Jaylene saw the worried look on the woman's face. Now what?

"Miss Sable, we have a problem."

"What is it?" Jaylene made no attempt to hide the weariness in her voice.

"Mrs. Gallagher, she's in reproductions—"

"Yes." Jaylene nodded her head impatiently.

"She says she needs management approval before she can do a rush job on the transparencies. Could you come down and talk to her?"

Jaylene tried to keep her voice calm and polite. "You hold a management position, don't you, Rita?"

Rita's jaw tightened, but her gaze dropped from Jaylene's hard stare.

"Take care of it," Jaylene ordered quietly but firmly. She went back to her work, remembering the "A" rating she had recently seen in Rita's file. How could someone so incompetent get such high ratings?

Rita Kastle closed the office door gently, even though her hands were shaking. Mr. Corbin would never have talked to her this way. Poor dear man. It was wrong of the company to force him into retirement just so they could open up a position for Miss Sable. This equal opportunity and ERA nonsense was causing a great deal of trouble. Women were not meant to be managers.

Damn. Why did Lowell have that accident and get himself killed? He had promised to take care of her, yet she'd had nothing but grief from his precious company for the last twenty-five years.

She hurried down the hall into the ladies' room, restraining the urge to swear aloud as she entered. In the old days, when all managers were men, this had been a woman's refuge. She could say what she liked without worrying who overheard her, but one never knew these days when a manager was around.

Dampening her wrists with cold water, she felt her bitterness fade and checked her appearance in the mirror. She was forty-eight years old, but with the help of Miss Clairol and Maybelline, she looked ten years younger. Today, maybe even fifteen. The thought cheered her.

Her blond hair looked just right and her pink dress was one of her favorites. No mannish suits for her. She was a woman and happy to be one, unlike some others she could name who seemed determined to push into the realm of men, where they didn't belong. If she didn't need her job, she'd tell Jaylene to shove it. In a ladylike way, of course.

But she did need the job. There was no doubt about that. After Lowell failed her, she had tried marriage. Twice actually, though neither had lasted. There were so few real men these days. The two losers she had hooked up with didn't seem to realize that behind every successful man there was a woman. She had tried to encourage them and they had folded. Damn weaklings.

She turned from the mirror, seeing no way to delay her task any further, and left the ladies' lounge. She turned a corner and collided with a solid male body. "Oh, Mr. Margolis," she apologized. "I'm so sorry. I wasn't watching where I was going."

She had recognized him immediately from the pictures she had seen in the company newspaper, except that he was much handsomer than the pictures had revealed. His dark hair had only touches of gray at the temples and the bulk of his body covered by a heavy suit emanated strength and power. He was considerably taller than she was in her high heels and she liked having to look up at him. A woman should have to look up to a man, an AA to her superior.

"You're Miss Kastle, aren't you?"

She could not hide her surprise, and pleasure, at being recognized also. Her hand ran slowly along the embroidered edge of her collar, the silky feel of the fabric echoing the wave of femininity that grew under his unfaltering gaze. "Why, yes. How did you know who I am?"

His smile warmed her heart, his brown eyes causing that warmth to race through her blood. "You're well known in all levels in the company, Miss Kastle. Everyone is aware of your contributions and loyalty to TIE over the years. And now you have to guide Miss Sable while she learns the ropes."

Rita returned his smile, flattered beyond belief at his words. But that was the kind of thing that a man would do, go out of his way to give credit to the little people. She couldn't understand why he wasn't an executive vice president and Miss Sable was.

"Thank you, Mr. Margolis. It's nice of you to say so, but Miss Sable needs very little help."

"Ah, you're being much too modest."

Rita laughed quietly, and reached up to touch the locket hanging around her neck, gently sliding it back and forth on the chain. Her hands were one of her best features, small and lady-like, with pink polished nails. "Thank you again. It's a pleasure meeting you after hearing your name so often."

"The pleasure's all mine, Rita." He took her hand in his, holding it gently, like a gallant about to kiss it. Not like some of these younger men who clutched a lady's hand as if they wanted to wrestle with her. "You're originally from New York, aren't you? Do you think DeLucia's still serves those marvelous lunches?"

"Goodness, I haven't been there in years."

"Neither have I." His smile was contagious. "What do you say we find out? I have a lot of time for lunch today and I'd love some company. Do you think you could get away for lunch? My treat."

"Oh, Mr. Margolis, I'd love to."

"Fine. Shall we meet in the lobby around eleven-thirty?"

Rita nodded and then watched him saunter toward the elevators, a small smile playing about her lips. It wasn't often that a man invited her out to lunch these days. Certainly not a real man, like Mr. Margolis.

Dave Margolis sipped his wine. He had been tense when the meal had begun, but as it progressed he could feel his stomach relaxing. Yes sir, everything was coming up roses.

He thought he would have a coronary when he learned of the corporation's intent to consolidate the two foreign subsidiaries. He wasn't worried that he'd be out of a job, for at his level the odds were high that he would be retained. His real fear lay in being transferred to the domestic subsidiary where he'd lose all the opportunties he had now to supplement the salary TIE was paying him.

Gazing across the top of his glass, Margolis smiled at Rita, the sweet little plum that had dropped in his lap. He saw now that the consolidation could be a real blessing. If he could get the presidency of the new expanded foreign subsidiary, he could double or triple his present ancillary income. In another three years his Swiss bank account would hold enough to buy his own island.

He smiled at the thought. He might even let Margie and the kids visit occasionally. Often enough for him to play the benevolent husband and father, but not often enough to get on his nerves.

He put his irritation aside to develop the potential at hand. "I don't think there's anything in this world that can beat a French wine," he told Rita with a smile.

"Well, no other wine, certainly." She laughed coyly.

He let his smile deepen. She was probably close to fifty years old but didn't look too bad. A few wrinkles around the eyes, but otherwise her skin was pretty tight. The dim lighting of the restaurant helped, but her real attraction lay in her hatred for Jaylene. She kept that dislike hidden below the surface, but not very far down. He reached over and topped off her glass.

"California wines are all right for everyday occasions,

but for something special I'll always take a French," he said.

She looked over the rim of her glass at him and took a slow sip. "This certainly has been a special occasion for me," she admitted softly. "It's not every day that I get to sit at the same table with one of TIE's key executives."

She certainly knew how to make a man feel good, he thought. Although she wouldn't draw the hungry looks a sixteen-year-old would, she still knew just what to say. And do, probably. Twenty-five, thirty years ago, she must have really been something. He could see why Lowell Cabot had had the hots for her instead of his blue-blooded wife.

He leaned across the table so that he was closer to her. "It's not every day that I have such a charming luncheon companion, either," he said smoothly. Maybe he should take her up to his room tonight. Older women were so grateful for anything they got, and it might be just what he needed to secure her loyalty.

"What's it like to work for one of TIE's anointed?" he asked.

For the fleetest moment her face grew hard and ugly. "It's all right," she said, and then laughed. "I guess I'm from the old school. I just think that men are physically and psychologically better equipped to handle the pressures of management."

"I'm not sure the feminists would agree with you, Rita."

She smiled. "I know I don't agree with them."

Dave shook his head with a pleased laugh. He didn't know how yet, but old Rita was going to help him settle some scores. He could pay Jaylene back all that he owed her, plus a little interest. It would be so easy, because she wasn't clever enough to recognize him as a threat. She still believed that working hard and playing by the rules were all she needed to be successful.

Margolis swirled the remains of his wine in the goblet. He could see now that Jaylene had done him a favor by getting him derailed when she had in Texas. He had been close to the presidency of a domestic division, but that title wouldn't have gotten him the fat Swiss bank account he had now. But if a man didn't have his principles, he had nothing. Margolis quickly swallowed his wine to keep himself from laughing out loud.

Chapter Four

Dr. Rayburn Carroll tapped his fingers on the steering wheel as he waited for the light to change. He was tall and thin and looked younger than his forty-one years. The streaks of gray at his temples added dignity to his appearance, not years, or at least that's what he'd been told a number of times by various female acquaintances. He took a deep breath and looked around him. It was the beginning of September, and he was glad to be in Miami again. He had always liked the city, with its constant pulsating energy, its exciting Latin rhythm. He wished he was staying longer than just overnight. He would have liked to rediscover some of those little Cuban nightclubs. Well, if everything went smoothly with Miss Jaylene Sable later this morning, this would not be his only trip here.

The light changed, and Ray moved forward with the traffic. It was funny the way some cities seemed to match one's personality. Miami was like that for him, and so were Paris, Rio, and Singapore. Places where he could laugh and play all night long.

He had visited a lot of cities over the years, both with his work at the Harvard Business School and with his private consulting. New York, Chicago, and L.A. were as well known to him as Boston, his home. They had lost that aura of excitement and mystery that they had when they were new, when there were still secret places to be discovered. Any city, like any woman, lost its allure when it became too familiar. Thankfully, his life provided him with a great deal of variety in both areas.

After checking into his hotel, Ray drove out to the TIE compound. He wasn't expecting any problems in setting up the case study. After all, Malcolm Cabot himself had okayed it. But Ray knew that just because TIE's CEO was his godfather, he would not necessarily get wholehearted cooperation from the people he had to deal with. No, he needed Miss Sable's help with that.

Hoping to get a clue on how best to handle her, he had read everything he could about her, and that had amounted to quite a bit. Every business magazine and newspaper in the country seemed to have devoted space to her over the last few years—and usually more than once.

He had learned that she was thirty-eight years old and had gotten her MBA from the University of Chicago. She was the youngest woman to have been made an executive officer with a corporation the size of TIE, and she had justified their trust in her many times over with unbelievable deals. She was articulate, had a sense of humor, and was extremely competent. If she couldn't quite walk on water, it certainly wouldn't get much above her ankles.

Without ever reading it, he knew also that she was single, with very little, if anything, in her life besides her work. No one, man or woman, rose as fast as she did without single-minded determination. He understood that, but it also provided him with a problem. Just what could he make small talk about?

He pondered the problem as he was cleared through the gate, as he parked the car, and as he was escorted by a tall, good-looking, blond woman through one of the buildings to Miss Sable's office. When he passed through her outer office, he took a quick glance at the magazines on the end table. *BusinessWeek, Forbes,* and *Fortune.* No clue there. He'd have to rely on his marvelous charm.

The blond opened the door and showed him into a richly furnished office. He had a vague impression of light, paneled walls and leather-upholstered furniture, but his eyes were drawn to the woman seated at the desk. She looked younger than he had expected, and softer. Somehow, all the photos had failed to capture her youthful glow or the soft, rich brown of her hair. She rose as he entered and walked around her desk toward him. He hadn't expected her to be so small, either.

"Hello, Dr. Carroll." Her voice was impersonal, with a hint of iron in it.

"How do you do, Miss Sable?"

They met in the middle of the room and shook hands. Her grip was every bit as firm as his, but her skin was a lot softer. She might be one hell of a businessperson, but she also was one gorgeous lady. He wondered briefly what she would look like dressed in an outfit more daring than the trim navy suit she was wearing. This case study might be a lot more fun than he had expected if he could get her to loosen up a bit.

She indicated some overstuffed leather chairs off to one side of the room. "Why don't we sit here? Would you like some coffee?"

"Yes, that would be fine."

"I'll get it," the blond spoke up.

Ray walked over to the sitting area with Miss Sable, noticing the vivid paintings on the wall. Obviously, her trips to South America produced a number of results other than purely business. It was an opening, at least.

"Your artwork is stunning," he said with a smile once they were seated. "Are they from your trips to South America?"

"No. Our corporate interior decorator put the paintings there. He decided that since we're the Latin American subsidiary we should look Latinish."

He felt a sense of disappointment that he hadn't actually found a clue to the person hiding behind that cool exterior.

"I really don't have time for shopping on my trips," she added.

No, of course she wouldn't. He hadn't been thinking straight. He wondered what she would say if he told her it was because her beauty had befuddled his mind. She'd probably refuse the case study and have him thrown out on his ear. He smiled inwardly at the thought. Somehow he doubted that his usual lines would work on Jaylene Sable.

There was a knock on the door, and the blond woman came

in with a tray, bringing it over to the table between them. She put a cup of something near Miss Sable, and a coffeepot, a creamer, a sugar bowl, and an empty cup near him. "Shall I pour your coffee, Dr. Carroll?" the woman asked.

He shook his head. "No, thank you. I can use the practice."

"Is there anything else you need to practice?" she asked with a hopeful smile.

He laughed, relieved to know that his charm had not deserted him. "The list is too long to cover right now," he replied.

The blond left laughing, and Ray glanced over at Miss Sable's cup as he poured his coffee. He had thought she might have tea, but if it was, it was the strangest tea he'd ever seen. He put a dash of cream in his cup and sipped at his coffee. "What kind of bean did they use to make your coffee?"

"It wasn't a bean, it was a chicken. I have a cold, and Nancy, the woman who just left, thinks chicken broth will cure me."

"Ah, I see," he said, delighted to have a nonbusiness subject to discuss at last. "It's bad enough to have a cold in the winter. It must be horrible down here surrounded by sunshine and healthy tanned bodies."

She looked surprised at his sensitivity, and momentarily confused. She nodded slowly.

"If the chicken soup doesn't work, I know a lot of other remedies that we can try," he went on. "Their history of curing colds isn't fully verified, but they are guaranteed to make you feel good."

Her confusion fled, leaving behind a look of irritation, and he knew he had gone too far. She cleared her throat. "I do have a busy day, doctor. The quicker you state your request, the quicker I'll be able to make my decision."

"Decision?" He had been caught off guard, thinking they'd approach the study more gradually. He hadn't wanted to use the big guns unless they were necessary, but it looked as if she had already decided against him. What had happened to all that charisma he thought he had?

"I understood from Malcolm that my case study had already been approved," he said carefully.

"Malcolm? You mean Mr. Cabot?"

Her tone was wary, but he kept his voice soft and apologetic. "I'm sorry. Our families have known each other for years, so I forget myself. Malcolm is my godfather, and Lowell was like a big brother to me."

"Lowell?"

"Yes, Malcolm's younger brother."

"I know," Jaylene replied brusquely. "He was killed in an automobile accident years ago."

He doubted that she knew that it had happened while Lowell had been in northern Italy with his latest mistress, though, or that Malcolm had flown over quickly to pay the woman off so there'd be no scandal. He could still remember Lowell's wife arguing over where that money would come from. She had not been willing to part with a cent of her inheritance just to keep her husband's name free of scandal.

Were all women so greedy, or only the ones he had come in contact with? He wondered what things Miss Sable gave top priority to. From her tone when she began to speak again, he guessed she thought staying on good terms with her CEO was important.

"Actually," she said, "I'm concerned whether we have resources available right now to support you and your case study."

He hid a smile at her newly pleasant tone. "As I'm sure Malcolm told you, we'd like to do our study in your capital funds appropriation area. Why don't you let me take a quick look at that area this afternoon? I can give you an estimate of our requirements later in the day."

She stood up and looked at him with a confident, easy smile.

"That would be fine, doctor. I'll put you in Neal Aldridge's care. He's my director of staff services. Then check with Nancy, the lady who escorted you in. She knows when I'm free at the end of the day."

He decided to see how far her amiability would stretch. "Why don't we cover my estimate over dinner tonight?"

She looked surprised. "I don't think it should take that long," she said, then sneezed.

"The estimate wouldn't, but my cold remedies are rather complex. They would require more time."

Her laugh of honest amusement lit up her face and ignited a spark of desire in him. "You're very persuasive, Dr. Carroll."

"Call me Ray," he said with a smile as he moved toward the door. "I'll work with your secretary on this. See you at six?"

"Fine."

Ray was quite pleased with himself as he closed the door behind him. He had always known that a godfather was useful for more than just sending a card each time his birthday rolled around.

"Give these top three reports to Neal," Jaylene told Rita. "The staff work was inadequate, and I've indicated where more detail is needed."

"Yes, Miss Sable, I'll take care of it." Rita handed Jaylene her signature book, then hesitated. "Was that man here this morning the Harvard professor?"

"Dr. Carroll? Yes, that was he." Jaylene's voice was vague because her mind was elsewhere, but she glanced at her watch as Rita left the room. It was past four already. She was going to have to get things wrapped up here in a few more hours if she was meeting him for dinner.

She opened a file that had been lying on her desk and stared down at it. It was fairly typical. Dick Matthews had been hired in the sixties. He had married young and had good potential, starting night school soon after he was hired to increase his skills. Words like "hard worker" and "dedicated" were scattered through his early appraisals. Then, about eight years ago, the problems started, and his ratings had gone down, although his managers had all written comments about his problems with a sick spouse. Unfortunately, such explanations of extenuating circumstances were not considered part of the pertinent data that went into the computer. She closed the folder, wishing she knew what to do about him.

She picked up her signature book and started going through the documents in it, but after signing a few, she closed it. She didn't seem to be able to think at all today. It was this damn cold. There was nothing worse than a summer cold. Especially in Florida where summer lasted so long.

She walked over to her small refrigerator cabinet and poured herself a glass of orange juice, using it to wash down another couple of aspirin. Then she kicked off her shoes and stretched out on the sofa, willing the medicine to start working. She had too much to do to be sick.

For a brief moment, she was sorry she had lost Ken. It would be nice to be going out to dinner with him tonight for fun instead of having a business meeting over the meal. She needed to feel free of the pressures occasionally and actually to talk to people, not just to issue orders. It would be wonderful to have time to relax without feeling that she was on display.

When she broke off with Ken, she'd assumed that she would find someone else to take his place, but the reality of her situation was only starting to sink in. She worked unbelievably long hours and had watchdogs guarding her every minute. When would she be able to meet some eligible men? No one here at TIE was suitable; dating someone she worked with would be a fatal mistake. She had learned that long ago from the experiences of others. Being thirty-eight didn't help, either.

Maybe she should try again to get Aunt Sophie to come for a visit. She hadn't been to Miami yet, and they could relax and have a good time together. It was more than a year since she had seen her aunt, and she realized suddenly that she missed her. She could be herself with Aunt Sophie.

Her intercom buzzed, and Jaylene sat up quickly, slipping her feet into her shoes. "Yes?" she asked, feeling a little dizzy from getting up so fast.

It was only Nancy. "Anything on your agenda for tonight? I'm supposed to call Sue if she's needed."

Jaylene rubbed her eyes tiredly. She opened her mouth to tell Nancy of her dinner plans with Dr. Carroll, but

closed it again abruptly. She didn't have to wait until
Aunt Sophie came for a visit. This was a chance to be herself and have a little fun. Dr. Carroll—Ray, she corrected
herself—was not a TIE employee. Although he was not totally divorced from her work situation, there was no reason why she couldn't combine business with pleasure.

She was tired of the constant baby-sitting, and it was
time to cut some of the strings that made her TIE's puppet.
This was the first time in ages that she had been invited on
a date, even if it was a business one. She was going to enjoy
herself without a watchdog.

"No, I won't need her. I'm going to have an early night
and try to get rid of this cold. I'll grab whoever's on duty to
take me home."

Stepping back from her intercom, Jaylene fell into her
chair, and a laugh escaped her lips. She had done it, and it
felt good. Security would be furious if they ever found out,
but how would they? She wasn't as recognizable as they
seemed to think.

She'd have to figure out how to give Rose the slip, but
that shouldn't be a major problem. Certainly nothing
unsolvable.

She smiled. Either the aspirins were working or her cold
wasn't as bad as it had seemed. Suddenly she was feeling
much better, and more excited than she had been for ages.
Dr. Carroll was a handsome man and looked as if he knew
how to have a good time. And his voice! She could listen to
it all night. It was deep and rich, as if he had stereo speak-
ers buried in his chest. She got shivers just thinking about
it. Tonight was going to be one terrific night!

Chapter Five

Ray looked around The Jolly Pirate. It was a typical singles bar with lots of plants, dark wood decor, and shapely young waitresses. Actually, he was surprised at the type of restaurant Jaylene had chosen. He had expected something sedate and businesslike, something that matched her personality. Could it be that he had misjudged her, and that underneath her cool exterior beat the heart of a swinging, liberated lady?

Maybe she was even a wild nymphomaniac, he thought, sipping his drink. And maybe in order to keep the case study running smoothly, he'd have to satisfy her voracious appetites constantly.

He had a sudden vision of her office as he had seen it that afternoon, except that Jaylene was stalking him around those leather chairs. He tried to fend her off, but she was too much for him and seduced him on the couch. She impatiently ripped his clothes off, her hands roaming over his body in delight, as she challenged him to quench her burning fires.

Ray gulped at his drink, needing to quench a few fires of his own and keep his imagination from running away with him. She would most likely show up in her business suit, get the case study disposed of in a few minutes, and leave—probably to return to her office to get in a few more hours of work tonight. If she did anything to excess, it was most likely work, not sex.

"Sorry I'm late. I got lost."

He glanced up, coming out of his thoughts with a shock

as he saw a young woman sitting down across from him. Her voice sounded like Jaylene, but the form-fitting jeans and the lacy white blouse did not look like her. She smiled, her green eyes sparkling and her soft brown hair curling on her shoulders.

"I've passed this place a million times, but couldn't get onto the frontage road."

"No problem," he assured her, his gaze lingering over her body appreciatively. Maybe his daydream had been right. Maybe she was going to lure him into the darkness and ravage his body. "You're well worth the wait."

She looked slightly uneasy about his compliment, and he smiled in encouragement. Okay, so she wasn't a nymphomaniac; she still looked terrific, and they would have a good time tonight even if he had to mention Malcolm in every other sentence. The waitress appeared at their table and Jaylene ordered a whiskey sour.

"You know, I almost didn't recognize you," Ray admitted once they were alone again. "I was expecting someone in a business suit."

She blushed slightly. "It's after business hours, you know."

"So it is." His smile grew even warmer as his eyes caressed her. She was a gorgeous lady. He reached over and quickly touched her hand. "A lot of executives don't make that distinction between business and their personal lives. I'm glad to see how different you are."

She didn't seem to know what to say and retreated to safer ground. "Well, Ray, just how much are you going to bug us?"

"Only as much as you let me."

She looked unprepared for his suggestive remarks and he took pity on her, pulling a small notebook out of his coat pocket. "We ought to be able to complete the case study in about six weeks. Preferably we'd like to start around the first of October and finish up before Thanksgiving."

"How many people would you be bringing in?"

"Three graduate students. We'd need a secretarial contact for supplies and that sort of thing. Then I'd like a management-level person to act as a liaison between your management and professional staff and us."

She was silent for a long time, spinning her drink slowly. "Well, as I said," she sighed, "the powers that be have already made the decision."

His hand reached out to cover hers on the table, squeezing it gently. Her skin was warm, and he wondered how that hand would feel sliding across his body. Would her touch be gentle or demanding?

"I really do appreciate all that you're doing for us, Jaylene," he said softly. "Let me buy you dinner."

She seemed to hesitate, then laughed lightly. "Sure, that's what I came here for."

Unable to take his eyes off her, he waved the waitress over. Jaylene opened the large menu and bent her head to study it. He gave his only a cursory glance, preferring instead to watch her, to watch the way her hair fell forward onto her face, the absentminded way she pushed it back. She did not seem a hard, take-charge businesswoman, but a soft, alluring lady. He wanted to feel her wiggling in delight beneath him.

"You know what I'd like?" she said suddenly, putting down her menu. "A pizza with everything."

He glanced down at his menu, frowning. "It doesn't appear to be served here."

"I know. But I'd still like one. I can't remember the last time I had a pizza."

Impulsive behavior was a good sign. "Do you know a place around here that makes good pizza?"

"If I haven't had any in years, how would I?"

"Very good," he said, and grinned at her. "I was just testing you."

Jaylene broke into a grin herself, and he found it totally disarming. All sorts of plans began to form in his head. This was a lady he wanted to get to know.

They rose to their feet as he tossed some money for their drinks onto the table. Then he took her arm and they walked from the restaurant, stopping next to her Porsche. That, too, was a good sign. Stodgy, dull businesspeople did not drive Porsches.

"Now how are we going to find this pizza?" Ray asked.

"I thought we could just drive around. There have to be lots of pizza places in this area, and we'll just chose one."

He had a better idea. "That's no guarantee it'll be any good," he pointed out. "And there's nothing worse than bad pizza."

"So?" she asked suspiciously.

"I bet the doorman at your building would know a good place."

"So?"

She sounded even more suspicious, but he hurried on. "Well, you drive home and have him order a pizza for you."

"You know, you're about as subtle as a sledgehammer," she pointed out.

He ignored her comment. "I'll get my car and find a good New York–style deli and pick up some wine and salad. Then I'll meet you at your place."

She was silent so long that he thought he had pushed his luck too far. He found her desirable, there was no denying that, but he wasn't actually intending to seduce her to-night. After all, he had to be careful of Malcolm, also. All he needed was some affronted virgin running to Malcolm with a tale of how he had molested her, and he wasn't sure how much good this godfather relationship would do him. And it would be a trifle difficult to explain to Harvard why one of his case studies got canceled.

"All right," she said suddenly, her eyes flashing. "But if the pizza gets there before you do, I'm not waiting."

Rose was in the foyer waiting for her when Jaylene opened the apartment door. The woman's hard look seemed to soften when Jaylene stepped in.

"Were you going out, Rose?"

"No, I just was making sure it was you at the door," she replied as she took her hands out of the pockets of the full skirt she wore. Nancy wore the same kind, and Jaylene was sure that Rose had a thirty-eight strapped to her thigh, just like Nancy. A shiver went through her body.

She moved by Rose and went toward her bathroom.

"George is ordering a pizza for me. I'm going to work here tonight."

"Okay," Rose replied.

"I'll be working with a gentleman by the name of Ray Carroll. He's a professor at Harvard. They're going to do a study down here, and we have to review some plans. He's already passed TIE's security check."

Jaylene left her purse on her bed, then slipped out of her new sandals. Two red spots had appeared on the outside of each foot. She touched up her makeup and went back to the kitchen.

"I've had a hard day," Rose said. "I think I'll turn in early tonight. Call if you need me."

"We'll work quietly."

"Oh, don't worry about disturbing me," Rose said. "I survived my kids' teenage years in a tiny house. This place is so big, I probably won't even hear you."

Jaylene frowned as Rose went back down the hall. She was suddenly aware of how little she knew about Rose, just that she had been a policewoman in Cleveland before she retired and moved down here. They had been living in the same apartment for a couple of weeks, and yet Jaylene had never asked about her family or why she had moved to Florida.

When had she become so distant and uninterested in the people around her? Growing up in the closely knit Polish community in South Bend, she had always been sensitive and aware of others. Even when she had been working as a maid to put herself through school, she had trained herself to watch the people she came in contact with.

Of course, that had been more to copy their manners and social ease than because she cared about them. And then at TIE she had been working so hard to get ahead that she always seemed to be transferred before she had time to get to know anyone. Unless it had been someone who could be useful to know. Like Jesse.

She was glad when the intercom sounded. She didn't really want to dwell on the unhappy conclusion that she had become single-dimensional and uncaring. She told the doorman to send the pizza up. Ray arrived a few minutes later.

"Am I too late? Did you eat it all?" he asked, making exaggerated panting sounds.

Jaylene laughed and held the door open. She felt better seeing him. Ray was just what she needed to banish her melancholy thoughts. "Don't worry, I was going to give you a few minutes' grace. The pizza is in the oven staying warm."

She led him down the hall and into her white and stainless steel kitchen. He seemed impressed by its efficient look.

"Are you a master chef as well as a master financier?"

"Oh, definitely." She laughed. "I have so much time to slave over a hot stove."

As she watched, Ray slipped out of his jacket and unpacked the bag he had brought in. She was more and more attracted to him, she realized. He was so relaxed, yet still very much in control. Her eyes followed the line of his arms, and she wondered what it would be like to be held by them.

She turned away abruptly and carefully folded up the box the pizza had come in. They were working together, or would be soon. It was a sticky situation, and she had to be careful.

"Got a bowl?"

His voice startled her, and she quickly grabbed a salad bowl from the cabinet, then a corkscrew and some wineglasses. He grinned at her.

She forced a slight smile. "Have you ever been to Miami before?"

"A few times." He dumped the tossed salad into the bowl. "Looks like I got a bit too much. Got any pet rabbits?"

She reached over and took a piece. "I like salad."

He opened the wine. "This looks pretty big, too. Got any pet winos?"

She just laughed and took a glass. "I like wine, too. Here's to a successful case study."

He shook his head. "Here's to continued goodwill between the alumni of the Harvard and University of Chicago business schools."

She was surprised that he knew where she had gone to school. So he had investigated her background. Was he interested in her as a person, or was she just part of the case study? She'd like to think he was curious about her, but what was there about her or her accomplishments to fascinate anyone? Unless they were also studying TIE.

She refused to give in to any depressing thoughts and took the pizza out of the oven. "Why don't you bring your wine and the salad?" she suggested. "I thought we'd sit in the living room."

"Great."

He picked up the salad and went ahead of her through the door. When she brought the pizza in a few moments later, she found him studying an elaborate painting of geometric designs. It was an idiotic thing to hang on the wall; its only value was in its complementary color scheme. For some reason, she wanted to distract Ray's attention from it.

"You're certainly an art connoisseur," she said as she put the pizza on the low table before the sofa. "You commented on my office artwork and now you're fascinated by a picture in my home."

"People's collectibles are a reflection of themselves," he replied as he came over to her.

"Well, you should know TIE's interior decorator quite well by now."

He looked around the room slowly. "Did the interior decorator do the whole apartment?"

"Yes," she replied.

He turned back to her and intoned in a melodramatic voice, "Somewhere in these cold furnishings is buried the soul of the real Jaylene Sable."

Jaylene shook her head with a laugh. "Well, if you can find it, you'll be doing better than I."

"Maybe you just need a guide," he said quietly, his brown eyes firmly holding her, eyes so soft, yet so surprisingly strong.

The urge to melt into his arms was almost irresistible, but somehow Jaylene managed to pull her gaze away. She

had been cautious so long that she didn't know how to be
anything else where her feelings were concerned.

Yet when his hand came up to brush aside a stray curl,
all thoughts of caution vanished from her mind. Her heart
began to race, and desire sped through her blood. She tried
to pull back but found that she couldn't. Her body wanted
to stay close to his; she wanted to feel his hands on more of
her than just her cheek. But was he really attracted to her,
or was this all part of some game he was playing?

The safe business world she had surrounded herself with
for the past fifteen years had not prepared her for the sen-
sual onslaught of someone like Ray. She didn't know how
to respond to him. No, that was wrong. Part of her certainly knew how. But her stubborn mind was sending out
warning signals. Should she heed them or throw caution to
the wind for a change?

The warning signals won for the moment. "We'd better
eat this pizza before it gets cold," she said briskly.

Ray did not seem surprised by her abrupt change of
mood and sat down next to her. After a few bites of pizza,
she felt more confident and directed the conversation to
safe topics: school, travel, work. When everything was
gone but the wine, she felt exhausted. She hadn't talked
that much about her life in ages. It had been a release for
her, and she could think of nothing else to talk about.

Ray refilled their glasses. "So tell me about yourself."

She leaned back on the sofa and laughed. "I thought I
just did. You've just heard all there is to Jaylene Sable."

"You sprang to life in graduate school?" he probed. "Rising like a Venus out of a corporate accounting text. What
about your childhood? Where did you grow up?"

"Indiana." An unwelcome image of her poor neighborhood flashed into her mind. She preferred to think about
the present, about being here with him. She was suddenly
thirsty and drank most of her glass of wine. He refilled it.

"A farm girl, eh?"

She shrugged to avoid answering. "What about you?"

"A dyed-in-the-wool easterner. Old family. I've lived in
New England for three or four generations."

They both laughed at his exaggeration and then lasped

into silence. She watched him as he sipped his wine. Professor Carroll and the alcohol. It was a heady combination, and she felt her body begin to burn with desire. There was something about him that made her crave his touch and long to feel him lying beside her.

He was attractive and intelligent, and he seemed strong yet gentle. She wondered what fires his hands could kindle in her. Stronger and deeper than those Ken had found smoldering, she knew, for there had been nothing about Ken that had attacked the innermost reaches of her soul as this man's presence seemed to.

She closed her eyes slightly and imagined his body covering hers, his hands and his lips demanding her passionate response. She could almost feel his flesh beneath her hand as she would succumb to the desires of her own body and his. Together they would make a protective haven for their love and find safety within each other's embrace, for a short time at least.

Somewhat startled by the path of her thoughts, she realized there was one topic they had not even touched on all evening.

"Are you married?" Her question seemed to stun him, and she felt embarrassed. "I guess that was kind of abrupt, but, well, I just wondered."

He laughed easily. "No. I tried it years ago, but it didn't fit. How about you?"

"Are you kidding? I've been TIEd down for years." Suddenly it seemed too true, and she longed for even a few hours of freedom and release.

"I guess your career would keep you busy."

She nodded. "Same with you?"

"It's hard to travel as much as I do and have any kind of a home life." He looked toward the spectacular view. "I do consulting along with my academic work at Harvard, and it keeps me on the road a lot. I can find the bathroom in any major airport in the world with my eyes closed and I can call a taxi in sixteen languages."

She laughed, though she felt somewhat sad. He seemed to enjoy the constant travel and unsettled life. Why did she find it too much at times?

"If I'm not going to some Latin American country," she said, "I'm planning a trip to New York. There's always something."

He smiled in agreement, and a companionable silence seemed to envelop them like a large, soft cocoon, holding relaxation and peace in while keeping out the cares and tensions of the outside world.

Suddenly Ray leaned forward. "Do you ever feel like chucking it all for a picket fence and the pitter-patter of little feet?" he asked curiously.

The spell was broken, and she frowned at him angrily. Hadn't he felt that powerful attraction that she had? Or was she just an extension of TIE to him? A vague curiosity to be studied? "Why should I want to chuck it all? Because I'm a woman? It's all right for men to devote their whole lives to their careers, I suppose, but not for a woman."

He leaned back, apparently surprised by her vehemence. "I'm sorry," he said tightly. "It was a dumb question."

"Actually, I've never wished things could be any other way," Jaylene went on, ignoring his apology and feeling hurt. She had wanted him but he had not wanted her, and she suddenly had to convince them both that she was perfectly happy. "I decided a long time ago what I wanted out of life, and I've got it all. A great job. A nice home. Enough money to buy all the clothes and cars and extras. There's never been anything to regret."

But even as she said it, mocking thoughts flooded her mind, thoughts of the lonely nights she had spent in the past, and of the lonely nights that loomed ahead. That night in particular, once Ray had gone and she was alone. No, not even alone. There was TIE's security guard watching her every move. She had thought TIE was everything to her, but it wouldn't be much comfort tonight when she went to bed by herself.

Ray said nothing, and she wondered if he, too, had seen the emptiness in her words. But he just reached for the wine bottle. It was empty, and he put it down with a sigh.

"Just as well, I guess," he said. "It's time I was going anyway. Thanks for the pizza and the company."

"Thanks for the salad and wine." She stood up also, barely reaching his shoulders in her bare feet. "I hope you didn't catch my cold."

"I'm not worried," Ray said as he took her by the shoulders and quickly kissed her on the lips.

"Now you'll get my cold for sure," Jaylene warned.

He just laughed. "You only live once, kid. Go for the gusto." He let himself out the door and, just before closing it, looked back and winked. "See you in a few weeks." The door shut quietly after him.

Jaylene sighed and walked into the living room to clean up. She stared at the magnificent view for a moment. Then she shook her head and bent to pick up the empty glasses. The view could fill the windows, but it did nothing for the hollowness inside her.

Chapter Six

In his California office, Dave Margolis shoved papers and folders around his desk. Damn it. Where was that stupid report? He had to get those figures in today before everyone left for the Labor Day weekend.

"The hell with this." He pushed the intercom button and barked, "Laurel."

Almost immediately, a tall black lady walked into his office. "What can I do for you, Mr. Margolis?"

"I had an earnings projection report and it isn't here now."

"I gave it to you yesterday."

"I'm not talking about yesterday," he snapped. "I need it now."

"All those files are online," Laurel told him. "You can look at them through your terminal."

Margolis glanced distastefully at the little CRT and keyboard near his desk. "I don't like playing with little toys. I want that damn report and I want it now."

"I'll get you another copy," she replied coolly and walked out the door.

He glared after her as he gulped down the lukewarm remains of his coffee and then hitched up his pants slightly. It was getting harder to keep the old belly flat, and that damn handball court seemed to get bigger every time he went in. But he couldn't afford to give up his exercise. Personal appearances counted in TIE, and if he let himself get fat and sloppy, he'd never get the foreign sub presidency. They'd figure if he couldn't control his body, he couldn't control a worldwide business.

The coffee caused a burning sensation in his stomach, and a pained expression came to his face. TIE liked promptness. He'd better call Jesse and explain the reason for his delay. He pulled the phone toward him and dialed the number.

"Mr. Whitmore's office," a female voice said.

"Give me, Jesse, sweetheart."

There was a pause and then, "Tom Jordan here."

Damn. Who'd they think it was? Some idiot selling aluminum siding? "I asked for Jesse."

"He's tied up, Margolis. You got those numbers for us?"

"I'm getting them. I just wanted to explain the reasons for the delay." Why the hell should he be making excuses to some underling administrative assistant?

"We're full up on excuses today, Margolis. Just give us the numbers."

"You'll get them real soon." He could feel the anger churning in his stomach. He'd never liked that jerk Jordan.

"Well, I'm going to be tied up the rest of the morning, so call Ruthie when you've got your data." He paused for a split second, then noted, "All the other foreign subsidiaries have turned theirs in."

Margolis slammed the phone down. All the other foreign subsidiaries, hell! There was only one other foreign subsidiary, and that was Jaylene's. Of course, she'd have her numbers in on time. She probably wasn't working with an incompetent staff.

He began to tap his fingers on the desk as he always did when he was irritated. Good old Jaylene. Trying to outshine him again. But it wasn't going to work this time. When that consolidation rolled around, he was going to be president, not Jaylene.

Foreign subsidiaries had advantages no domestic division could match. There was a lot of extra income just waiting to be picked up. Various governments, all anxious for American dollars to flow into their country, were willing to pay for the privilege. Lots of suppliers were willing to kick back a good percentage of their TIE business to a friendly executive.

Margolis chewed on his thumbnail. Rumors had it that Kareau was destined to move over to the corporate staff. Senior vice president of marketing. And Burnbridge, his own boss, was ready to retire. That just left him and Jaylene shooting for the presidency.

The pain in his stomach became severe as the muscles twisted even tighter. He chewed on his knuckles to keep from crying out. He had to do something. Not only did he have to pay Jaylene for services rendered in the past, but he had to derail her train to the top. That pipeline that fed his Swiss bank account was his life's blood.

His thoughts turned to Rita Kastle. She was perfect. From the old school. She disliked working for a woman. Twice divorced. She knew she was likely to remain alone. She was a woman who could be persuaded to do anything in exchange for a little flattery and attention. Best of all, Jaylene couldn't really dump her. Old man Cabot would see to that. She could help him, but how? He picked up his phone and quickly dialed a number.

"Good afternoon. Rita Kastle speaking." An obviously tired voice came over the line.

"Hello, Rita. Dave Margolis here. Cheer up. It's almost quitting time for you folks at that end of the country."

"Quitting time for our staff usually stretches out into the evening," she replied, a touch of bitterness creeping into her voice.

"Sounds like old Jaylene is a real slave driver." He was careful not to sound critical.

"She's quite ambitious, Mr. Mar— Dave." There was a pause. "She's not here at the moment. Could I take a message?"

"Actually, I didn't want to talk to her, Rita."

"Oh?"

There was a definite smile in her voice that pleased him. He had known she'd be a snap to win over, and he was silent for several moments for effect. "I'm sorry, Rita. I really shouldn't bother you like this. Busy as you are, you certainly don't need somebody calling you cross-country with inconsequential items."

Rita's laugh was light and flirtatious. "I enjoy the break, believe me."

He laughed with her. "You know, I really enjoyed our lunch in New York. Do you think we could do it again soon?"

"I'd like that. Maybe we should coordinate our trips more." There was a short silence, and then she continued with a heavy touch of bitterness. "Of course, I don't travel as much as I used to. Miss Sable prefers that I manage the administrative requirements here at home base."

Margolis was silent again and then cleared his throat as if in embarrassment. "Actually, Rita. I have a favor to ask. I've come into some money recently. A trust fund my father set up years ago has matured."

"You're lucky. The only thing I have maturing is my body."

"Like a fine wine," he said smoothly. He knew from her quiet giggle that his flattery was working. "Anyway, my broker has indicated to me that Florida real estate is a good investment right now. And I'd like to look over some stuff, especially in the Miami area. Unfortunately, I know nothing about the city and really could use a guide. Someone I could trust."

"Well, I do know Miami."

"I know you're busy, but I'd sure appreciate it if you could help me look. I'm going to New York next week and thought about flying down to Miami on Friday."

"For the weekend?"

"Is that a problem?" Damn. He had never thought about her having other plans. "If you have something else planned, that's all right."

"No, I don't. Shall I pick you up at the airport?"

"If it wouldn't be too much trouble. I'll call you in the middle of the week with the details then, shall I?" He paused, then lowered his voice. "I'm looking forward to seeing you again."

"Me, too."

He hung up the phone slowly, a satisfied smile lighting his face. Rita was going to help him. All he had to was figure out how. He left his office for his luncheon appointment and pondered on what use Rita could be to him. As he pulled into the parking lot of a small restaurant and bar not far from the Santa Monica beach, he relaxed. He could count on Brewster to think of something.

The Pink Pony was a dirty little joint that served grease and ptomaine along with strippers for lunch and dinner. Once in a while a young comer showed up among the girls, but most of them had had their moment in the sun. It was Brew Merrill's favorite spot, and Margolis only agreed to meet him there because it was dark.

He paused in the entryway to let his eyes become adjusted to the dimly lit interior. He saw the private detective at his usual table in front of the small stage, on which a dancer was gyrating. A disco record was playing, but the dancer was following her own tune. She looked thirty going on sixty-five.

Ignoring the bouncer who also served as the maître d', Margolis went directly to the table. Brewster was engrossed in the woman making erotic love to a customer's necktie and did not immediately acknowledge Margolis's presence.

Margolis had only glanced briefly at the pathetic woman. She was as repulsive as the fat little detective across the table from him. He was shaped like a pear, with large hips that accentuated the shortness of his arms and legs. Each pudgy finger ended with a dirty fingernail. A piranha would find it hard to love Brewster Merrill, but he served a purpose.

Once the tie was properly anointed, the dancer tossed it back to the customer. Margolis remained still while Merrill joined in the general merriment.

Finally Merrill turned to him. "Boy, I guess you corporate types never lighten up."

"I prefer a little more class in my entertainment."

Brewster had turned back to the dancer, and Margolis grew impatient. "I don't have all day, Merrill."

"Okay. Okay." Reluctantly, he turned his attention back to Margolis. "Your money will be in Switzerland by today or tomorrow. Cheng says he don't want no more trouble with your quality control guys. If he does, no more bonuses.''

"I've taken care of it.''

A bored dancer took her turn on stage as a waitress came by. Brewster ordered a hamburger with a double order of french fries and a pitcher of beer. Margolis ordered his usual: Old Style, in a bottle.

"I have a very special project for you, Brew.''

The other man merely nodded, his eyes straying slightly back to the dancer.

"There's a lady in Florida. Works for our Latin American subsidiary. Her name is Jaylene Sable, and I want you to find all her weaknesses.''

Their order came and Brewster immediately attacked his plate. Margolis nursed his beer, drinking straight from the bottle. He let some of the beer slop over, hoping that the alcohol would kill the germs if the bartender or waitress had touched the rim.

As Brewster ate, Margolis filled him in on Jaylene's background, or the little he knew of it, and the impending consolidation. He emphasized that if he was out and Jaylene was in, the gravy train would cease running. If the reverse happened, the haul could more than double. The possibility so unnerved Brewster that he asked for another double order of french fries.

"We're gonna need someone to watch her every move. An inside person is best.''

"I got her administrative assistant nibbling on some bait,'' Margolis replied. "I should be able to reel her in in a couple of days.''

Brewster's head bobbed up and down on his scrawny neck like one of those toy dogs some people put in the rear windows of their cars. "Good, good. How about outside of work?''

Margolis shrugged. "I don't know who, if anyone, she socializes with.'' Brewster's face twisted in a semblance of a smile. "One of those dedicated corporate types, huh? Does anyone live with her?''

"Yeah,'' Margolis replied. "Corporate security has hired

a housekeeper, personal security type. I don't know anything about her."

"Sounds like I'm gonna have to go to Miami," Brewster mumbled through a soggy mass of chewed potatoes. "I can check the housekeeper out. They probably hired her through some local security outfit. A lot of my old friends are still around."

"I didn't know that you'd lived in Miami, Brew."

Brewster snickered around a handful of french fries. "I used to have a little entertainment business down there. Offshoot from my Cleveland operation."

Margolis glared sharply at him. "I don't want you into that crap anymore."

Brewster just smiled.

"I mean it, Brew," Margolis said through clenched teeth. "There is too much at stake here to have you blow it fooling around with little boys."

This time Brewster laughed outright. "Don't worry, Davie. It's just a hobby with me now."

Margolis rose to leave. "There's big bucks in it if I can get the whole enchilada, Brew. Three, four, five times what we pull in now."

Brewster just nodded slowly, an ugly smile on his face.

Margolis turned quickly to leave the joint, shaking his head. As he walked out the door into the bright sunlight, a hard smile came to his face. The man was slime, but he knew his business. Jaylene was as good as buried.

Chapter Seven

"She can hold her head up all by herself now."

Ray sighed inwardly as he stared at the colored snapshot of the bald-headed, cross-eyed, jug-eared baby. But he and George Kors, professor of accounting, had been friends for many years, and Ray had to come up with something nice to say about George's child. With his limited knowledge of babies, he was out of his league.

"She looks like a happy child," he said lamely.

"Yes, she is," George agreed. "Very much so. And you realize, I'm sure, that a sense of humor is one of the best indications of a superior intellect."

"Yes, I . . . I believe that I read a research report to that effect," Ray replied.

"Here, Ray, pass that on to John. I have a good number of shots that I took over the Labor Day weekend that you'll find interesting."

Ray held the photograph out to John Lithford, professor of statistics, who was looking at it as if the photograph were covered with maggots. He did not put his hand out for it.

"Come, come, John," George scolded. "Take it and pass it on. There are others who want to see it."

John slowly took the photograph in hand while three other glum faces stared at him. What had started as a regular, pleasant Tuesday lunch in the faculty cafeteria for the six of them had suddenly turned depressing. They had been discussing strategy for the annual freshman/faculty lacrosse scrimmage scheduled for that afternoon when

George, for some reason, had hauled out pictures of his child.

"Now, this picture clearly demonstrates that intelligence and strength are not mutually exclusive," George said as he shoved another picture of the cross-eyed child at Ray. "In fact, the latest thinking goes back to the ideal of ancient Greece: that strength, beauty, and intelligence go hand in hand."

Ray nodded solemnly. "Yes, I see that she's grasping a finger."

"That's my little finger," George said. "And you've probably noticed the small white spots on the tip."

Ray nodded in agreement although he didn't see a thing. He had learned quickly to accept all George's pronouncements about the child. Any question or expression of doubt just prolonged the agony.

"That's an indication that the skin is lacking in oxygen. Melissa's grip has restricted the blood flow in that finger to twenty-three to twenty-six percent of its normal volume."

"Very interesting," Ray responded, and shoved the picture to the man next to him. "Here, John. Would you like to see this?"

"Certainly," John answered through clenched teeth.

"Now here's Melissa—"

A tiny buzzing sound interrupted George's discourse. Kent Vogel, who was also in the accounting department, turned off his wristwatch and popped out of his chair. "I have to be off, gentlemen," he said cheerfully. "Department meeting in ten minutes."

George looked quickly at his watch. "Right you are, Kent. Let me gather my things and I'll walk with you."

"I have to stop by my office first."

"Very good," George replied as he inserted the pictures into an envelope. "So do I."

Kent swallowed painfully. "See you all at the match later," he called, keeping a small smile on his face.

As the two of them left, George's voice floated back to the table. Something about supermarket shelves meeting a child's need for color stimuli.

John finally broke the silence. "It's obscene, that's what it is. Hell. He's at least fifty years old."

"I hear his wife is about thirty-seven."

"The miracles of modern medicine," another man grumbled. "It solves one problem and creates several others."

"Come on, gentlemen," Ray cajoled. "It's George's first marriage and first child." A sly grin slipped across his face. "At least the first he's admitting to."

The others all joined in the laughter.

"I don't mind old George's pride and all that. But, damn, he's constantly shoving pictures in your face or talking your ear off about that kid."

"Yes, you'd think he found a cure for cancer and eliminated the national debt, all in one fell swoop."

John had been silent after his initial outburst and now he sadly shook his head. "George used to be so much fun. He was always going to conferences around the world and coming back with the wildest stories to enliven our own dull lives. Remember that summer you and he spent some time at the London School of Economics?"

Ray grinned. "You mean when he decided we should write a paper on which part of the British Isles produced the best lovers? That was quite an undertaking. We compared girls from Wales, Britain, and Scotland. Extensive research. Took us all summer."

Jolly, comfortable male laughter echoed around the table.

"As I remember, he said it was a tie," John murmured. "Didn't want to hurt anyone's feelings in case he ever went back there."

"Small good it would do him now," someone sighed.

"If he did go back, the only stories he would share with us would be about Melissa in London anyway," someone else added. Silence descended on the table as they sadly pondered the truth in the statements.

John turned to Ray suddenly. "You're the only one left, Ray. If you get married, there'll be no one left to live out our sexual fantasies."

"No need to worry about that, gentlemen," Ray replied as he began gathering his dishes onto his tray.

"That's what George said," someone reminded him.

"Yes, but there is a difference between George and me," Ray pointed out. "I've been married before and got it out of my system."

John laughed and slapped him on the back. "Good show, Ray. I knew that we could depend on you."

They made plans to meet in a couple of hours to warm up for the scrimmage game, then Ray left. It was a beautiful Indian summer day and he decided to take the long way back to his offices.

There was little need for his colleagues to worry, he told himself. He had the best life imaginable and was not about to tamper with perfection. Trading his freedom for a wife would be the height of folly. All he'd get was someone who'd spend his money and tell him he was too old to play lacrosse, like Kent's wife did. It was ridiculous. Kent had been their best player, and now he was relegated to the sidelines because she was afraid he'd hurt his knee again.

"Dr. Carroll. Oh, doctor."

Ray looked up to see a young woman running across the lawn toward him. Her long blond hair streamed out behind her and her peasant-style dress slipped off one shoulder. She was barefoot and carried her sandals in one hand.

She stopped in front of him, breathless. Her lips were parted and there was a healthy glow on her cheeks. "I'm so glad that I saw you, Dr. Carroll. I wanted to tell you that I'm switching my major to finance."

Ray blinked, trying to concentrate on what she was saying instead of how she looked. "That's good, Dianna. We work hard, but I'm sure that you'll find it interesting, challenging, and fun."

She laughed softly, deep in her throat. "I'm counting on that," she almost whispered. "I understand that you're not only a good teacher, but also a very fine gentleman."

He took a deep breath. Did she emphasize the *man* in gentleman, or was his mind playing tricks on him? "I'll look forward to seeing you in class," he said quickly and then stepped around her. "You'll have to excuse me right now. I'm rather pressed for time."

"Good-bye, doctor."

Ray just waved without looking back and hurried on. Dianna Edwards was a very good student, but she also had a reputation as a huntress. The scalps of several graduate teaching assistants dangled from her belt. It looked like she was setting her sights on bigger game this year.

He blew his breath out and shook himself violently to suppress the physical desire clouding his mind. Women like Dianna could break up homes and bring down kingdoms, much less turn a bachelor's head. But Ray knew enough to avoid those kinds of entanglements. He didn't want to be accused of favoritism or have some young thing expecting marriage. No, give him a woman who knew the rules every time.

That was why he preferred women in their thirties, dedicated to their careers. Like him, they were interested only in temporary, pleasant company, and lacked the desire to entangle him or get emotionally involved themselves.

Jaylene was a perfect example. Of all the women he'd known, she was probably the least likely to get emotionally involved with anyone. To reach her present position, she had had to manage her emotions very tightly and was probably suited by nature for that. He could easily have dinner with her one more time without putting anyone at risk.

Maybe he was being overly cautious, but he had seen too many one-sided affairs in the past, and the heartbreak they brought. The route he chose was safer, both for himself and the women he dallied with, and that was the way he preferred it. He guessed it was a gift of sorts from Lowell.

He and Lowell had been as close as brothers for a time. It seemed only natural that Ray spend all his vacations at the Cabots' summer home in Maine, for Ray's mother had been Lowell's and Malcolm's first cousin. After she died, Lowell's mother had been only too happy to include Ray with her family.

Malcolm and his sister were almost grown by that time, but Lowell was only five years older than Ray. Lowell was like no one Ray had ever met before. The youngest of the Cabot children, he was treated more like a spoiled grand-

son than a son. Everything he wanted was handed to him
with pleasure, and the trouble he got into was laughed
away. Ray watched Lowell with awe, marveling at his
exploits and envying his recklessness.

Lowell seemed to enjoy Ray's hero worship and allowed
him to tag along with him and his friends. He taught Ray
how to sail and how to drive. He gave him advice about
girls and love and life. Ray wanted nothing more from life
than to be like Lowell.

Once Lowell went off to college, though, their relationship changed. Maybe it was partly because of the whispers
around the small resort town about the garage owner's
family who had moved away suddenly. The daughter had
been sixteen and pretty enough to attract Lowell's attention. Rumor had it that she was pregnant and the Cabots
had paid the family to disappear quietly.

Or maybe it was because of the girl Lowell had met at
college who came to the house in tears when he dropped
her. She had been hysterical and had driven away wildly
when he had refused to see her. A few days later, Ray
learned she had been killed in an automobile accident.
Haunted by the memory of her grief, Ray wondered if it
really had been an accident. Lowell had only shrugged off
the news, too busy with his present girl to care.

It didn't take long for Ray's hero worship to fade. As
Lowell grew more and more reckless, Ray became more
and more careful. Lowell laughed at him and called him
his "little conscience," but Ray didn't care. He had seen
people hurt by love. He was not going to be one of them.

One summer, Lowell ran around with the daughter of
another prominent family in New England. No one was
willing to be bought off when she became pregnant, so
there was a quick marriage. The ink was barely dry on the
wedding lines, though, before Lowell was chasing after
someone else.

TIE provided Lowell with a new array of women to play
with, and Ray knew that Malcolm kept up the practice,
started by their father, of buying the women's silence.
Some agreed to an abortion, some accepted the settlement
offered and disappeared with their child. There was one,

Ray heard, who took her life. Lowell's merry-go-round ended in Italy when he had too much to drink and crashed his car. There was one final mistress to pay off, and it was finished. Except for the legacy of memory Lowell had left each of them.

Ray went slowly up the steps to his office. Whenever Malcolm or his mother mentioned Lowell these days, it was always with sad fondness. Was he the only one with bitter memories? Was he the only one fearful of inadvertently repeating Lowell's mistakes?

"Dr. Carroll, I'm sorry to interrupt you, but there's a Mrs. Prescott out here who insists on seeing you."

Ray frowned at his secretary. "I don't know any Mrs. Prescott," he said. He had to leave for the lacrosse game soon. "What does she want?"

His secretary shrugged. "She says it's personal."

"Look, tell her I'm really busy now and ask her to make an appointment."

The door closed and Ray went back to loading his briefcase. He wanted to get out to the field a little earlier than usual. This was the first game of the season, and he wanted to be sure to stretch out properly. He couldn't afford an injury now.

There was a quick knock on the door before it swung open. Now what? he thought irritably. He looked up to see his ex-wife walk in.

"Dr. Carroll," his secretary called as she followed Linda in. "I tried to tell her—"

"It's all right, Mrs. Whitaker." He waved her out of the room. "I can spare a few minutes."

Once the door closed, Ray indicated a chair for Linda and sat down himself. "Mrs. Prescott? I thought you were an O'Neill."

"Oh, that was ages ago," she said with a laugh. "You haven't been keeping up."

He said nothing. She looked as if she had put on some weight, and there was more gray in her hair since the last time he'd seen her about five years ago, but she did look happy. "So who's Mr. Prescott?" he asked.

"Dr. Prescott," she corrected. "Dr. Philip Prescott, head of psychiatry at Boston General."

He smiled. "Quite a catch."

She smiled back. "Quite a nice man."

He sat forward in his chair, slightly embarrassed by his cynical remark, but then the Linda he had been married to hadn't been into nice people, she had been into money and position. "So what can I do for you?"

"Actually, it's what I'm going to do for you," she said, and opened her purse, taking out a velvet-wrapped package. "I'm finally being fair and returning your mother's jewelry." She laid the package on his desk.

He was surprised and unwrapped it slowly. It was his mother's pearl necklace. "You didn't have to give it back," he pointed out. He noticed the large diamond on her left hand. "Or were they too insignificant for your attention now?"

"Ray, that's unfair." Then she stopped and shrugged. "Well, I guess I can understand your thinking that way. After all, I only kept them to spite you, but Philip has made me see how childish that was. Even if their monetary value isn't that large, they do have sentimental value for you."

Ray wrapped them up and put them in his briefcase. "Hardly, Linda. I have no memories of my mother at all."

"You still haven't forgiven her for dying when you were three, have you?"

What kind of a question was that? This conversation was getting ridiculous. "There's nothing to forgive," he pointed out tersely.

"Philip says that's the basis of all your problems."

Terrific. He was delighted to provide them with a topic of conversation. "Just which problems are these?"

Linda did not seem to notice the sarcasm in his voice. "Your inability to make a commitment," she said, crossing her legs. "You see, Philip says that when a boy loses his mother around age three, it interrupts his bonding process, and he may have real trouble later in life making an emotional commitment to a woman."

"Have you forgotten I made a commitment to you?"

She smiled and shook her head. "No, you didn't. That was the whole problem. And I'll bet that in the fifteen years since our divorce, you've never come that close to a commitment again."

"Maybe it's because I prefer the type of life I have now," he pointed out.

"I'm sure you do. It's safer."

He was getting annoyed and rose to his feet. How could he have forgotten that it was impossible to argue with Linda? "Look, this has been just fascinating, but I have a lacrosse game in less than an hour and have to leave."

She got to her feet, too. "Don't you think you're getting a little old to be playing that?"

"No, I don't. You're only as young as you feel, and I feel about twenty. Now I suppose you've got a theory about that, too?"

"Phillip says you're trying to keep busy so that you won't notice how empty your life is."

"Tell Philip I appreciate his concern, misplaced though it is." He picked up his briefcase and went to the door. "It was wonderful seeing you again."

Linda came after him and patted him on the arm. "You should come over one evening for dinner. Philip would love to meet you."

So he could psychoanalyze him in person? "I have a pretty busy schedule," he said. "You know, I'm doing consulting work along with my teaching, and it takes me all over the world."

"Right, and keeps you too busy to get involved with anyone, even as a friend."

He pulled open the door. "Good-bye, Linda."

She smiled. "Good-bye, Ray. And be careful at that game. You heal slower when you're over forty." Thankfully, she left before he had a chance to reply.

Ray winced and gritted his teeth as he stepped gingerly out of the shower. The red, purple, and black spot on his thigh seemed to be growing by the minute, both in color and in pain. The lacrosse field had been in terrible condition with all those potholes concealed by the grass. He was lucky he was in such good shape; he just got bruised when he fell instead of breaking something.

He limped into the bedroom, noticing how tight his knees were. Probably from his fall, too. Although it could be from all the running. The ground was as hard as a rock, and probably everybody who played was a little achy about now, even the freshmen. His age was immaterial. He put on his robe and walked slowly into the kitchen, where he filled an ice bag.

Pain tended to make one weary, he thought as he sat down in the living room. He put his feet up on a low table and balanced the ice bag on his thigh. Linda didn't know what she was talking about. He had always healed fast, and would this time, too. In two or three days, he could play another full game.

A deep frown creased his forehead. He could play another full game if the coach had any sense. All this putting him in and yanking him out was ridiculous. No wonder they had lost by seventeen points. He would just be getting into the flow of the game when Dan would tell him to "take a breather" on the sidelines. Take a breather! What did Dan think he was? An old man? Maybe Linda had been talking to him.

He moved the icepack down on his leg a little. He was going to have a chat with Dan. He knew that being the coach of the faculty lacrosse team was a headache with little glory. He had served a term himself about five years ago, but Dan had accepted, so he should do the job right.

And that didn't mean making the players feel like yo-yos. In and out. In and out. Dan would have to realize that once he put a person in, he should leave him in. But then Dan wasn't exactly the swiftest, even though he was a doctor of sports medicine. Once, after pulling Ray out, he had given him a strange look and asked if he was all right. Obviously the man could not tell the difference between a flush and a healthy glow.

Ray's back was starting to ache slightly, so he hobbled over to the sofa and stretched out. Unfortunately, that put him right under a crack in the ceiling.

His apartment could certainly use some redecorating.

Some new furniture, too. The lumps of the sofa were suddenly more noticeable when they met the lumps on his body. He'd have to talk to the management. After all, he'd lived here long enough to warrant some consideration. With all the money he'd paid in rent, they could have refurnished the place five times over.

He turned to gaze around the room. All the furniture was old and uncomfortable. He shook his head. Just the other day, he had seen the building maintenance people redecorating the apartment down the hall, replacing a lot of the furniture. All that for some new graduate assistant who was just moving in. And here he was, one of the oldest tenants, living with the furniture nobody else wanted.

Sliding down a little farther, Ray put his arm over his eyes, cutting off the image of the cracked ceiling. He really should move. This place was getting a little down at the heel.

He'd moved in right after his divorce. It was convenient to the business school and inexpensive. Plus they were good about taking care of his mail and that sort of thing when he was traveling. But now he was used to staying in the finest hotels, and the contrast always struck him when he came home.

Ray sat up suddenly, knowing now that he really had to move. He had avoided getting attached to people, and now he was getting sentimental about a place. Calling this dump home.

The phone rang, but he did not move. It was too much trouble to go over there. The answering machine could get it. But after the fourth ring, he got wearily to his feet. What was wrong with that damn machine? He hobbled over and picked up the receiver.

"Yes?" he answered curtly.

"Hi, Ray." An annoyingly cheerful feminine voice pierced his ear. "This is Jerelyn. Say, a bunch of us are going into the North End for a little Italian. You know, a little pasta and a lot of vino. You interested?"

He leaned against the table to ease some of his weight from his throbbing leg. The last thing in the world he wanted to do was go barhopping with Jerelyn. She was a bundle of energy and a lot of fun, but she could be just a little too frenetic. At times, a man needed a certain quiet maturity.

"I would like to very much," Ray replied, "but I have some other commitments this evening that I really can't get out of."

"Okay," she responded cheerfully. "Some other time maybe. Nice talking to you."

The line went dead before Ray could reply, but he smiled fondly as he hung up the receiver. The really nice thing about Jerelyn was that she always handled her disappointments very well.

He limped over to the answering machine to see why the call hadn't been picked up. The indicator was set on PLAY instead of RECEIVE. The maid must have knocked it over when she dusted. He set it to RECEIVE and went out into the kitchen to change the ice in the bag.

As he sat down the phone rang again. He breathed a sigh of relief as he heard the machine pick up the call.

After his message a female voice came on. "Ray, this is Lorie. I wasn't paying attention and I made much more food than I can possibly eat in a week. Why don't you come over and help me out? I won't eat until seven, seven-thirty, so call anytime."

Ray sighed as the line went dead. Lorie had been rather clingy lately. She was a managing editor of a book company. He had thought her quite sensible, somehow missing that matronly gleam in her eye. Well, he'd better stay away. He couldn't prevent her foolish dreams, but, as a gentleman, he certainly wouldn't encourage them.

He stared blankly at the window, wondering who he'd find to replace her. Jaylene suddenly came to mind and he smiled. Maybe he ought to cultivate the potential there. She certainly had her head on straight and her priorities in order. Neither was she likely to use the too-much-dinner ploy.

The file for the TIE case study was on the end table next to his chair. He took it and quickly reviewed his notes. Probably should drop her a line and fill her in on the latest details. He remembered her reluctance about the study.

On the other hand, she probably got a ton of mail already and wouldn't even see a letter from him. It would get intercepted by some administrative assistant and routed to the appropriate person on her staff.

He looked at his watch, it was about twenty to five. If she was in town she should be in her office. Maybe he ought to give her a call. Malcolm had approved the study, but its success still depended on Jaylene's cooperation. Looking back, he was afraid that he might have laid it on a little thick about his relationship to Malcolm. He'd definitely better call her.

Ray found her business card and dialed the number.

"Good afternoon, Miss Sable's office. Rita Kastle speaking."

She sounded as tired as he had felt just moments earlier. "Hello, Rita. This is Ray Carroll from Harvard. It's good to hear a sunshine voice from the Sunshine State."

"What can I do for you, Dr. Carroll?" The sunshine disappeared as the Ice Age hit.

"May I speak to Miss Sable, please?"

"I'm sorry. She's in conference at the moment. May I give her a message?"

Ray could see that it was no use chipping at that wall. He'd freeze to death before he got through, so he just left his name and number and hung up.

He limped to the refrigerator for a Pepsi and took a hefty swallow. The more he thought about it, the more convinced he was that this case study would require Jaylene's personal touch. The woman's touch, so to speak. He smiled as he thought of all the ways her touch might be beneficial.

He drained his glass and went over to the kitchen phone. This time he dialed TIE's general number in Miami. Good thing he was proficient at remembering names.

"Good afternoon. TIE Corporation." The voice was professionally pleasant.

"Nancy McConnachie, please."

After a few moment's wait, another voice came on. "Nancy McConnachie speaking."

"I'm sorry to bother you, Nancy. This is Ray Carroll. I

don't know if you remember me. I'm from Harvard, and you escorted me into Miss Sable's office last week."

"I wouldn't forget you, Dr. Carroll."

Ray was disconcerted for a moment. "Actually I was trying to get hold of Miss Sable. The operator must have dialed your extension by mistake."

"Uh huh," she said laconically. "They do that sometimes. Do you want to talk to Miss Sable?"

"I would hate to disturb her if she's busy. I could leave a message. Do you take shorthand? It's a rather long message."

"Why don't I just put you through?" There was a chuckle in her voice as if she found him amusing.

Before he could answer, Jaylene was on the line. "Hello, Ray."

He was startled. "How did you know who it was?"

"Nancy told me."

Of course. That was a stupid question. He shook himself mentally to get into a more businesslike frame of mind. "Do you have a few moments, Miss Sable?" he asked briskly. "I want to cover a few items with you."

"For a person with your connections, Dr. Carroll, of course."

He must have come on too heavy about Malcolm. Good thing he had called. "I want to make sure that you would be personally available for our case study team. One of the doctoral students is a woman, and I think your being a high-level executive would add a positive contemporary flavor to the final write-up of the case."

"I'd be happy to help."

Ray swallowed nervously. That had been taken care of rather quickly. He scanned his mind to determine if there were some other things that should be covered. His notes were in the living room and he really didn't want to drag his leg that far.

"School start yet?"

Her soft voice jerked him out of his thoughts. "Oh, yeah. Classes started about two weeks ago." He cleared his throat. "I'm a doctoral adviser, though, so I don't actually have any teaching assignments. My day consisted of re-viewing thesis topics and a lacrosse scrimmage."

She sighed. "Must be nice to have the time to sit on the grass and just watch some game."

He smiled slightly at her misinterpretation. "I wasn't watching," he told her quietly, but with a certain amount of pride. "I was playing."

"You?" He thought he detected a laugh in her voice. "Isn't that the game where the players beat each other up with sticks?"

"There's a little more to it than that," he told her. "But why did you sound surprised that I'd be playing?"

This time she cleared her throat. "I thought it was a game that was restricted to undergraduates."

How old did she think he was? "It is an amateur sport, but there are many different leagues. Even for us old fellows."

She just laughed again and didn't seem at all concerned that she might have hurt his feelings. "I guess I don't know too much about it."

He took pity on her. "For a midwesterner and a woman—no insult intended—you could be considered quite knowl-edgeable."

"No insult taken, sir. I read the sports page each day, but I don't claim to have great interest in what it says. However, Jesse's told me for years that you've got to get along to get ahead."

"You appear to have done that quite well."

Her laugh warmed his heart, and he wished she wasn't eight hundred miles away. He'd like to take her out to din-ner to some quiet little restaurant with candlelight and good food. Then maybe a little dancing. He shifted his weight and his leg protested. Well, maybe they'd skip the dancing and come back here for some serious conversation. The cracked ceiling and the rummage-sale furniture came into his mind. Just as well she was where she was.

They covered a few more items and then Ray hung up. It was only a little after six. Still too early to eat, but plenty of time to read some of those professional journals that were awaiting him. He limped out to the living room and found the crossword puzzle in the *Boston Globe*.

Chapter Eight

"More coffee, Dave?" Rita asked.

He shook his head and smiled across the table at her. "No, thanks. It was a marvelous meal."

She smiled, then rose to her feet and began to clear away the dirty dishes. "It's been a marvelous weekend and one I shall remember for a long time."

What a thrill it must be to have the money to buy anything they had looked at! Some of those condominiums were gorgeous, and not one was rejected because of the price. She really envied Dave.

"I'll remember it, too," he said, coming right up behind her. He slid his arms around her waist and pulled her close.

Rita was startled at his misinterpretation, but not unpleasantly so. Dave was an attractive man, and not too many of them paid much attention to her these days. They were all off chasing younger things and too busy to think what a more mature woman might be able to offer. It was nice to know that Dave was a bit more discriminating, although she did wonder just why he was singling her out for this attention.

"You're a very special woman, Rita," he whispered, his lips close to her ear. "Is it presumptuous of me to want to know you better?"

"Not at all." She turned in his arms and smiled at him. "Is it presumptuous of me to have been hoping you'd want that?"

He bent down and kissed her. It was a pleasant, if not

91

earth-shattering event, but then Rita had seen Camelot fall a long time ago. The knights were all dead.

"You know, I think we make a terrific team," Dave said. "I could sense that the first time we met."

Rita just smiled in agreement, letting him do the talking. Everybody was after something, usually money, sex, or power. Which did Dave want? He had more money than she did, and her forty-eight-year-old body drove few men wild with desire, so that left only power. But what power did he think she could give him?

He reached down to nuzzle her ear, then pulled her body to his. At the same time, he pressed her back up against the kitchen counter. It certainly appeared that he had an appetite he wanted satisfied.

He looked at her, his dark brown eyes burning. "I don't beat around the bush, Rita. I want to make love to you."

Now that he had taken the first step, Rita felt that she could let herself go. She pulled his head down to hers and pressed her body into his. "I thought you'd never ask, Mr. Margolis."

She moved out of his grasp and led him toward the bedroom. She could feel her body tingling. It had been too long since she had had a man.

"Well, I plan to thank you properly for this weekend, Dave. With all the money you've spent the past few days, you could have bought three young women."

He kissed her again. "I prefer quality to quantity, Rita. Besides, most of those youngsters are just raw meat. I like my food properly seasoned."

Rita walked into her bedroom and turned on the bedside lamp, keeping it low. She looked better in dim light, her wrinkles hidden by the shadows.

She left Dave to undress in the bedroom while she used the bathroom. After throwing her clothes into a hamper, she donned a short bathrobe, then brushed her teeth and combed her hair.

It was going to be nice to have a real man for a change. Once a woman crossed into her forties, there wasn't much to choose from, just losers from the divorce battles, or else wimpy little momma's boys who had never had a woman.

The married men around never had the money to support their appetites. It certainly wasn't like the old days.

Dave whistled softly when she came back into the bedroom. Her health club membership was worth the price, for it had kept her skin reasonably taut. Dave had a bit of a potbelly, but otherwise he wasn't in such bad shape, either.

Rita lay back on her bed and assumed the submissive pose that most men liked. She knew she had guessed right when Dave moved in to lie on top of her. He was heavy, but Rita was strong and gently massaged him with one thigh.

He came up and then quickly entered her. A happy grunt escaped his lips before a smile split them apart. He leaned forward to bury his face in her hair and murmured into her ear. "I like a woman who's primed and ready to go on short notice." That was due to the tube of vaginal cream she kept in her medicine cabinet, but she didn't tell him that. Instead, she began groaning and complemented his rhythmic pumping with an undulating motion of her own.

She was just starting to get a pleasant sensation when he came. She let a moan escape her lips and let her body relax to match his. He continued to lie on her, and she could feel the perspiration go from his body to hers.

After a while he lifted his head and kissed her on the lips. "Like I said, babe, we could make a real team."

He rolled off her and onto his side. Rita figured he would want more, and even if he didn't, most men enjoyed a pleasant massage. She rolled toward him on her side and slid her top leg between his, gently massaging him again with her thigh.

"Are you going back to the hotel?"

A satisfied smile was on his face as he adjusted himself to her rhythm. "Not unless you want me to."

"This isn't as fancy as the Omni, but you're welcome to stay."

He flopped over on his back. "Your turn to ride the soldier, Rita."

The closeness of his body and his first entry had aroused a strong hunger in her. She mounted him, and within moments her pleasure began to reach higher and higher peaks. Before she moved onto the summit, though, Dave spent himself again.

Her body shivered, and he mistook her frustration for fulfillment. His face broke into a large smile and he slapped her bare bottom. "You're a real woman, sweetheart."

She got off him, and rolled into a sitting position on the side of the bed.

"I need to go to the bathroom," Rita said hoarsely.

Dave just shook his head and laughed.

She went into the bathroom and quickly reached a climax herself, feeling comfortable and relaxed. Not perfect, but certainly better than doing the whole thing herself.

She got dressed again before she came back out. Dave was already dressed, and they moved back into the living room.

"You want to help kill off this wine, sweetheart?"

Rita nodded. Dave filled her glass and brought it over to her. What was he after? A mistress? But why in Miami? She watched him toy with his wine. She knew he wanted something, and she was sure he was getting around to telling her what it was.

"What's it like working for Miss Hotshot?"

Rita was surprised at the question. "You mean Miss Sable? Oh, it's all right. She works us pretty hard, but I imagine from the way Mr. Whitmore acts, she'll be promoted and out of our hair before too long. I can last until she's gone."

"Yeah, she does seem to be his pet, doesn't she?"

Dave sounded surprisingly bitter, and she raised her eyebrows as he took a drink of his wine. "Do you think there's anything going on between them?" he asked.

"Not at all." She laughed. "She's such an emotionless bitch. The only thing she's having an affair with is her calculator."

He laughed. "Have you heard the rumors about the consolidation of the foreign subsidiaries?"

"Everyone must have by this time."

"Well, it's going to happen. They're just laying in the finishing touches now. Your old Jaylene proposed it, and

Jesse loves anything she suggests." He gulped his wine. "But I'm going to level with you, sweetheart. When the changes are made, I plan to come out on top."

"Vice president of finance?"

"No, I mean the top of the heap." He read the question in her eyes and went on. "I plan to be the president of a new and larger foreign subsidiary."

"I'm sure that there are a few others with those same plans," Rita said as she tried to keep a pleasant smile on her lips. So that was Dave's brass ring.

"Kareau's going to corporate. He'll be VP of marketing. And Burnbridge is retiring. At least, he'll make it official. He's been mentally gone for a year."

"So that leaves you, Miss Sable, and whoever else corporate has in mind."

Margolis nodded.

She smiled and lifted her glass in a toast. "Good luck."

"I need more than luck."

"You have that, too," she murmured.

"Thank you, madam," he replied, bowing slightly. Then he finished his wine and put the glass on the end table next to him. "Actually, my only obstacle is your little friend, Miss Sable. My sources tell me that she and I are the only ones under serious consideration."

Rita did not know what to say, so she remained silent.

Margolis cracked his knuckles. "She gave me the shaft once, and she'll probably try again." He reached for his empty glass and drained the last drops. "I need to know what she's doing, Rita. I can't have any more surprises."

She looked down into her glass and swirled the wine around. "I suppose I could call you every so often."

He leaned forward in his seat, and she could see the hardness in his eyes. Very quietly he began talking. "I need to know everything. When she sneezes and how many times she goes to the john. I want a copy of every scrap of paper that goes in and out of her office."

Rita finished her drink. "That's an awful lot of paper. Are you sure you want to see it all?"

"Everything."

"It'll be a lot of work to reproduce. I'll probably have to

stay even later then Jaylene, and that woman has nothing else but her work."

"I'll make it worth your while, Rita."

Bitterness flooded her. Malcolm had said that when he came to Italy right after Lowell was killed. If she had the abortion, he'd make it worth her while. So she agreed to it and to the silence he wanted, trusting him do what was right. And what did she get? The privilege of working damn hard for every penny TIE paid her.

"When I'm president you'll be my AA, Rita. That's worth another eight or ten K in salary alone."

"An extra ten thousand a year sounds good," Rita replied. "But at my age, you don't make too many bets for the future."

"Hey, Rita." Margolis laughed. "Sometimes you just have to take a chance. When the brass ring comes around you have to reach out and—"

"I tried that once, Dave."

He glanced at her a moment and then looked down at the floor. She knew that he knew all about her and Lowell. Well, that was only to be expected. Some rumors never seemed to die.

Margolis licked his lips and then looked up at her. "I could make you an advance against your salary increase."

Rita stared quietly at him. Little beads of sweat were appearing at his hairline and on his upper lip. He wanted the presidency, and he wanted it real bad. She smiled tightly. This was a tough world, and there were no freebies. She'd found that out long ago. "I told you I don't like making bets on the future. Anything I get is up front and nonrecoverable."

"You're asking for a lot," Dave said, staring hard at her.

"I'm taking all the risks," she snapped. "What happens to me if I get caught sending you this stuff? Miss Sable's not going to be pleased, you know."

"Then be careful not to get caught." A mean look crossed his face. "Anyway, with your connections, that shouldn't be any kind of problem."

Rita's lips tightened. Her so-called connections were growing rather tenuous. Malcolm didn't bother returning her calls anymore, just leaving it all in his secretary's hands. If she was caught in this, Jaylene could put her out on the street with little more than the clothes on her back.

"I want twenty-five thousand up front and a thousand a month until the consolidation goes through."

He was stunned. "Come on, Rita. Be reasonable."

They argued and negotiated for several hours. Then Dave gave in and, as a show of faith, made out a check for five thousand dollars. She'd get an additional thousand a month until he was named president of the new subsidiary. If she got caught and fired, he'd pay her a year's salary.

Rita felt almost giddy with triumph, and she felt her loins tingle with excitement. She could see why men enjoyed business so much. Winning gave a person a real high. "Would you like to stay until it's time to get your plane?"

"No. I'd better go back to the hotel and clean up. Then I'll head straight for the airport."

Rita was disappointed, but kept a smile on her face as she followed him to the door. He kissed her on the cheek. "Good-bye, sweetheart. We're on our way to the top."

Rita closed the door after him and stood with her back against the wall. Suddenly she was starting to come down with a thud. He had finally agreed so quickly that she was concerned that she had asked for too little. Then a bitter realization came to her. Or else he was planning to welsh on her. Their handshake agreement could hardly be taken to court.

Her needs were almost painful, and Rita moved quickly into the bedroom. Her face had a hard set to it. Mr. Margolis had better stay current with his payments, or he was going to have an empty mailbox.

She plugged in the vibrator and put it to work. It lacked even the little warmth that Margolis had, but the relief was quick. As she relaxed, she began to consider her insurance options.

Chapter Nine

On the day in October when the case study was due to start, Jaylene dressed for work with special care. She brushed her hair until it gleamed. Her black fitted suit was as conservative as all her business suits, but the white silk blouse beneath it had a narrow ruffle at the collar and cuffs. It was her only concession to the warm, feminine feelings Ray aroused within her.

She could hardly believe how anxious she was to see him again. Ultraconservative, ultrabusinesslike Jaylene Sable was actually looking forward to seeing a man. It was because he was so easy to talk to, she told herself. They had a lot in common. It had nothing to do with his looks. She'd be this anxious to see him even if he were overweight and bald. But a tiny smile came to her lips as she thought of how very not overweight or bald he was.

She knew she had been slightly irritated with him when he had left a few weeks ago. His question about marriage had hit her the wrong way, but now that she looked back on it, she saw that it was a perfectly normal thing to ask. It showed that he was interested in her and wanted to get to know her better. She should have been flattered by his interest, not angered.

Because she was so anxious, the morning seemed to drag. She had a meeting with Kareau, then one with the legal staff. There was a civic luncheon that PR wanted her to attend, and of course it was on the other side of town. By the time she got back to the office, it was almost three.

"Dr. Carroll and his students arrived," Rita told her.

"Where are they?" Jaylene asked, glancing around her. Knowing Rita, she almost expected to see them sitting in the waiting area.

"Mr. Aldridge is taking them around."

Jaylene nodded. "Let me know when they're back." She went into her office and sat down.

She had done a lot of thinking since Ray had been in town a few weeks ago, and she had decided that it was time she had some fun, time she broke free a little. She didn't have to give her every breathing moment to TIE; it had never asked that of her. She needed to learn again who she was, Jaylene Sable the person, not just Jaylene Sable the executive vice president.

It had seemed only natural to include Ray in these plans to break free. He was interesting, attractive, and available. Now that he was actually here, though, she was slightly worried. What if she had assumed too much? She was not exactly an expert in personal relationships. What if she had decided he was interested in her because she wanted him to be? He said he wasn't married, but that didn't mean he didn't have a girlfriend, or live with somebody.

She got to her feet and walked over to the window. That night they'd shared dinner in her apartment, she had been a little edgy. Maybe she had misinterpreted the things he had said. All those looks, all those silences, maybe they were natural mannerisms. They didn't have to mean that she was the sexiest thing he'd ever seen. After all, men had been fighting off this magnetic charm of hers pretty successfully for years. Why would somebody who'd been around as much as Ray suddenly fall victim to it?

"Miss Sable, Dr. Carroll's here." Rita's voice came over the intercom.

Jaylene hurried over to the security of her desk. "Send him in, please."

He looked as gorgeous as ever, tall and strong. His dark brown hair had just a touch of gray that seemed to match the gray of his suit perfectly. No wonder Nancy had been drooling over him. How could he be attracted to her?

"Good afternoon, Miss Sable," he said. His smile was

friendly and warm, but she would not let herself read any-thing more into it.

She came around her desk to meet him, forcing her smile to match his. "Hello, Ray. We needn't be so formal."

She extended her hand. His grip, when his hand met hers, was firm and confident. His touch, though, was elec-trifying. She would have liked for it not to stop with her hand, but continue up her arm, across—

"Shall we sit down?" she suggested brusquely. Her face felt warm, and she was horrified to think she might be blushing.

"Sure."

They crossed the office to the chairs in silence. Had he been reluctant to let go of her hand, or was that just her imagination? Why was she thinking about him this way? She had the sudden feeling that she should have worked harder at replacing Ken in her life. She could see the head-lines now: "TIE Executive Ties Up Professor." Mr. Cabot would not be pleased.

"My students are really looking forward to this study, although they did think I should have scheduled it in Jan-uary and February," Ray joked lightly to break the uneasy tension.

She forced another smile. "I'd have to agree with them. I'd rather be in New England in the fall, but Florida is bet-ter in the winter."

"Unless you ski."

"To a Floridian, skiing means water skiing," Jaylene re-plied.

"Oh, right."

There was a long, awkward silence. "I'm sorry I wasn't here when you arrived."

He shrugged—probably because he hadn't noticed her absence, she decided.

"I realize you're quite busy, and this case study isn't the most important thing you're involved in."

That was true, but it certainly was in her thoughts a great deal. Or, rather, he was. She cleared her throat. "I assume that Neal introduced you around and that the ar-rangements are satisfactory."

"They seemed fine."

"Anything special you want me to say at our kickoff dinner this evening?"

Ray laughed. "Just that you're glad to have us."

She laughed also. She'd be glad to have him anywhere. Anytime. She shifted her position. Maybe she needed a vacation. "I am glad to have you and your team here. And so is my staff."

While she was speaking, he reached into his briefcase and took out a few papers. "I put together a couple pages on what other executives have said about the value of our case studies."

Jaylene quickly glanced over them, conscious that his eyes were on her the whole time. What was *he* thinking? she wondered, barely aware of the words on the pages before her. Did he notice the little bit of frill on her blouse? Did he see the warm and feminine woman beneath the business suit? Maybe she should take her jacket off and be sure.

She bit her lip to keep from laughing. Yes, she definitely needed a vacation. "That sounds like what I had in mind," she said, and returned the papers to him. "By the way, I hope you have no objection to having our kickoff dinner tonight in our executive dining room."

"That's all right."

She was almost embarrassed to tell him the reason. "It has nothing to do with cost. It's just that our security department doesn't want to let me off my leash, and they vetoed any restaurant. It's easier to protect me here from all the dangers of life."

He looked concerned. At least she thought he did. "Have there been some recent threats?"

"No." She hesitated. "Well, not really. I've had a few nasty letters. You know how it is when you're in the limelight a lot."

"No, I don't."

She was sorry she had brought it up. He was probably sure now that people were taking potshots at her every place she went and he'd want to stay clear of her.

"A lot of it is actually my fault," she said with a wry

smile. "When I first came to this job, I got a lot of PR, both print and video. You know, the young wonder-woman stuff. TIE liked it and so did I. I guess there are just a few weirdos out there who get a kick out of writing threatening letters. No one's ever done anything in person."

"No doubt because of your security."

Her heart sank. There was no chance he'd want to see her away from TIE. He sounded like part of TIE's security. She stood up and briskly walked back to her desk.

"Anyway, that's my tale of woe, not yours. But I do apologize for dinner in the executive dining room. It's not too lively at night."

He got up more slowly and followed her across the room. "I'm beginning to see why it's a problem. My students would like to see some of the nightlife of your city." He rubbed his jaw with his hand thoughtfully. "Is there someone who could show them the city afterward?"

"Drew Hanson, our staff economist, is young and a bachelor again, so I'm sure he'd love the assignment. Anyplace special you want to go?"

His smile grew warmer and his eyes took on a teasing gleam. "I think my students would prefer not to have the old professor along. They wouldn't say anything, but I know it would be a burden on them to keep an eye on me."

"Oh." Did she dare hope again?

"Actually, I was wondering if you were well known up in Fort Lauderdale."

"Probably not like in Miami."

His smile deepened. "I enjoyed our dinner at your apartment, but I'd like to take you out this time. My treat. If you're free, that is."

"As a matter of fact, I am." She smiled back.

Ray was seated down the table and across from Jaylene. Too far away to converse during dinner, but just the right position to watch her during the welcoming speeches. She seemed aware of his eyes on her and smiled back at him slightly while trying to pretend her attention was on Frank Kareau. Ray had no idea what Kareau was talking about and didn't really care. He had heard these opening session speeches a hundred times before and could recite them in his sleep. He was much more interested in Miss Jaylene Sable.

There was a smattering of applause and Ray joined in. So did Jaylene, but her eyes slid over to meet his. He winked, and she actually blushed. It was her turn to speak next, and he grinned as she rose to her feet, but he would behave and resist the temptation to get her flustered.

While he only half listened to her speech, his eyes, and his mind, were sliding over her graceful body, wondering what delights were hidden by that demure, conservative suit. She had beautiful hair, a gentle kind of brown with highlights that dared him to touch. How he'd like to see it loosened from the elegant chignon and down on her shoulders. Or better yet, lying against a pillow.

Lisa DeNapoli, one of the graduate students on the study, leaned over toward him. "Boy, I wouldn't mind being where she is in fifteen years."

"Yes, she's done quite well for herself," Ray agreed, although Jaylene's business successes were far from his mind. It didn't matter to him whether she was a department manager or an executive VP, she had the right attitude, and that was what counted. She had complete dedication to her job and time only for brief affairs, just as he did. They could have a marvelous time together.

Suddenly the speeches were over, and everyone was standing, getting ready to leave. Drew Hanson was talking with the three students, obviously planning their evening, and Ray was anxious to plan his own evening. He sauntered over to Jaylene.

"Nice speech, Miss Sable," he said.

Her smile had a hint of suspicion in it. "Name three things I said."

"You were happy to have us, you were sure that TIE would benefit as much as the students, and you hoped we all had a good six weeks."

She raised her eyebrows in surprise. "I could have sworn you weren't listening."

He grinned and leaned a bit closer. The gentle scent of her perfume tickled his senses. Then footsteps approached and someone slapped Ray on the back. He turned to find Frank Kareau next to him.

"Great to have you aboard," he said enthusiastically as he reached for Ray's hand. "Be sure to let us know if there's anything else at all that you need. Don't be shy, just ask."

Before Ray could say a word though, he was gone. Jaylene's green eyes were laughing.

"I hadn't realized how generous TIE was," Ray murmured. "Most companies are willing to help, but to offer me anything I need—now that's really something."

"Need a new car? A new house?" she asked.

"Actually, I had something in mind that was a bit softer and warmer than a car."

"Oh?" Ray heard a definite invitation in her voice, and he knew it was time to get out of there.

"So what's our plan for tonight?" he asked quietly.

She glanced around before she spoke, and Ray knew that whatever she had in mind, she didn't want the rest of TIE to know. That was fine with him. Something private and cozy was always best. Otherwise, there would always be some busybody who didn't know the rules trying to rearrange their lives.

"I thought I'd go home and get my car, then pick you up at your hotel," she said.

"We can take my car," Ray offered.

"And add all those miles onto your bill? Besides, my car can use the exercise."

"Okay. What time shall I expect you?"

She glanced at her watch. "How about in a half hour?"

"Great," he said, then she was gone, drifting over toward the students where he could hear her asking about their arrangements for the evening. Drew must have had a full schedule planned, for she laughed and shooed them out of the room.

Ray left soon after she did, and a few minutes after he parked his car at his hotel, she pulled up in her Porsche. She hadn't changed her clothes, but she looked different. Relaxed, perhaps, and more alive.

She got out of the driver's side and looked across at him. "Want to drive?"

"Sure," he said.

The inside of the car was close and he was intensely aware of her nearness. Without even turning toward her, he could see the curve of her thigh and the swell of her breasts. His hands wanted to reach out and touch her, to feel the softness of her skin beneath him. He exhaled slowly.

"Well, where to?" he asked.

"What?" She turned to face him, but her eyes seemed to linger on his lips. In the light from the hotel, he could see the flush on her cheeks. The sound of her breathing matched his own. Suddenly she was in his arms, and he was crushing her closer to him, totally ignoring the stick shift that was jabbing into both of them.

His lips found hers. They were soft and warm and invited his touch to linger. He was only too happy to oblige as her arms echoed his tightening hold.

She was a marvelously delightful creature to have in his arms. That spark of attraction he had felt between them from the first seemed to burn more brightly with each second that they were together. He wanted to touch her, he wanted to see her, he wanted to explore quite slowly the many intrigues her body held for him. As tantalizing as her lips were, he did not want to feel limited to discovering their secrets alone.

A rapping on the window broke them apart, and Ray turned to find the hotel doorman frowning at him. "Come on, buddy, move on."

Ray laughed slightly as he put the car in gear. That was just what he hoped to do.

"That was a nice place," Jaylene said, hours later as they left a small bar on the outskirts of Fort Lauderdale. She leaned back in the Porsche and relaxed as Ray turned on to the highway. She smiled over at him, but he was staring at the road ahead. She slipped her feet out of her shoes. The carpet on the floor was soft and felt good. She had never sat on the passenger side before and was enjoying the luxury of having a man drive her. It was very different from having a chauffeur.

Jaylene barely suppressed a giggle. Her chauffeur was a conscientious young man who took his duties seriously. She'd never had any desire to smooth his hair or tickle him on the neck. It felt wonderful just to let herself go. The impending consolidation was a sure thing, and morale was plummeting among her staff. To say the least, things were very tense at work. Maybe that was why she needed to relax.

"I had a wonderful time," she said. "It's been ages since I went dancing just for fun. Usually it's been at some place that PR thought would bring us good press."

"Well, they wouldn't have sent you there. The only press those guys knew about was the bench variety, and I don't even want to think about how much they could lift."

She just laughed. "You have to admit it was a change from the kickoff dinner with all that china, silver, and crystal."

"I'm not sure I was looking for quite that much of a change, thank you."

Jaylene moved closer to him, resting her head on his shoulder. He put his arm around her, and she was very comfortable in spite of the bucket seats.

They seemed to be alone on the road; few other headlights disturbed the darkness. The stars were reflected on the water off to her right and—

She sat up abruptly. "Why is the ocean over there? We're going in the wrong direction."

Ray seemed remarkably unperturbed. "No, we aren't."

She glanced behind her as if she expected to see Miami glittering in the background. "We're heading north. I know we are."

"I know we are, too. But it's not the wrong direction."

She eyed him suspiciously. She had always thought professors were a little strange. "Are you planning to circle the globe and come into Miami from the south?"

He made a face at her. "It's too early to go back. Don't you have any adventurous blood in you?"

She leaned back in the seat, realizing that she was quite

happy in his company and was in no hurry to get home. Unless, of course, she could persuade him to stay there with her for a while. Maybe he was thinking of something along the same lines. "It depends on the adventure. What did you have in mind?"

"A beach."

"A beach? We've been passing beaches for miles."

"A secluded beach."

"Why secluded? Are you planning on feeding me to the sharks and don't want any witnesses?"

"That depends on you," he replied, and glanced over at her. She pulled away from him and leaned against the door. "What do you mean, it depends on me?"

"You'll see."

A few miles farther along, the highway moved inland and, rather than lose sight of the ocean, they turned onto smaller roads. After a few more miles, they found a beach that seemed to satisfy him. It was protected from the road by trees and undergrowth, and seemed as deserted as it could possibly be.

"We're probably trespassing," Jaylene worried as he turned down a narrow drive to the beach and cut the motor.

"There's not a house for miles."

"That doesn't mean anything."

"Sure it does. It means no one will know that we're trespassing." He got out of the car and reached for her hand. She wiggled back into her shoes and joined him reluctantly.

"We'll probably be mugged."

He laughed and took her hand, leading her between the trees to the beach. There were no lights in sight, but the stars and the moon lit the deserted sandy stretch. The only sound was the gentle lapping of the water on the shore. It was beautiful.

Ray slipped off his shoes and she did the same, and they stood silently in the sand that was still warm from the heat of the sun. It was wonderful, but she still felt strange. It had been so long since she had just slowed down and enjoyed the beauty of nature.

"I hope there aren't any broken bottles in the sand. I'm not good with blood."

"I promise not to cut myself then," Ray said.

They walked down toward the water, and Jaylene began to relax. There was nothing else she had to do, no meetings awaiting her presence, no major decisions awaiting her signature. She breathed deeply of the night air and listened to the rhythmic beat of the waves upon the shore. Gently, but constantly, the water was washing up near their feet. It had done so for ages already—before TIE was even thought of—and would keep on, long after TIE was gone. It gave her a tremendous sense of peace.

They stopped at the water's edge. The waves gently rushed around their feet, then slipped away, pulling bits of sand in the current. The water was cool but not cold, and seemed to be tugging her gently toward its depths.

"Well, are you game?" Ray asked.

She had been lost in her own thoughts. "Game for what?"

He nodded toward the water. "Swimming."

"I don't have a bathing suit."

"Neither do I."

She didn't need the moonlight to know he was grinning. "Skinny-dipping in the moonlight?" She laughed. "Are you serious?"

"Oh, yes," he assured her. "It's a very popular activity."

"Oh?"

"That's what the students tell me," he quickly soothed her.

She couldn't help laughing. God, he was just like a little boy. "It's insane."

"Look, if you're embarrassed, don't be," he went on. "It's so dark, I won't be able to see a thing."

"Sure, you won't."

He leaned over and gently brushed her lips with his. His touch was warm and seductive. She realized she wanted it to go on and on, just as the waves went on and on, and she leaned into his embrace. His arms went around her, his hands gliding over her back, pulling her ever closer into the shelter of his body. His touch was as magic as the setting, and when he released her, she moved away slowly, reluctantly.

"There might be dangerous currents," she whispered, not thinking only of the water.

"We won't go in over our knees."

"Then why take our clothes off?"

He smiled as he bent to kiss her again. "I don't think it would be as much fun with them on."

They moved away from the water and slowly began to undress.

Jaylene had always thought she had a good figure, but now she hesitantly removed her blouse. Her breasts were firm and high, but would he think they were too small? She let her skirt fall to the sand, then carefully folded it and laid it aside. She knew Ray was watching her, a bit more openly than she was watching him. Would he find her body attractive, or would he think she was too thin?

Under the cover of her slip, she slid her stockings off, then turned to find he had moved close to her. He put his hand under her chin and lifted her face gently to his. His lips teased hers, brushing and caressing, then drinking deeply of her warmth. His hands seemed to burn her skin through the thin silk of her slip, and she could feel his nakedness pressing against her.

He pulled away from her slightly, then lifted the slip over her head. His eyes never seemed to leave hers; they told her of her beauty and erased any hesitancy she felt without a word being spoken. His hands slid over her breasts and onto her back, finding the back of her bra and opening it with ease. The lacy piece of lingerie fell among the tangle of their clothes.

"Do you know how beautiful you are?" Ray's voice was quiet.

She smiled back up at him. "You're not bad yourself." His body was slender, but as she ran her hand over his chest, she could feel the muscles beneath, taut and firm. Her fingers spread out and moved with pleasure across him, tangling slightly in the hair on his chest. She was surprised at how much hair he had on his body. It made him seem very different from the immaculately dressed professor, and her breath quickened. She turned then and ran down toward the ocean. Ray was right behind her as she splashed into the waves. The water was cool and felt good against her heated skin. She dove in, and when she came up for air, her hair hung like a thick curtain covering her shoulders.

Ray was right next to her, standing in the water that was just barely over his waist, but up to her chest.

"Is this a mermaid?"

"Only at night on secluded beaches." She laughed, then splashed water at him and dove away, but when she came up again, he was at her side.

They frolicked in the water like children, laughing and splashing and racing away as fast as the water would let them move. The moon and the water and Ray seemed to weave a hypnotic spell, pulling her deeper into its power until they were the only two people in the world. When they finally left the water and collapsed on the sand, it seemed right and natural that their laughter should stop, and they melted into each other's arms.

"Do you know that I've been dreaming about this since we met?" Ray whispered as his lips met hers in a blinding kiss.

His hands caressed her body, setting it aflame with primitive wanting. He seemed to be a part of the sand and the sea and she wanted him so. She clung to him, reveling in the delight of his touch and wanting more of it, much, much more.

His lips ran from her mouth down her neck and onto her breasts, feasting on her skin and setting her flesh on fire. Her back arched against him, her hunger for him so strong that even the sound of the sea was lost to her. Her breath came in gasps, her body weakened by its urgent needs.

She ran her hands over his back. He was hard and strong, and his body became her universe. She could see only him above her, and she wanted to know nothing more than the pleasure of his touch. She closed her eyes and inhaled the sweet fragrance of him. Sweat and salt water and his after-shave all mingled into an intoxicating scent of love.

Suddenly, they were one, and she clung to him in a passion so powerful that it was frightening. The world was shaking and crumbling, yet he remained the one source of strength. Locked in his embrace, she soared above the stars and rode the crest of the waves, higher and higher as the water threatened to engulf all else, just as their hunger consumed their every breath.

"Smile, sweetheart. You're on candid camera." Brewster Merrill laughed harshly as he snapped pictures of the couple locked in an embrace on the beach. He had been following that Sable dame all evening, and he was glad he was finally getting a little something for his trouble. A picture of a smooch or two in the car wouldn't help Davie.

When the camera beeped faintly to indicate that he had used up his roll of film, he quickly put it into its case and pulled out a nightscope. He had plenty of pictures, but he hated to leave in the middle of a show.

Jaylene stood up, and Brewster examined her body appreciatively. At this distance, with her small breasts and slender figure, she almost looked like a boy, and Brewster could feel desire tickling at him.

The couple dressed and walked arm in arm toward their car. Brewster waited in the bushes until he saw the movement of the headlights indicating that the Porsche was leaving the beach area. Then he got up and almost ran to his car. This was unbelievable. Just beautiful. He and Margolis really had that broad by the short hairs. She'd do anything they wanted now.

Chapter Ten

Jaylene rested her head against the back of the seat. She could vaguely hear Nancy and the chauffeur chatting in the front of the limousine, but their conversation did not hold her interest. Instead, her mind kept replaying scenes from the last few nights. She could hardly believe that Ray had been in town two days and was leaving tomorrow.

She felt wonderfully different since he had come, as if something vital in her core had been changed in the last forty-eight hours, but she knew it was nothing that drastic. Everyone needed a vacation occasionally. She couldn't take two weeks to lie about on a beach in Mexico, so she had condensed her vacation into a two-day period. She had relaxed, unwound, had fun, and now felt terrific—ready to throw herself back into her work with renewed vigor and enthusiasm.

Ray should go into business for himself as an instant vacation for busy female executives, she thought with a smile, for he had been the most important part of her rejuvenation. Ken had never had that effect on her, but there was something about Ray that blew away all her carefully designed defenses. He touched her in a way that no one else ever had, and apparently it was just what she needed. She felt whole again and ready to give her all to TIE, although she wouldn't mind a few more of these mini-vacations before the case study ended.

Jaylene spent her morning in a series of meetings and found the hectic pace enjoyable. She felt more and more invigorated as the day went on. Lunch was a quick snack

113

grabbed in her office, and then she was off to another meeting.

"Ah, Miss Sable, just the person I hoped to see."

She stopped in the middle of the hallway and turned to Ray with a carefully polite smile. "Hello, Dr. Carroll. I hope there's no problem with the case study."

His eyes seemed to caress her as they lingered for a moment on her lips, then eased gently down her body. "No, nothing major," he said. His brown eyes came back to hers and they seemed to be laughing. "But I think there are a few little items we somehow didn't touch yet. Do you think you'll have some free time when we might be able to cover them in greater depth?"

She felt her cheeks redden and quickly glanced around. The hallway where they were standing was far from empty, but no one was giving them a second glance. She allowed a small smile to play on her lips as she turned back to him.

"Actually, my schedule is awfully crowded, but I could try to squeeze you in at the end of the day."

"I certainly would appreciate it." His eyes were twinkling. "Although I hate to take up more of your time when you've been so generous already."

"Nonsense. TIE has made a commitment to your case study and would want me to do everything I can to ensure its success."

"Do you realize what you're getting into?" he murmured. "There can be so many areas that'll need your personal attention. We may have to meet fairly often while I'm here."

"Mr. Cabot himself put me at your disposal," she reminded him, trying hard to remain serious. "He wouldn't want your needs to be ignored."

"Miss Sable."

Jaylene's teasing manner faded at the sound of Rita's voice. She glanced over her shoulder to see Rita hurrying up, then spoke softly. "Why don't you come over to my place about eight o'clock?"

He nodded and went on down the corner.

"Miss Sable, a package just arrived from corporate. It's marked urgent."

Jaylene followed Rita back to her office, taking the thick envelope and tossing it onto her desk. She knew without opening it that it was the final outplacement list awaiting her approval. Some of her lightheartedness slipped away as she slowly pulled the list out of the envelope and flipped through it. As much as she would have liked to sign it quickly and send it back, she forced herself to read the names listed.

Personnel had done a very thorough job. Some women and minorities, but not too many, and few people over forty-five. There would be few, if any, discrimination suits, and very little pension to be paid, just severance pay and vested rights, which was cheaper in the long run. She ought to be pleased.

Dick Matthews's name caught her eye, and she got a funny feeling in her stomach. He was high on the list, and from his work record, he deserved to be. Except that it wasn't quite that simple. She picked up her phone and put through a call to Jesse.

"I got my outplacement list this morning," she told him. "And I have a problem with one of the names."

"Did somebody goof?"

"No, no. He fits all the criteria for outplacement." She was hesitant to explain, fearing that she knew what his reaction would be. "It's just that he has special family problems."

"We don't meddle in our employees' personal lives."

"We make exceptions for upper management personnel," she reminded him.

"Upper management involves a few people who are unique," Jesse explained. "Lower-level personnel involves too many people. You open up a can of worms anytime you do something special for one of them. You either set a precedent that you have to live with the rest of your life or you leave yourself open to a suit for preferential treatment."

Jaylene didn't know what to say. She knew that a big corporation like TIE had to be concerned with precedent and equal treatment, but it still didn't seem right to let Dick go.

"How long has the individual in question been around?" Jesse asked, interrupting Jaylene's stewing.

"A little over fifteen years." Just as long as she had been with the company.

"Hell, Jaylene. That boy'll get almost a year's salary in severance pay. He'll be all right."

Boy? A man in his forties was still a boy? What would he do once TIE let him go?

"You've been through these large-scale cutbacks before," Jesse pointed out. "What's the problem now?"

"It's just that I know the situation and—"

"Let me tell you a little story," he said brusquely. "When I was twelve, my dad gave me a young steer to raise for the 4-H fair. I lived with that animal for nine months, feeding it, grooming it, taking care of it. I loved it like a pet. When the fair came, that steer won first prize in its class."

"That's nice," Jaylene replied coolly, wondering what the point of his homey little tale was. "I imagine you were very proud."

"I had forgotten something important, though." His voice was quiet and emotionless. "A steer is raised for only one purpose, and that's not to be a pet. I found that out when he was auctioned off after the fair. A local restaurant bought him and advertised Jesse Whitmore's prize steer on their menu for a month."

"Oh."

"But I learned my lesson, Jaylene. Never get close to anything expendable. Use the employees to meet TIE's goals and objectives, but don't get involved with them. If you do, you don't belong where you're at. Talk to you later." He hung up the phone.

Jaylene hung up slowly. She felt shaken. All that boundless energy and enthusiasm from this morning were gone, replaced by confusion.

Here was Jesse on the one hand scolding her for caring about an employee, while on the other hand, she herself felt that she'd been too uncaring for the past few years.

She had blinded herself to the people around her, never caring about them, sometimes not even realizing they were there. Who was right?

She frowned thoughtfully and tried to decide what Aunt Sophie would say. Probably not to let herself be distracted from her goal, but what was her goal these days? She had reached financial security; she was successful in her work. Hadn't she achieved what she wanted? Then why was she so moody these days? Why wasn't she satisfied with what she had, instead of starting to question everything?

She sighed and got to her feet. She needed Ray's touch even more than before. She only hoped the relaxation and peace would be there for her once again.

Margolis's intercom buzzed and he turned toward it, glad of the interruption. This last pile from Rita was practically worthless. "Yeah?"

"You have a collect call from Florida on line two, sir. A Mr. Rooster, I think he said."

Margolis frowned. "I'll take it, sweetheart."

He snatched up the phone and waited as the operator established the connection with his secretary. "Go ahead, Mr. Margolis," the young voice said cheerfully.

He waited until the click told him that his secretary was off, then shouted into the phone, "What the hell are you doing calling me on this line? And a collect call, yet."

"I forgot the number of your direct line," Brewster whined. "Anyway, I've got some really good stuff for you."

"It better be," Margolis grumbled.

"I got some pictures of that Sable broad. Pictures of her getting humped by some guy on a beach. He's a Harvard professor doing some work for your company."

Margolis could hardly believe what he was hearing. Little Jaylene? TIE's vestal virgin getting screwed on a beach? "You're not trying to pull something on me, are you, Brewster?" Margolis asked suspiciously.

"Hey, I swear on my mother's grave."

"You told me a few weeks ago that you needed money for her doctor bills," Margolis reminded him.

"Well, she's as good as dead," Brewster replied. "But

you're going to love the shots. I think they'll come out real good."

"If they do, Brewster baby, I'm going to throw a few extra K in your pot."

"Real good, Davie. I could use it."

"Yeah, I know. Your sick mother."

"Huh?" Brewster grunted.

"Never mind. Just mail me the pictures. Express mail or whatever. Just get them to me fast." He hung up before Brewster could reply.

Margolis was so excited that he began to pace around his office, punching his right fist into his left hand. He almost squealed with delight. Jaylene was as good as dead. She was a walking corpse once he started circulating some pictures of her indiscretion. A stuffy old corporation like TIE didn't want its executives, especially the female ones, running naked around Miami.

He could hardly wait for the consolidation so that he could take over the new division. There was all of Latin America just waiting to join the Margolis appreciation club. He was going to be so rich that he could use hundred-dollar bills to blow his nose.

"You'd better be careful, Rose," Ben said as they stood on the balcony of Jaylene's apartment. "You'll get used to this kind of living, and then when this job's over, what'll you do? Marry some rich widower with one foot in the grave and the other on a banana peel?"

Rose laughed quietly as she put two glasses of iced tea on the patio table. Ben pulled his chair up to the table and she sat down with him.

"It's okay," Rose said, taking a sip of her tea, "but it'll never feel like home. There's nobody to talk to all day and there are hardly any kids. I'd settle for a smaller place and some good friends any day. I really miss chatting with the neighbors over a cup of coffee."

"You know what I miss?" Ben asked. "Sometimes I really miss the snow. After spending most of my life in Cleveland, half of it in a beat car, I really miss it. Must be old age. I keep forgetting the flu, the sniffles, my feet not thawing out till the end of April."

"I miss the fall," Rose responded. "The trees never change here. How do the kids know when the football season starts?"

"Christmas was just awful last year," Ben said, nodding his head in understanding. "It didn't seem right without the snow. Even gray snow is better than no snow."

"You going to visit your kids over the holidays?"

Ben just shrugged. "I don't like to butt in. Besides, both of them live in the Southwest now, so there isn't any snow there, either."

"So take your vacation and go to some ski resort or something."

"It's no fun going alone, and who'd go with an old geezer like me?"

"Old is in your head, Ben. There must be a lot of people who would go places with you." She would, if he asked. He was always good company.

They sat quietly for several minutes looking out at the view before he spoke. "I've had a hard time tracking your friend, Rose, but I think we finally got a break. He was spotted here in Miami the other day."

"You mean he's moved back?" Rose's throat suddenly seemed tight.

"I don't think so," Ben said, shaking his head. "He was staying at a Holiday Inn over near the airport. One of my guys was taking his brother-in-law to look for a job and he saw him."

"Are you sure it was him?"

"Well, he's lost a little more hair. But this guy said that he'd recognize that bubble ass anywhere in the world."

Rose did not speak. Her pulse quickened and she got to her feet, going over to the railing to calm herself. It was hard to believe. Was she really getting closer?

"Anyway," Ben continued, "we still think he went to L.A. I'll follow up with this lead and we'll see what we can get. I think we're getting close."

Rose just nodded.

"What are you going to do if it's him, Rose?"

What was she going to do? Would anything pay him back for all he'd done? Then why was she following him after all these years? Did she still feel guilty because she blew the case in her eagerness to nail the scum? Rose turned and gave him a small smile. "I don't know, Ben. I don't know what I'm going to do."

Ben finished his tea and then stared at the ice cubes in the bottom of the glass for a moment. "How are you and your boss lady getting along?"

"Real good," Rose said. "She seems more relaxed the past couple of weeks. I think she's found herself a boyfriend."

"That'll improve a woman's disposition," Ben replied.

Rose stared at him in surprise. His cheeks turned red and he looked down at his feet. "I know a girlfriend improves a guy's disposition. I just figured it worked the same for a gal."

Rose laughed heartily. "It does, Ben. It works exactly the same."

Jaylene got out of her limousine at the same time that Ray was parking his car in the visitor area by the side of her building. She waited in the lobby for him.

"Afraid I'd get kidnapped?" he teased. Although there was no one in sight, they maintained a cool, dignified demeanor.

"No, afraid you'd get lost," she replied.

Once the elevator door closed, Jaylene moved quickly into his embrace. It felt so good to be held. The pressures of the day seemed to vanish when she stood in the warmth of his arms.

"I had wanted to get home a bit earlier than this and have some dinner sent over," she told him. "Now we have the choice of eating around ten or taking pot luck with whatever's in the kitchen."

His hold on her tightened slightly. "Well, if there's nothing edible in the kitchen, I might be able to suggest something we could do to pass the time while we wait for the food to arrive."

She laughed and looked up at him. His lips came down

on hers again, softly, yet demanding her response. Just as her arms were tightening around him, the elevator door opened.

"That's the fastest elevator ride I ever got," she grumbled as they went toward her apartment.

Rose met them at the door, her right hand in the pocket of her skirt, as always.

"You remember Dr. Carroll," Jaylene said. "We have some work to catch up on, and I thought it would be more comfortable to do it here."

Rose nodded impassively, but Jaylene thought she detected a twinkle in the older woman's eyes. Jaylene couldn't understand why she felt like a teenage daughter when she was the one who paid the rent.

"I was just cleaning up after my dinner. I'll be through in a few minutes."

Rose went back toward the kitchen and they followed her. The delicious smell of spaghetti sauce greeted them.

"That doesn't smell like pot luck," Ray whispered.

Rose picked up a towel and began to wipe off the counter. "Have you eaten?"

"Not yet," Jaylene said.

"Well, there's plenty of sauce left, if you want it," Rose said. "But you'll have to make more pasta." She folded up her towel and hung it over the rack.

"Thanks." Jaylene laughed. "I had offered Ray pot luck, but I never figured he'd get this lucky. I was trying to remember how to scramble eggs."

Right now, though, she was trying to remember where she might have some spaghetti. She pulled open one cabinet. Dishes. Another was canned goods. At least she was getting warmer. Rose opened a cabinet, took out the spaghetti, and handed it to her.

"Thanks," Jaylene mumbled, and pretended to study the directions. Where were the pots? In the ten months she had lived here, she didn't think she had made more than a cup of coffee in this kitchen. She had warmed up a few frozen dinners, but that didn't require pots and pans.

Rose must have read her mind, for she silently got out a

pot and began to fill it with water. "Why don't I fix this for you while you set the table?" she suggested.

"I think I can manage that," Jaylene admitted, and put down the package. She and Ray went into the dining room.

"I haven't cooked in ages," she told Ray in embarrassment.

He just laughed. "You should see me in my kitchen. I've lived in the same apartment for over fifteen years and don't know half of what's in there. The other half I don't know how to use."

She laughed with him and felt better. Just because she was here with a man she found attractive and whose company she enjoyed, that was no reason to feel she had to prove herself domestically. Lord, she had come a long way beyond that, she hoped.

By the time they had set the table, Rose had reheated the sauce and cooked the spaghetti. She also brought out tossed salad and some crusty bread.

"This is marvelous, Rose," Jaylene sighed. "You've saved us both from starvation."

"No problem." Rose stood back and surveyed the table. Apparently satisfied, she nodded and headed back toward the kitchen. "It's nice to cook for someone else for a change. I'm going to watch some television in my room. I'll do the dishes later."

"We can handle the dishes," Jaylene pointed out with a laugh. "I think I can find the sink."

"You have a dishwasher." With that Rose left.

"Well, obviously you didn't come here tonight because of my great skill in the kitchen," she said to Ray. "Lucky thing I'm so good at my job. Look what a lousy housewife I'd be."

She had meant it as a joke, an attempt to hide the embarrassment she felt at not being able to find things in her own kitchen. It didn't matter that he had said he couldn't find things in his own place.

He leaned forward, though, and put his hand over hers. "I think you'd be great at whatever you wanted to be great at. We're both nondomestic for the very same reason: we live our lives with the same priorities and the same rules.

Personal relationships take second place to our careers. Our jobs are the real loves in our lives."

"You're right," Jaylene said, marveling at how closely his words reflected her own thoughts. "In fact, I've often thought that I was married to TIE, and liked the feeling. Most of the men I've dated haven't quite understood, though," she added with a shrug.

"Most people are possessive creatures," he replied. "They need to possess something totally. For some, it's another person. But for others, it's control over our own lives. That's why you and I are so perfect together."

He lifted his wineglass in a toast. "Here's to us, the perfect couple. Wedded to our careers, yet willing to share a few moments of happiness together."

She raised her glass and touched it briefly to his. He was right, they were the perfect couple. When they parted, there would be no tears, no clinging, no unspoken promises. They both already had everything they wanted. There was no need to complicate perfection with unwanted attachments.

Chapter Eleven

"I think you're worrying about nothing, Jaylene," Frank Kareau told her. It was almost the middle of October, and she'd had that outplacement list for a week and a half before she'd had this chance to talk to him about it. "This guy'll be fine. Where do you think all our taxes go? Into social programs to help people just like this guy Matthews."

"It looks to me like the current administration is cutting a lot of those programs."

Kareau just waved his hand impatiently. "That's just propaganda that some sob sisters put out. All they're doing now is cutting off the deadbeats so that the money is available for people who really need it."

Jaylene said nothing, just stared down at the pen she was tapping against the desktop. That was basically what Jesse had told her, without the political message that Kareau had inserted. Her job was to take care of TIE. The employee would take care of himself, and if he couldn't, society would step in.

Frank was on his feet and moving toward the door. "If he was pulling his fair share there'd be no problem, but we can't turn TIE into a charity service. Profits would evaporate. Then TIE would die, and everybody would be out on the street. You know that, Jaylene."

"Yes, I do," she replied tersely. The last thing she needed was a minilecture in economics from someone to whom a deep thought was thinking while scuba diving.

"And making money is what our jobs are all about," he went on. "It's the bottom line that counts."

Jaylene put the pen down and pulled a folder toward her. "Thanks for stopping in."

He paused, his hand on the doorknob. "Sure thing, any time. That's what I'm here for." He smiled brightly, then left.

Jaylene frowned at the door. That's what he was there for, all right, to dispense meaningless advice. She was no closer to knowing how to solve the problem of Dick Matthews than when she first saw his name on the list of potential outplacements in New York two months ago.

She got a can of diet cola from her office refrigerator and absently poured it into a glass. Maybe she was worrying for nothing. Maybe Dick and his family would be all right. After all, she didn't know much about his situation, and certainly he couldn't be the first person with a sick spouse to lose his job. Others had survived, and so would he.

She sighed as she walked back to her desk. She'd sign that list and send it back before Jesse started accusing her of being soft again.

Her intercom buzzed. "Dr. Carroll on line two," Rita said quickly. Jaylene's initial reaction was pleasure, but it was dampened slightly by some indefinable note in Rita's voice: almost a sneer, as if Rita knew she and Ray were not just working on the case study together, no matter what they tried to pretend. How could Rita know about Ray, though? Jaylene shrugged off her question as she reached for the phone. It was just her imagination. Things had been tense at work lately, and she was starting to see bogeymen everywhere.

"Dr. Carroll, how are you?"

"Missing your warmth."

She smiled with remembered pleasure. "Yes, I heard Boston was in for some chilly weather."

"I tried to convince the university to set up a southern branch in Miami, which I would head up, of course, but they refused."

"What a shame!" It was good to hear his voice, surprisingly so, considering her normal aversion to close relationships.

"So how are my kiddies behaving? Any problems?"

"Not a one, I've actually seen very little of them." Maybe she should have invented a problem. Then he might have hurried down, and an evening with him could be just what she needed right now.

"That's good to hear," he said. "I'll probably be there some time next week to check on their progress. Will you be available for a midstudy meeting?"

"It depends." She sighed with disappointment. "I'm going to Haiti and the Dominican Republic later this week, and I won't be back for eight days."

"You sure like to remind me that I'm stuck in a cold climate, don't you?" His laughter was light, and the sound refreshed her. "Well, try not to get too sunburned."

"No chance of that."

Suddenly he was saying good-bye and the line was dead. Was he going to postpone his visit because she'd be gone, or was he coming anyway? He hadn't seemed disappointed when she said she would be out of town. Maybe he didn't care if he saw her again. The thought was slightly depressing, and that irritated her.

She had only been out with the man a few times. What difference did it make if she saw him again? He had been easy to talk to, but she'd find someone else, someone who lived in town. She'd get out and meet someone as soon as things slowed down a little at the office.

She sat for a moment with her hand still on the phone, then impulsively picked it up and dialed. After several rings, her aunt answered.

"Aunt Sophie, it's Jaylene."

"Janie?" The old woman sounded astonished. "What's wrong?"

"Nothing." Jaylene laughed. "I haven't been able to reach you lately and thought I'd try now."

"You have more important things to be doing than calling me in the middle of the day," she scolded. "How are you ever going to get ahead if you let your mind wander?"

Jaylene laughed again. "I'm already ahead," she assured her. "Now when are you coming down to Miami for a visit?"

"A visit? You with your busy schedule and me up to my ears with work at the hospital? Who has time for a visit?"

"We both get vacations," Jaylene pointed out. "I miss you. It's been far too long since we saw each other."

Her aunt sighed. "I know, but things change. You have your life now and I have mine. You're going to be somebody one of these days. You don't need an old woman around your neck holding you back."

"I already am somebody," Jaylene said. "Somebody who has nobody to talk to. Why won't you come down here? You don't need to work anymore, and I've got plenty of room. Come live with me."

"Janie, we've been through all this before," her aunt said impatiently. "Didn't I teach you anything all those years you lived with me? This is a tough world. Don't get involved with other people. Take care of yourself. You could be the first woman president of a large corporation. You'll only hurt yourself if you take your eyes off your goal."

"Aunt Sophie, I'm not going to hurt myself."

"You have so many chances I never had," her aunt went on as if she had not spoken. "You can do all the things I wasn't allowed to do. I want to be proud of you, Janie."

"Aren't you proud of me now?" Jaylene teased.

"Don't make a joke of it. Things are better now, but you're still a woman, and that doesn't help."

"I guess you're not going to come down and visit, then."

"There's plenty of time for visiting," her aunt replied brusquely.

"Yes, you're right. Maybe we can get together over Christmas."

"Maybe," her aunt said. "Just stop worrying about me. I told you years ago, when you left South Bend, not to come back. There was nothing for you here then, and there's nothing for you here now. You'll never get ahead by looking back. I'm part of your past, not your future."

"I'm feeling a little down today, and I just wanted somebody to talk to." Maybe it was because her "ulcer" was due next week.

"Just be tough, Janie, always be tough."

"Right." She forced her voice to be stronger, more confident. "You sound a little tired yourself. Are you feeling okay?"

"Just a little cold," she said. "You remember how the weather is in the South Bend."

"That's why I was trying to invite you to Miami," Jaylene reminded her.

"That discussion is closed," her aunt snapped.

Jaylene chuckled indulgently. Aunt Sophie was one tough cookie. "I love you," Jaylene said, and then swallowed the small lump in her throat.

"I am proud of you, Janie."

Jaylene hung up the phone. She was tough; she had forced herself to be over the years. She sighed and clenched her teeth. Tough was fine, but it was also lonely.

Rita tapped her fingers impatiently on her desk, her phone to her ear. She hated being put on hold, and Angie was doing that to her a lot lately. Every time she called Malcolm, she had to wait, and then she was always told he was too busy or had just stepped out. She had the feeling that it was all Angie's doing, too. Malcolm was a man of honor. He wouldn't forget what Rita had done for his family.

"Rita?" Angie was back finally. "I'm sorry, but he must have stepped out. Would you like to leave a message?"

What for? He'd probably never get it. "I'll call back," she snapped, and hung up.

How in the world was she ever going to reach him? Angie guarded all access to him more jealously than his wife. She stopped. Maybe that was it. Maybe she should write a letter to him and mail it to his home.

She wouldn't have to go into a lot of detail about her latest appraisal session and how unfair Miss Sable had been to downgrade her to a "B" performance level. All she needed to do was ask him to call. Maybe even slip in a sly reference to the fact that she'd been having trouble reaching him lately. She hoped he'd really dress Angie down for that.

She mentally started to compose the letter when her

phone rang. Could Angie have actually told him she'd called? She picked it up hopefully.

"Rita Kastle speaking."

"You're sending me a lot of garbage, sweetheart."

She said nothing for a moment, rather stunned by the angry tone. It definitely wasn't Malcolm. "Dave?"

"Why the question? You got the same deal with someone else?"

"No," she stammered slightly. "It's just that your tone of voice surprised me."

"Oh, yeah. How about this?" Then, affecting a solicitous and pleasant tone, he again said, "You're sending me a lot of garbage, sweetheart."

What the hell was he so mad about? She didn't have to take this crap from him. "I'm sending you exactly what you asked for. Which is everything."

"I didn't know you'd follow that request so blindly. An invitation to the TIE Employees Club Halloween party? Now come on, Rita."

"You said no screening, and that's what you got."

There was an angry silence for several moments. Then, "I'm getting a lot less than I expected out of our deal, baby," Dave snarled. "A hell of a lot less."

"So am I, baby," she snapped back. "I'm still waiting for you to finish your down payment."

That must have got him, for the silence was suddenly a lot less belligerent.

"I've been busy," he replied evenly. "The check's in the mail. Anyway, screen out the crap from the next load."

She let her anger die also. At least for the moment. "I'm going to have to be a little careful, Dave," she told him. "Corporate's reprimanded Miss Sable about those leaks to the other divisions, and we've put together a task force to find the source."

"So get on it."

"I am, but I'm still concerned."

"What's to be concerned about? You're on it, you control it. I have to run now."

She hung up the phone. That damn check had better be in the mail, or he was going to be surprised at just how much crap she screened from the next load. The envelope would arrive empty and stay that way until he was caught up on his payments.

Dave Margolis was disgusted. He had had such high hopes only a week ago. He had been certain that Jaylene was as good as gone, but where was his ammunition? Brewster could have walked those pictures from Miami and been here by now. There must have been a problem with them.

He wrote out Rita's check and stuck it in the mail on his way out of the office. He'd like to dump her. Every pile she sent him was nothing but junk. She was a worthless investment. Oh, he'd had a little fun spreading tidbits from Jaylene's confidential memos throughout the corporation. Hell, even Jesse had perked up when the management payroll list wound up in the corporate word-processing center. But, so far, there had been nothing to help him get the edge on her and keep it.

He drove down to the The Pink Pony to meet Brewster. It had been a bad day so far, and he was sure Brewster wasn't going to brighten it any. He walked through the door and wiped his hands on his pants, feeling a shiver of revulsion down his back. He saw the pear-shaped private detective at his table, laughing with two of the dancers, but they were gone by the time he got there.

He sat down and waved the waitress away. "I thought you didn't like girls. Why do you always want to meet here?"

"The bimbos give me a laugh," Brewster said, stuffing french fries into his mouth. He chewed a moment. "Actually, I like the fries here. Most places make them too dry. Fries taste better if they have a chance to swim."

Margolis looked away with disgust.

"Where are those pictures you were supposed to send me?" he asked.

Brewster held up his hand for him to wait, then mopped the remaining french fries in the grease at the bottom of the plate before popping them into his mouth. He was still chewing as he scooted his chair up closer to Margolis.

"Okay, Davie. Now—"

"Don't call me Davie."

"Sorry."

Margolis knew then that Brewster did not have good news. He normally wasn't penitent about anything.

Brewster downed a bottle of beer and turned toward him. "There were some technical difficulties, so I didn't send them to you right away. Then since I'd waited this long, I thought I'd just bring them with me."

Margolis did not reply but stared at the man. Droplets appeared on Brewster's face, but he couldn't tell whether they were grease or sweat. He certainly wasn't going to touch him to find out, either.

After digging in his pocket, Brewster pulled out an envelope. "These are the shots after they were first developed."

Margolis flipped through them, his anger growing by the second. "What the hell is this?" he snarled, looking at the shadowy figures in the black and white pictures.

"It would've helped if I was closer, but there was nothing but open beach and—"

"You can't even tell if they're male or female, much less who they are," Margolis interrupted him.

"Yeah, yeah. I know," Brewster hastened to explain. "So I had a friend of mine do a little work."

Again Margolis was silent as he accepted the new group of photos. Initially there was a spark of anger as he saw a blowup of the woman's face. Even if she hadn't been partially obscured by the man's head, it still would have been difficult to determine who it was. The spark passed quickly though, replaced by a sense of defeat. Thousands of dollars spent on Rita and Brewster for nothing. Absolutely nothing. He was doomed.

"Hey, I got a line on something else," Brewster told him.

Margolis looked up slowly, his face clearly showing his skepticism.

"That Sable broad's been married before."

"For Christ sake, Brewster," Margolis snapped impatiently, "the pope's probably been married before."

"Hey, just hear me out."

Margolis remained silent.

"She was married to some guy by the name of Josef Switek. He's a small-time hood. Been in the joint for peddling junk, stealing cars, and armed robbery. While he was there he was a hit man for the Aryan Brotherhood."

"What's that?"

"An organization of Caucasian prisoners."

Margolis was intrigued, but not too excited. Lately, Brewster's schemes had a way of falling through. "That's good, Brewster. We might be able to put that to good use."

"Yeah. If nothing else, we could give him to the newspapers. He's been hard to get a line on, though. Last I heard he was in Baltimore. Should I go find him?"

"Might as well." He paused slightly. "Let's hope that this venture will be a little more damaging to Miss Sable's career than your last attempt."

Brewster shrugged off Margolis's lack of enthusiasm. "Hey, he's gonna be our ace," Brewster assured him.

"He'd better be, Brewster," Margolis replied tiredly, "or it's bye-bye gravy train."

"Don't worry, Davie. I got a good feeling about this."

Margolis's jaw clenched, but he chose not to respond, rising instead and nodding shortly to Brewster. Then he hurried out into the relative purity of the smog-filled L.A. air.

Brewster was turning out to be an absolute zero. He'd better get back to his office and go though that stuff from Rita again. He dearly hoped there would be a pony someplace in that pile of crap.

Chapter Twelve

Jaylene's smile was not a reflection of her inner feelings, but part of her makeup. It did not waver even though she viewed the reporters before her more as enemies than as friends. She was glad, though, that the press conference was almost over, and she was looking forward to seeing Ray later that day. It was almost a month since he had last been in and that was too long. She nodded to another reporter.

"How can TIE condone doing business with the Communist government of Cuba?"

Her initial statement had covered exactly that point, but this wasn't her first repetition, and probably not her last. "TIE is not doing business with Cuba. We own part of a sugar refinery in Honduras, and that part ownership does not allow us to make decisions on where the sugar cane will be purchased."

"Just how large is TIE's share of the refinery?" a reporter from the *Wall Street Journal* asked.

"We are not majority owners," she said, purposely sidestepping a direct answer. "If we were, we would choose another supplier."

"But surely TIE's size and economic standing must give you substantial influence, regardless of the actual percentage of ownership," the reporter persisted.

She remained calm and patient. "TIE's partners' decisions are based solely on the bottom line. They are not feeling any political repercussions, and the fact that TIE is, is unimportant to them."

Jerry Dentman, the PR official who had arranged the press conference, nodded to her, and she stepped back from the podium, relieved. She felt as if she had just been before the firing squad, but somehow the bullets had missed.

"Good job," Jerry told her quietly as they left the room.

"Yeah, you had me convinced," Nancy said.

Jaylene just shrugged. "I wish we had an idea who leaked that information to the press in the first place."

"We'll probably never know," Jerry pointed out.

Rita was waiting for them when they got back to Jaylene's office. "Mr. Whitmore wanted to talk to you as soon as the press conference was over."

"Fine," Jaylene said, going past her into the office. "Get him for me, will you?"

She got some pineapple juice from her refrigerator cabinet and took a long drink. A conference to justify TIE's actions was not her favorite way to start a Monday morning. Her intercom buzzed and she picked up the phone.

"Did you satisfy the sharks?" Jesse asked brusquely.

"Hopefully," she said, sinking into her chair. "Nobody seemed too belligerent."

"They never do," he noted. His voice was sharp with irritation. "How the hell did that information leak out anyway?"

"I haven't the faintest idea. If I did, there'd be a new name heading that outplacement list." She paused for a moment, truly puzzled. "I didn't even know myself about them buying from Cuba until last week when Neal happened to find it buried in a minority holdings operating statement."

"Well, it didn't do TIE's image any good to be caught unawares like that. Don't let it happen again."

"Kareau's the president of the subsidiary. Maybe you ought to tell him if you can find him. He did one of his disappearing acts again."

Jesse didn't seem to care. "You're better at handling the press. Anyway, that's not the first leak of confidential data from your area. I've told you before, now I'm going to emphasize it. Plug that goddamn hole." The phone went dead.

Jaylene hung the phone up slowly. It was barely ten

o'clock in the morning, and already she was exhausted. It would be good to see Ray. She leaned forward and pressed her intercom button.

"Send Dr. Carroll in as soon as he arrives," she told Rita.

Ray had not come to Miami while she was out of town, but instead had called Rita for an appointment during the last week in October. Jaylene had accepted the information nonchalantly enough, but inwardly she had been quite pleased. Perhaps he, too, had felt that overriding passion.

And no matter what Aunt Sophie thought, she was not being weak or losing sight of her goals by looking forward to his arrival. No, she was as dedicated as ever. All Ray was doing was providing her with an outlet for some normal human desires. Since her emotions were not involved, he was not distracting her in any way. He just refreshed her so that she went back to TIE better able to perform. She was more productive because of him.

Yet some nagging worries seemed to linger and grow as she waited for his arrival that morning. She always dressed carefully, but she had wanted to look especially nice that day and had dressed in a favorite silk dress that she seldom wore to the office. What if someone at TIE suspected Ray was the reason?

It didn't matter if they did, she told herself, and walked over to stare out a window. She was free to date him. He was not a TIE employee, or politically active like Ken. No one could object to anything about him. Yet she could not rid herself of the desire to hide their association. She felt almost as if she were cheating on TIE by dating someone else, by allowing something other than her work to creep into her thoughts.

She told herself she was being ridiculous. Dating Ray did not make her unfaithful to TIE. She remembered that she hadn't responded to Nancy's teasing about her slightly different hairstyle today. Why didn't she tell Nancy that she hoped to have dinner with Ray that night?

It was just this strange attitude here at TIE. Everyone admired her work, but lately she doubted that anyone saw her as a real person. She was an executive VP, not a woman. Why couldn't she be both? Maybe that was why she enjoyed Ray so much. He let her be whatever she wanted to be.

She wondered if they would continue to see each other occasionally after the case study was finished. It wouldn't be too hard to do if they were both so inclined. She traveled a great deal, and so did he. Their paths ought to cross some of the time.

"Miss Sable," Rita's voice came over the intercom, jarring her back to reality. "Miss Osborne is on the phone. She says it's imperative that she speak to you."

Jaylene walked back to her desk, wondering what had happened now. Karen Osborne was her newly hired director of information services, and since she had started last week, she had uncovered a good deal of sloppy record keeping. Jaylene picked up the phone. "Jaylene Sable here."

"Karen Osborne, Jaylene. I just wanted to let you know that you and I are now an item."

Jaylene was confused. "I don't understand what you're saying."

"We've made the west wing men's room. One of my male managers saw it and took me in to see it for myself. The message accuses us of playing Tarzan and Jane and asks who plays who."

What? Jaylene felt as if all the air had been knocked from her and she sank into her chair. "I don't know quite what to say. This is a first for me. At least, that I know of." She found she was trembling with hurt and anger.

"Me, too," Karen replied. "Want me to have my managers check some of the other washrooms?"

Jaylene shook herself mentally. "No, I'll call security and have them check all the washrooms. The women's johns have walls, too."

They both forced a laugh at Jaylene's attempt at humor.

Jaylene dialed the number for the director of security and explained the situation to him.

"Well, you're certainly moving up in the world, Miss Sable," he said with a laugh. "Now you're up there with Whitmore and Cabot."

"I beg your pardon." She saw nothing funny in the matter.

"When I worked in corporate, we were always having to clean Mr. Whitmore's and Mr. Cabot's names from the walls. Those two were favorites on the urinal journal."

"I see," Jaylene said, ice still coating her voice.

"Don't worry, Miss Sable," he said. "We'll have it all spick-and-span by morning."

"Thank you."

She stared at the phone for a moment after she had hung up. A man just wouldn't understand. Men have hired men for centuries, so no one gave it a second thought. But if a woman hired another woman, she was immediately open to such attacks. It wasn't fair.

Suddenly she had a strong urge to see Ray. Tonight seemed too long away.

"Well?" Margolis prompted. "Anybody find our little love note?"

"Oh, yes, have they ever." Rita's snicker reminded him of the hiss of a snake. "Things have been quite exciting around here this morning."

Margolis couldn't help chuckling. Maybe this little idea of Brewster's would help. He had thought Brewster was just tossing out wild ideas to cover up the fact that he hadn't had much luck in tracking down her ex, and he had only agreed to try it because it gave him a laugh. Maybe it was helping his cause too. "So what's been happening?"

"Miss Osborne has been tearing around like a real hellion. My goodness, that woman can be harsh," Rita told him. "And the girls in the secretarial pool can talk of nothing else."

"I don't care about the other broad or a bunch of typists," he snapped. "How is little Jaylene faring?"

"Very tight-lipped and stiff."

"Did Whitmore call?"

"No," Rita answered. "She just sent out a directive to security and all managers."

Margolis felt a little twinge of satisfaction. He'd also had the homosexuality rumors spread in corporate headquarters. Jesse would probably call her about it, too. "Things look good for us, sweetheart."

"It certainly seems that way," Rita purred. "Did you get my latest package?"

"Yeah," he replied. "It came this morning. I'm about halfway through it."

"You should really let me screen the contents and pull out the routine office communications before I put the package together for you," Rita said. "I was sure after our last conversation that you'd want me to do that."

Margolis laughed indulgently. "I was a little under the weather that time, sweetheart. So I was a little grumpy. You just ship it all to me."

"Okay, Dave. Whatever you say."

"Now you're talking like a good AA. See you, sweetheart."

He hung up the phone with a satisfied smile on his face. That rumor might just do in little Jaylene. It probably wouldn't get her fired, but it could knock her out of contention for the presidency of the new subsidiary. After all, a fine upstanding corporation like TIE had to be careful about who it selected as president of one of its major business units.

Then he sighed as he looked toward the pile of papers on his desk. A large unwrapped package stood next to them. Hell, he was a day behind all that crap Rita was sending him. Maybe he *should* let her screen out the useless junk. But what if she threw out something important? That damn broad would never know the difference.

He fingered some of the papers on top of the pile. With that rumor, Jaylene was in deep political trouble. Did he really have to plow through this pile looking for more crap to pin on her?

Ray looked across the table at Jaylene as the waiter poured their wine. He thought she seemed tired. Her eyes didn't have the sparkle he'd remembered, and it seemed to take a lot to get her to laugh. It was their first evening together in almost a month, and he had wanted it to be perfect.

"A penny for your thoughts, milady," he said, once the waiter had left.

She forced a smile. "That's more than they're worth."

"Maybe you should tell the doctor about it."

A bit of sparkle returned to her eyes as she gazed suspiciously at him. "I thought your doctorate was in economics."

"We Harvard grads are very versatile."

A soft glow came over her face. "Yes, I remember."

He was relieved that her gloom seemed to be evaporating. He was more comfortable with the old, fun-loving Jaylene than with this new, sad one. "Good thing," he teased. "I hate teaching refresher courses. I was hoping to go on to the advanced level."

Her lips formed a semblance of a smile, then she seemed to sink into her blue mood again.

"Seriously, Jaylene. You look like you've had a bad day. Anything you'd like to talk about?"

"Not really," she said, shrugging her shoulders. "I guess my tolerance for some of the political nonsense of my job is at an all-time low today." There was a long silence as she stared off behind him. Her eyes clouded and looked troubled.

He was touched by her dejection and felt an inexplicable need to comfort her and make her smile. "I'm a good listener," he prodded gently.

Jaylene didn't reply, but took another sip of her wine.

"I'll even turn my collar around if you like."

Reluctantly, she smiled. "You're crazy. Maybe that's why I feel like I can relax around you. I thought last time you were in that being with you was as refreshing as having a quick vacation. I hope your curative powers are as great this time."

Touched by her words, Ray didn't know what to say. He reached for her hand as he stared into her eyes. The confusion and pain in her eyes seemed to ease slightly.

"Excuse me, please."

Ray jerked back. The waiter served their salads and left. An awkward silence descended while they ate, and it wasn't until they were well into the main course that Jaylene finally broke it.

"There are times when I really don't care for myself." Her voice was quiet and sad.

He looked up to see pain in her beautiful green eyes. He wanted to kiss them both to ease the hurt. The strength of that feeling surprised him and he forced himself to reply mildly, "There are times when we all can say that."

She twirled her wineglass slowly, staring down at it. "I know. But I'm at a level where I affect the lives of so many people. They've come to depend on me and plan their lives with certain expectations."

Ray thought he understood now. "You mean TIE's planned cutbacks I've been hearing about?"

She nodded.

"Sometimes you have to sacrifice a few for the benefit of many," he pointed out.

"I just never planned on being a general."

He shrugged his shoulders. "You didn't choose it, but you are in a war. It's an economic war, but it can be vicious.

"I know that, too," she admitted. "The organization comes first. If a few must be sacrificed for its health, then so be it." Her voice sounded very weary.

"TIE is big, Jaylene, but it has to adapt to survive. Remember what happened to the dinosaurs."

She didn't reply, but nodded her head.

"Are you firing one of your boyfriends?" he joked.

Jaylene laughed shortly and shook her head. "I don't know any of the people well, but I do know that one of them has some special circumstances."

"If you can't do anything about those special circumstances, you'd better put them out of your mind."

"I've been told that," she snapped. Her lips were suddenly compressed into a thin angry line.

For some reason, he could not bear the thought of her being mad at him and he reached out to squeeze her hand. "You'll just tear yourself apart, Jaylene, and still not help anybody."

Her anger seemed to ease. "I know."

She pushed her plate away, and, of their own volition, his hands moved over to hold both of hers. They looked at each other silently until the waiter came with their coffee, then they broke apart.

"Anyway," she said, forcing some vigor into her voice after the waiter picked up their dishes, "I'll be glad when the next few months are over."

He smiled. "I didn't know our case study was such a burden."

"That's not what I mean," she said. "I'd like these cutbacks to be over. It looks like things may get mean. There have been a few attacks," she said.

Ray was immediately concerned. "I presume your security people took care of it."

She shook her head. "It wasn't anything physical," she explained. "It was just some name-calling."

He was relieved. "It wasn't really you they were vilifying, Jaylene. It's TIE. You're just a representative of the corporation."

"I'm not sure they see the difference."

"That's not important," Ray replied. "What is important is that you see the difference."

The pain returned to her eyes. "You know that saying about sticks and stones?" she asked in a tight little voice. "Well, it's a lie." She was trying desperately to smile. "Words can hurt you. They can hurt real bad."

His grip on her hands tightened, but his touch seemed somehow inadequate. Too superficial. She was hurting deep inside, in places where his hands could not soothe. He ached for her, wishing he knew that to say. Normally he was quick with the words, jokes and flippant remarks just rolling off his tongue, but now he felt himself in deep water, and stayed silent. When words were needed, he only hoped he could find the right ones.

He saw the tears hiding just beneath the surface, and he wanted to sweep her into his arms, to hold her tight against the cruelties of the world. At the same time, though, he felt such a tremendous surge of anger at the people who had hurt her that he longed to strike out at them. How could he feel such tenderness and such hatred at the same time? The strength of his emotions frightened him. He was totally out of his depth and knew it, yet he couldn't back off. Not while that look of suffering was in Jaylene's eyes.

"Would you like dessert, sir?"

Ray stared stupidly at the waiter for a moment, then gathered his wits. "No, thank you. Just the check, please."

The interruption by the waiter had given Jaylene enough time to compose herself. Her eyes were still clouded with tears but otherwise she seemed cool and collected.

Ray took a deep breath, relieved to see her recovery. Talking out the hurts might work for some people, but it wasn't a method he was comfortable with. Tears and raw pain were not something he knew how to deal with. No, he was much better with laughter and a little fun. And that's what he could give to Jaylene. He'd keep her laughing and smiling until she had forgotten all about her hurt.

He left some money with the check and turned toward her. "Well, what now? Dancing? A movie?"

She just stared at him, the pain in her eyes deepening. Ray did not stop to think, he just put his arm around her shoulder. All he wanted right now was to make her feel better.

"I don't know about you," he said, "but the only thing I want to do is to take you to my room."

"I'd like that very much," she whispered.

They went out into the hotel lobby and waited for the elevator, standing close but not touching. Two sophisticated professionals out for an evening. Yet Ray could sense her iron self-control.

The elevator took them to Ray's floor and, still silent, they walked to his room. He opened the door and let her precede him. The door closed behind him and they stood looking at each other.

Then Ray went to her. He stroked her hair gently and pulled out the pins that held it and it fell in a soft cloud onto her shoulders. He ran his fingers through the thick waves, then leaned forward to kiss her forehead.

All the while she just stared at him, her eyes wide and dark, hesitating.

He pulled her into his arms and kissed her neck and ears, his lips brushing her skin tenderly, trying to ease away the sorrow and the hurt. He kissed her forehead again, and then her cheeks, then finally he kissed those suffering eyes.

Somewhere Jaylene crossed the boundary between uncertainty and confidence. The pain was supplanted by desire.

Discarding their clothes, they lay on his bed. On the beach, she had been a young girl surrendering to her love. Tonight she was a woman surrendering to her passion, feeding hers and inflaming his.

Later, much later, the room was dark. Jaylene slept like a satisfied tigress. Ray, exhausted, knew he had never before experienced such joy. He was good at sex, making sure that both he and his lady enjoyed themselves, but tonight he had done more than pleasure Jaylene. He had rejuvenated her spirit. He felt good. He felt triumphant, yet humble. And, as he drifted off to sleep, he felt fear.

Chapter Thirteen

October turned into November, and before Jaylene knew it, the case study was drawing to a close. The unexpected calls from Ray that brightened many a day for her would soon end. So would those days of whirlwind passion when he would fly down to work with his students. Although she had dropped a few hints about them getting together when their schedules coincided, he had not heeded the suggestion. Sadly she could only assume he was not interested.

But it probably was for the best, she reasoned with herself. She was lonely at times, but otherwise she was very satisfied with her life. She liked devoting all her energies to TIE, and she did not want to risk that relationship by allowing herself to be distracted by Ray. It already seemed different, almost as if she and TIE had been separated while Ray was around. She was anxious for it to return to normal, as it surely would once Ray was gone.

The only marriage she wanted was to TIE. She had tried the more conventional type years ago, and it had cured her of ever wanting it again. As a young girl, she had had the same dreams as all her schoolmates: a husband, a house, children. A place of her own where she really belonged. It sounded so simple, but getting it had turned out to be impossible.

After her miserable years in grade school where she had never felt accepted, Jane Louise had been glad that her mother could not afford to send her to the Catholic high school. She didn't even care that the local Polish National Alliance scholarship went to another student. She would be a misfit at the Catholic high school as she had always been a misfit. When Aunt Sophie offered to pay her tuition, Jane Louise had turned her down in a rare show of independence.

The summer before high school she worked in a local drugstore. She got along well with her co-workers; they said that she spoke so well that nobody would know she came from the west end. If they could like her, surely there would be more people at her new school just like them. She would have lots of friends.

The reality of Central High School came as a complete shock to Jane Louise. The students were black, Latin, hillbilly, and the poorer white ethnics whose parents could not afford tuition at the Catholic high schools. It wasn't at all like she had dreamed it would be.

Central High was not safe; it was ruled by fear, and that even extended to the teachers. A full-time policeman was assigned to the school, but there were over twenty-five hundred students, so he could do little; everyone was pretty much on his own. No one wanted to get involved.

Jane Louise was a timid child, only wanting to be liked and to live down the shame of an alcoholic father. Here, no one cared about her father, but no cared about her, either. The stong preyed on the weak, and the weak on the weaker still. She was too frightened to concentrate in class and her grades began to fall.

Then, suddenly, after spring vacation of her freshman year, she met Josef. She had seen him around school before that; it would have been impossible not to. He was not particularly handsome, his face scarred from fights, but he was one of the toughest of the gang leaders. He was three years older than she, but only a grade ahead.

She thought he had been watching her outside of school for several days, but didn't know why he would. She was small and not very well developed, certainly nothing like Stephanie, his girlfriend. But then one day a girl was taunting her, and he sent someone over to stop her. The girl ran.

Strangely enough, for the next several days, no one bothered Jane Louise. She didn't know or care why, she was just glad to have a little peace. When Josef asked her to carry some things into school for him, she was happy to.

Once she was under Josef's protection, the teachers turned hostile toward her, but she didn't care. They hadn't helped her when she had needed it, and Josef had. He deserved her loyalty, not they.

One day, early in her junior year, police officers came to the school. Jane Louise, along with some other students, was searched. The package she had been carrying for Josef that day contained narcotics. They questioned her for hours about who she was carrying the packages for and how many packages she had carried.

Jane Louise didn't say anything. She was scared, but Josef had said that they couldn't do anything to her. A few teachers were brought in and told her that she was in serious trouble. They urged her to give the police the information they needed, promising protection.

They sounded ridiculous. The police and teachers might live by rules, but the gangs did not. There was no way they could protect her. She stayed silent and was suspended from school. Her mother was horrified and ashamed. Such a thing had never happened to anyone in the family, or to anyone in the neighborhood. Aunt Sophie was grim and angry.

The drugstore where she had worked during the summer would not take her back. Aunt Sophie offered again to pay her tuition at the Catholic high school, but Jane Louise knew that there was no way she could return to school. Everyone would know she was tainted.

She started working in neighborhood hash houses where the work was hard and the pay was low and the male customers badgered her.

Josef again protected her. He was tough and smart, and when he wanted to have sex with her, she let him. She didn't enjoy it much, but was happy just to have someone who was watching out for her, someone who cared about her.

Just after her seventeenth birthday, they eloped and were married by a justice of the peace in Roseland. Afterward she called her mother with the news; surprisingly, her mother had not minded missing the ceremony. She had always dreamed of Jane Louise getting married in church and wearing a white dress.

Jane Louise knew she had hurt her mother, but she believed that everything was going to be wonderful now. She wouldn't have to work anymore and could keep busy making a home for Josef and their family. She kept on believing that until the first time he came home drunk and blackened both her eyes and bloodied her nose.

Ray drove up the long, palm tree–lined drive and stopped in front of the Bayshore Golf and Tennis Club. A valet hurried over to open his door, then drove the car to a discreetly hidden parking lot as Ray walked up the winding sidewalk.

It looked as if Jaylene was trying to wind up the case study with a bang, he thought. This place just reeked of money with its long white veranda. The green canvas awnings on each of the second-story windows matched the green of the finely manicured lawn. Trees and bushes grew in perfect symmetry. Ray went into the lobby, and a white-suited gentleman greeted him.

"I'm Dr. Carroll, here for the TIE dinner."

"Ah, yes, Dr. Carroll. Your party is this way."

Ray was led through the lobby and down a corridor where the thick carpeting muffled the sounds of their feet. They stopped in the doorway of a private dining room. Ray recognized some of the people milling about with drinks in their hands.

Ray entered the room and was immediately greeted by a waiter with a tray of drinks. He took a glass of wine, glancing around. He didn't see Jaylene. He guessed he had beaten her here and wandered about aimlessly. Without her to talk to, the party seemed routine and boring.

He had really enjoyed this case study and was sorry it had ended so quickly. Jaylene had been marvelous. A lot of fun, easy to talk to, and one very sexy woman. It was hard to believe that he wasn't going to see her again.

Over the years he had met and enjoyed countless lovely ladies, but he couldn't remember a single one who had been quite like Jaylene. He was so comfortable with her, he felt as if he had spent a lifetime in her company, not just an occasional day during the past six weeks. He had found himself really looking forward to each visit.

Of course, it was probably just as well that it was over. As much as he enjoyed her, he wasn't looking for a long-range relationship. No, a few dates and a few laughs, and then on to the next fascinating female.

He heard some people arriving and turned to see Jaylene at the door followed closely by her security guard, Nancy. He went over to them.

"This is very plush, Miss Sable," he said quietly, leaning down so that he would not be overheard. "I'm not sure this poor schoolteacher can ever go back to his ordinary life."

"The grapevine says that a full professor at the Harvard Business School with a consulting firm partnership is not a candidate for food stamps."

"We try to get along."

"How brave," she mocked, her mouth curving into a teasing smile.

One of the waiters brought her a drink and another offered them some hors d'oeuvres.

"My goodness," Jaylene said sarcastically as she gazed across the room. "I think that's Frank Kareau."

"Don't you recognize your own boss?"

"Of course, he's the one who disappears at the first sign of trouble. I guess I should feel relieved that he's here. It must mean the natives aren't too restless." She paused. "Then again, maybe he figures that since I'm here, he can throw me to the wolves if need be."

Ray was not amused. Maybe it was a good thing that he was leaving. He was getting a little old to be worrying about anyone but himself.

Kareau saw them and his face broke into a wide smile as he hurried over. "Can I steal her for a minute, doc? We really have to talk. We're both traveling so much that we have to make our appointments six months in advance."

Ray had no time to protest as Jaylene and her manager walked off to the side by themselves, and entered into an animated discussion. Although Kareau's smile never left his face, it was obvious they were arguing. Jaylene seemed to be coolly holding her ground, but Ray wondered if he should go over. Maybe she needed his support.

"Care for a glass of wine, sir?"

Startled, Ray looked up at the gray-haired steward. "Sure, thank you."

He took another glass and looked back over at Jaylene and Kareau. Kareau was still smiling, but his shoulders seemed to have a dejected sloop to them. Just as well he didn't go over. She was a big girl and had demonstrated any number of times that she could take care of herself.

Kareau left, but before Jaylene could return to Ray, another man intercepted her. Ray wasn't sure who it was, but it looked like her controller. Damn. This was their last night together. Didn't she care?

"The younger women are always the popular ones, aren't they, Dr. Carroll?"

"Hello, Rita." Ray had turned slowly so that his pasted-on smile had a chance to warm up. He had tried to be cordial to the woman, but from the day they first met there had been friction between them. Ray had gotten the strong impression that Rita did not like him.

"I really appreciate all the help you've given my students," he told her. "Without it, our project would not have been as successful."

"We try our best in administration, doctor."

Her humility seemed false, but he just nodded. "That's all anyone can ask."

He looked around for Jaylene and saw that she was with yet another man. His jaws tightened and he gulped his wine. He was starting to feel totally useless. His eyes strayed around the room and fell on a group of women fashionably dressed in bright clothes—the corporate wives. Their dress contrasted sharply with the more somber clothes of Jaylene and the other businesswomen. He stared morosely at the wives. Maybe he should join them. He was just another decorative appendage.

"Hi, doctor."

His mind preoccupied, it took Ray a moment to recognize

the bright young lady in front of him as one of his graduate students. "Hello, Lisa. You're looking very nice tonight." That was a stupid remark. "I mean you look less formal tonight."

She took a sip of her wine and giggled. "I know what you mean, Dr. Carroll."

"It just threw me when I saw you without your glasses."

"Boys don't make passes at girls who wear glasses."

"What?"

"Didn't they say that when you were in school?"

"I don't remember."

Lisa drained her glass of wine. "I had a real nice talk with your lady."

"My lady?" Ray asked, confused.

Lisa's fingers flew to her lips. "Oops. Wasn't I supposed to say that? It must be the wine."

Ray shook his head. All young women were romantics. They saw deep personal relationships around every corner, but he and Jaylene were only having fun.

"Anyway, as I was trying to say—" Lisa interrupted his thoughts with an exaggerated clearing of her throat. "Jaylene—I mean Miss Sable—and I had a long talk."

"Oh, that's good." Ray's eyes wandered around the room again. Jaylene was working her way toward him, but it seemed to be taking forever.

"She told me that I was smart and worked hard, but that I didn't have any flair. She told me hard work would just get me more work and give somebody else the glory."

"She's probably right," Ray replied absently. Jaylene still had not reached him. Should he start moving toward her?

"Miss Sable said that women have a special problem in business, because they grow up expecting somebody will take care of them. She said that I had better learn to take care of myself, because no one else was going to."

Yes, that sounded like Jaylene, all right. She hadn't reached her position without knowing how to take care of herself. He guessed he'd wait here for her. She'd get to him in due time—if she wanted to. The waiter came by with the wine again and he took another glass.

"More wine, Lisa?"

"I shouldn't, but I will. I don't know when I'll ever run across all these free goodies again."

Lisa took her glass and then squinted across the room. "Speaking of goodies. Is that Drew Hanson over there by the table?"

"Yes, it is."

She drained her glass of wine. "Well, this is our last night in town, so I'm going to shoot the moon."

Ray had to smile as he watched his student cross the room with a determined tilt to her shoulders.

"Do all Harvard professors ogle their students that way?"

Ray was suddenly irritated as he glanced over at Jaylene. She could talk to everybody in the room, but apparently he wasn't even allowed to talk to one student. "I don't ogle my students. I was just thinking."

"I'm sorry. Something bothering you tonight?"

He shrugged his shoulders. "I guess I'm just a little tired. Must be old age slowing me up."

People were moving into the inner dining room, so Jaylene took his arm and moved close to him. "When a woman gets to my age, she likes a man with a slow hand."

Ray did not reply, but his irritation seeped away. It was a real shame that the case study wasn't going to take longer. Much as he hated to admit it, he knew that of all the women who had filled his spare time, Jaylene was the one he would remember the most.

Frank Kareau interrupted Ray's reverie. "That was a real fine job you and your students did, Ray. I think TIE got more out of your study than Harvard."

They shook hands. "Thanks, Frank. I know we got what we wanted out of it."

Kareau was patting him on the back and moving up the line to another couple almost before Ray had finished his sentence.

"Your boss is very smooth," Ray commented to Jaylene.

"Oil usually is." The question in his eyes must have been very obvious, for she continued after a pause. "It wasn't Frank's idea to hire me. I was on Jesse's personal staff, and he highly recommended me. Frank is not one to leave an apple unpolished, so here I am."

"Being in the right place at the right time has a lot to do with most promotions."

Jaylene made a slight face. "I guess."

They both nodded politely to Rita as they walked to their table. "Anyway, the experience has been very interesting. I've learned how to take care of myself in some pretty dirty infighting."

Ray held her chair as she sat down, a cold pall settling over him. He might remember her, but would she remember him? Or had he been just a momentary diversion from her hectic business life? Since that was how he regarded her, why should the thought bother him so?

"Why don't you make us both a drink?" Jaylene suggested as they entered her apartment. "I want to change out of this suit."

"Sounds promising," Ray joked.

She forced herself to smile and went down the hall to her bedroom. She had known from the beginning that it was not going to last. He had been in and out for six weeks as he guided his students, but now that the data gathering was finished, she wouldn't even have his occasional visits. Neither of them had pretended that it would be otherwise, so there was no reason for her to feel all mopey and sad. They'd had some fun, and it was over.

She ignored the lacy nightgowns hanging in her closet and took out a terrycloth romper. It was cool and comfortable, and the blue violet color certainly matched her mood. She ran a comb through her hair and went back to the living room.

"That looks comfortable," Ray said as he handed her a drink.

"It is." She knew he was comparing it to the sexy outfits she had worn on other occasions, but she didn't care. She accepted the glass from him without really looking at it, and took a swallow.

"It's brandy," he warned, but a little too late.

The fiery liquid burned its way down her throat.

Strangely enough, it felt good. It was something to concentrate on instead of her rapidly growing depression.

"Don't you always gulp your brandy?" she teased when she was able to speak.

"Not recently."

He seemed to be watching her more closely than usual. Was her dejection that apparent? She'd better make an effort to cheer up or he'd think he was at a wake.

She sat on the sofa stretching her legs out to rest on the edge of the table. "Oh, it feels good to sit down. It's been some week."

He sat on the sofa, too, but near the other end. "Tired?"

"A bit." Better he think that than decide she was a clinging vine going into a decline because he was leaving.

"Want me to go?"

She sat up abruptly. "Goodness no. I'm not that tired. There's still a spark of life left in this old body." She patted the sofa next to her playfully. "Maybe you're too far away to see it."

He moved closer, a relaxed grin on his face. "I thought you were giving me a little hint."

"What's the matter? Worried that your charm wasn't working?"

He put his arm around her shoulder and she rested her head against his chest. She could hear his heartbeat. The sound was soothing, making her feel safe and not so alone.

"My charm is always working," he said, whispering the words softly into her ear. His fingers moved across her arm and into her armpit.

"Ray, stop that," Jaylene ordered, trying to squirm away from his tickling fingers. "If you don't, I'll call Rose and have her shoot you."

"You told me in the car that she's locked herself in her room and won't come out."

"I lied," Jaylene squeaked. She was caught in the corner of the sofa with no escape from his hands, but then his touch changed. His tickles became caresses and his teasing manner turned serious. They were in each other's embrace, and her only thought was to savor these last few hours before he left.

Silently, they moved into her bedroom. The lights were out and the drapes were open to the night view of Miami, but neither of them seemed to notice. They fell across the bed, on top of the smooth satin bedspread, too lost in each other to care about their surroundings.

Their needs were immediate and they shed their clothes quickly and came together with frantic urgency. It was as if by filling her body and soul with him, she could erase the knowledge that she would be alone tomorrow.

Spent, they lay back against the pillows and began a more leisurely seduction of each other. She tried not to think of how she would miss him as she ran her hand slowly across his chest. She had tonight, and would make the most of it.

They made love again and then lay in each other's arms. Ray drifted off to sleep, but Jaylene fought the need to rest. Even though her eyelids drooped, she lay in the dim light, listening to the sound of his even breathing and trying to memorize the feeling of peace and security she felt in his presence, that wonderful sense of being needed. But she knew she'd never recapture it once he was gone.

Jaylene felt a movement next to her and awoke with a start. The room was filled with the gentle glow of morning. By the dawn light she watched Ray getting dressed.

"I never meant to sleep this late," he said, feeling her eyes on him. "I should have been back at the hotel hours ago."

"Your students are old enough to take care of themselves."

He pulled his shirt on. "I know, but we've got an early flight out and I still have to pack."

She lay on the bed watching him button his shirt, then put on his socks and shoes. How did one say good-bye to a casual lover who had added so much to her life?

He stopped next to the bed, all dressed, yet silent. Maybe he wasn't sure how to say good-bye, either.

"I didn't know case studies could be so much fun," she joked. "The next time I'm offered one, I won't be so quick to turn it down."

His smile seemed regretful. Apparently her attempt at humor had misfired.

"It's been great knowing you, Jaylene," he said quietly.

Lord, what a terrible line.

"Maybe we'll see each other around sometime," she said. That was even worse. Why hadn't she taken the time away from business to have a few more affairs so she could handle this better?

"Well, if you're ever in Boston, look me up."

"Same if you ever come back to Miami."

She was either going to cry or throw up if they didn't stop all this ridiculousness. Why didn't he just get it over with and go?

He leaned over her suddenly and kissed her lips. "If I have any questions about the data, I'll give you a call."

"Sure," she said, but he had already gone. She heard her front door close quietly. Then the apartment was deathly still.

One tear ran down the side of her face, but no more. It was all right that he had left. It was fine, in fact. She had needed a diversion from all her work and he had provided it. True, she was left with only her work again, but she could fix that. She'd find somebody else to laugh with and somebody else to love with. And if it took some time, that was only to be expected. It was harder to find a man at thirty-eight than at twenty-eight. She was just lucky she hadn't become emotionally involved with Ray.

Chapter Fourteen

Jaylene closed the door with her foot, leaning against it for a moment as she caught her breath. Then she went into the kitchen and dumped her armful of packages onto the table.

Why had she thought getting out of the house would be fun and relaxing? Was she so far removed from reality that she had forgotten that the day after Thanksgiving was the busiest shopping day of the year?

It was just that the rooms had been so deadly quiet. Rose had left earlier in the week to stay with her daughter who'd just had a baby, and the apartment had seemed like a tomb. Jaylene had spent Thanksgiving alone, trying to read some reports she had brought home, but the silence had become more and more overwhelming as the day wore on.

Had she become so dependent on Rose that she was unable to function here alone? she had wondered yesterday as she ate her Thanksgiving dinner of roast turkey, sweet potatoes, cranberry sauce, and stuffing, sent over for a fee from an exclusive restaurant down the road. She had had the right menu for a perfect holiday, yet a certain bitterness kept her from really enjoying the meal. Was this what she had fought for over the years, the right to dread each holiday for the loneliness that accompanied it?

At least Rose had her memories to warm her. A husband she had loved, children, and now grandchildren. What did Jaylene have? Would TIE send her cards at Christmas? Would one of the divisions she started spawn new divisions that would send her letters scrawled in crayon?

She picked through her packages, angry at the maudlin sentimentality that had been washing over her lately. Ninety percent of the women in America would give their eyeteeth to be in her shoes. A position of power. Outstanding salary. Not dependent on a husband. The freedom and money to go anywhere, do anything she wanted. Why wasn't she satisfied all of a sudden?

She opened one bag and removed some books. Now that she had them home, she wasn't sure she was interested in any of them. Just knowing that she had time to read one of these six-hundred-page novels made the weekend seem even longer. What had she done to pass the time other years?

Last year, she had been Jesse's administrative assistant and had been living in New York. She and her then current boyfriend had gone to Cape Cod. What was his name? He was before Ken.

Some other years Aunt Sophie had come to visit. She smiled as she remembered the year she had been living in L.A. and they had gone to Disneyland the day after Thanksgiving. Now that had been a nice holiday.

The phone caught her eye. She picked it up and tried again to reach her aunt. But the phone rang and rang in an empty house, just as it had yesterday.

Jaylene replaced the receiver and stared at it thoughtfully. Maybe what she needed was a real, old-fashioned holiday to get it out of her system once and for all. Maybe she ought to go home for Christmas. She could surprise Aunt Sophie and stay for a couple of days. They could catch up on all sorts of gossip and just relax.

The idea appealed to her, and the thought of the next few days seemed almost bearable because Christmas would be so different. She picked up one of the books she had bought and took it into the living room. She settled down on the sofa and began to read, but her mind refused to cooperate. After a half hour, she had read only five pages. Hell. She tossed the book onto the cocktail table.

Why hadn't she thought about visiting Aunt Sophie earlier? She could just as easily have gone over Thanksgiving as over Christmas. And then she wouldn't be sitting around here, moping.

She let her eyes close as she leaned her head on the back of the sofa. When had she become so restless? She knew, but almost hated to admit it to herself. Ever since that case study had ended and Ray had gone out of her life, she hadn't been herself.

It had been so nice to have something other than work to look forward to. Would she ever see him again? Too bad she hadn't thought of him earlier, too. Maybe they could have gone away together for a few days. Unless, of course, he had someone that he spent the holidays with.

She looked at her watch, but not even an hour had passed since she had returned home. She sighed. Maybe this was the eternity that the good sisters in grade school had always told her about.

She walked over to the window and stared out at the afternoon sun. It was a bright summer day outside. Stupid place couldn't even have a real Thanksgiving.

She resisted the temptation to check her watch again. This long holiday weekend was going to kill her yet. Thursday, Friday, Saturday, Sunday. She counted the days on her fingers. Four days in all, and she still had a little more than two and a half days to live through. She had never gone through a holiday like this before. Was she the only one in Miami who was alone?

There ought to be an organization that rented out kids. Or maybe even a family. When she felt lonely or domestic, she could hire a husband and a child named Laura Michelle, age ten, to keep her company.

She blanched suddenly. Laura wouldn't be ten, she would have been almost twenty-one by now.

Jaylene walked over to the windows and stared blindly out at the water. Why had her thoughts fastened on Laura after all these years? She was part of the past, dead and buried with a great many other useless memories. Things had worked out for the best, no matter how terrible they had seemed then.

But, unwillingly, her mind took her back to that time when nothing but pain had filled her life. She had been incredibly naive and trusting then, believing that the fairy-tale world in books was going to be hers even if she had the wrong cast of characters.

And how wrong her cast of characters had been! Josef had not been hero material. Why had he married her? That was something she had wondered about for years after she had left South Bend and all its bitter memories. She knew why she had married him: girls were supposed to get married. They were supposed to want a home and a family, and she was no different. She had hoped that with Josef she would finally have a place where she belonged.

But dreams have a way of disappearing when they come up against reality. At best, Josef had been unemployed, but most of the time he had been hatching some illegal schemes. When they failed, as most did, he took it out on her. She took to wearing long-sleeved dresses to cover the bruises, no matter how warm it was outside.

The house she had longed for, with a big kitchen for her to bake in and a yard for their children to play in, remained a dream. They lived in a two-room apartment above a butcher shop where the smell of dried blood and spoiled meat clung to everything.

Because Josef couldn't find a job, she had continued to work in the neighborhood diners. The one where she worked most frequently was more than a mile from their apartment, but she walked the distance, even in the worst weather. A week's bus fare could buy enough meat for two dinners, though often enough Josef just drank it away. No matter where she hid her money in the apartment, he found it.

Her mother had become very ill soon after she and Josef were married, and Jane Louise began to work double shifts, trying to help her mother with doctor bills and to keep food on her own table. Her mother suggested several times that they move in with her, but Jane Louise couldn't bear for her mother to know the truth about her marriage.

When they had been married for seven months, she discovered she was pregnant. It was not the happy occasion her dreams had told her it should have been. She was already exhausted, both physically and mentally. How could she cope with another life dependent on her?

She did her best for a time, learning that what she had thought was exhaustion was only a vague weariness. Real exhaustion was something new, something she was learning more and more about with each passing day.

Then one evening, Josef came home in a frenzy. He had tried to rob a liquor store and had been recognized. He wanted all the money she'd saved to leave town and he didn't believe her when she claimed she had none. With her mother so ill and the baby coming, how did he think she was able to save anything?

In his fear and rage, he had lashed out at her. It wasn't the first time, but she had been afraid for the baby and tried to run. He caught her at the top of the stairs. The last thing she remembered was falling.

When she woke up, she was in the hospital. Aunt Sophie was at her side. Late that night she gave birth to a tiny little girl, three months premature. Laura lived barely an hour, and before Jane Louise was well enough to leave the hospital, her mother died also. Aunt Sophie made arrangements for the funerals and gave her a place to live. She was the one who convinced her to break all the marriage-is-forever rules she had grown up with and to divorce Josef. He was in jail by that time, and she had never seen him again. Aunt Sophie had given her a new life, and she was ready to begin living it.

Jaylene turned away from the window, brushing aside some tears, furious at herself for getting weepy over some might-have-beens. She had been very lucky to escape the mess she had made of her life, and compared to that, a lonely Thanksgiving was not much of a hardship.

She went over to the table and picked up the book again. This time she was going to read it.

Chapter Fifteen

"Well, I think this is going to work out splendidly," Malcolm Cabot said, leaning back in the rich leather booth and taking a sip of his brandy.

"I certainly appreciate your giving the assignment to Cambridge Associates, sir," Ray assured him.

It was the middle of December, and he and Malcolm and Jesse Whitmore were having lunch together to discuss a consulting job that Malcolm had given to Ray's firm. Ray picked up his own brandy and cast a surreptitious glance at Jesse Whitmore. He sensed that Jesse was not as pleased as he and Malcolm were, and wondered why.

"This consolidation is a tricky project," Jesse said. He stared into his glass for a moment before looking up at Ray. "We want to really study it from all sides before a decision is made. A sloppy implementation could lose us more than we'll save."

Ray nodded, although he was reasonably certain that they had already made a decision. His firm was just needed to confirm what TIE wanted to do. And to provide a convenient scapegoat when the flak started to fly.

"We'll certainly do our best."

"We know that, since you'll be doing the study yourself," Malcolm said. He finished his brandy and rose to his feet. "I hope you'll excuse me, gentlemen, but I do have an appointment in a few minutes and had better get back to the office."

Once Malcolm had left, there was a long silence at the table. Jesse lit a cigar and worked at it thoughtfully while

Ray sipped his drink. He hoped that Jesse would get around to his objections, knowing it would be a lot easier to get the job done if he knew just where he stood.

"Ray, I'm going to be honest with you," Jesse said suddenly.

"Good."

"Malcolm put me in a real bind when he said he wanted to hire you to do the consolidation study. My first reaction was negative because of you and Jaylene." He hesitated, looking definitely uncomfortable.

"Because we'd had a few . . . dates?" Ray suggested. He did not bother to ask how Jesse had known. Things like that tended to get around.

"Yeah, because you had been seeing each other," Jesse said gruffly. "We all could be opening ourselves up to a lot of grief before this thing is done."

"So why didn't you hire another firm?"

Jesse stared down at his cigar for a moment. "TIE needs to close down some plants that Malcolm's father opened years ago. It's been a long while since they've been profitable, and it's time we stopped being sentimental about them. Unfortunately, Malcolm may not agree with me, and it'll help if I go along with him on some other issues."

"I see," Ray said slowly. He understood Jesse's dilemma completely. The bottom line was what counted the most. "What is it you'd like me to do? Refuse the contract?"

"Hell, no," Jesse said, and shook his head. "That would only start Malcolm asking questions. I just want to be reassured that there's nothing between you and Jaylene."

Ray relaxed. "That's easy to do," he said, and finished his brandy. "We had a little fun, but nothing serious. It was over when the case study was over. I haven't given her another thought." That wasn't strictly true; she had strayed into his thoughts a number of times, but Jesse needn't know that—or just how much he had enjoyed her company. And it was true that it was over. Neither of them was in the market for anything but a brief affair.

"That's the best news I've had all day." Jesse laughed and raised his hand for the check. "Actually, I was afraid that I had started something."

"You had?" Ray was puzzled.

"Yes, when I was telling her about the case study, I joked about her having a fling with you."

"Oh?" He wasn't sure he wanted to hear the rest.

"She had just dropped her latest boyfriend and I suggested you as a temporary replacement." The waiter brought the check over and Jesse signed it quickly. "I hadn't expected her to take me seriously, though. Do you think she thought it was an order?"

Ray joined in Jesse's laughter, but he felt vaguely hurt inside. Oh, he was sure she hadn't really thought it was an order, but the very fact that she and Jesse had joked about it bothered him. He had thought their attraction had been spontaneous and right, not something she had planned because she was between boyfriends.

Somehow Ray made proper good-byes and left, hurrying through the snowy December afternoon back to his hotel. His mind was on Jaylene all the while. She had seemed so special to him, so different from the other women he had known. Not that he had hoped for any future between them. No, she had just been a particularly nice companion, one that he would remember fondly for years to come. Now he was no longer sure that she deserved to be remembered.

He went through the lobby and up to his room, determined to put her from his mind. He was due to fly to London tomorrow and had the rest of the afternoon and the whole night ahead of him. A lot of fun could be had in twenty-four hours in New York. And he was game for all of it.

He took his address book out of his briefcase and paged through it. He should have called someone before he left Boston and made sure she was free. The trouble was, he couldn't decide whom to call, so he had put it off.

He sighed and tossed the book onto the bed. He didn't really want to spend the evening with any of his old girlfriends, that was the problem. He needed some new names in his book, some new territory to explore. Jaylene might have been better than anyone in that book, but she wasn't unique. There were others out there just as much fun as she was. All he had to do was find them.

* * *

Jaylene knew she was being ridiculous. There was absolutely nothing wrong with a woman calling a man in this day and age. Still, she was nervous as she dialed the phone.

She had decided to do this yesterday when Jesse had called and told her to come to New York for a meeting. New York wasn't that far from Boston, and she wanted to see Ray again. Why shouldn't she give him a call and see if he was free?

It had taken her some time to get up enough nerve to call his office at Harvard, and then she had been given another number to call. Someplace named Cambridge Associates, his consulting firm. Still moving on the same flow of determination, she called the new number. Ray had not been available because he was in New York.

Jaylene had not been able to believe her luck. With a little persuasion, she had managed to get the name of the hotel he normally stayed at, and now, newly flown in from Miami and installed in her own hotel, she was calling him.

The phone barely rang once before he answered. A shiver of excitement went down her spine when she heard his voice. She knew she had done the right thing. They'd have a marvelous time tonight!

"Ray, it's Jaylene."

There was a moment of silence, and she smiled, thinking how surprised he must be.

"How are you?" he finally asked.

"Great, now that I've tracked you down." She laughed, kicking off her shoes and relaxing on the bed. "I'm in town for a day or two and thought we might be able to get together."

"I'm flying to London tomorrow," he said.

"Well, that leaves us tonight. What are you in the mood for? TIE's got great connections. I can get us tickets to any show you want to see." She was glad that she had packed that black evening dress just on impulse.

"I'm not sure," he said. For the first time, she realized that he didn't sound as excited over the prospect of an evening with her as she had hoped.

"Look, if you've already got plans, I understand." She sat up quickly, her excitement fading. "I did try to reach you yesterday when I found out I'd be in town, but I didn't have any luck. We can do it some other time." Or more likely not do it, she told herself. It seemed pretty obvious all of a sudden that he hadn't been lying awake at night dreaming of her.

"Don't be silly," he said quickly. "I'd love to see you. You just caught me off guard, that's all."

"You would?"

"What are you in the mood for? Sophisticated or tourist?"

"What's tourist?" She laughed.

"You poor deprived girl. How about if I pick you up in a half hour and introduce you to New York?"

"Sounds marvelous."

She hung up the phone and changed into slacks and a sweater, something more suitable for New York's wintry weather than the suit she'd had on. Then, after touching up her makeup, she grabbed her coat and went down to the lobby to wait for Ray. She didn't care if she seemed overly anxious to see him. She was.

Suddenly he was coming across the chrome and deep red lobby toward her. He looked as handsome as ever in casual slacks and a down ski jacket. His dark hair was windblown, his brown eyes searching eagerly for her. She thought she would burst with excitement and longing as she rushed into his arms. They closed around her, and for a moment she was in heaven. His strength surrounded her, and the memory of all the good times they'd had clouded her senses.

"My, that was some welcome." He laughed.

She stepped back, smiling. Although his tone was teasing, his eyes were serious; he seemed as stirred by the meeting as she was.

He helped her with her coat, then hurried her out the door and into a cab. "Want to go ice skating?" he asked.

"Fine." Suddenly she realized she didn't really care what she did as long as she was with him.

He told the driver to take them to Rockefeller Center,

then sat back, putting his arm around her shoulder and pulling her close. "It's good to see you again."

She laughed. "You sound surprised."

"I am," he admitted. "I hadn't realized until I heard your voice just how much I'd missed you."

She just smiled, then let the smile fade as his mouth came down slowly to meet hers. Their lips touched gently at first, as if they, too, were surprised by this chance meeting. Then a wave of passion seemed to shake them. The kiss deepened and she and Ray clung together, hungry for each other's touch. They broke apart when the cab swerved around a corner.

"So how've you been?" she asked.

"Okay." He gently reached up to brush a strand of hair from her face. Then they were locked in an embrace again.

The afternoon passed in a haze for Jaylene. She hadn't skated in years, but she managed to do reasonably well. Maybe it was something one never forgot how to do, or maybe it was Ray's hand in hers that provided the magic. She only knew that her feet seemed to fly over the ice, just as her heart was flying.

Lost in the same haze, they went back to her hotel and ordered dinner from room service. While they waited, they lay in each other's arms, talking a little, but mostly just touching, touching as if discovering something new and wondrous. And for her at least, it had been.

Sometime during their magical day, she had made a discovery. She was in love with Ray. All of her great plans to stay free and devote herself only to her work had somehow been ignored.

Her heart had been wiser than her mind, but, as they lay together that evening, she knew it was right for her. She needed to give herself completely to another. She didn't know how Ray felt about her, but she wasn't worried. How could he not be touched by the magic? How could their bodies love so beautifully if their spirits didn't also?

Ray got out of bed, careful not to disturb Jaylene, and went into the bathroom. He saw by his watch that it was almost six o'clock and there were faint sounds of stirring in the hall outside.

Why in the world had he agreed to see her yesterday? What had he been thinking of? Especially in light of what he'd told Jesse about their relationship. He grimaced as he turned on the shower. He had not been thinking, that was the problem. He had been reacting. She was an attractive lady and, as soon as he had heard her voice, his glands had put his mind on hold.

The water was cool to the touch and he stepped under it, muttering a curse when he felt just how cold it was. But he stayed under it, soaping himself liberally as he tried to cool down the heat that Jaylene had awakened in him.

Sure, she was attractive, but it was goddamn idiotic of him to have risked that contract with TIE just for another evening with her. He had decided years ago that no woman was worth a risk, and he had not changed his mind. Jaylene was a lot of fun. He enjoyed her company, but he could find any number of women whose company he enjoyed just as much.

He pushed away the bitter memory of how uninteresting all the women listed in his address book had seemed yesterday and how glad he had been to hear Jaylene's voice. Companionable women were a dime a dozen. Contracts that brought him the money and prestige that this one would were rare.

He got out of the shower before icicles formed on his body and dried himself briskly. It was time he made Jaylene understand that he wasn't husband material. He wasn't even boyfriend material. He traveled light because that was the way he preferred it and that was the way he would always prefer it.

Jaylene was lying in bed awake when he went back in the bedroom, a towel wrapped around his waist. Her eyes were dark with memories of the night they had spent in each other's arms, and her deep brown hair fell over her shoulders and across the pillow. He could feel its softness beneath his touch and he remembered the faint scent of perfume on her skin.

"You're up awfully early," she said with an inviting smile.

Although it hurt, he steeled himself to look away. "It's a brand-new day," he said briskly. "And we both have things to do."

"But not this early," she protested with a puzzled smile.

"I like to get started early," he said. "Morning's my best time."

"Oh, yeah? Come prove it to me," she teased. "Come on back to bed, professor. I think I need a little work on my technique."

His resolve threatened to melt at the passion in her voice, but he wouldn't let it. He loved his job. He loved the travel. He especially loved his freedom. Jaylene was becoming a threat to all that. She was sweet and wonderful, but deadly to his way of life. He wouldn't give in to her again, even if it killed him.

"I didn't notice any problems," he said lightly as he walked over to the chair where he'd tossed his clothes. He was careful not to look at her; she represented temptation. "There comes a time for every student when she has to go out into the world and fly on her own."

"Ray?"

The hurt was evident in her voice, but he pulled on his pants, his back to her.

"Ray, what's the matter?"

He put on his shirt, only stopping to button every other button, then pulled his sweater over his head. Dressed, he felt armored against her charm, and he turned to face her.

"Who says anything's the matter?" His voice was nonchalant and his casual shrug provided the finishing touch. He sat on the edge of the bed, his back to her again as he pulled on his socks. "It's just time I left, that's all."

"I thought you'd stay through breakfast at least," she said. "You told me your flight doesn't leave until two o'clock. What's the big rush?"

He pulled his shoes out from under the bed. "Because you've got to get to work. Or have you forgotten?"

"Hardly," she snapped, and threw back the covers.

He tried to keep his eyes intent on his shoes, as if tying

the laces required his full concentration. But, straying of
their own accord, his eyes followed her slender body from
the bed to the chair where her robe lay. Even when she had
wrapped it around her, he could picture her flat stomach
and her firm, high breasts. He could feel her lying beside
him, and his body demanded that he stay. He rose to his
feet.

After running a brush through her hair, Jaylene turned
to face him, leaning back against the dresser. She was obviously irritated, and hurt. "I think I ought to tell you that
while you may be quite good in some areas, your exit lines
stink."

Ray tried to avoid looking directly into her eyes or at her
partially covered body. He chose instead a spot on the wall
behind her.

"I've never been good at long good-byes," he said.

"You did fine in Miami."

"That was different," he said with a shrug. "I thought it
really was good-bye."

"And this isn't?"

He didn't know what to say. He didn't want to hurt her,
but neither did he dare see her again. Somehow he had to
make her understand. "This has to be," he said lamely.

"Fine. Just say so then. Say it was fun while it lasted but
the magic's gone. I'm a big girl, I can take it. You aren't
the only fish in the sea, you know."

The anger in her eyes hurt him. He knew he was doing it
all wrong. The magic wasn't gone; it was as strong as ever.
That was the problem, and that was what he didn't dare
say.

"Take care, Jaylene," he said quietly, and let himself
out the door, a bitter taste in his mouth.

She had been insane last night, Jaylene decided as the
door closed behind Ray. Or maybe it had been a rare form
of indigestion. Whatever it had been, it had not been love.
She was too sensible to let herself get involved with something as futile as love. And certainly not with someone like
Ray.

Refusing to feel sorry for herself, Jaylene went into the

bathroom and took her shower. Sure, Ray's strange departure hurt, but she would get over it. Get over it easily, in fact. She still had TIE.

Her reaction to Ray had not been normal for her. She had clung to him for some reason, even as she insisted she did not want any close relationships. She wanted to be on her own, dependent neither financially nor emotionally, yet she had been acting as if she had changed her mind—as if she wanted to be married.

What an idiot she had been! she fumed as she moved briskly into the bedroom and pulled a suit from the closet. Her actions had probably reeked of orange blossoms and white lace and she had scared Ray away!

After a quick breakfast, Jaylene went over to TIE's corporate headquarters. Her pep talk had not cheered her up as much as she had hoped, but she ignored the depression settling around her. She was determined to get on with what she was good at. And that was making money for TIE.

Jesse was waiting for her and she was shown right into his office. She didn't know the reason for his summons, but she was strangely uncurious. He'd get to it soon enough.

"You got a handle on who's throwing your confidential information to the winds?" he asked her.

"Not yet." Since he'd brought that up first, that wasn't the main reason for the meeting. Getting things over with wasn't Jesse's style. "We've set up a task force to track it down. We're going on the assumption that it's an inside job and is being done for revenge or kicks. Right now we've got an operative planted in the cleaning crew to watch the copying rooms in the evening. I think we'll plug the leaks shortly."

He nodded his head and grunted. "I hope so, but that's not the reason I called you up here. I wanted to discuss your relationships," Jesse went on. "One in particular."

Jaylene gazed suspiciously across his desk. The summons suddenly took on a new, more sinister meaning, and a cold wariness spread through her body. Just how was TIE going to interfere in her life now?

Jesse cleared his throat and leaned forward. "Let me

confirm a rumor. It's almost a sure thing that we're going to merge the two foreign subsidiaries. So we've decided to hire a consultant to check our assumptions out. You know. Make sure that we do it right."

She was not distracted. "What does that have to do with my private relationships?"

Jesse shifted his position. "The outfit we hired is from Boston. Cambridge Associates."

Jaylene froze slightly. So that was it.

"They're a bunch of business school professors, and the one heading up the study is familiar with TIE. And yourself."

"Dr. Carroll," she said, and Jesse nodded.

She should have known. That was what all that nonsense had been about this morning. He didn't want to jeopardize his contract. Why hadn't he thought about his precious contract when she called yesterday? Had the promise of a little free sex been too much for him to pass up? she thought angrily.

"Now, I talked to Ray yesterday," Jesse continued, "and he assured me that there's nothing going on between you two. You got together a few times in Miami, had a few dates." He hesitated a moment as he pursed his lips. "Now you're each traveling separate paths on to bigger and better things."

No wonder he had been so curt this morning; he had lots of tracks to cover. "So what do you want from me?" she asked bitterly.

"I want to know that you feel the same way," Jesse snapped impatiently. "I want to know that when he comes down to study your operations the most he'll get is a handshake."

Jaylene was angry now and jumped to her feet. "Damn it, if you're so afraid I'm going to molest the guy, why don't you just hire someone else?"

"I can't," he informed her, equally irritated. "Malcolm's got some bee in his bonnet about hiring Carroll's firm, and he's going to be pretty curious if I start hedging." He paused for a moment. "Maybe you'd like to chat with him about it?"

Jaylene sat with a sigh, all her anger deflated. "No," she said quietly.

Jesse's anger seemed to disappear also and he leaned forward, looking straight into her eyes. "Jaylene, I've gone with my balls hanging out into some pretty rough places for you. I need your word that nothing's going to jeopardize the impartiality of that study."

She looked at him and nodded. It was a little late to get so upset about TIE's prying into her personal life. She had made her choice years ago and had just reaffirmed it that very morning. TIE was her whole life. Jesse had known how she felt, and that was why he had brought her along as far as he had.

"You needn't worry," she said quietly. "Neither of us is carrying any torches."

Chapter Sixteen

"God damn!" Margolis put the phone down calmly enough even though his hands were shaking and he was close to tears. What was happening to the company? Sweat had broken out on his brow and he wiped it with his handkerchief. Ray Carroll had been hired to do the study for the foreign subsidiary consolidation. Good Lord. How had that happened? There were thousands of consultants out on the street. Why him?

The pain in his stomach and the hate in his heart caused his face to twist. He knew why. Good old Jaylene. She was up to her old tricks again, and he was the one that would end up paying. He frowned at the miniature Christmas tree Laurel had put on his credenza, and took some antacids out of the drawer. Damn Christmas junk. What kind of a Christmas was he going to have now?

He drank some water but it didn't help the antacid start working. He'd have to take a tranquilizer. He opened a drawer and looked at the array of colored pills, selecting a blue capsule. His hand was shaking violently as he pushed his intercom button.

"Yes, sir?"

"Laurel, I have some items that I have to take care of. See that I'm not disturbed until I tell you," Margolis instructed.

"Yes, sir."

He pulled up the lever on the side of his chair and put it into a recliner position. It would be about fifteen or twenty minutes before the pill took effect and his stomach stopped twisting into knots, but just knowing that relief was on its way made him feel better.

He stared up at his ceiling, wondering if those jerks in corporate knew about their consultant and Jaylene. Probably not. They lived in their own little world. He sat up and reached for his phone, dialing the number of Jesse's administrative assistant.

"Tom Jordan."

"Hi, Tom," Margolis boomed jovially into his receiver. "How are ya?"

"All right."

Margolis clenched his teeth, fighting to keep his tone light and friendly. "Understand you guys hired a consultant to study the foreign subsidiary consolidation."

"I haven't seen any announcements to that effect." Jordan was curt.

"Damn it, Jordan," he snapped. "Don't play cute with me. I don't need some damn letter from corporate. I know one was hired and I know his name is Ray Carroll."

"There is a Ray Carroll that is known to corporate. Dr. Ray Carroll. Professor of international finance at the Harvard Business School. A partner in a small but highly respected consulting firm known as Cambridge Associates. He has—"

Margolis couldn't stand that sanctimonious voice anymore. "He has been screwing Miss Jaylene Sable on the beaches of Florida. Or did you guys somehow miss that?"

There was a long silence and Margolis felt a tightness in his chest. That hadn't come out right.

"I haven't been to Florida recently," Jordan replied dryly. "And when I do go, I don't spend much time on the beaches. I burn too easily."

Margolis could not reply. His mouth was so dry that it pained him to open it.

"Anyway. What I was trying to say was that Dr. Carroll has a strong connection to Malcolm." Jordan paused a split second and then went on. "As in Malcolm Cabot. I understand that Mr. Cabot is his godfather."

Margolis clenched his teeth in anger. Damn that Jaylene. She had really wormed her way in good this time.

"The feeling here is that Dr. Carroll has Mr. Cabot's

highest respect," Jordan went on. "In fact, Miss Sable also has his respect. Both are recognized as competent professionals. Properly discreet in their personal lives."

That tightness was still in his chest. "Yeah, well, you know how these things go, Tom. You hear things."

"If you think there is any substance to what you hear, Margolis, perhaps you'd like to cover it with Mr. Cabot."

"Hell no, Tom. You know how it is with people in our position. Everyone is trying to tear you down. If there was any substance to such rumors, I'm sure you people would know about it."

"That's true."

"I think we both should forget this conversation, Tom."

"That seems wise."

Margolis hung up his phone as the pain in his chest increased. He pulled open the drawer, and this time took a pink and yellow pill. That damn Jaylene.

Ray was irritated with himself as he drove toward his consulting office to clear up a few things before he left for his Christmas holiday in Aspen.

Why had he been so damn indecisive about where to go for the holidays this year? He could remember other years when he had to choose among three or four great possibilities. This year, he hadn't been able to find even one.

The problem was not Jaylene, even though she did have an irritating way of creeping into his thoughts. No, the problem was that he had left everything too late. He should have been making plans in November or even October. That would have given him months to work up some excitement. It was stupid to wait until the last week before Christmas and then to have to struggle to find a place. And he only had a place because someone had dropped out of the YMCA trip at the last minute. It wasn't his usual kind of trip, and he would drop out, too, if something better came along, but he knew nothing would.

"Oh, Dr. Carroll." His secretary followed him into his office. "I've got that letter and your itinerary at TIE typed up. If you sign it I can still get it in today's mail."

Ray took the papers from her and glanced at them while

she waited. The letter to Jaylene was brief and businesslike—just the way he wanted it. No sense in looking for trouble. He glanced at the other papers. They seemed fine, so he picked up his pen and scrawled his signature across the bottom of the letter, then stopped, his pen still poised above the paper.

Should he just add a little note to her? He could wish her happy holidays, nothing unprofessional about that.

"Is something wrong with the letter, Dr. Carroll?" the secretary asked.

He started. "No, no, it's fine." He straightened up and handed the papers to her. She left him alone with his thoughts.

What was Jaylene doing over Christmas? Something exciting probably, with one of those other fish in the sea that she mentioned. He doubted that she'd have to resort to a YMCA ski trip.

He remembered how much fun they'd had that afternoon and evening in New York. She was an extraordinary woman. It would be good to see her again, even if only professionally. Maybe they could have lunch occasionally. She was so easy to talk to, so easy to relax around.

He thought of her lying in bed that last morning. Maybe he'd better skip the lunches. She was too easy to relax around. If he wasn't careful, he'd jeopardize the consulting contract and his freedom. He was glad he hadn't added anything to the letter after all.

"The call is for you, señor."

"I'll take it in my study," Margolis told his Mexican housekeeper. He had had a drink and a good meal, and the world was back in focus. He could handle any little problems that came up. If he couldn't, he sure didn't deserve the presidency of that new subsidiary. He smiled at his cleverness and went down the hall.

Margie had lined the hall with poinsettias and it looked kind of nice. He'd have to tell her when he saw her. He guessed that she and the kids had gone out somewhere tonight. Christmas shopping, he thought. He supposed he'd better send Laurel out to do his. It was less than a week away.

Margolis picked up the phone in his study. "You can hang

up now, Nina," he called out, and waited until he heard the click of the other receiver.

"Hey, Davie. What's happening?"

Margolis clenched his teeth momentarily, but he wasn't going to waste time arguing over his name. Jaylene had to be handled, and quickly.

"We've got to do something drastic, Brewster," Margolis said. "Corporate's hired a consultant on that consolidation."

"So what?"

"The consultant is the guy you saw rolling around on the beach with our little Jaylene. Based on that activity, I'd say she's got an in with the guy who's going to be making some key recommendations."

Brewster snickered. "I think it works the other way, Davie."

"Huh?"

"The guy has the in, Davie. What's the matter, you forget how it works?"

"Shut up and listen," Margolis snapped. "We can't waste time smearing her a little bit. We've got to knock her out of the race, and in a hurry."

"Now you're talking, Davie. I got a line on some guys that can take her out. Real clean. No fuss. They can guarantee it'll look like an accident."

Margolis bit back a curse. "That's not what I want and you know it. I've never authorized that kind of violence in our dealings."

"Hell, Davie, make up your mind. One minute you want her out, and the next you're backing off."

"I'm not backing off of anything. I just don't think we need to resort to murder."

"Well, I don't know what else to suggest right now," Brewster said slowly. "I got another lead on her ex. If this one pans out, maybe he can be of use."

"Good," Margolis snapped. "Call me when you have something."

"Sure, Davie. Maybe I can even be your Santa Claus."

Margolis's mouth opened to speak, but the line was already dead, so he slowly hung up his phone. Brewster had been getting a little big for his britches lately; he was starting to feel indispensable. Well, when this job was over, he'd dump him. When Dave Margolis was in the catbird seat he wouldn't need that scum anymore.

Jaylene had everything arranged. In only two days, on the day before Christmas Eve, she'd fly to Chicago and rent a car to drive to South Bend. She'd arranged to stay for three whole days. It was going to be great to see Aunt Sophie again; it would rejuvenate her spirits. All the distractions would be knocked away, and she'd return to TIE with her priorities back in order.

Her intercom buzzer interrupted her daydreams. Two shorts and one long. Jesse.

She punched the button to cut into her waiting line. "Jaylene Sable speaking."

"Good morning, Miss Sable. I got a little Christmas present for you."

"You don't sound too happy about it, Mr. Whitmore," she teased. "Is it coming out of your pocket?"

"It's coming out of mine and yours, little lady," he snapped. He was not into the Christmas spirit and disgust was heavy in his voice. "Old Malcolm's got religion and thinks he's Santa Claus."

"You want to give me a better clue? I don't know what you're talking about."

"Malcolm doesn't want to pink slip any outplacement candidates until after Christmas. In fact, he wants to wait until the end of January."

"So we'll carry an extra two mil a month in payroll expense for the next couple of months. That shouldn't send TIE to bankruptcy court," she said, surprised at how relieved she felt that the layoffs were delayed until after the holidays.

"You must be sipping heavily of the Christmas spirit, too," Jesse grumbled. "Check your figures and then maybe you'll start thinking like a financial officer again. It's going to affect our bonus and it'll flatten profits next quarter, which will affect the price of TIE's stock. In case you don't remember, both you and I have some big options coming due early next year."

Jaylene knew that was all true, but it didn't make any difference. Somehow, she didn't care about the money that much this Christmas. "Maybe you should tell Malcolm your prize steer story," she suggested.

Jesse's voice grew more irritated. "I did. Then he looked down that long, goddamn patrician nose at me and gave me a lecture."

"Oh?"

"Basically he told me that I have to share everything I've busted my ass for with all the lazies of the world. I guess you have a different view of the world if you're born wealthy and neither your father nor your grandfather had to scramble for a living."

"I guess," she said noncommittally.

He was silent for a moment. "Well, pump the numbers through and give me a new profit projection by quarter for next year ASAP."

"Will do," Jaylene said. Even the thought of working late into the night didn't dampen her excitement for the upcoming holiday.

"Good. Get back to me with those projections."

"Happy holidays," Jaylene said, unable to resist the temptation, but the receiver was already dead.

She dialed Neal's number, realizing that she had even more work to finish before she left, but she didn't mind. In fact, she was really going to enjoy the holiday. There was something to giving instead of receiving. She wasn't going to spoil the holiday for anybody. Dick Matthews would have a good Christmas.

"Wanna buy me a drink, fella?"

Josef turned cold eyes toward the young bargirl. Her face was overly made up, and she was trying for a bored look of sophistication. Dirty little slut.

Although she was young, she was apparently streetwise. The picture of boredom on her face quickly turned to uncomfortable concern. "You don't have to if you don't wanna," she slurred and hurried over to a black man who had just entered the bar.

Josef could feel his left cheek twitching. Harlot. Filthy whore. The fires of hell would be too good for her.

Staying just inside the doorway, Josef looked around the

run-down bar on the edge of New Orleans's French Quarter. Across the room, in a tarnished mirror behind the bar, he could see his own reflection. Small, wiry body, pale skin and dark eyes that kept watching. They moved past his own image and saw a fat, white man sitting alone in a far corner.

That had to be his man. He slowly walked over and stopped at his table.

"You Brewster?"

"Maybe," came the careful reply. The pig eyes glanced up at him and shifted back to the table.

Josef sat down. This was his man. "I'm Josef Switek."

The fat man waved to a bargirl.

"Beer?" he asked.

Josef nodded.

"Two of the same," the fat man ordered, indicating his own bottle. They waited in silence until their drinks were served.

Josef broke the silence first. "Tiny said you might have a job for me."

The fat man nodded his head. "I might. What's your trade, Joey?"

"Odd jobs," Josef said. "But mostly pest control. I specialize in rodents." He took a sip of his beer. "The two-legged kind."

"I hear you, Joey." The fat man's face twisted into what was probably a smile. Yellow, cigarette-stained teeth showed from behind his lips. "I hear you real good."

"You got a job for me or ain't you?" Josef looked coldly at the man. He didn't have time to fool around. If balloon ass didn't have anything he was heading out to L.A. He'd heard that the gooks and the spics were trying to move in on the drug trade there. Josef could feel a bubble of anger rising to the surface. He was a professional willing to go anywhere white men needed help.

After a pause, the fat man replied. "It depends, Joey. You got any references?"

"The best." Josef raised the shirt sleeve on his arm to show the underside of his left wrist where a small swastika with a dagger was tattooed. He was proud of that mark, just as he was proud of what it meant: that he was an elite soldier in the Aryan Brotherhood. "I was in Statesville for four years and removed twenty-five rats in that time. Eighteen black and seven spic."

The fat man just nodded and pointed to the copper bracelet Josef wore on his left wrist. "Old age creeping up on you?"

Josef's eyes glittered as he removed the bracelet. It was a new tool and he enjoyed showing off. He turned it so the man could see the inside. "I just pull it out here and it unravels into a nice little piano wire. It can break a man's windpipe easy." Josef chuckled happily. "It goes through airport security slick as can be."

"Nice." The fat man looked more impressed, then drained his bottle of beer. "What are your terms?"

"I bid on jobs. The money depends on how hard it is to take out the pest. You know, how much security I have to get through and that kind of thing."

"You work on a retainer basis?"

Josef nodded. "Yeah. Three hundred a day, plus a bonus for any rat I gotta exterminate."

There was a silence as the fat man drew pictures on the table with the water from the rings the beer bottles left. Finally he lifted his head and looked at Josef. "Your rates are a little on the high side, but competitive."

"I'm worth it," Josef stated.

The fat man nodded. "The job I got for you may be different from your others, but you're the only one that can do it."

"Oh yeah?"

The fat man ordered another round of beer. They waited in silence until the bargirl had left. Then the fat man hunched over the table. "Your ex-wife is giving a friend of mine a lot of problems."

"Ex-wife?" Josef was confused for a moment and could feel a hot anger coming on. He didn't want one of his real bad headaches, so he took a deep breath and let it out slow.

"You were married, weren't you, Joey?"

In and out. Real slow. Josef concentrated on deep breaths. "I was married." In and out. Real slow. That's how the doctor in prison had told him to do it. "And I'm still married."

The fat man looked puzzled. "I thought she divorced you about twenty years ago."

"I don't believe in divorce." In and out. Real slow. "There's never been a divorce in my family."

"Okay," the fat man said with a shrug. "Your wife, then. She's running loose around Miami and giving my friend a lot of problems. We gotta put a chain on her. Are you in?"

One more time. In and out. Real slow. Was he in? He didn't even have to think about it. Hell yes, he was in. He'd been a little busy for the past few years, but now it was his duty to go home and take care of family business. Little Janie was running around Miami saying she was a divorced woman. She was bringing shame to his family. Their people always married for life. A wife served her husband for life.

"Sure, Brewster," Josef answered, speaking slowly. "I'm in."

Chapter Seventeen

Jaylene shifted the brightly wrapped packages from one arm to the other and rang the doorbell again. The fresh snow on the sidewalk had not been shoveled and was up over the top of her shoes. Her feet felt like blocks of ice.

When there was still no answer, Jaylene leaned over the wrought-iron railing to look into her aunt's front window. The drapes were open, but the late afternoon sun was too weak to send much light into the room. She could see that there was no Christmas tree in its usual place by the window, but that didn't really mean anything. Lots of people living alone skipped traditional Christmas decorations. She did herself.

Knowing that if she stayed in the snow much longer she'd be sick by Christmas, Jaylene trudged back to her rented car. She put the presents into the trunk with her suitcase and climbed into the front seat. She had planned to surprise Aunt Sophie at home, but she'd go to the hospital instead.

She glanced at her watch. It was almost three-thirty. The second nursing shift started at three. She hoped Aunt Sophie was just getting off work, not starting. Jaylene had only been able to manage three and a half days off and she had already used up most of the half day with traveling. She would hate to waste more time sitting around waiting for Aunt Sophie to get off work.

Jaylene drove slowly through the slush-covered streets. South Bend looked the same and yet it didn't. The houses were as small and close together as she remembered, but they seemed shabbier than they had.

An obviously closed-down plant caught her attention for a moment. She blinked her eyes momentarily as she tried to remember how many she had seen today. Four? Five? A lot.

The shopping district was still along Western Avenue, but there weren't as many shoppers as she expected only two days before Christmas, but maybe it was just a slow time of day. As she passed, though, she saw that a number of the stores were closed and boarded over. It gave her a strange feeling. The greasy diner where she had labored so many hours was now a parking lot.

Jaylene pulled into the lot at St. Joseph's Hospital. It looked different, too. A new wing had been added, and the old one renovated.

She had been gone twenty years, but it had never seemed that long until now. She supposed she had changed just as much as her old neighborhood had.

The inside of the hospital was different, too, and Jaylene had no idea how to find her aunt. She used to work in emergency, that was how she had been with Jaylene when she had fallen down the stairs and lost the baby. But her aunt was older now and might work in a different section, one where the pace was less hectic. Jaylene went up the front desk to ask for help.

"I'd like to find my aunt," she begun. "Her name is Sophie Domelski."

The woman turned to a computer terminal and began to key something in. "Do you know what she was admitted for?"

"I'm sorry," Jaylene said quickly. "She's not a patient, she's a—"

"Oh, here we are," the woman said and reached over for a large red visitor's pass. "Room 4126. That's in the south wing."

"No, she's a nurse," Jaylene explained. "She works here."

The woman frowned at Jaylene over the tops of her glasses, then turned back to the terminal and hit a few more keys. "Sophie Domelski of 437 Ford Street, South Bend. Born 5-17-1922," she read off impatiently.

"That's her," Jaylene said in shock. "What's the matter with her?"

The woman did not reply, but handed her the visitor's card. "Room 4126. Take the elevator to the right of the desk."

Jaylene felt numb as she walked through the hospital corridors. Aunt Sophie couldn't be sick; she would have called and told her if she was. It was probably nothing serious. She was getting on in years and was just in for a checkup. Yet somehow Jaylene was not convinced.

She stopped outside room 4126 and took a deep breath before she went inside. At first she didn't see Aunt Sophie, but then she realized that the shriveled old woman sleeping in the far bed was her aunt. She walked softly over to her side, wondering what had happened to the long black hair she always wore in a bun. This woman's hair was short and almost pure white. It had been more than a year since she had last seen her aunt, but surely a year wasn't time enough to have wrought all these changes.

The woman's eyes opened suddenly. They were the same: dark and hard and very much alive.

"Aunt Sophie?"

"Janie? What the devil are you doing here? Who called you?"

Jaylene stared. The brusque, uncompromising manner was that of her aunt, but the voice was that of a poor, sick old woman.

"No one called me," Jaylene said quietly. "I came to spend Christmas with you. Why didn't you tell me you were sick?"

Aunt Sophie's smile was hard. "I'm not sick. I'm dying."

She had always been brutally honest, but her reply stunned Jaylene.

The old woman's smile softened slightly. "If I were sick I would have called you, Janie. You would have helped me get better. But I have cancer and it's spread throughout my whole body. There isn't even the slightest hope that I can be cured."

"You shouldn't say that," Jaylene said sharply. "There should always be hope."

Her aunt shook her head. "Everything that has a beginning has an end, Janie. I'm just coming to my end."

"I could at least make life comfortable for you," Jaylene replied quietly, desperately, trying to hold back the tears that threatened to well over.

"You've done better than that. You've made me proud."

Jaylene did not know what to say, and a tear escaped to run down her left cheek.

"Someday you'll be president of that entire corporation," her aunt went on. Her face grew intense and she leaned forward to grasp Jaylene's wrist. "That's why I didn't tell you about my problems. You can't afford to let yourself get distracted now that you're almost at the top."

Jaylene just patted the wrinkled old hand as a nurse came into the room. Her success seemed to mean more to her aunt than it did to herself lately.

"It's time for you to rest now, Sophie," the nurse said as she fixed the pillows behind her head.

"I have a visitor."

"She can come back later," the nurse replied.

"She doesn't have time to waste sitting around hospitals," Aunt Sophie snapped. "She's an executive for the TIE Corporation."

"I don't care if she's the President of the United States. You're taking a nap." The nurse lowered the bed and straightened the blankets around her.

"You're nothing but a bully, Nadia."

A smile broke the nurse's frozen features. "I had the world's best teacher." Then, as she moved to leave, she nodded for Jaylene to follow her into the hall.

"Don't stay here too long," Aunt Sophie called after them. "South Bend hasn't changed and you have more important things to do."

Outside the room, the nurse stopped.

"How serious is it?" Jaylene asked dully, the shock of Aunt Sophie's illness numbing her mind.

"She has cancer."

"She told me that."

The nurse shrugged. "In some ways she may be luckier than many others. She has a poor heart that could go at any moment and relieve her of the suffering."

Jaylene said nothing. It was what she had feared deep down, yet hearing it said aloud was a blow. Her aunt had always been her source of strength. That was one reason she had come to see her: she needed some of that strength to tell her she made the right decision all those years ago. How could she stay true to her goals without Aunt Sophie behind her?

Jaylene turned on the television to provide some companionable noise while she waited for her frozen dinner to cook. Her aunt's house had changed since Jane Louise had lived there. Only the bare minimum of furniture was in the rooms, and the overabundance of knickknacks that used to cover the shelves was gone.

Months ago, her aunt had started clearing things out, getting ready for her death. She had not wanted to leave sixty-odd years of memories for someone else to go through, so she had disposed of most things. Jaylene understood it, but could not help feeling saddened. Was she so far removed from her aunt's life that she was not to be leaned on in the times of trouble? She felt very much alone, as if all the things she had thought were behind her, giving her support, were gone.

The buzzer rang on the stove and Jaylene went to take out her dinner. She hadn't wanted the hassle of eating out and had picked up something at the store on her way home from the hospital. It didn't look too appetizing now, but she sat down at the table and picked at it as memories raced around her.

After she had lost the baby, Jane Louise had gone home with Aunt Sophie. Physically she had recovered in a few weeks, but she hurt emotionally for a long time. Why was she to be deprived of so many things that everyone else took for granted?

Josef had run up some debts and she had hospital bills to pay, so Jane Louise sold her mother's house. It was small and run-down, so it didn't bring in much, but she used what was left to pay for her divorce.

Aunt Sophie said she was well rid of him, that marriage didn't have to be forever. She didn't need a man; she could succeed on her own.

Aunt Sophie was right, she decided. On her own, she could go as far as she wanted.

At Aunt Sophie's suggestion, she enrolled in night school to get her high school diploma. She was among peers there and accepted for the first time. Like her, they were all trying to escape their past and their present. And they all had a future. Suddenly she had a million choices ahead of her and didn't know which to pick. She knew one thing, though: she was through dreaming and wishing for things to be the way she wanted. From then on, she was going to make things happen.

Once she had her high school diploma, Jane Louise made plans for college. She'd go part-time and work at the hash house as much as she could. But Aunt Sophie had other ideas. There was nothing in South Bend for Jane Louise, she pointed out. She ought to go away to school and see what the world was like. There was little money, but she'd make up the difference with determination.

Things raced along after that. With Aunt Sophie's confidence bolstering her, she applied to DePaul University and found a job as a maid near the campus on the north side of Chicago. She learned a lot at the university, and just as much on her job as she studied the manners and speech of the people she served. She saw how power and money were a protection from the meanness of life and vowed that one day she'd have enough of both to be really happy.

When Jane Louise Sabelski graduated from DePaul, she disappeared, and Jaylene Sable was born. She was created from Jane Louise's determination and Aunt Sophie's strength and would succeed at any cost.

Jaylene put her fork down and pushed away the half-eaten dinner. Why had all that determination seemed so right years ago, and so blind now? Why, when she had fulfilled all of Aunt Sophie's dreams, did she still feel empty and lost? Where had she gone wrong?

Aunt Sophie died the day after Christmas, and Jaylene extended her visit by a few days to take care of the funeral. There was little to plan, actually, for Aunt Sophie had spelled out just what she wanted in a very specific letter she had left with her lawyer. She had even specified the menu for the reception after the funeral.

It was an old-fashioned ethnic funeral but, surprisingly, Jaylene got a great deal of comfort from it. Although her memories of the old neighborhood and its residents were not good, the old traditions gave her a strong sense of peace.

Afterward, she drove back to the house to collect her things. Once she was gone, the house would be sold, along with the remaining furnishings, and the money would go to the parish for a day care center. Aunt Sophie really had everything planned.

She stopped for a moment just inside the doorway, shivering in her lined Burberry raincoat and boots. She'd never come here to stay again, she thought as she gazed slowly around the faded room. It was a long time since she had left, and during all those years she had never really missed the place, but just knowing it wouldn't be here for her anymore made her sad.

With Aunt Sophie gone, she truly was on her own, alone in the world in a way that frightened her. She had no one to care about and no one who cared about her. Who would share her joys? Who would cry over her hurts?

There was nobody in the whole world who cared if she was happy, or sad. There was no one who'd come all the way across the country if she was sick and needed help as she would have for Aunt Sophie or as her aunt would have for her. All TIE wanted was her best work effort. She had given it her life.

Her suitcases were packed and waiting in the living room, so she carried them slowly out to the car. There was no reason to linger, no good-byes to say.

Chapter Eighteen

"I think January second ought to be a legal holiday, too," Nancy remarked as she checked over Jaylene's office. "A body needs time to recover."

Jaylene glanced up from the paper she had found on her desk. "I thought most people celebrated on New Year's Eve. That would have given you yesterday to recover."

"If you can say that, you didn't have the kind of New Year's I did." Nancy plopped down in a chair with a sigh.

"No, I probably didn't," she admitted, and turned her attention to the paper in her hand. It was a copy of Ray's itinerary for the next few weeks, and she would dearly love to burn it.

She had come back from South Bend emotionally exhausted and hoping to immerse herself in her work, only to find a letter from that bastard waiting for her. She wished she didn't have to see him again, but there was no way she could avoid that. He was coming to Miami this morning, in fact. He had treated her like dirt, but she was not going to respond in kind. She would be cool and polite, the perfect businesswoman, the perfect executive vice president, she thought as she took some papers out of her briefcase, aimlessly rearranging them on her desk. Unfortunately, although she knew she could control her actions, she was not as certain about her emotions.

Why had she found Ray so attractive? Why had he kept straying into her thoughts? She had met handsome men before. Why had Ray touched her so much more deeply?

Why had she clung to him so? Maybe the answer lay in her New Year's Eve, the one so different from Nancy's.

It had been just an ordinary evening to her, except that she had known the excitement it held for most people. The lights of the city seemed to twinkle even brighter as if mocking the fact she was alone. She had had one glass of champagne, but toasting in a new year by herself had held little enchantment, so she went to bed about eleven.

Maybe it was this unsettling loneliness that she feared. Maybe she had wanted to hold on to Ray so she wouldn't have to spend another Thanksgiving or New Year's Eve alone. Maybe he had just been her security blanket, there to ward off all sorts of vague evils that seemed to be creeping up on her. It could not have been anything more, she had assured herself. She had not been in love with him.

"Rose back yet?" Nancy asked.

Jaylene shook her head. "No, she'll be back tonight."

Nancy shrugged and got to her feet. "I think I'll go scowl at Rita."

Jaylene nodded, relieved that Nancy was going. She was tired of pretending to read the papers on her desk and wanted a few minutes alone. Once the door closed behind Nancy, she wandered over to the window.

She was not lovesick, she told herself, she was just plain angry at him. Or maybe she was angry at herself, she admitted ruefully. She had been vulnerable when he had entered her life, and she didn't like knowing that her guard had been down.

And she was still vulnerable now; that was the problem. Ever since South Bend, she had been feeling strange. Restless and dissatisfied. Even though she was an adult, she felt orphaned by her aunt's death. For the first time in her life, she felt totally alone.

Suddenly she was afraid to think about the future, which seemed to hold nothing but loneliness. She realized then that she had to be on her guard against Ray. Just because they had shared a few hours of passion didn't mean that he was her knight in shining armor. He was another workaholic, like her, and she mustn't let herself depend on him or on anyone else.

No, what she had to do instead was start depending on herself again. She had become too much of an extension of TIE. They owned her body, it was true, but maybe it was time she started reclaiming her soul. She turned away from the window, took a piece of paper from her purse, and dialed the number written on it.

"Multiple Sclerosis Society. Rochelle Winston speaking."

Jaylene cleared her throat quietly. "Yes, my name is Jaylene Sable and I was wondering if I could get some information from you about the support available for the patients. Does your organization offer help with doctor bills and things like that?"

"No, unfortunately we don't have that kind of money. Our funds go primarily for research and education. None of the catastrophic illness organizations helps with personal bills."

Jaylene picked up a pencil and tapped it lightly against her desktop. She had suspected that was the case, but had been hoping it wasn't. "I guess the government provides that kind of help," she said.

"Well, a lot of people assume the government programs step in and help in these cases, but it isn't quite that simple. There are financial requirements to be eligible for Medicaid. Many families without adequate insurance are forced to choose between a loved one's continued medical care and their life savings."

Jaylene felt an emptiness in the pit of her stomach. "That must be awful."

Rochelle agreed. "It's especially hard on the patient himself. Just because his body isn't functioning properly, that doesn't mean his mind isn't. He watches his family's future being traded away for extra care for him. Sometimes the patients are driven to drastic measures just to stop such things from happening."

Jaylene took a deep breath to try to clear her mind. "With this unstable economy and high unemployment, you must be seeing more of these cases," she said slowly.

"Unfortunately, yes."

There seemed to be nothing else to say. Kareau's vague assurances that Dick's family would be fine were wrong. Certainly, if she had followed his advice and not gotten involved, she would not be so upset now, but would that have helped Dick? Could she help him now, though?

"I appreciate all your information," Jaylene said. "I wondered how people managed those huge medical bills."

"Do you have someone in your family with MS?" Rochelle asked. "Are they aware of our organization? We do provide some patient services that they might find helpful."

Jaylene hesitated and tossed the pencil down as she leaned back in her chair. "No, it's not a member of my family, but the wife of someone I work with. His name is Matthews. Dick Matthews."

"Oh, Dick." Rochelle laughed. "Yes, he certainly knows we're here. In fact, he was one of the people I was going to refer you to. He heads a family support committee that helps spouses and families of patients learn to cope, and is also active in many other ways. I'm surprised he hasn't hit you to buy some of the boxes of candy we sell each year at Christmas."

Jaylene felt embarrassed. "Well, I don't know him really well. Certainly not enough to ask him personal questions."

"Oh, Dick wouldn't mind. He's marvelous. Helped lots and lots of people through some pretty rough times."

Who would help him though his rough times? "He seems like the type who'd get involved," Jaylene said vaguely.

After thanking the woman for her time, Jaylene hung up slowly, a worried frown on her face. She might not be able to help the other three hundred people on the outplacement list, but she was going to save Dick Matthews's job for him.

A knock on the door woke her from her thoughts and she looked up as Nancy poked her head inside.

"Security just called, and Dr. Carroll's here. I'm going down to get him."

"Fine," Jaylene said as she checked over some folders on her desk.

"I thought you'd want to know," Nancy went on.

"Yes, thank you." She picked up a couple of the folders. "I should have time to say a quick hello before my staff meeting."

"Righto." Nancy was gone.

Actually, she had a full half hour, but she was not going to spend it in his company. There were only a limited number of polite phrases she could spout before her emotions took over. Telling the CEO's godson that he was a first-class bastard who ought to rot in hell was probably better left unsaid.

Why was she getting so upset? She sat back in her chair and forced herself to take a deep breath, then another. He was not worth getting angry over, he was *not* an important part of her life.

Brewster's scowl matched Josef's dark look. Normally the man had ice water in his veins. He seemed like a cool professional who'd kill anybody or anything exactly as ordered. He seemed like someone to depend on.

That is, except where his ex-wife was concerned. In fact, he didn't even buy the *ex* business. Like he was in some kind of time warp. He kept calling her Janie instead of Jaylene and still referred to her as his wife.

"Why should I just hang back and watch her?" Josef asked sullenly.

"Because that's what I want, and since I'm paying the freight, I'm the boss."

Josef nodded. "Yeah, but if I quit I could do what I want."

Brewster kept his scowl but considered the problem. Would this thing Joey had about his ex be a problem? Maybe he should have Joey removed. A nobody like him could be whacked out for five hundred bucks or so. The city was filled with illegals willing to work for anything.

Trouble was, it'd be best not to get involved in something like that right now. He had a few little plans up his sleeve that were rather sensitive, plans that had nothing to do with Margolis. Well, not directly. Their success did depend pretty heavily on Margolis's success, but Brewster hadn't figured on sharing any of the wealth with him. It might not hurt to have Joey on his side, though.

"Look, Joey," Brewster said finally to the man sitting on the other bed in the room they were sharing. "I got some sensitive business that I want to get into. You stick with me and maybe we could be partners."

"What kind of business? Hauling junk?"

"Coke mostly," Brewster said.

Josef was silent for a long while and Brewster assumed that he was thinking it over.

"That dame fits into the plan, Joey," Brewster pointed out. "So we gotta let her sit."

Josef laughed harshly. "How can that little bitch fit into a business plan? She don't know enough to breathe unless someone tells her."

"She's real important to it," Brewster assured him. "My client wants the job she may be headed for, and it's my job to make sure she don't get it. If you start hassling her now, her security'll double and we'll never get a chance to get near her. And if my client don't get what he wants, our chances for scoring big are real small."

Josef frowned and shook his head. "Hey, I don't care about all that. It just gives me a headache to hear it all." He shook his head and stood up. "I'm with you, Brew. But, remember, after you don't need her no more, you give my wife back to me."

"Sure, Joey."

"As long as I'm cleared by security, can't I just go find my own office?" Ray asked the TIE security guard.

"We'll have an escort here soon, Dr. Carroll. This complex is pretty big, and we don't want you to get lost."

"I've been here before," Ray persisted.

"Why don't you have a seat, sir?"

Ray turned away and pursed his lips slightly. He might as well listen to the man. No doubt he had his orders to make sure that newly hired consultants didn't go wandering all over the damn complex. Ray sat down hard and snatched a copy of *Fortune* off the end table.

As he idly flipped through the pages, Ray couldn't help but recall the other times he'd been here. He remembered the pleasure of seeing Jaylene unexpectedly in the halls. The seemingly innocent conversations they'd had would be filled with special meanings for the two of them. They would enjoy relaxing together after a hectic day. He frowned and tossed the magazine back onto the table.

He had to stop thinking of those things, he told himself as he got to his feet and wandered over to a window. He was here for business purposes, that was all. He could take the strain of seeing her often. Certainly the memories of their times together were with him, but they wouldn't affect his attitude toward her. No, he had to protect her, just as he'd had to that last day in New York. She probably thought he'd been really rough on her, but men had to do that sometimes to protect a woman from the consequences of her emotions.

"Hello, doctor. Nice to have you with us again."

Ray turned to find a tall blond woman standing next to him. Damn. It was Jaylene's personal security companion. "Hello, Nancy."

He would rather have not had much to do with Jaylene or her personal staff, but it was all right. He could handle himself. Forcing one of his charming smiles onto his face, he followed her to the elevators. He was a gentleman, and gentlemen specialized in difficult situations.

"Here we go, doc."

He looked up to find Nancy holding an elevator door open with her hand. He bowed slightly from the waist and gestured for her to precede him. "In my circles, a lady always go first."

Before either could move, the doors started to close and Nancy had to chop at the door with her hand. It retreated and she grabbed Ray's arm lightly with her free hand.

"Go," she ordered quietly but firmly as she ushered him into the elevator. "These doors are a little hyper, and I would hate for them to crush us."

"My body will forever be in your debt," Ray joked, though he felt a little embarrassed.

"I'll remember that."

Ray left the smile on his lips, but it wasn't in his heart. He had remembered Nancy as having a rather hard edge, and it was still there. It wasn't that he didn't like strong, competent women, but he liked them to temper their strength with feminine softness. Like Jaylene did so well.

The elevator door opened and Ray looked about him, slightly bewildered. This was Jaylene's floor. He was sure of it. Why was he here?

Nancy ushered him out again and they walked down the carpeted hallway. He could see Jaylene's face everywhere and feel her presence all around him. At any moment, she might step out from behind one of those doors. He felt a little warm and loosened his tie a bit.

"I forgot to ask where my office was going to be." He hoped his voice sounded stronger to her than it had sounded to him. He was probably just coming down with a cold; he didn't want her to think he was speechless at the prospect of seeing Jaylene again.

"Right here," Nancy said, pointing slightly ahead of them. "It's just a few doors down from Jaylene's. Mr. Kareau thought that it would be the most convenient spot since you'll be working with her so much."

"Yes, of course. That makes sense," Ray replied brightly, though his stomach tightened. "That's exactly what I would have chosen. You people are certainly efficient and organized. I guess that's why TIE is the successful company it is today."

Nancy stopped at one of the doors and opened it. "Here you go, doc. Home sweet home."

"Thank you." He took an uncertain step inside, but the room was empty. What had he expected?

"I'll tell Jaylene you're here."

"Very good, Nancy. Thank you for all your help," he called briskly as she closed the door.

He took a deep breath and wandered over to the desk. His and Jaylene's first meeting was bound to be difficult, but he'd been in sticky situations before and handled them well. The key was to leave the woman with her self-esteem intact. That was what a gentleman did and that's what he would do.

He pulled open a drawer aimlessly and saw that the desk was filled with supplies. Internal and external telephone directories. Paper clips, pads of paper, pencils.

There were some bound reports on the desk, and he flipped through them quickly. They covered sales by product and territories, cost and profit figures, plant locations, and much more. All the information he would need to design the consolidation. Someone was very, very thorough, and it had to be Jaylene.

He sat down with a weary sigh. He would have to do everything possible to make these next months easy on her. He couldn't allow that intimacy to return, of course, but neither would he do anything to hurt her. That meant that he mustn't get involved with anyone else while he was here. In fact, he probably shouldn't date at all until he was done with the study.

Ray sighed. Sometimes sacrifices were required, so he'd just have to stick with his resolve. But, truthfully speaking, he hadn't met too many women who appealed to him lately. His tastes had been changing, and he admitted he was looking for more than surface prettiness. Some substance and personality were needed, along with—

There was a light knock on his door and Jaylene came in. She strode forward with her hand out. "Hello, Ray. It's good to see you again."

There was a tightening in his chest as he rose to his feet. She was wearing a powder blue suit that was cut softly to emphasize her feminine figure. Her hair fell gently around her face, and her eyes were light and glowing as always.

He came around the desk and took her hand in both of his. "Hello, Jaylene. You're looking very well."

Then, as quickly as he had taken her hand, he dropped it. This would be a difficult enough situation without the added pain of touching her. The gentle warmth of her touch lingered in his hand as he retreated behind his desk and indicated a chair to Jaylene.

She shook her head, a brave smile on her face. "Sorry, I

don't have the time to chat. I was just on my way to a staff
meeting and only wanted to see that everything was to
your satisfaction."

Her voice had a musical quality to it, even now when she
was doing her best to sound businesslike. He had to force
himself to concentrate on what she was saying and not on
her soothing tone.

"Everything is fine, thank you. I'm especially impressed
with the homework you've given me," he said, patting the
bound reports. "I can see that I'm going to be awfully busy
tonight." That had been a clever way to clue her in. Now
she would know not to expect anything, yet the excuse was
strictly impersonal.

"Sorry about that," she said. She'd always had a beautiful smile and she forced it into her lips again. "But the
troops are rather tense about this consolidation. The
sooner we get it resolved, the better."

"That's true," he agreed. "From what I've seen so far,
I'll need about six weeks. Two months max."

"Good." She looked quickly at her watch. "Sorry, but I
have to run. Let us know if you need anything else. My
staff has been instructed that they are to give you the
fullest cooperation."

"Thank you," he responded, then she was gone.

Ray turned slowly and looked out the window. That was
certainly an exceptional lady. He knew that scene in New
York had been a little sticky, but she seemed fine. Pleasant and charming, as if nothing had happened.

He frowned. Maybe he had been worrying for nothing.
Maybe, in her mind, nothing *had* happened. Otherwise,
how could she have acted so cool and unconcerned? If she
had given the incident even half as much thought as he
had, surely he would have seen some sign, some indication
of the pain of being apart.

Of course, that was all for the best, he reminded himself
briskly. If things continued so well, there'd be no reason to
keep each other at arm's length. They could get together
and have some fun. Discreetly, of course. When he returned to his desk, he was smiling.

Chapter Nineteen

Jaylene escaped into the hall. Her hands were shaking, and she made a conscious effort to still them. Putting a careful smile on her face, she hurried over to her own office and breathed a sigh of relief once she was safe behind the door.

Lord, she was such a fool! Her feelings toward Ray hadn't changed, no matter what she told herself. She had been furious with him for weeks, but seeing him standing in that office, looking the same as ever, had knocked the wind from her sails. She had known then that she still loved him. The few stupid little scoldings she had given herself had done nothing but hide the issue temporarily. They had not erased the longings she felt when she was with him. Her pride had kept her businesslike facade in place, but it hadn't been easy. More than anything, she had wanted to be back in his arms, to know the peace and security of his embrace.

She took a deep breath and walked over to her desk. She had to stop thinking that way. Whatever they had had, it was over now. Seeing Ray often might be hard, but each meeting would get easier. She'd learn to revive her anger against him, and, little by little, she'd kill the love that had grown. It might be hard, but she had never flinched from doing something just because it was difficult. By the time Ray left Miami for good, she'd be over him completely.

Jaylene spent the rest of the day in meetings and kept herself too busy to give Ray another thought. She knew his office was just down the hall from hers and that she might meet him in the hall anytime, but that was just an unpleasant fact she'd have to get used to, like working with Rita, or having her name scrawled on the wall of the men's room. She was tough and she could handle it.

She was exhausted, though, by the time she got home, and craved a little peace and solitude. The apartment was too still, however, even with Rose's company. It just wasn't conducive to wrestling with her feelings and coming to grips with them.

After washing off her makeup and changing into a running suit, she went into the kitchen. "I'm going out for a walk."

"Darn it," Rose complained. "Why do you always wait until I'm busy?"

"Relax. I'm just going to walk around the grounds. I'll be back in a half hour."

"Wait. I'll be putting this in the oven in a few minutes."

"I'm gone," Jaylene called.

The best way to solve a problem, she told herself as she waited for an elevator, was to face it head on. She had to examine it, pick it apart, and really identify it. Then she could begin to fix it.

Falling in love had been stupid and certainly not suited to career plans, but it was not the end of the world. Neither should she feel that everything she had worked for was in jeopardy. No, she just had one little problem that could easily be remedied.

The elevator stopped, letting her out on the ground floor. She knew Rose worried when she went out alone, but it wasn't necessary. The Belle Isle apartment complex was a safe place and the grounds were patrolled after dark. Besides, without her makeup and with her hair pulled into a ponytail, she looked more like a college student than the woman in TIE's publicity photos.

"Evening, Miss Sable. A little on the cool side tonight," the doorman said.

"Hi, George," she replied. Aunt Sophie might scold her that it was unnecessary to know the names of the people around her, but it made Jaylene feel better. As if she wasn't quite so alone.

"Walking in the gardens, ma'am?"

"Yes, I am." Jaylene stopped outside in the cool night air and took a deep breath. She felt more relaxed already. Ray's presence no longer seemed so threatening.

"Fred'll be on duty soon with Butkus. I'll tell him you're out there."

She waved in reply as she took off briskly down the sidewalk. It was starting to get dark, but lights illuminated the walkway. She skirted the silent swimming pool and strolled down a path through the gardens.

Ray had said the study would take about two months, and part of that would be spent in L.A. with Margolis and in TIE's foreign locations. That wouldn't leave much time for them to be together.

Jaylene felt her confidence returning as she walked past the tennis courts. She had done very well that morning. She had been perfectly calm and businesslike. No trace of her feelings had been visible. If she had done it once, she could do it again. She could do it as often as she needed to.

She rounded a corner where some tall bushes screened the tennis courts from the street beyond. A figure stepped out of the shadows a few feet ahead of her.

Jaylene jumped, more because she had been startled than because of fear. It was only when the man came a step closer that she became uneasy.

"Hello, Janie."

The voice woke some nameless fear from the past. She took a step backward, then forced herself to stop. She didn't even know who this was. He was old and beaten-looking and could be some former crony of her father's. Just because he called her Janie was no reason to panic.

The rough voice came again. "What's the matter, Janie? Don't you remember all the fun we used to have?"

The voice was harsh and raspy and unfamiliar, but the mocking hatred in it was not. Her stomach twisted in fear. It couldn't be he. There was no way he could have found her.

"I've missed you," he said softly. He rubbed one hand over his fist as he smiled slightly at her.

All the pain, the fear, and the humiliation came rushing back. She wanted to run but knew he'd catch her, and when he did his anger would be worse. Her mouth was dry but she forced the words out.

"What do you want, Josef?"

His smile grew, but it only emphasized his evil expression. "What kind of a question is that for a wife to ask her husband?"

"We aren't married anymore," she told him quietly. "I divorced you years ago."

She saw his nostrils flare and heard the swift intake of breath. He was angry. "I don't believe in divorce, Janie. A good wife stays by her husband." He took another step closer, so that she could smell the scent of stale tobacco clinging to him. "But then you always needed me to teach you how to be a good wife."

She could feel his anger building, his desire to strike out at her almost palpable. The air that had seemed so refreshingly cool now seemed cold, but she would not let herself shiver. He would take it as a sign of weakness and fear. She shifted her weight slightly and her arm brushed against a bush.

Suddenly she remembered where she was and who she was. She wasn't the poor timid little Jane Louise anymore who didn't know how to stop the abuse. She was Jaylene Sable and in control of her life.

"Get lost, Josef," she told him. "Find some other poor sucker to push around. I'm not available anymore."

"You're my wife, damn it. Until death do us part." His voice was like the hiss of a snake, soft but deadly.

She felt the all too familiar fear, but she hid it. "No, I was through with you years ago. There's nothing you can do about it."

There was something very heady about standing up to him, but when she felt his rage tremble through the air, she thought she might have gone too far.

"There's plenty I can do, bitch," he snarled, and reached out to grab her wrist.

His hand was like a claw, squeezing tightly as he twisted her arm. She knew from experience that his other hand would be the one to worry about. It would be the one to strike and punish, to cause the pain. She kept her free arm bent and ready to ward off any blow.

If only he'd turn slightly, she thought, remembering Nancy's advice to strike an attacker in the family jewels. She had to do it right the first time, though, because he sure wasn't going to let her get a second shot.

He didn't turn, but he seemed surprised at her attitude. He had, no doubt, expected her to start whimpering. She hadn't, so he hesitated.

"Hey! What's going on there?" a deep voice cried. From somewhere close by, a dog barked. "Miss Sable, is that you?"

Josef dropped his hand. "Shit." He glanced around wildly, then let go of her. "I'll be back, Janie. You can count on that." Then he was gone, back into the shadows and out of sight.

Rose knew immediately that something that happened. "What's wrong?"

Jaylene tried for an offhand shrug, but fell a little short. "Nothing really. I ran into a panhandler, that's all."

"Are you sure that's all he was?"

"Of course." Jaylene did better with her laugh. It came out sounding almost normal, but she didn't think she could keep it up for long, so she started down the hall toward her room. Rose followed her.

"Actually, you would have been proud of me," she said. "By the time Fred and Butkus came along, he was just about on his way."

Rose snorted. "Let that Doberman take all the chances he wants to, but you be careful. Any two-foot midget becomes a giant when he's got a Saturday night special in his hand."

Jaylene sat down the the edge of her bed, her hands shaking. She busied herself with removing her shoes. She had never considered that Josef might be armed.

"I think I'll take a shower."

Rose was watching her closely, but she just nodded. "Dinner'll be ready when you are."

Jaylene was relieved when she was alone and could give way to her trembling. She couldn't believe he was back. After all those years, what could he want? She had worried about his reappearance in her life when she was in college and he got out of jail. When the years passed and he made no effort to contact her, she had relaxed. They each had gone their own way. Why was he back now?

The questions only increased her worry, for she had no answers. She took her shower and changed her clothes. She thought of the cutbacks and Dick Matthews. How could she help him? Then instead she thought about the consolidation and the fact that Ray would be around often. How would she deal with that? She tried to think of anything but Josef.

"You almost done?" Rose asked from the doorway.

"And hungry as a bear," she insisted, hoping that she'd be able to eat something.

She followed Rose into the kitchen where a chicken casserole was waiting on the counter. The table was set for two and wine was at each place.

"I don't know about you, but I thought a glass of wine would be nice," Rose said.

Jaylene sat down. "Marvelous."

They began to eat. "I got some of my Christmas pictures back today," Rose said after a moment.

"Oh? I'd like to see them." Especially tonight, for it would be another way to keep her thoughts in safe areas.

"You don't have to," Rose protested. "I mean, there's just pictures and more pictures of me and kids."

"You don't want me to see what I'm missing, is that it?"

Rose didn't laugh, but fingered her wineglass thoughtfully. "Did you ever wish you had a child?" she asked.

"A child?" The question stunned Jaylene.

"Sure," Rose said. "I can't imagine what it would have been like not to have any kids."

"I don't have time in my life for a family," Jaylene said stiffly.

"I wasn't talking about a whole bunch of kids, I was

talking about one. Somebody to love and tuck into bed at night. I thought all women went through a stage when they longed for a child."

"I guess some of us don't," Jaylene said. "Besides, I'm not even married."

Rose smiled, looking like a contented grandmother. "Hey, this is the age of the liberated woman. All over the country women who aren't married are having babies. At least you have the money to take care of one."

"I'm quite happy with things the way they are, thank you."

Rose did not argue, but chatted about other things through the rest of the meal. Once the dishes were done and put away, she brought out a stack of envelopes.

"Are you sure you want to see all these?" she asked.

"Of course."

They really weren't such a struggle to get through. The baby was darling and the other children cute. Rose was obviously so proud of them all that Jaylene was surprised to feel a little jealous.

Later that night, unable to sleep, Jaylene kept seeing the pictures. Mostly the ones of Rose's daughter and granddaughter. There had been so much love and warmth in those pictures. So much of the things she didn't have in her own life. Rose's earlier question echoed through her mind.

Have a baby? The idea had seemed ridiculous when Rose said it, but the more Jaylene thought about it, the more it appealed to her. She lay there and considered the possibilities. She was lonely, and wouldn't a child solve that problem? It would give her someone to love, someone to love her—a reason for being alive besides making more money. And Rose was right, that stigma of unwed motherhood was gone.

She turned over restlessly and told herself she was crazy. How could she possibly think of having a child? For the last week, she had done nothing but bemoan the mess that her life was in and question the choices she had made years ago. And into that mess, she was thinking about bringing a child! What kind of a life could she give a child, when she could barely manage her own?

On the surface, it seemed so simple. A child would bring light and warmth into her life, but she had to stop and ask herself what she could bring to a child. Not a father, that was sure.

Certainly there were ways of finding a biological one, but what about someone who would help tuck the child in at night, give horsey-back rides, or play baseball? Her own father hadn't been much of a presence in her childhood, but would things have been better without him? Did she really have such confidence in herself that she thought she could be both father and mother to a child? Especially when she hardly seemed to know who she was?

Still awake several hours later, she got up and wandered into the living room. She just couldn't do it, she realized. No matter how much she would like a child, she had no right to bring one into her world now.

She smiled, thinking how upset Aunt Sophie would be if she knew Jaylene was even considering it. Aunt Sophie, who lectured against distractions. Surely a child would not be allowed in her aunt's master plan. And it was her aunt's words that really helped her make a decision.

When Laura died, Aunt Sophie had told Jaylene not to cry for her. She said that any child had a difficult road even with two good parents to guide his or her steps, but with only one, there were many ways for a child to get lost.

Jaylene had the feeling that she had made a wrong turn somewhere along the way and had gotten lost. She wondered if she'd ever find the way back.

Chapter Twenty

"I know that a lot of the employees are worried about rumors of cutbacks and the consolidation," Jaylene said. "And it's unfortunate that we can't give them any hard and fast details right now. All we can do is keep our own spirits high so that morale doesn't get any worse."

Rita nodded carefully, a polite smile on her face in spite of her inner anger. The last thing she needed was a little pep talk from the ice queen. Rita knew far more about duty to TIE that Jaylene Sable ever would.

"This should all be over in another few months and things will settle back to normal," Jaylene pointed out.

"We can hope so," Rita pretended to agree with her. Except if things went well, there'd be a few major changes just around the corner.

Jaylene went on, but Rita barely listened. Miss Sable wasn't looking too chipper these last few days, she thought. Her hair seemed dull and there wasn't much sparkle to her eyes, yet Dr. Carroll had been in town for more than a week now. Could it be that the romance of the century had fizzled out?

Rita bit back a sardonic smile. The mood the past week was certainly different than it had been last fall when Dr. Carroll had been around. Could Dr. Carroll have gotten tired of being frostbitten and dumped her? That thought was enough to brighten Rita's day.

"Well, I'm sure you understand what I mean," Jaylene was saying.

Rita nodded again and rose to her feet. "Of course, Miss Sable. Will there be anything else?"

"Do you happen to know where Dr. Carroll is? I'd like to see him before he flies down to San Juan this evening."

Rita smiled slightly. She had no idea where the professor was right now, but she couldn't resist having a little fun. "I think he was having a cup of coffee with Nancy, so I'm sure I can find him. You know how that woman is after anything in pants."

Rita was pleased to see the surprised look on Jaylene's face, and walked smoothly toward the door. It looked like her suspicions were right. Dr. Carroll must have dropped her.

"Any calls?" Rita asked Judy, who had been watching her desk.

"Nope," the girl said, and rose slowly to her feet. "Okay if I go for lunch now?"

Rita nodded and reached for the phone as soon as Judy was out of sight. Finding Dr. Carroll could wait. It was around starting time in L.A. and she had some more urgent business to cover. She quickly dialed a number.

"Margolis here."

"Hello, Dave." Her voice was cheerful and businesslike, even if her mood was not. "This is Rita."

"Yeah?"

He must be in one of his sulking moods. Poor dear. Lately he reminded her more and more of her ex-husbands. "I was just calling to see how things were going. I haven't heard from you lately."

"I'm a vice president of a large corporation, goddamn it. So you think I have nothing to do but call around the country all day?"

"No, I—"

"And since when were you promoted to president? I don't report to you."

She let him rant and rave, angry herself, but not about to join in a shouting match.

"Just remember that, sweetheart. I'm running this little operation. You just follow orders."

He paused and she took her opportunity. "I'd follow orders a lot better if you made good on your promises," she said, a little more sharply. "You still owe me this month's fee."

"It's in the mail." His belligerency was suddenly subdued.

She let that pass unchallenged, certain that it would be in the mail very soon. He knew that he needed her. "The consolidation study seems to be progressing well, although I don't think that Carroll and Miss Sable are an item anymore."

"What a shame!" he mocked.

She bit back a sigh of impatience. She was beginning to think that he was more interested in revenge than in getting ahead. Since she would most likely be out if he was out, he'd better get his head on straight.

"I thought that information might be of some use to you," she pointed out.

"Yeah, well, we'll see. I got things under control." He paused a moment. "Listen, sweetheart. I got an operative in Miami. He's got everything under control down there. His name is Brewster Merrill. Give him a call at 555-8409. Maybe he could use your fine hand."

"I'd be glad to help him, Dave, but—"

He had already hung up. Rita tapped her fingers on her desk. It didn't look good. It didn't look good at all. She could smell a loser even as far away as California. Maybe this Brewster would know how to salvage something from this wreck.

Margolis scowled at the telephone after he hung up. That bitch was a real ray of sunshine. Reluctantly, he pulled out his personal checkbook. She hadn't really been worth the price, but now was not the time to cut her off. They were entering into a tense phase. He had to maintain the status quo a little longer.

A tense phase? Hell, more like a critical one. This Carroll guy's connection to Malcolm was like a three-inch steel cable.

He poured himself some orange juice and flavored it with a bit of vodka. Jesse was coming in later that afternoon, and he didn't dare take one of his pills. The vodka wouldn't be any problem, though. He wouldn't have more than one; besides, he'd have lunch in a few hours and it would be all out of his system by the time Jesse arrived.

Just then the intercom sounded. "Yes," he barked into it.

"Mr. Fletcher is here for his nine-thirty," Laurel's soft voice came back at him.

Margolis swallowed the nervous lump in his throat. Boy, that broad had it easy. She didn't have anything to do but sit on her ass at that desk all day. There was never any pressure on her.

"I'm expecting a conference call. Tell him I'll get to him later."

A male voice came over the intercom before Laurel had a chance. "This is our third postponement, Dave. We either do it today or forget about it."

"Okay, okay, Sam. I'm sorry about the delay. Things have been pretty tense around here lately. You know, this consolidation study and all that kind of stuff."

"I'm free at one, Dave. That's it."

"Sure. Fine. That's good with me, Sam. One o'clock will be fine." His voice took on a stern note. "See that that's put on my schedule this time, Laurel."

"Right, Mr. Margolis."

He turned away and quickly finished his drink, then made another. Maybe he should have sent those pictures of Jaylene and Carroll to Malcolm or Jesse anonymously. Hell, but how would anyone have known who it was then? All it looked like was two people screwing; even the beach was barely discernible. That damn Brewster had really fouled that up.

Hell. He supposed he ought to call Brewster and tell him about Rita. Maybe the two of them could bug each other instead of him. He reached for the phone.

Brewster answered after one ring. "Yeah?"

"Your telephone etiquette stinks," Margolis snapped. "We instruct all TIE employees to give their name and department when answering their business phone."

"That's swell, Davie. But I like to know who's calling before I let them know who I am."

Margolis grimaced. Yeah, a sleazeball like Brewster would need to do that.

"So what's coming down?" Brewster asked.

"What the hell are you asking me that for?" Margolis demanded. "You're supposed to be fixing things out there."

"Hey, I'm doing what I can," Brewster assured him. "You just okay some nickel-and-dime stuff and expect it to do the job. It ain't gonna. If you want to win big, you got to play hard."

"We're not going through all this again," Margolis said. "There's got to be another way. Hell, politicians are always thrown out of races for some stupid little reason. Why can't we do the same with her?"

"Because it ain't the same."

Margolis sighed impatiently. "You're going get a call from a dame by the name of Kastle. Rita Kastle. She's Sable's administrative assistant. Maybe you can use her."

Brewster just grunted, and Margolis changed the subject. It was about time that slimebag remembered who was running this show. "So what's the word on Sable's ex?"

"We're working out a plan."

Margolis frowned. "What plan? I thought you were going to feed him to the press."

"So I changed my mind," Brewster said. "Do you really think anybody'd care that twenty years ago this bigshot dame was married to some loser?"

"Then why the hell did you chase after him?"

"He's got possibilities, Davie. Real possibilities. Shit, he hates her worse than you do. You just say the word, and he'll take her out of your life permanently."

"I told you no rough stuff, and I meant it. Find another way."

Before Brewster could start an argument, Margolis hung up. His glass was empty and he stared down into it, swirling the ice cubes. Hell, all he needed was for Brewster to start some real trouble and it would backfire on him for sure. He just wanted that dame out of the race for the presidency; he didn't want her murdered. A little bending of the law was all right, but more than that just wasn't his style.

He drained the last few drops of ice water. Brewster had better start coming through or he was going to be out. A sourness twisted his stomach. If somebody didn't come through with something soon, Dave Margolis was the one that was going to be out.

The door slammed violently just as Brewster hung up the phone. He glanced quickly at Josef's scowling face but didn't say anything and returned to his game of solitaire. What worried him right now was that Margolis was scared.

"I'm tired of just sitting around watching Janie," Josef burst out. "She's hiding out at her office most of the time. Comes home real late and rushes right into the building. There ain't anything else about her to know."

Brewster shrugged. "Just keep an eye on her for a little longer." Keeping an eye on that dame wasn't too exciting, but it kept Joey out of his hair. He gave Brewster the creeps, but Joey had a number of useful characteristics. Hate and pure viciousness for a start. Brewster didn't know how or where, but he just felt in his heart that there would be a good use for Joey and his talents.

"This ain't right," Josef cried.

Brewster looked up from his solitaire game. "What ain't right?" he asked.

"She's my wife," he said bitterly. "A wife is supposed to be submissive to her husband. The Bible says she's supposed to obey him in all things. How the hell can she do that, living away by herself?"

Brewster watched Josef pace the floor, mentally feeling the weight of the thirty-eight in his belt. It looked like a couple of Joey's cylinders were going to go out again, and he wanted to be ready in case there was a need for some heavy persuading.

Josef stopped. "I'm gonna go over there. She belongs to me and so does all that goddamn stuff of hers."

"She'll just call the law on you. And then it'll be back in the slammer."

"She won't do that. She's my wife," Josef insisted angrily.

"That ain't the way the law sees it, Joey. She divorced you, remember?"

"The laws of God don't recognize divorce," Josef said hoarsely. "The laws of God take precedence over the laws of men."

Josef's eyes seemed to glaze over and Brewster became nervous. Living with this guy was like living with a Doberman that had fits. "Cool it, Joey," Brewster snapped.

"She's my wife," Josef said determinedly. "She has to live in my house and submit to my rule. The word of God commands her."

"You ain't got a house," Brewster said.

He stared blankly at Brewster. "You mock the word of God?"

Brewster shifted so that he could reach his gun more easily. "No, I'm not," he assured him. "Anyway, don't the Bible say all good things come to him who waits?"

The glazed look in Josef's eyes turned to confusion. "Yeah," he said uncertainly.

"So right now we gotta wait, okay?" Josef did not reply. "Okay?" Brewster repeated.

Josef blinked as if he were trying to focus his eyes. "Yeah. Okay."

"Why don't you go out and have some lunch?" Brewster suggested. Josef nodded in silence and left.

When the door closed behind Josef, Brewster swept the cards off the bed and onto the floor. Then he leaned against the backboard with his hands behind his head. Things looked a little shaky right now. Joey walked a fine line between human and animal, and little Davie sounded real down. Like he was ready to throw in the towel. That would put a severe crimp in Brewster's own plans.

There was more involved than just his cut from Margolis's racket. That was a nice piece of change, but he had a few irons of his own in the fire. Since he had arrived in Miami, he had made a couple of new deals. Sweet little ones that needed those TIE jets that flew back and forth between Miami and South America. When Margolis took over, they would carry more than just some fat-assed executives. There'd be a little extra freight tucked here and there.

He had made some pretty firm commitments with his new partners, and they weren't going to like it if he had to back out. Should he clue Margolis in on his plans?

No, what good would that do? That greedy little bastard would just want a cut of the profits, without doing any of the work. The key was to get the Sable dame out and Margolis in. Period.

He got up from the bed and walked to the window to stare down at the parking lot below. Maybe this dame that Margolis talked about might turn out to be useful. She could tell him all he needed to know about the Sable broad: her working schedule, her security, maybe even a few of her weaknesses. He laughed suddenly. When this was all over, little Davie would owe him more than he realized.

"Oh, Dr. Carroll." Rita stopped Ray in the hallway. "I've been looking all over for you. Miss Sable would like to see you before you leave for San Juan tonight."

"Fine." Ray glanced at his watch. It was already five o'clock. "Is she free now?"

"I'm sure she's in a meeting, but I can call you just as soon as she gets back."

Ray nodded and went into his office. It was getting late in the day, but that didn't matter. Staying here close to dinnertime to see Jaylene worked in well with his plans.

It was over a week now since he had come down to study her subsidiary. His nervousness of the first day or two had subsided. She had shown no signs of being bothered by his presence or of expecting that their relationship would continue. Though there had been a few moments when he sensed a softening of her glance, he seemed to be the only one haunted by memories, the only who had to hold himself in check when they were together. His hands kept wanting to reach out for her; his arms kept wanting to hold her.

He took a deep breath and paced his office. It was time to take a risk, he decided. He wanted to spend some time with her, and he was going to ask her out. Their meeting would be late and it would seem natural that they have it over dinner.

He'd go slowly, keep everything on a purely business level, but if it went well, maybe they'd do it again once he got back. Maybe with a few more personal touches. By the time the consolidation report was finished, they might be well on their way back to the relationship they'd had before.

He glanced at his watch again. Damn. He wished she'd get back to her office. He could hardly wait to see her.

Chapter Twenty-one

Jaylene walked wearily down to her office. It was almost six. That meeting had taken far longer than it should have, but she had known her managers would object strongly to the cuts. Kareau had finally settled them down by pointing out that this was a good way to get rid of the deadwood. When business picked up, their headcount would go back up and they could hire some young tigers.

She had heard cutbacks discussed in such a way before, but found it distasteful today. No one seemed to consider the people being fired. She brushed her hair back from her forehead. Maybe Jesse was right. Maybe she was getting soft.

Rita was still at her desk and trailed Jaylene into her office. "What kind of damage have I wreaked on the schedule?" Jaylene asked.

"You had Mr. Kareau."

"I spoke with him after the meeting."

"Mr. Samuels from accounting."

"Ditto."

Rita closed her appointment book. "That was all, except for Dr. Carroll."

Jaylene did not speak for a moment. Did she want to see him? Yes and no. Part of her wanted much more than just to see him; she wanted him to ease her weariness away. But the other part kept reminding her she was a fool. Seeing him would only bring more pain. Unfortunately, the only part of her she was allowed to listen to was the part owned by TIE.

"Yes, send him in please. Then you can go on home."

Rita closed the door behind her and Jaylene leaned back in her chair with a tired sigh. Actually, everything seemed to fall apart last week. First Ray had come back into her life, then, that same evening, so had Josef. And Josef was definitely the greater jolt to her equilibrium. It hurt to see Ray, but just the thought of seeing Josef terrified her. She still wasn't over the shock of his appearance.

She could feel his hand grip her wrist and hear the hatred in his voice. He knew where she lived, and that frightened her. She felt vulnerable, lying awake at night wondering where she would see him next. She thought she had seen him twice since then, but she couldn't be certain.

She rose slowly to her feet and walked over to her refrigerator, taking out an orange. Then she sat on the sofa away from her desk and carefully tossed the rinds into the wastebasket.

The only place she really felt secure was at the office, so her hours were growing longer and longer. But the pace was becoming grueling. She was already exhausted, and Neal had asked her today if she felt all right. She had snapped at him, rather unfairly she knew, but she was just so worried. Why had Josef come back after all these years? What did he want from her?

Once the orange was peeled, she leaned back and slowly ate a piece. It was juicy and sweet, and she supposed quite good, but nothing seemed too enjoyable these days. She felt so tired all the time, and she couldn't care less about food.

She put the remaining pieces of the fruit on the table and leaned back on the sofa. Her feet up and her eyes closed, she willed herself to relax. She wasn't feeling well because she was so tense. That was all. Everything she had worked so hard for seemed to be coming apart lately. Where would it all end? Six months ago, she had been so happy with her life. Now there were problems everywhere she turned.

Falling in love with Ray had been enough of a disruption, and then she had lost Aunt Sophie. Josef was just the final straw. She felt trapped by circumstances and was trying not to lose the confidence she had struggled to gain over the years. If only she didn't feel so damn lonely most of the time, she was sure she could cope with the rest.

What she'd really like was a night away from all the pressures, but the companion she'd choose would be Ray. He would have been able to relax her. He would have known how to make the threat of Josef disappear. In his arms Josef would seem so unimportant. But that was impossible.

There was a knock on her door, and she sat up quickly, grabbing the orange. She shoved the pieces into the refrigerator, then called, "Come in." By the time the door opened, she was at her desk.

Ray looked as tanned and relaxed as always. Obviously he was not haunted by memories of their earlier relationship. "Hello, Jaylene. You're looking good."

"Thank you." His soft tone of voice might have convinced her that she was, if her mirror hadn't been reflecting her haggard look for the last few days. "I hope you're finding everything you need."

He just nodded and sat down across the desk from her.

"Things seem real hectic for you," he said quietly.

His eyes still had that warm, caressing look. He was the same old Ray and would never change. He had probably been born knowing how to make a woman feel like a woman and would still have them flocking around when he was ninety-five. The trouble was, she had foolishly assumed that that attentiveness had meant personal involvement on his part. Now she knew better. It was just how he treated everyone. She forced her thoughts back to the conversation.

"Things are usually hectic," Jaylene admitted. "But they are worse now. The cutbacks are upsetting a lot of my management people."

Ray nodded sympathetically. "But you'll be in good shape after the consolidation and won't have to do much cutting then."

Ah yes, the consolidation. That's what they were supposed to talk about. "I hope you weren't staying here so late on my account," she said. "I did want to go over a few things before you went to some TIE sites in Latin America, but it wasn't really imperative."

Ray's face broke into a broad easy smile. "No problem," he assured her. "My flight's not until ten, and I was hoping that you'd be able to spare me a little time."

Jaylene leaned forward, putting her elbows on her desk and resting her chin in her hands. Ray had missed his calling when he went into teaching. He should have become a politician. He had a way of making whomever he was with feel like the most important part of his life. She knew it was just a lie, though, part of his charm that he had developed over the years.

"Did you bring a copy of your agenda with you?" she asked.

He patted the folder in his lap. "I did, but actually I have a suggestion to make first."

She said nothing, just raised her eyebrows questioningly.

"I think it would be much nicer if we could cover the details in a more relaxing atmosphere. Like over dinner. I'm sure that there are any number of places we haven't been to yet."

They hadn't been to her place for a long time, she thought, but kept a cool silence. She'd love to take him back home with her and slip into something more comfortable. It was barely six, so that left them plenty of time for dinner, some business talk, and some loving. She sat up suddenly. All the loving would be on her part. To Ray, it would just be sex.

"I don't think that would be wise, Ray," she said coolly.

"Why not?"

His smile was so persuasive she could almost feel herself falling under his spell again.

He went on. "I've taken Kareau out to lunch and I'll be doing the same with Dave Margolis and Sam Burnbridge. No one will think anything of it."

No one but her, that is. But she did need to eat, and if they sat here discussing his trip, it would be even later before she did. And he was right, no one would think anything of it. She could control her feelings. She could be just as cool and uninvolved as he was.

"It would be nice to get out of the office," she said with a smile as she rose to her feet. "Did you have any place in mind?"

She refused to read anything special into his smile or the way he took her arm. It would be a business meeting combined with a meal, that was all.

The steak house Jaylene suggested was well lit and busy, and not conducive to romance. There was a half hour wait for a table, so they went into the bar.

"It's a shame you're only spending a week on this trip of yours," Jaylene said once she had a glass of wine. "Some of the places you're going to are really lovely, and the manager of that plant in Haiti always invites me to stay with his family for a few days. They have a gorgeous house right on the beach."

"Maybe I'll have to plan a trip down there once the study is done," Ray said.

"I'm sure you'd enjoy it."

Ray's smile grew warmer. "I'd enjoy it more if I had an experienced guide."

The look in his eye left her no doubt about whom he was thinking of, but she kept her smile cool and impersonal. "That's true. I've found that some of the best restaurants aren't on the list you get from a travel agent."

"Neither are the best beaches," he pointed out softly.

She felt her face warm and took a sip of her wine. She was doing fine, she told herself. She could be having this conversation with anybody—Jesse, Frank, Mr. Cabot. But, still, she was glad when they were called for their table.

It was relatively easy to keep the conversation on the consolidation. Ray had some questions, and she filled him in on the details of some of their operations. They ate their salads amid discussions of the economic stability of Latin America. The main course was accompanied by a discussion of the impact of a strong dollar on a multinational organization like TIE. By the time they had both refused dessert and were sipping their coffee, they were engaged in an amiable argument about personal investments.

Jaylene let herself relax as Ray signaled for the check. She had done it. She had had a pleasant, businesslike meal and had not once felt that she had lost control of the situation. It had been no harder than conducting business when she had terrible cramps. All she had to do was ignore what was hurting, in this case her heart, and concentrate on the business at hand.

Ray gave the waiter his credit card.

"Why don't you let me pick up the check?" she suggested.

He shrugged. "Either way TIE pays for it."

"That's true."

He signed for the bill. "Want to stop back in the bar for an after-dinner drink?" he asked.

"Sure." She was feeling confident. The dinner had been fine. Great, as a matter of fact. There was no need to fear a little extra time with him.

The bar was far less crowded now. The lights had been dimmed, and Ray chose a booth in a far corner. The intimacy of the situation sent little prickles of uneasiness down her spine, but she ignored them and ordered a brandy.

"You know, I'm glad we have this chance to talk," Ray said quietly.

"Oh?" She glanced around trying to find something impersonal to focus on, but the room was too dark. Her eyes kept coming back to Ray.

"I don't mind admitting that I was worried about returning to Miami," he told her.

He stopped as the bargirl put their drinks in front of them. She clutched her snifter gratefully. It was something else to watch.

"I didn't know how you'd react," he went on. "Things were going pretty hot and heavy when I left, and then we met again in New York that time."

The mention of the night in New York stiffened her spine. After the way he had treated her there, he shouldn't have had the nerve to mention it. She wouldn't have if she had been he, but then it was becoming apparent that he viewed a number of things differently than she did.

She leaned against the back of the booth, her glass in one hand as she watched him coldly. "And you were afraid I would expect to pick up where we left off?" she finished for him.

"Well, no. Not exactly." He looked slightly uncomfortable. "I just didn't know what you were expecting."

"A consultant doing a consolidation study," she said dryly.

A wry smile crossed his lips and the tension left his eyes. "I guess I should have known you'd handle it right."

She sipped her brandy for courage before she spoke. "Handle it right? What would I have done if I had handled it wrong? Molested you in my office that first day?"

Feeling confident, he laughed and drank some of his liqueur. "No, that I could have dealt with. I'm always afraid that any woman I see more than twice is going to start hearing wedding bells and expecting declarations of love."

"Does that happen to you often?"

"No, because I'm too smart."

She nodded, but had trouble looking directly at him. She took another sip of her brandy instead and shifted her position. There was a pain deep inside that threatened to engulf her, but she tried to ignore it. She forced a smile and looked right at him.

"I guess I may be a little backward in these things, but just how are you being so smart?" she asked.

"In my choice of women," he explained. "I was suckered into marriage once but I learned my lesson. Now I don't go anywhere near the marriageable ones."

"I see," she said, although she didn't. The pain was growing, matched with anger, and seemed to slow her mental processes. "So I was one of the nonmarriageable ones."

He reached over and squeezed her hand. The touch was both wonderful and abhorrent to her, but she did not pull away. She needed his warmth, even if only for a few minutes.

"Actually, it's a compliment," he told her. "You see,

what I usually do is look for a woman who's too involved
with her career to want any type of entanglement. We
have a few laughs and then say good-bye. No one sheds any
tears."

"Sounds sensible," she agreed. Too bad he hadn't known
that she had been *too* involved in her career, and had been
ripe for love. She probably could have fallen for Godzilla if
he had been as nice to her as Ray had been.

His voice was soft and caressing when he began to speak
again. "It is sensible, but I never expected it to work as
well as it did in our case." His hold on her hand tightened
and he leaned across the table toward her. "When I saw
you again last week, I knew that we had found the perfect
relationship, and I didn't want it to end."

There was no great bubble of happiness rising inside
her. She had the uneasy suspicion that his idea of a perfect
relationship was not the same as hers.

"This consulting contract I have puts a crimp in things,
but once it's completed, I think we should give serious
thought to reestablishing our relationship." He looked remarkably pleased with his suggestion, but she wanted to
be certain she knew what he was saying.

"Just what kind of relationship are you suggesting?"
she asked quietly.

"The perfect one for people like us," he said, enclosing
her hand in both of his.

The delight of his touch was almost as painful as his
words. People like us? What did that mean? It had the ring
of something he thought was a compliment, but would
hurt.

"We both understand the rules," he told her. "Neither of
us wants to be tied down, because our careers are all-
important to us. We aren't like the rest of the world. But
we can still have a great time together. Just without all
the trimmings that other folks think they need."

"Like marriage and a family?" she asked.

He nodded quickly. "Right. I've thought it all out over
the last few days. We could have a close, loving relationship. It would be semipermanent, and, most importantly,

mutually satisfying. There would be no suffocating entanglements and restrictions to get in our way."

Surprisingly, Jaylene did not feel the intense pain she expected, just a numbing coldness. She knew herself well enough now to know that Ken had been right in a way when he had called her an old-fashioned girl. She might not be waiting for a knight in shining armor, but she did have some rather outdated standards that she lived by. Trust, honor, fidelity. But she was also smart enough to know that when someone wanted to change the rules, it was because he had something to gain by it.

"A semipermanent, nonrestrictive relationship?" she said slowly.

"Right. We'd meet when convenient, maybe take a few trips together, but when we were tired of each other, it would be a simple good-bye."

Was there such a thing as a simple good-bye? she wondered.

"But while we were apart, we'd be free to see others," he said.

"I see."

He smiled, apparently thinking she intended it as a play on his words. "It'll be perfect," he repeated. "We can have fun and not worry that the other one is getting emotionally involved. We're both too smart for that."

If it took brains to avoid emotional involvement, then she ought to be declared mentally incompetent. She finished the last few drops in her snifter and put it down. The numbness was fading and she had her choice of tears or anger. She picked anger.

"So what you're asking is that I become your mistress?"

He looked stunned. "No, we'd both be—"

"We'd have sex whenever we happened to be in the same town," she said. "But then you'd be free to sleep with whomever you wanted when I wasn't around."

"But so would you," he pointed out.

She waved the bargirl over and gave her a credit card. "Sorry if I hurt your feelings, Dr. Carroll, but your idea stinks. When, or if, I ever commit myself to another person, it won't be in such a half-assed way."

"Half-assed?" he snapped. "What kind of commitment are you looking for? What kind are you willing to make? I suppose you'd quit your job for the right man and move to Timbuktu."

"I might," she said. "But that's not the point at all. I wasn't the one suggesting this weird arrangement."

"What's weird about not wanting to be tied down by a lot of meaningless promises?" he asked. "Lots of people are following that route these days."

"Then it shouldn't be hard to find someone else for your scheme."

The ride out to Belle Isle was silent and chilly. About halfway across the causeway, she felt him glance at her.

"I'm sorry if I offended you," he said stiffly. "I had no intention of doing so."

She almost laughed aloud at the absurdity of the situation. Offended, no. Hurt, yes. The man she loved wanted a loving relationship free of entanglements. How else was she supposed to feel?

"Don't give it another thought," she said. "It was not the first such proposal I've had and I doubt that it'll be the last."

"I merely thought that since we had enjoyed each other's company in the past, we might want to continue to do so in the future," he said.

She was glad of the protective darkness. It was getting too hard to hide the hurt. She would have loved to continue enjoying his company—but not as a mistress. She wanted to give love and receive it. She wanted to feel secure in their relationship, not fear that he would meet someone else and be through with her. What she wanted was a real commitment, and that was something she'd never get from him. She felt close to tears, and was glad when he turned into her driveway. Two cars were parked near the door, and he stopped down the drive from them.

"I'll just get out here," she said, and reached for her purse and briefcase.

"Don't be silly. The cars'll be moved in a minute or two," he snapped.

Yes, and in a minute or two she'd be sobbing like an idiot. She jerked open the car door and stepped out. "Thanks for the dinner, Dr. Carroll. Hope you have a good trip."

"Anytime, Miss Sable." His voice was equally chilly.

She slammed the car door and stepped onto the sidewalk. She heard him put the car into reverse, then heard footsteps hurrying up behind her. For a second, she had the wild notion that he had changed his mind. That he loved her just as she loved him and didn't want to part this way.

Her fantasy lasted just long enough for her to turn around. Ray's car was still backing down the drive, and the person rushing toward her was Josef. Before she had time to think or scream, he was at her.

"You dirty slut," he shouted. He slapped her face hard and she fell, landing sharply on her left hand.

"A married woman cleaves only to her husband." He spat the words at her.

Finally her paralysis left her and she began screaming. At the same time she heard an alarm wailing. Josef looked up and then turned and ran away.

"Miss Sable, are you all right?" The doorman got to her just as Ray did.

"Jaylene, you're hurt."

"I'm fine," she said impatiently. She struggled to her feet with help from Ray and the doorman.

"The police should be here any minute, Miss Sable."

"Thank you, George." She turned toward the door, brushing some sandy dirt from her hand. She had scraped her palm and it stung slightly. She could feel her face stiffening up where the hand had struck.

"Are you sure you're all right, Jaylene?" Ray worried. He retrieved her purse and briefcase. "You look like you took a hard blow to your face," he said worriedly.

"Thank you, Dr. Carroll," she snapped. Then she grabbed her purse and briefcase. "You'd better go or you'll miss your flight."

"I can get another flight," he said. "I'll stay with you while the police look for the guy. I didn't see him, but—"

She stopped walking. Josef's attack had not changed her

anger at Ray. "I don't need you to hold my hand. No entanglements, remember?"

"Jaylene—"

"Good-bye, Ray." She followed George into the building.

Chapter Twenty-two

"This is ridiculous, Rose," Jaylene protested. "I'm fine. I only got pushed down, not run over by a truck."

"That wrist isn't fine," Rose argued as she brought two plates of bacon and eggs over to the table. "Last night, you said it was sore, and you aren't moving it any easier this morning."

"It's just stiff, that's all."

"When did you get your medical degree?"

Jaylene gave up and concentrated on eating her breakfast. It was true her wrist was still a little sore, but it wasn't broken. She couldn't take time out this morning to go to the doctor's.

"I think you ought to get a complete physical," Rose said suddenly. "You haven't been feeling too good for the last few weeks."

"I feel fine," Jaylene insisted.

"Well, you look awful."

Jaylene smiled. "Thanks, Rose. You do wonders for a person's morale." She pushed away her half-eaten meal and got to her feet.

"Promise me you'll make an appointment."

The buzzer sounded and Jaylene went over to the speaker. "Yes, George?"

"Your car's here, Miss Sable."

"Thanks. See you tonight, Rose." She hurried out before Rose could give her any more flak about the doctor.

It was ridiculous, she told herself as she rode to work.

She was fine. But by lunchtime her wrist was so sore she had to go down to the nurse's office.

"I think it's just sprained, but you ought to have it X-rayed just to be certain," the nurse told her.

Swell. She had too much to do to run around having her wrist X-rayed. Trust Josef to really screw things up for her.

"Shall I call one of our doctors and tell them that you're coming over?"

Jaylene frowned. She couldn't spare the time, but neither could she get much done with her wrist the way it was. "All right," she agreed. "But I hope it won't take long."

The doctor's office was in a large hospital only a few miles from TIE and she was taken immediately, but then the doctor seemed to fuss around terribly.

"How have you been?" he asked as he poked and probed at her wrist.

"Fine," she said. "Well, a little tired, but I work long hours."

"Sleeping all right?"

"Yes."

He twisted her hand and moved each of her fingers. "Appetite good?"

"It's been okay. I've never been a big eater."

He put her hand down. "It's just a sprain. We'll wrap it up and it'll be fine in a few days."

"Great." She reached for her jacket, but he stopped her.

"I've got a few more blanks I have to fill out on my form," he told her. "Can you roll up your sleeve?"

She tried to be patient as he took her blood pressure.

"It's kind of high," he told her with a frown.

"I've been under a lot of pressure lately," she said. And even more right at that moment. She had to get back.

"When was the last time you had a complete physical?"

She shrugged. "A few years ago, I guess." She couldn't really remember.

"How about your last Pap smear?"

She shook her head.

He sighed and put his stethoscope back into his pocket.

"What I'd really recommend is a complete physical," he said. "One where we admit you to hospital for a few days and run some tests. You're getting to an age where you have to be a bit more careful of your health."

"I know how old I am," she said.

He smiled. "We all do, but rarely believe it. Now, can I schedule you for a stay with us?"

"Look, doctor, I appreciate your advice, but I really don't have the time."

He nodded. "I knew you'd say that, so I have an alternative. Not as good, mind you, but better than nothing. Stay for a few hours and we'll do a less extensive exam."

Jaylene got to her feet and picked up her jacket. "I don't even have time for that."

His smile did not waver. "Sure you do. You've got as long as I insist on."

She stared at him in confusion.

"TIE sent you to me and won't let you back without the completed form."

"What?"

"They want to be certain that you're fit to work and won't come back and sue them later for making you work when you weren't able." He laughed at the shock in her face. "Actually, it's more for the protection of the employees so the company won't force them back on the job instead of giving them a sick day, but it works the other way too."

Jaylene sank down in the chair. "I can't go back to work unless you say?"

He nodded slowly. "I promise it won't take that long. A few hours at most. Okay?"

"I don't have a choice, do I?"

The meal was pleasant. Rose and Ben chatted about the old days, but as they lingered over their coffee she brought up the subject on her mind.

"Have you been keeping track of our friend?"

Ben took a sip of his coffee before he answered. "Yeah, I have. I talked a little with some Miami plainclothes and the DEA."

"The Drug Enforcement Agency?"

He nodded. "Yeah. You remember Joe Heiser, don't you? Well, his nephew is with the agency down here."

"I didn't think the DEA was interested in kiddy porn."

"Your friend is trying to move into a higher stakes game."

Rose did not reply and sipped her coffee.

"The profits are enormous," Ben pointed out with a shake of his head.

"That would draw him." Rose's face took on a hard set.

"You ought to just forget about him. From what I hear, he's in over his head. No life insurance salesmen are knocking on his door."

She had hated him too long to quit now. "What's he up to?"

"He's teamed up with some ex-con name of Switek. Josef Switek. And the two of them are lining up with Raoul de Noaguira and some Young Turks who want a bigger share of the local drug business for themselves."

"Anybody gonna do anything about it?"

Ben shrugged. "You know how it is. The good guys have limited budgets, limited manpower. They just keep an eye on things, make a few busts, and hope that no civilians get hurt."

Rose nodded. Yes, she did remember. It always seemed that the cards were stacked in favor of the bad guys. "He could come out of it smelling like a rose."

"There isn't a bookie in town who would give you odds on that," Ben said, reaching over to touch her arm. "Forget about him, Rose. He's playing in water way over his head and doesn't even know about the undercurrents. You get too close and you're liable to get sucked in with him."

She saw the obvious concern in his face and a warm feeling came over her. "Don't worry, Ben. I'm not an avenging angel. I enjoy life, and I don't plan to do anything foolish."

"Then what are you going to do?"

She stared straight ahead for a long time. "I don't know. I didn't really plan this out." She paused, then turned toward Ben. "I'm just hoping that when he does get in over his head and he's clawing to come out, I'll be there."

"Then what?"

"I'm going to step on his fingers." She patted Ben's hand, which rested on hers. "Just a little."

"I can't be pregnant," Jaylene protested.

The doctor's eyebrows raised slightly. "You haven't had sex in the last few months?"

She backed down. "Well, yes, but . . ."

He shook his head. "Why don't you get dressed and come down to my office and we'll talk about it?"

She nodded and put her clothes on quickly, her mind too shocked to think clearly. All she kept thinking about was the night last week when she had thought briefly that a child would be the answer to all her problems. Now she was going to have one, and it didn't seem like the answer to anything.

The doctor was waiting for her and had her sit down. He was gently reassuring, but it didn't really help.

"I take it this pregnancy wasn't planned."

"Hardly," she said with a grimace.

"You don't have to go through with it. You're still in your first trimester. Termination would be a fairly routine procedure."

She nodded, though a shiver ran down her spine. "I don't know what I want to do."

He understood. "Take some time and think it through, but either way you should be seeing a doctor soon. Your blood pressure is too high and you may need vitamin supplements. Do you have a gynecologist here in Miami?"

She shook her head. "Can you recommend one?"

He wrote out the names of several doctors for her on his prescription pad. "Good luck."

She took the paper and rose to her feet. "Thanks."

There was no way she could return to work that day, so she took a cab home. Rose was out, she was relieved to discover. She called Rita and told her she wouldn't be back at work and then changed into jeans and a T-shirt and decided to go for a drive.

She needed some time by herself to think. She drove her Porsche north of the city until she came to a deserted

stretch of beach. It wasn't the same place that she and Ray
had made love, but it reminded her of it and made her remember all the pleasant and happy times they'd had together. She sighed and sat down on the sand. The sun was
warm and comforting; the constant motion of the water
was relaxing.

What was she going to do? Keep the baby or have an
abortion? She crossed her legs, leaning forward to draw in
the sand with her fingers. The idea of an abortion made
her uneasy. It was not just her upbringing; she had so
many questions about her whole life, so many doubts
lately about the choices she had made years ago. She had
to think this whole thing through, not rush out and do
something she'd be sorry for later.

She brushed the sand from her hands and leaned back,
closing her eyes to the brilliance of the sun. If she had an
abortion, everything would go on as it had been. The same
long hours of work to fill her life because there was nothing else. The same loneliness, but with the added haunting
of what might have been. She opened her eyes. She didn't
think she could have an abortion.

She got to her feet and slipped out of her shoes to walk
along the water's edge. If she didn't have an abortion, then
she'd have the baby. What kind of changes would that
make in her? What would TIE's reaction be? Were they lib-
eral enough to allow an unwed mother to hold a high executive office? She didn't think so.

Of course, she wouldn't exactly be destitute if she left
TIE. She had enough money saved to live well for a while,
or live a bit more moderately for even longer. And she was
sure she could get another job without too much trouble. It
might not be as prestigious, or pay as much, but she
wouldn't be likely to go on welfare.

What about the child itself? She had lots of love, but
would that be enough?

She felt something hard beneath her foot and dug in the
sand, hoping to find a shell. It was just a rock. She tossed it
back into the water.

That seemed to be the whole stumbling block: could she
raise the child by herself and do a good job of it? Could she

be everything to her child, both father and mother? She didn't know how to be either. She didn't even know how to change a diaper.

Somehow she seemed to be making decisions without even knowing it. She had ruled out an abortion rather quickly, and had accepted the fact that she'd have to leave TIE. That only left one other problem: Ray. Should she tell him?

It was his child, too, whether or not she liked the fact, whether or not she thought he would care. From their last conversation, she sincerely doubted that he wanted that kind of involvement, but she supposed he did have a right to know. And that meant she had to tell him.

What would his reaction be? She gazed out over the water but didn't see the waves, imagining Ray as she told him the news. She had a sudden vision of his face lighting up with joy, of his declaration of love for her and the child and his insistence that they marry because he could not bear to be apart from her anymore. She laughed aloud and the vision faded.

No, that was not likely to be his reaction. She wasn't sure Ray was capable of loving anyone, but she was pretty sure that her announcement was not likely to inspire such devotion.

She turned and walked slowly to her car, then sat in the open doorway, brushing the sand from her feet. The next few months were likely to be a bit rough, so she supposed she'd better see one of those doctors soon and find out how to take care of herself. If she was going to go ahead and have the baby, she wanted to do it right.

She stopped and gazed out at the ocean. What in the world was she doing? How could she so easily abandon the dreams she had cherished for the past fifteen years?

Maybe there was more to her than just a businesswoman, she thought, and slipped into her shoes. But, Lord, she didn't even know how to talk to a child. Then she smiled. Of course, babies didn't come knowing how to talk, either. Maybe they could learn together.

"I ought to blow your fucking head off," Brewster screamed at Josef. Brewster was angry, but still knew enough not to do anything he might regret later. He needed time to think things out. "Sit down," he ordered Josef, pointing to the bed with the thirty-eight.

Damn. That idiot had come running into the room with that wild-eyed look of his. It didn't take much prodding to get the story out of him. He had hit that Sable broad and run, never thinking that the police might have followed him. Or that Jaylene might swear out a warrant or get a peace bond. She had enough pull to do a lot in this town. Their only hope was that she wouldn't want any publicity and would cool it.

Calmness was returning to Brewster, but he kept his gun pointed at Josef. That bastard wasn't going anywhere until he settled down, too.

"What the hell's wrong with you?" Brewster demanded. "Why did you have to go slapping her around?"

"She needed it," Josef insisted. "She's running around with other men. She's got to be taught a lesson. She's my wife."

"She ain't your wife." Brewster found himself screaming again. "She divorced you. According to the laws of the civilized world, she's a single woman."

"The laws of God—"

"Don't give me that laws of God and men shit." He was shouting because he was tired of the stupid discussion, not because he was angry. "You left over twenty years ago and she divorced you. What the hell's the big deal?"

"A man's got to go where his work takes him," Josef replied. "Marriage is forever. A woman should wait. It is her duty."

Brewster shook his head in exasperation. Joey was usually a real cool character, but get him near that Sable broad and he turned flako.

"Look," Brewster said patiently. "My plans are entering a very sensitive stage right now. One little sneeze and we all could be dead. I don't want any fooling around. Leave the broad alone until I tell you."

"She's my wife," Josef said sullenly.

Brewster pulled the hammer back. "I'm gonna be rich, Joey. Filthy rich. I don't want anyone to queer my deals."

Josef scowled at him and did not reply.

"When it's all under control, Joey. The wraps will be off. You can have her."

The scowl went away, but he continued staring at Brewster.

Brewster's face broke into an ugly smile. "You can rape her every hour of the day. You can have all sorts of fun."

"Sex isn't fun," Josef said. "It's a duty."

Brewster released the hammer of his thirty-eight and put it back in his belt. He'd wished he'd seen how crazy Joey was before he took him on. Once it was all under control, though, Brewster would see that he and that Sable broad went to hell. She'd cost a lot to whack away, but it would be worth it to get rid of Joey.

"Get us a beer, Joey."

Chapter Twenty-three

"If you let all those people go, I'll only be able to maintain our existing programs. New development will be out," Karen Osborne said.

Jaylene nodded wearily. She had been at this all morning with her managers, reviewing their outplacement candidates just to make sure that there would be no problems. Like Karen Osborne, they all warned of decreased service levels in their departments.

"Sorry," Karen said. "I guess you're tired of hearing the same record over and over."

She forced a smile. "The biggest problem is that I agree with most of you. But the powers that be want the cuts."

Karen stood up, gathering her papers. "Yeah, well, cheer up, things are bound to get worse."

Jaylene grimaced. "Thanks," she said. Karen grinned and closed the door behind her.

At least most of these interviews were over, Jaylene thought with a sigh as she poured herself a glass of orange juice. One more left, and then a different type of agony for that afternoon: she was going to tell Ray about the baby. It was the end of January and two weeks since she had learned she was pregnant. Time Ray knew, also. She would have told him sooner, but he had been in Latin America, and when he got back, she'd been gone for a few days. Now they were both in Miami and there was no reason to wait any longer, but she would certainly be glad when the day was over. Her intercom sounded.

"Mr. Dentman here to see you, Miss Sable," Rita announced.

"Send him in, please." Maybe Jerry would help her mood.

The door opened and a short, nattily dressed man rushed in. "Jaylene, how can you do this to me? You're crippling my department, the lifeblood of this organization."

"Come off it, Jerry. Public relations only has to cut two people."

"I know," he replied calmly. "But isn't that the way a manager is supposed to act? I didn't want you to think I was doing a lousy job."

"Do you have your outplacement candidates identified?"

"Yeah, Irma and Jeff."

"Any problems with them?"

"No, Irma's getting married and moving out of state and Jeff's going back to school."

Jaylene took a deep breath and sighed. "If they were quitting anyway, how come they're outplacement candidates?" She checked her list. "Now they're eligible for three month's severance pay."

Jerry Dentman just shook his head with a sad expression on his face. "You mean they were going to quit anyway? Why didn't they tell me that?"

Jaylene could not suppress a laugh. "Jerry, you're incorrigible."

He shrugged. "Yeah, I know, but as long as we're on the subject, how'd you like to buy a ticket to a Heart Association dinner honoring the governor?"

"All right, I guess," she said. "But what'd he do for the association to be so honored?"

"Nothing," Jerry laughed. "But he's a popular speaker and will draw a good crowd."

Jaylene was confused. "You're honoring him, yet he hasn't done anything for you?"

Jerry didn't seem to see the contradiction. "If we gave awards to the guys who deserved them, nobody'd come and no money would be raised. Then what would the organization do?"

"You mean those awards are more for raising money than giving recognition to someone who's worked hard?" Jaylene asked. "That doesn't seem fair."

"Maybe not," Jerry admitted. "But the little guys do get some recognition. You have to understand that a nonprofit organization's the same as TIE. What counts is the bottom line. They need money to keep going and they get money from having big names appear."

"So if I bought out the banquet hall, I could probably name who the award should go to," she suggested.

"Probably. We do have some principles, but money does talk. Especially if it would be somebody who'd give a fair bit of change on his own." He rose to his feet. "Well, this isn't getting your work done. Anything else we have to cover?"

Jaylene shook her head. "No, we're set. Good luck with your ticket sales."

After Jerry left, Jaylene sat staring at her desk for a while. An idea was forming in her head, and she thought it might work. It would have to be done just right, but if it was, Dick Matthews would be in the clear. She picked up her phone and slowly dialed her personal lawyer's number. TIE's name had to be kept out of it for now.

She was feeling hopeful as she listened to the phone ring. Even the thought of her talk with Ray that afternoon did not worry her as much anymore. Optimism was growing. If she could solve Dick's problem, surely she could solve her own.

Ray walked briskly down the hallway to his office. The cool, distant smile on his face was meant to discourage idle chatterers. The longer he stayed in the hall, the more likely he was to see Jaylene, and he didn't think he was ready for that. He had still been smarting from her rejection when he got back from his trip, but then she had been out of town herself and he had flown up to New York, so he hadn't had to see her. Now, though, they both were back. He knew she was there without anyone telling him. He could sense it in the air.

"I hear you're heading out again tonight, eh, Ray?"

Frank Kareau came up next to him. "L.A. this time, isn't it?"

"Yeah," Ray agreed. "I'll spend a day there and then I'm going to take a swing through the East."

"Sounds good. Singapore, Hong Kong, Sydney. I envy you."

Ray forced a bright smile to his face. "Yes, I'm looking forward to it myself."

They parted and Ray hurried along. Actually, he'd be looking forward to a trip to East Podunk. Miami was getting a tad old for him. He would be glad to be gone.

He went into his office and put down his briefcase. He wasn't looking forward to seeing Jaylene again, but it probably would be better to get it over with. He had opened himself up for her and she had walked on his face. It had hurt, but sooner or later he was going to have to see her again.

His phone rang. It was Rita. "Miss Sable would like to see you if you're free."

"Sure," Ray agreed briskly, wondering what the summons was for. The only thing he could think of was that preliminary report on his South American trip. Maybe she was bothered by something in it, for she sure wasn't bothered by him.

He took a deep breath and squared his shoulders as he marched down the hall. He was tough, he was fine. It wasn't as if his feelings had been involved.

"Dr. Carroll's here," Rita said.

Jaylene tried to keep her eyes on the papers she was scanning. "Good. Send him on in." Jaylene sat back in her chair and closed her eyes briefly. Lord, how terrified she was. Her hands were ice cold and she felt like throwing up. Now that would be a great way to great Ray. She smiled in spite of her fear.

How would he take the news that she was pregnant? She was getting excited about it, now that the initial shock had worn off. Would he be excited, though? They had not exactly parted on the best of terms.

The sound of Ray entering made her sit up straighter.

There was no smile on his face, and he didn't look the slightest bit glad to see her again. Her stomach churned some more, but she ignored it.

"Hello, Ray."

"Hello, Jaylene."

She indicated a chair before her desk as she pressed her intercom button. "Please see that we aren't disturbed." She barely waited for Rita's murmured agreement before her eyes were back on Ray. She wished this afternoon were over.

"I hope that report didn't cause you too many problems."

Report? What was he talking about? She stared at him in confusion for a moment, then a faded smile came over her lips. "There's no problem with your report, Ray. I read it a few days ago and thought it was well done. I sent you a note about it."

"Oh, well, I haven't really looked through the mail on my desk yet," he stammered.

She leaned back in her chair and took a deep breath, knowing there was no sense wasting time beating around the bush. "What I have to talk about has nothing to do with business," she said quickly.

He said nothing. His eyes remained passive. If there was any warmth in them, she could not see it.

"I've stewed about this for days," Jaylene went on. "I tried to think of the best way and the best place to tell you. I finally came to the conclusion that there was no best, and I had just better tell you straight out."

She fell silent for a moment and looked directly at him. Her mouth was dry and she had trouble speaking. After clearing her throat, she forced the sentence out. "I'm carrying your child, Ray."

The words seemed to echo around the room as Ray just stared at her. She thought she saw his cool reserve slip slightly, but then he appeared to go into shock. It wasn't the reaction she had dreamed of, but then neither was it what she had feared.

He opened his mouth, but no words came out. He closed

it again and swallowed, then cleared his throat. "You're pregnant?" His voice sounded strangled.

He seemed so stunned that she felt sorry for him and let a tender smile creep onto her lips. She understood the shock that he was experiencing. Hadn't she felt the same way when she'd heard?

"It does happen sometimes, doctor," she teased gently.

He nodded. "Yes, of course. You just caught me by surprise."

"I was rather surprised myself."

He nodded again and shifted position in his chair. After a moment, he shifted back again. "I don't exactly know what to say," he said lamely after the silence seemed to drag out to eternity. "I guess I never expected this from a woman of your maturity and experience."

Her tender understanding disappeared and anger darkened her face. Was he saying what it sounded like he was saying? "I resent your implication, Dr. Carroll."

His control also seemed to slip. "Hell, that's not what I meant," he snapped, and ran his fingers through his hair.

She stared at him. She did not care about his agitation and no longer felt any sympathy for him. She had far more at stake here than he did.

He sighed and visibly tried to control his impatience. "I only meant I was surprised," he assured her. "I never expected to have this conversation with you."

She said nothing, continuing to gaze at him coolly. She knew she had been cherishing some foolish hopes, but that did not ease the pain of seeing them burst before her eyes.

He cleared his throat and seemed to regain his businesslike manner. "Have you made any decisions about the future yet?" he asked. "I'll be happy to help you in any way I can."

He sounded as if he were discussing the consolidation, and that hurt her deeply. Didn't he know how to be a human being instead of the perfect businessman?

She tried to copy his tone. "The decision is already made. I am going to carry and keep my baby."

"Fine." His voice was brisk. "I assume that I am the father and, therefore, I am available to you for marriage."

She stared at him, unable to believe her ears. He was available to her for marriage? Just like he might be available for a meeting that afternoon! No mention of love or affection or even fondness. Not the slightest indication he wanted her or the baby. Just a macho announcement that he would do the proper thing by her. Well, he could go to hell!

"Is this another one of your semipermanent, nonrestrictive relationships?" she mocked. "Well, I hate to tell you, but I haven't changed my mind about them."

"What?" He must not have expected her refusal and was really stunned.

She laughed bitterly. "Read my lips," she said. "I have no intention of marrying you or anyone else."

He rose to his feet, his manner suddenly reasonable and conciliatory. "Look, Jaylene. The only people who have children out of wedlock are movie stars and welfare mothers. You're neither." He paused as if to let the sense of his words sink in. "We don't have to stay married. But once we establish the legal relationship I can help you. The child will have a legal claim against my estate. Most of all, it will have a name."

Legal claim and estates! Why was he calling it a marriage? Why not a temporary merger? How about consolidating their assets to finance a new division? She needed love and he was handing her corporate bullshit.

"I have a substantial estate of my own, Dr. Carroll. Plus a perfectly good name." She wanted to hurt him the way he was hurting her. "I don't need you or your marriage."

He appeared calm, but she could see the muscle twitching in the side of his face and knew he wasn't.

"You needed me once," he said.

She stared at him but did not reply. She needed him still, but what difference did that make to him? He wasn't willing to offer himself, just his name and his estate.

"Didn't you?" he repeated, almost shouting through clenched teeth.

She would not let him know how she was hurting, how frightened and alone she felt. When she had decided to have the baby, she had figured she'd be alone. Ray was not upsetting any carefully laid plans, just a few dreams.

"I needed a man, doctor," she said coldly, emphasizing the *a*.

It took the wind out of his sails, and she got a fleeting sense of victory before the pain set in. He rose to his feet.

"I'd like to wish you good luck and good health," he said quietly.

Her reply was just as quiet. "I wish you the same." Then he was gone.

Ray did not see anyone or anything in the hall as he hurried through. All he knew was that he needed the privacy of his office before he exploded.

That woman was insane! He closed the door behind him, wishing he could slam it to relieve his frustrations. There was no getting around the fact. She must have completely lost her mind.

He stalked over to the windows and stared down at the parking lot. The sun was shining brightly and the people outside were in their shirt sleeves. Stupid, obscene weather. It ought to be freezing in January. He crossed to his desk.

Maybe he was the insane one. For a while there in her office, he had actually thought she wanted to get back together with him. He had actually been hoping that was what she wanted. But she didn't want him, didn't even need him.

Her parting shot about needing a man ran through his mind. Maybe that was all she needed, he thought suddenly. Maybe she was one of those liberated females he'd read about who wanted a child but not a husband. Maybe the only reason she'd gotten involved with him was to get pregnant. Maybe he had been nothing more than a convenient stud.

Damn. How could he have been so stupid as to believe they had something special going?

Jaylene sat at the dressing table of her private bathroom, mopping the tears from her face with an already soggy Kleenex. Why hadn't she stayed calm? She had never meant to say all those things to Ray. She had wanted him and still did. But not on the terms he was prepared to offer.

She angrily threw the Kleenex into the wastebasket and took another. She shouldn't be sitting here feeling sorry for herself; she ought to be counting her blessings. And one, certainly, was this private bathroom in which to sob her heart out.

Jesse would probably be glad to know that she was getting such good use from it. He was forever reminding her how much more expensive she was than the men he had promoted. They only needed a urinal, a bowl, and a sink, but she cost three thousand dollars more for the additional dressing room. If he told her that one more time, she was going to write him a memo about misrepresenting the facts. In his figures he was adding the cost of the dressing room, but never subtracting the cost of the urinal.

She took a deep breath and stared at herself in the mirror. Why was she sitting here thinking of the stupid things Jesse had said to her? She could write a book about him by now. *Smart-Ass Remarks and Texas Folktales,* as spouted by Jesse Whitmore and collected over the years by Jaylene Sable. Maybe that's what she ought to do once she left TIE. She'd probably have some time on her hands.

The tears started again. She didn't really want to leave TIE. She didn't want Ray to feel like he had to marry her. What she really didn't want was to feel so alone.

She sobbed until the teary wave had passed, then glanced up at the clock on the wall. She had told Rita she wanted thirty minutes alone, and her time was almost up. She guessed she'd better start making some repairs. To her face, at least. What could be done about her life?

A spasm went through her body but she refused to let it trigger another bout of tears. Nothing much had gone right in the talk with Ray. She had been excited and scared at the same time. She was carrying their love in her and had wanted to share her excitement. It was all that nonsense about estates and giving the child a name that made something snap within her, that made her want to

hurt him. She bit her lip before the tears could start again.
She knew she had succeeded.

Sighing, Jaylene took off her jacket and her blouse. With
her red eyes and streaky face, it would take her forever to
look presentable. She took out a jar of cold cream and began to remove the remains of her makeup.

As she was wiping it off with a tissue, the intercom
buzzer next to her sounded. The noise seemed to echo all
around her. She ignored it and continued cleaning off her
makeup.

The buzzing continued, sounding as if somebody was
leaning on the button. "Stuff it, Rita," she said aloud. "I'm
indisposed."

The buzzing went on and on. "Damn it," she finally
cried and picked up the telephone handpiece. "Rita, I
don't—"

"It's Mr. Whitmore," Rita interrupted her. "He said
that he had to speak to you immediately."

Before she could reply, Rita had cut out and Jessie's
voice broke in on her. "Damn, Jaylene, where were you?
Sitting on the throne getting a new perspective on life?"

Jaylene clenched her teeth. "There are some things in
my life that are my own damn business, Mr. Whitmore."
Maybe it was just as well that Jesse had called. She was
spoiling for a fight, and it might as well be with that
bigmouth cowboy.

Chapter Twenty-four

"Would you like some wine, sir?"

Ray looked sourly at the JAL hostess. She was pretty and very pleasant. Normally that would have inspired him to make some response, but tonight he was in an exceptionally foul mood.

"No," he grumbled. "Just get me a martini. Extra dry." Then he turned back to the window.

January had certainly ended with a bang. First, Jaylene dropped her bomb on him, and then the trip to L.A. was a bust. What would February bring? Probably his trip to Singapore was jinxed.

The drink came and he murmured his thanks to the hostess. Her beautiful smile was enhanced by her slight curtsy.

Maybe he should find himself an Oriental wife, he thought as he sipped his drink. It was certainly extra dry and almost choked him. Or had it been his thoughts? Damn it. He didn't want a wife. No, a mistress would be more to his liking. Irritation washed over him. He didn't want a mistress, either. He didn't want anybody.

He stared glumly out at the darkness. They were over the Pacific Ocean and everything was black beneath them. He didn't want anybody and he didn't have anybody. So what the hell was there to grump about?

Maybe it was the drink, he thought, and put it aside. He should have learned by now that most foreigners don't know how to make a good martini. He eased the seat back and tried to relax.

He had a right to be grumpy. It wasn't every day that one of his girlfriends gave him such happy news. Jaylene had to be different.

He stared up at the ceiling of the plane, the engines softly droning on in the darkness. She was different, all right. She was so different that she was special.

Ray impatiently turned over. Damn it. He was doing it again. He wasn't treating her properly, and that was the cause of all his problems. For years, he had had a successful set of ground rules, and now he was the one who was breaking them.

Determined not to think of Jaylene anymore, he forced his thoughts back to his L.A. visit. Now, that Margolis was a real gem. How did a guy like him get to where he was?

Margolis had raised hell with his secretary because none of the reports Ray had requested were available, although Ray suspected she had never seen his list. She had just ignored Margolis's ranting, though, and found everything Ray needed. As it was, he had had to bring some of the material along with him to review on the plane.

L.A. sure didn't match up to Miami, but then Margolis wasn't the executive Jaylene was. Well, at least she had that going for herself.

He stirred uncomfortably. What was she going to do now? It wouldn't be easy to be a high-powered executive and a single mother. Not even for someone like Jaylene.

Angrily, he got a pillow from the compartment above his head, then threw it down on the headrest and swore under his breath when it fell on the seat. That's what Jaylene wanted and that's what she had. She was a big girl and she knew what she was doing. If she didn't, she should. He sat down and closed his eyes.

After several minutes of stirring he got up and went to the bathroom. When he returned, he lay with his eyes wide open, staring at the ceiling. His eyes refused to shut.

Finally he gave up, raised the seatback, and turned on the reading light. Might as well finish reviewing those reports. They were preferable to more thoughts of Jaylene.

He cruised through the data rapidly. The figures weren't quite as good as those for Jaylene's unit, but still not too bad. The differences might be due to the exchange rates of the Far East countries or something else beyond any TIE officer's control.

He was almost ready to stop and try again to sleep when he noticed something in the quality control section that just didn't jibe. Puzzled, he started searching.

Hours later, he stared thoughtfully out his window. His lap-size computer lay on the tray table. It had been an interesting and informative night and it all came from paging through an obscure quality control report.

The monthly reports illustrated one thing very clearly: someone was bleeding the Far East subsidiary. But why? Ray had a feeling that this part of his study would be just what he needed to take his mind off Jaylene.

Margolis was running through the woods. His lungs were on fire and ready to burst. Sweat dripped from his brow, salt burned his eyes. He didn't see his enemy, but he heard it behind him. Screaming and howling. An ungodly sound. As if Satan had released all the hounds of hell.

He tore at the blankets wrapped around his body and woke up. He was soaking wet. He was safe in his own bedroom, but the howling still rang in his ears.

"Goddamn it. It's just the phone," he mumbled. He dropped his head back down on the pillow. "Margie, get the damn phone."

It rang again and he put his arms around his head. Would she ever answer it? "Margie. Margie," he screamed. His sat up, his breath coming in short gasps. There was no one in her bed. Where the hell was that woman?

He reached for the phone himself, and almost dropped it as he put it to his ear. "Hello," he mumbled.

"Mr. Margolis?" asked a foreign-accented voice.

"Yeah. Who the hell is this?"

"It is Chung Kee, sir. TIE/Singapore."

There were spots before his eyes and his breathing was still rapid. His mouth was dry and he really didn't feel like talking. "Call me in the morning, will you, fella?"

"Is it not morning where you reside?" the man asked him.

"Yeah," Margolis snapped. "But it's damn early in the morning." He took a deep breath and slowly let it out. As he did that he could see the clouds clearing. "Kee? What the hell you calling me now for?"

"It is at your request, sir. Your very words were as soon as I could."

"Where are you?" Margolis asked.

"I have left work. I am calling from Hung's establishment. It is not far from my office."

His head was starting to pound now. "So what do you have for me, Kee?"

"Information, sir. It is, I think, good information."

"Yeah?"

He leaned back, massaging his brow, while Kee filled him in on Dr. Carroll's visit. When the consultant arrived he went straight to see Lai Chou, the department director of quality control. The professor spent a good part of the day with him. The two of them then went together to see Harry Cheng. After the meeting Cheng left his office much earlier than usual. He left in a most agitated state.

"It is good information?" Kee asked as he finished.

Terrific. Best news he'd heard all morning. It only meant the end of everything for him. "Yeah, it's great," Margolis snapped.

"I shall call again tomorrow."

What for? The details of the funeral? "No, don't bother." Margolis slowly hung up the phone.

"That bastard Cheng," he mumbled. He'd given the little rat enough money to pass on, but the greedy little bastard probably had kept it all for himself. That had put Lai's nose out of joint, so when Carroll showed up, he spilled the whole cookie jar.

He stared out across the room and suddenly realized that the other bed was still neatly made. Where the hell was his wife? He rubbed his eyes. With his job and all the traveling connected with it, they tended to have their own lives, but that didn't mean that she shouldn't be home in bed at three A.M.

He got up and stumbled toward the bathroom. Hell, she probably was out with one of her girlfriends. No. No, they wouldn't be out this late. Probably just at one of her friends' houses, yakking.

The light in the bathroom hurt his eyes and he closed them momentarily. When he opened them he was staring into a mirror. The face that looked back was sagging and gray.

"It's over," he told the man in the mirror. "It's all over. The gravy train ain't gonna run no more." Then he threw up.

After he cleaned himself up, he actually felt much better. He was getting tired of L.A. anyway. TIE wouldn't prosecute, and they couldn't touch those foreign bank accounts. He and Margie could take those Swiss francs and run. He wouldn't be the richest man in the world, but they'd have enough to get by. Maybe they could move back East. New York had a certain edge that L.A. lacked.

It was about six in Miami. Might as well roust Brewster's fat ass out of bed and tell him the good news. He dialed the number.

After what seemed like a hundred rings Brewster's sleepy voice finally came on.

"Yeah."

"This is Margolis, Brew. It's over."

There was a long silence, and Margolis figured that he either hadn't heard or hadn't understood. "The gravy train's over. No more gold flowing into Switzerland. That guy Carroll has cracked the code."

Brewster still didn't answer. Well, he was never too bright. He'd figure it out when he didn't get his cut. "I gotta go now. I just wanted to let you know." There was still no answer and Margolis found himself getting irritated. "Damn it. Are you awake, Brewster?"

"Yeah, Davie. Wide awake."

"Oh." Margolis was surprised at the clarity and strength in his voice. "Well, I want to call Kastle and let her know. We're shutting down the operation. Everybody's on his own."

"I'll call her, Davie. Save you a dime."

Margolis was surprised, but agreed and hung up. He stared dully at the empty bed across from his.

* * *

Brewster watched the hard-faced woman with the dyed blond hair argue with the hostess. It was obvious the blond wanted to be seated in a booth, while the hostess wanted to seat her at the counter, probably to save the booths for the couples who would come in during the lunch hour. Reluctantly, the hostess led her to the booth.

"Old broad looks as mean as a snake," Brewster muttered to himself. Once she was seated, Brewster put some money down for his coffee and walked over to the booth. He slid in opposite the woman without saying a word.

"I presume you're Brewster Merrill," the woman said after a moment. Her voice was like a winter's day in Fargo.

Brewster just nodded.

"I also presume that, since you called me, you're buying lunch." She picked up the menu and signaled for the waitress. She ordered an old-fashioned and a steak. Brewster didn't order anything. He knew that this was the type of place where the french fries would be dry.

After her drink came and she took a sip, he spoke. "I got a call from Davie this morning."

"Is that right?" Her voice was noncommittal, but her eyes narrowed.

"Yeah," Brewster replied. "He's shutting down the operation."

The knuckles of the hand around the glass turned white. Her lips stretched into a thin line. "That son of a bitch," she hissed through clenched teeth. "The dirty bastard."

"He might still come out this way," Brewster said mildly, not certain just what was the cause of her outburst.

She gulped at her drink and then stared out the window at the shopping mall outside. "I don't give a damn if he ever comes back."

"Any other problems then?"

She turned to look at him, a crooked twist to her lips. "Any other problems? I'm forty-eight years old, and have been working my behind off for the past twenty-seven years. I'm making a measly twenty-five thou a year and my prospects for better are now zero." She drained her glass. "Hell, no, there aren't any other problems."

She pushed her glass across the table to him. "Get me another one."

Brewster signaled the waitress and they sat silently until she had her second glass.

"What were you getting out of this?" Brewster asked. "Promises?"

"I got a few bucks out of it, but mostly it was promises," she agreed.

He nodded as he stared out the window. "I had a good gravy train that's derailed now."

"Fucking loser," Rita spat, the venom she felt boiling over.

Her food came and Rita attacked her plate, cutting her meat as if it were Margolis. Brewster didn't say much until she was done.

"At least you still have your job," he pointed out.

She ordered another drink. "Actually, I may not have that for much longer."

Brewster raised his eyebrows in reply.

"Margolis wanted a copy of all the documents that went through Miss Sable's office. That turned out to be a lot of copying, and I think somebody spotted me one night." She shook her blond head. "That potbellied ass. He had to have everything. I couldn't screen a thing."

Brewster ordered coffee for both of them and they sat in silence, nursing their cups.

"How much gravy was on that train of yours?" Rita asked.

"A lot." He sipped at his coffee. "Davie had a little kickback scheme with the suppliers to his plants. I picked it up in gold or dollars and put it in Switzerland for him."

"He's got a secret Swiss bank account?" Rita asked, the bitterness in her voice apparent.

"Yeah, he's sitting on all that gold, while my plans are all going down the tubes."

Rita stared moodily into her cup and didn't really seem interested. Selfish old bitch. Didn't care about anyone but herself, Brewster fumed.

"I was going to set up a little freight forwarding business," he said loudly to get her attention.

She looked up at him. "So Margolis was going to throw a few crumbs your way," she said. "Who cares?"

He laughed. "I had other merchandise and other customers in mind. All I wanted was to piggyback on the TIE corporate jets."

Her face had a puzzled look.

"My merchandise is very small, but valuable. And a lot of it comes from South America."

Her face relaxed, and Brewster thought that he saw a glimmer of understanding in her eyes. "I don't think you're the first with that idea, Mr. Merrill," she said. "Security is real tight around our planes. All the pilots double as security personnel. Slipping a little merchandise aboard wouldn't have been that easy."

"I had some ideas." He shrugged.

"Doesn't matter now," she said, and looked at her watch. "I'd better be getting back. The ice queen will be looking for me."

Brewster held up his hand. "Give me a few more minutes."

Her lips curled, but before she could say anything Brewster spoke. "We're both losing a lot. Maybe we can come up with something to recoup some of our losses."

She relaxed back in her seat, her curiosity piqued. "At this point I'm willing to listen to anything."

"I've been thinking," he said, cautiously gauging Rita's interest. "Do you think we might be able to get one load in?"

"Like I said, Brewster, security is tight."

He nodded in understanding. "I may have no choice. Would you be willing to help?"

"I don't want to know anything about it," Rita snapped.

"All I need from you is information."

She laughed harshly. "You sound like Dave."

"I don't want no copies," Brewster hurried to assure her. "All I want is to be able to call you once in a while and get travel plans and stuff like that." He paused, taking an educated guess. "And I promise to pay on time."

From the look in her eyes, he knew that Margolis was as slow paying her as he had been paying him. "Doesn't sound too hard," she replied slowly. "We could give it a try. I'd rather be getting the money than seeing it all roll into Margolis's lap anyway." An unpleasant smile stretched across her lips. "You know, it's almost funny. He was trying so hard to beat her, and all he had to do was sit tight and let her take herself out of the running."

Brewster just stared at her.

She leaned a little closer across the table. "Miss Jaylene Sable is pregnant," she told him. "And quitting TIE. Margolis could have been the president of that subsidiary if he'd covered his tracks better."

Brewster snickered, then laughed aloud. "Shit. How I'd love to be the one to tell him the news."

Chapter Twenty-five

"So where do you go from here, Ray?"

Ray looked across the dinner table at Charlie Lai, the slim young graduate of MIT and Cal Tech who was manager of quality control for the Singapore operation. They had gotten to know each other pretty well over the past few days and were having a last dinner together at Ray's hotel.

"First I hit Taiwan and then on to Seoul. I had a few other stops that I was scheduled to make, but I canceled most of them. Singapore took a bit more time than I had planned, but with Taiwan and Seoul, I'll have enough information about the Far East operations to write my report. Then I'll head back to New York."

"You will have to tell your findings to Mr. Whitmore."

"Well, I'll have to write a report with my recommendations. I've already covered Margolis's extortion scheme with Jesse by telephone."

"What will happen to Mr. Margolis?" Charlie asked.

"He's out. Fired," Ray replied. "Your plant manager Mr. Cheng is also on his way out."

"Do you know if the powers have given any thought to a new plant manager?" A pensive expression crossed his face.

"Do you want it, Charlie?"

He just smiled and shrugged.

Actually, Margolis and Cheng would not be the only ones out on the streets, Ray thought. He suspected that the Singapore scheme was only one of many illegal operations

Margolis had going. Corporate security would have fun cleaning house down here. He took a sip of his tea and was silent a moment, his thoughts drifting back to Jaylene, as they always seemed to. For some reason, this trip didn't have the excitement of his other trips, the ones he had taken before he met her. He shook himself mentally and asked Charlie, "What did you say your wife studied at Berkeley?"

"Pre-med," Charlie answered. "She is a gynecologist. Although now she is taking some time off after the birth of our third child, a boy."

"Oh. Congratulations, I guess."

Charlie frowned. "You Americans do not always appreciate your children, but we count them as a blessing. The state helps to take care of the body, but we need children to care for our spirits. How many children do you have, Ray?"

Ray felt his face twitching slightly. "None," he finally answered.

"Then you'd better hurry," Charlie urged.

Ray tried to laugh off the other man's serious expression. "Why? I'm reasonably well off financially. I can take care of myself."

Charlie shook his head. "Again you emphasize the body. I speak of your spiritual needs. We Chinese believe that without a family, children, grandchildren, and so on, your soul will never know peace. You will spend an eternity in loneliness."

The last few weeks had already seemed like that eternity. "I guess I'm lucky I'm not Chinese then." Shrugging, he tried to laugh, but it sounded weak in his own ears.

"Lucky?" Charlie's face showed puzzlement. "I do not understand."

"If I were Chinese I'd have to get married," Ray explained.

"A wife is a gift from the gods. She gives a man a taste of what you westerners call paradise. If I could afford it I would take another woman."

"It works differently with us. In America, we can only marry one woman."

"At a time," Charlie pointed out.

Ray had to smile too. "True. Anyway, our women expect a very close emotional relationship."

"I know a man with three women. He is very close and loves each very much."

"Well, I find it difficult to let anyone get close to me," Ray said, then picked up the glass of plum wine they had just been served. Why had he said that? He had never confided anything like that to anyone. Here he was with a man he had known for only a couple of days, and he was opening the depths of his soul to him.

Ray raised his eyes and found Charlie looking at him. He raised his drink to his lips but the glass drained all too quickly. When he put it down, Charlie was still studying him.

"It is said that the man who seals his windows because of the rain will never know the warmth of the sun."

Ray did not know what to say and was relieved when the waiter brought the check over. He paid it quickly, then he and Charlie parted company. Ray walked slowly to the elevator while he watched the other man leave the hotel, going home to his wife and family.

There was a bitter taste in Ray's mouth as he rode the empty elevator up to his empty room. That was how everything seemed these days: empty. Valentine's Day was a week away. The traditional day to celebrate love, and how would he spend it? Probably alone.

Charlie's words continued to ring in his mind. If a man seals his windows because of the rain, he will never know the warmth of the sun. Ray had an uneasy feeling that he had felt the warmth of the sun but had turned his back on it.

"Could your friend put his hands on the table, please?"

Brewster looked into the hard, smiling face of Raoul de Noaguira and began to sweat profusely. He and Josef had a meeting this evening at a bar just west of Miami that was owned by one of Raoul's many cousins. There were five tense men at the table, and a majority of the patrons probably worked for Raoul.

"Joey." The sound had come out squeaky and Brewster

cleared his throat to try again. "Joey, this is Raoul's home. Let's be polite and do what he wants."

Josef's snake eyes roamed the hard faces and the room. There wasn't any fear in them, and that bothered Brewster. The little weasel was too crazy to be scared.

"Joey," he hissed through clenched teeth. He didn't like dealing with these men, and the setup unnerved him.

Josef blinked once at Brewster and his muscles seemed to relax.

"Slowly, please," came Raoul's quiet command.

Josef slowly put his hands on the table in front of them. Brewster couldn't restrain his body from shivering. He had sweated so much that he was soaking wet.

Once Josef's hands were on the table Raoul spoke in Spanish to one of his men, then turned back to them, smiling. "I have ordered another round of beers. It will give your friend something to do with his hands."

They waited in silence until the beers came. Brewster was too worried to touch his, but both Josef and Raoul drank deeply.

"Now, Brewster," Raoul said with a quiet little smile, "we really must resolve some of the business issues that were raised here today."

"It's finished, Raoul," Brewster whined. "There ain't no way I can get at those corporate planes. My contact, my main man, is out."

Brewster licked his lips and fell silent. He looked nervously at Raoul and was sorry that he had slipped into street talk. Raoul was an honors graduate from Amherst and had two years at the Yale Law School. Although he hadn't been born in this country, he was proud of the fact that he spoke English perfectly.

"Those are very strong words, Brewster," Raoul said quietly.

"Look," Brewster said loudly, "I'm just as sorry as you are, but—"

Raoul held his hand up and Brewster fell silent. "To secure a fair share of the market, a number of people had to make commitments." He sipped his beer and stared intently at Brewster. "The risks in establishing ourselves, due to certain peculiarities of the other suppliers, are quite high. So everyone concerned takes these commitments very seriously."

"Honest to God, Raoul, I'm sorry, but I can't do anything about it."

Raoul pushed his beer bottle around in circles, forming trails of dampness on the table. "These are very old-fashioned men we deal with, Brewster," he said without looking up. "They have certain idiosyncrasies. One is extreme reluctance to accept the word *can't.* "

Sweat rolled down Brewster's face and dripped from his loose jowls onto the front of his shirt. His throat felt parched and constricted.

"They come from a world of honor," Raoul continued. "To them, a man's word is worth more than his life. If he breaks his word . . ." Raoul shrugged. "Then obviously he places little value on his life."

Brewster tried to speak, but all that came out was a hoarse squeak.

Raoul smiled easily. "Think about it, Brewster. You had a long-term commitment. We all understand that the world changes. But you still must fulfill your obligations. Think about how you'd like to do that." He nodded to his men and they stood up and stepped back a few steps from the table.

Brewster and Josef went out into the night. When Brewster reached the car, he leaned on the hood and threw up long and violently. Finally he just sat on the ground, leaning on the right front wheel, sweat pouring out of his body, in spite of the cool night air. He was shaking violently.

Josef didn't say anything and eventually helped him into the passenger side of the car. After they were back in the city, Josef turned to him and said, "You should've let me go for it back there. We could've taken a few to hell with us."

"We wouldn't have died there," Brewster snorted. "These guys know how to make you suffer and wish you were never born."

Josef drove in silence for a while. "This client of yours was supposed to be our ticket to those corporate jets?"

"Yeah."

"You were gonna use TIE corporate jets to bring the merchandise in?" Josef asked.

"Yeah," Brewster replied.

"Pretty slick," said Josef admiringly.

"Yeah, real slick." Brewster sniffed long and hard. "Then that goddamn wimp gets himself canned and we're all in trouble."

Josef shook his head. "We still got Janie."

"Nah," Brewster snorted. "That goddamn broad is a straight arrow."

"We can make her do what we want."

"No," Brewster said. "You've been following her around. You've seen how secure she is. Besides, we couldn't hold her forever."

"Too bad she don't have a kid. That's the best way to get to a woman," Josef said. "We could hold it while she hauled the stuff for us. Or at least made a few good hauls."

"She ain't dropped her kid yet," Brewster said absently. "And we can't wait until she does." He was concentrating on Raoul's friends and the ways they might express their displeasure when the car swerved suddenly and he fell against the side.

"Shit, Joey. What the hell you doing?" he cried, rubbing his shoulder. "It ain't enough that Raoul's gonna get us. You want to do the job for him?"

But Josef wasn't paying attention to him. "That whore," he muttered, his face twisted in fury. "That filthy slut."

Brewster stared at him, his troubles with Raoul fading from his mind somewhat as he enjoyed Josef's distress. "What'd you think, Joey? That she was saving herself for you?" He smiled slightly as Josef's hands clenched the steering wheel tighter.

"She's gonna have a baby," he exclaimed. "Hell. She must've been sleeping around like some woman of the streets. I thought you said she was a straight arrow."

"She may roll in the hay with a boyfriend once or twice, but it's nothing serious," Brewster assured him. He had found a way to needle Josef and it was fun; it made him feel better. He liked seeing the other man squirm. He liked seeing him suffer. "She probably makes so much money that she can do whatever she wants. Makes her own rules."

"That ain't right," Josef insisted. His breath was coming hard and his voice was tight with rage. "She's my wife, and I ain't been near her. She shouldn't be pregnant. She's got an office job and everything, but she ain't nothing but a slut."

Brewster turned back to the window. Seeing Joey rage was fun, but not profitable. What he needed was a good place to run to, and he wouldn't find it listening to this weasel.

"Who's the father?" Josef asked after a moment of silence. "Her pretty-boy professor?"

"Yeah." Raoul's threat began to grow in his mind again. Where could he hide from them? Was any corner of the earth safe?

Josef turned a corner sharply and Brewster banged his head on the door. "Damn it, watch your driving and stop mooning about your ex's boyfriends."

"Hell, I'd like to get my hands on her," Josef muttered. "And that pretty boy. I'd teach him not to mess with another man's wife."

Brewster was about to point out again that she'd divorced him years ago when an idea began to take shape. Maybe that was the answer. She had security around her, but her professor didn't. He didn't even work for TIE, so they didn't really give a shit about him, but she would. She wouldn't stand by and let them hurt the father of her child.

"Come on, Joey," he snapped. "Goose this damn thing. We have a lot of work to do."

Rose turned to Jaylene as she hung up the phone. "Your limo is here."

"Thanks, Rose," she replied, picking up a silvery shawl and wrapping it around her shoulders, left bare by the black silk designer dress. She was a little nervous and hoped everything went as planned.

"Who's this guy you're going with?" Rose asked. "I don't think I ever met him."

Jaylene just laughed. Rose was sounding more and more like a mother hen. She put her arm around the older woman's shoulders and gave her a quick hug. "Don't worry, Mom. He's safe. He's married."

"In my day, that wasn't safe."

"Jerry's not really a date, Rose," she said. "He's an escort. His wife tore a ligament a few days ago playing tennis, so he was going alone, also."

Rose just grunted as she followed Jaylene into the hallway. "A pretty young woman like you ought to be going out on real dates, not having escorts. You shouldn't have broken up with that nice Dr. Carroll."

"Right, Rose."

She was relieved that the elevator came immediately and she could go. Rose was a dear and meant well, but she just didn't know about some things, and Ray was one of them. It had been more than a week since that horrible meeting when she'd told him she was pregnant. Some of the pain was finally starting to fade, but maybe that was only because he wasn't in town. He had gone to L.A. and then on to the the Far East, and wouldn't be back in the country for another week. Even then he might not be coming back to Miami. Ever. The elevator doors opened and Nancy, also dressed in a formal gown, was waiting for her.

"You're going to break a lot of hearts tonight, boss lady."

"Thanks, Nancy. You look pretty smashing yourself. How's your date?"

"A little quiet right now. I think his wife gave him a long list of do's and don'ts before he left the house."

Jaylene chuckled as they went out to the car. Tom, her chauffeur/security guard, was a large, burly individual who tended to inspire respect quickly. They all knew that he was ruled by his tiny Latin wife, though. No doubt Tom was going to be a very circumspect date for Nancy tonight.

"How's Cherie?" Jaylene asked the PR director as she settled herself into the back seat.

"Not too bad," Jerry replied. "She's glad that you're my date. I guess she was worried that I'd get into trouble by myself."

The window between the front and back seats was open and Nancy turned slightly. "Way to go, Jerry."

"What did I do?" he protested.

"Forget it," Jaylene laughed.

They rode in silence for a while and then Jerry spoke again. "Compared to the heart and cancer societies, the Multiple Sclerosis Society is pretty small, but they're really doing a super job on this dinner tonight."

"Is that right?" Jaylene remarked mildly.

"I mean it's outstanding," Jerry continued. "Just a week ago, they were going to have one of their quiet little affairs, give some awards to a few unknowns, and now look at them."

"Yes," Jaylene agreed. "Now they have Mr. Malcolm Cabot himself coming down to accept a Corporate Citizen of the Year Award."

"That's really sharp of them, actually. Some nobody like this Matthews guy volunteers and they give him an award. Then to get some PR mileage out of it, they give the company he works for an award."

"Mr. Cabot's certainly coming down on short notice," Nancy said. "I always thought the chairman of the board had a tight schedule."

"Malcolm's from a long line of wealthy civic leaders," Jerry pointed out. "They go for this noblesse oblige stuff."

No one replied and they rode in silence for a moment before Jerry added, "Besides, my corporate source said that Angie wanted a few days in the sun down here."

"His wife?" Nancy asked.

"No, his personal secretary," Jerry replied. "A very personal secretary."

"She's Malcolm's executive assistant," Jaylene said.

Jaylene knew there were rumors about what else Angie was, but she never paid much attention to them. People should be allowed to do their jobs without being judged by others. She knew that didn't happen, though. Once her pregnancy became known she'd probably find that out all too clearly.

The limousine stopped and she looked up to find they were already at the Omni, the site of the MS Society's awards dinner-dance. She and Jerry were shown to a table with distinguished-looking Malcolm Cabot, Angie, a statuesque redhead, and Dick Matthews and his wife. Nancy and Tom were also there, trying to look like a dating couple rather than two security guards.

Malcolm was the perfect host and made everyone feel welcome, especially Dick's wife. She was in a wheelchair, but was dressed just as formally as the other women. What really made her stand out from the others, though, was the pride and love in her eyes for Dick. Pride and love that was returned in his eyes. Jaylene felt slightly envious of them. They shared something she'd never have.

After the dinner, the awards were presented. Dick was rather embarrassed when he got his, as if he couldn't understand all the fuss. He obviously preferred the background where he lived and worked.

Malcolm knew how to use the limelight a bit better and gave a beautiful speech about how proud TIE was of Dick Matthews and others like him. He spoke of TIE's sense of responsibility to the community and how an employee's volunteer work was rated quite highly by TIE, even so far as to be part of every employee's job objectives. Successful participation counted quite heavily in the individual employee's evaluation.

After the awards, the orchestra played big-band dance tunes. Dick and his wife didn't stay for that, but Malcolm danced with members of the women's board. Nancy and Tom got up to dance, and Jaylene, pleading a sore foot, was left at the table with Jerry and Angie, who said she didn't care to dance.

"Malcolm gave a very fine speech," Jaylene said to Angie.

"Yeah," Jerry broke in. "It was beautiful. We'll make the eleven o'clock news easy. Plus we had some national print media guys here too. It's super PR."

"That's good," Jaylene said. "I hope it will help."

"Well, it's hard to measure, Jaylene. But TIE will get a lot of good out of it, a lot of good. This is the type of PR you can't buy."

"Oh, I wasn't thinking of TIE," Jaylene said brightly. "I was thinking of Dick Matthews."

"Dick Matthews?" Jerry asked.

Jaylene took a deep breath. She knew that Jerry was going to catch a lot of flak about this because it had been his responsibility to check everything out before Malcolm agreed to accept the award. It was, however, the only way to save Dick's job.

"Yes," she said with a smile. "Dick is one of the three hundred people we're going to furlough at the end of the month."

Jerry's mouth dropped open and Angie shot a sharp glance at him.

"I suppose all this could be forgotten by the end of the month," Jaylene mused aloud.

Angie was still glaring at Jerry. "Honest to God," he squeaked, "I didn't know."

The sharp blue eyes then turned on Jaylene, but she just kept her smile innocent. "I don't know all the details," Jaylene said smoothly. "This all happened so fast and Kareau, who normally would be here, is out of town."

"Were you aware of Mr. Matthews's status?" Angie asked quietly.

"Of course," Jaylene said, deciding to lay the situation on the table. "His supervisor brought it to my attention. Mr. Matthews has suffered rather low ratings over the past few years, and his supervisor wanted to point out the extenuating circumstances of his wife's illness. I took it up with corporate personnel and they were quite adamant that it would not be wise to make an exception in Mr. Matthews's case. They were concerned with precedent."

"I see." Angie pursed her lips thoughtfully. She turned toward Jerry. "It would appear that with all the publicity generated today .corporate personnel should review the case again. Don't you think so, Mr. Dentman?"

"Definitely, Miss Shindelman," Jerry replied quickly. "There is no question in my mind."

Angie nodded her head. "I'll put your recommendation on Mr. Cabot's agenda for consideration, Mr. Dentman."

Before Jerry could voice his thanks, Malcolm appeared. "Don't we have an early day tomorrow, Angie?" he asked.

"Very early, sir," she replied, smiling. "I'll get the car. It was a pleasure meeting all of you." Malcolm graciously bid farewell to each person individually.

After Malcolm left, Jaylene looked cautiously at Jerry. Some color was starting to return to his face and he was frowning at her. She felt a twinge of guilt for the trouble she had caused him, but he wouldn't lose his job over it. Probably nothing more than a lecture.

She just smiled slightly and rose to her feet. What could he say to her, though? She was his commanding officer.

"I think I'm ready to leave myself," she said.

She told them to drop Jerry off first, then relaxed on the way back to her home, feeling good about the evening.

Sometimes it was nice to have power, especially when it could be used to help someone. She had accomplished something, and it felt good. If only she could use that power to help herself, everything would be perfect.

She sighed and looked out the window, refusing to do anything but savor the day's triumphs. She had a feeling that her future might not hold many more.

Chapter Twenty-six

On the way to Taiwan, Ray realized he was tired of traveling, tired of hotel rooms, and tired of his own company. Somewhere between TIE facilities, he realized he was tired of his barren little apartment, too. When his thoughts drifted ahead to the end of this consulting job, it gave him no sense of peace to think about returning to Boston.

On the plane to Seoul, he decided to consider seriously the request that he had received to write a textbook. The idea of staying a longer time in one place was becoming strangely appealing.

Throughout his stay in Seoul, he tossed about the notion of finding a new place to live. He considered a different apartment, or maybe even a small house. There were tax benefits he wasn't taking advantage of.

It wasn't until he was ready to return to the States, though, that the real shocker finally hit him. Whenever he looked forward to a nice, quiet, peaceful place to relax at the end of the trip, Jaylene was there. The actual surroundings were indistinct and somehow didn't matter. It was just her presence that made it seem like a home.

What had happened? Somehow, sometime, she had slipped through his defenses and had become a necessary part of his life. He had known that he hadn't wanted to let her go, but he hadn't ever stopped to find out why. He had thought he was opening himself up to her by suggesting that idiotic semipermanent, nonrestrictive relationship, but that wasn't what he had wanted at all. He just had been too afraid to look at himself any more closely.

He wanted her as a part of his life. A real part. A permanent part. He loved her. He wanted to marry her. He wanted their lives to mingle with that of their child.

The thought of his child stopped him cold as he remembered his and Jaylene's last meeting. They hadn't parted with any promises to meet again. In fact, she had acted as if she never wanted to set eyes on him again. Not that he could blame her. He had acted like an ass. Was it too late to win her back?

The desire to see Jaylene again was suddenly overpowering, and he changed his flight plans to fly to Miami before he went to New York. His flight from Seoul would arrive in L.A. around ten o'clock at night. He'd grab some sleep at a nearby hotel, then fly on to Miami and Jaylene in the morning. It would be Valentine's Day and the perfect time to plead his case.

When he called Rita to apprise her of his change of plans, though, he found out that Jaylene was leaving for Colombia the morning after his return. He would barely have time to see her before she'd be gone for almost a week. That was too long to wait. He told Rita to book him on a red-eye out of L.A. He could sleep anytime. It was more important that he see Jaylene.

The twelve-hour plane ride to L.A. was grueling. He tried to catch some sleep on the flight, but all he could think of was Jaylene. He wanted so badly to see her. Would she want to see him?

By the time the KAL jet landed in L.A., he was exhausted and stumbled getting off. A small, pretty Korean hostess grabbed at his arm to help him.

"Are you all right, sir?" Her beautiful almond eyes flashed concern.

"Sure," Ray replied. "I'm just a little stiff."

"Twelve hours in an airplane is very long. Do you want me to help you with your bag?"

"No, thank you. I'm old, but not that old," he growled as he walked off. He felt ancient, but told himself he just needed to walk around a little bit to get the kinks out of his system. Twelve hours on a plane was too long.

He felt bleary-eyed and dopey and certain Jaylene would refuse to see him. He had been such a jerk, purposely hurting anyone who got too close to him. It would serve him right if she wouldn't even let him into the TIE compound.

When he finally got through customs he was more tired than he could ever remember. His eyes stung and his muscles hurt. He jumped on a shuttle cart to catch a ride to the American Airlines terminal. He ought to get Jaylene some flowers or candy or something. He couldn't just arrive empty-handed on Valentine's Day. Maybe he could pick up something at Miami airport.

When he arrived at the American check-in lounge, he saw that he didn't have that much time. He checked in, entered the plane, and fell into his seat in the first-class cabin. He was so tired that he could barely move, but he was tired of sitting, too. He had been in airplanes so long that his mind and body screamed to escape.

It wasn't long before they were airborne and had settled into their flight lane to Miami. The drone of the engines aggravated a headache caused by tension and tiredness. His drink order consisted of a glass of water, two aspirin, and a cup of tea to settle his stomach.

The closer he got to Miami, the more uncertain he became. He knew he loved her, but he had no idea how she felt. The last few times they'd been together, she'd been anything but loving.

His thoughts went back to the case study he'd done in the fall. Every moment they'd spent together had been so special, and then when she had called him in New York, the magic had still been there. Until he had seen fit to spoil it. That was where the trouble had really begun, he finally admitted, that morning in New York when he had chosen the contract with TIE over her.

So exhausted that he couldn't sleep, he just leaned back and stared up at the ceiling. And what about the child? She had said that she was keeping it, but what if his stupidity the other day had caused her to change her mind?

He would back her up regardless of her decision, but he didn't want to feel he had forced her one way or another.

He looked anxiously at his watch. They had been in the air about two hours. What time would they get into Miami? He should probably ask the stewardess when she came by again.

Jaylene was shaking him by the shoulders and whispering in his ear. "Ray. Ray, wake up."

Good Lord. He had waited so long to see her and then he had gone and fallen asleep in her bed. Why was she keeping an old guy like him around? A beautiful woman could get herself a young man. Her tinkling laughter faded far away. Was she leaving?

"Honey," he called. "Honey."

The shaking increased and his eyes popped open.

"Sir," the stewardess was saying, a professional smile on her face. "We're about to land in Miami. You'll have to raise your seatback to an upright position, please."

"Oh, yeah," he mumbled and complied, feeling as if he were awakening from a drugged sleep. God, he felt awful. His hands and feet felt as if they had lead weights on them.

Two eternities later the plane docked and Ray was able to stumble into the terminal. He bought an overpriced and probably stale box of candy and put it in his briefcase as he moved automatically toward the baggage claim. He would pick up his bag and then catch a cab over to the TIE office complex. The clock on the wall said that it was just after seven in the morning. Jaylene ought to be there already.

He stopped for a moment. Was he supposed to call for a TIE limo when he came in? Or would they be waiting for him? For the life of him he could not remember what Rita had told him.

"Dr. Carroll?"

He looked up into a pair of pale blue eyes set into a hard, pale face. "We're your drivers from TIE. Do you have your bags yet?"

He looked from the man to his partner, a young unsmiling Latino. They were both wearing chauffeur's caps and black suit coats with the small TIE emblem on the outside of the handkerchief pocket.

"I was just going to pick them up."

'We'll go with you, sir."

"Fine," Ray said, and continued walking to the baggage claim. He found his claim tickets and handed them to the man.

While the Latino got his suitcase, Ray sat down. He hoped he wasn't so tired that he'd be incoherent when he saw Jaylene.

"Okay, let's go."

Ray's eyes popped open. He was surprised at the man's brusqueness, but he got up without saying a word. He was so tired that he probably couldn't recognize curtness or anything else. Besides, it wasn't worth making a fuss over.

The pale man led him out while the Latino followed with the bags. Ray didn't remember ever having two drivers pick him up before, but maybe the younger man was in training. Maybe with two drivers, he'd get there twice as fast.

The limousine was waiting outside. While the Latino put the luggage in the trunk, Ray climbed into the back seat. Another man was already there.

"We had to pick up someone else, Dr. Carroll. You know orders."

"As long as we're going to the offices I couldn't care less," Ray said, and settled himself down. The other man, fat and wearing dark glasses, merely nodded at him over the *Wall Street Journal.*

Just as well, Ray thought wearily. He was in no mood or condition to converse with anyone. He turned to close the car door when the Latino pushed in beside him. Ray blinked at him, trying to clear the fog in his brain enough to speak.

The other man turned as he was climbing into the driver's seat. "New security procedures, sir. One man has to ride in back."

Ray sighed but he moved over to the middle. All he wanted was to get to the goddamn office so he could talk to Jaylene. He had to see her before she left.

He stared straight ahead at the road as they left the airport and entered the expressway. No one spoke. He wiggled his nose at an unpleasantly sweet smell. One of these men certainly had a unique after-shave.

He tried to keep his eyes open and planned what he would say to Jaylene. He hoped she wouldn't have so many appointments today that he would have to wait hours before seeing her. Well, he'd just camp on her doorstep if necessary. He intended to see her and to make her understand that—

Suddenly Ray received a blow to his side just under his ribs and above his kidneys. He gasped in surprise and pain. Before he could move, his hair was grabbed and a rag soaked in that strange, sweet after-shave came down on his face. Then he felt himself falling.

The elevator doors opened and Jaylene found Rita waiting for her. "Oh, I'm so glad that you're here, Miss Sable," Rita whined as she wrung her hands. "Mr. Whitmore's been calling and wants to talk to you."

Jaylene glanced at the nearest wall clock. It was her normal time of arrival. What was Rita getting so upset about? "I always get here at seven, Rita. You could have told him that."

Rita hurried after her. "But he said that he wanted to talk to you."

"If I'm not here, I can't very well talk to him," Jaylene pointed out, trying to maintain a patient tone. "Can I?"

If Rita replied Jaylene didn't hear her. She and Nancy went into her office, where Nancy scanned her appointment schedule. "You don't have any outsiders at all today," she noted. "No little cupids coming to brighten up your day."

"Little cupids?" Jaylene asked.

"Sure," Nancy said. "The Easter bunny comes on Easter and Santa on Christmas, so it must be little cupids on Valentine's Day."

Jaylene forced herself to laugh. "I guess if it's romance and excitement you want, you've got the wrong office."

Nancy laughed as she left the room, and Jaylene turned her chair so she could stare out the window. Here it was

Valentine's Day already and how would she spend it? As she had spent New Year's Eve: alone.

She watched a bird flying high above their office complex. Should she call Jesse back or wait for him to call her? Her intercom buzzed. The decision had been made for her.

"Jaylene Sable speaking."

"Congratulations, you saved one of the minnows."

"Good morning, Jesse. Is corporate personnel going to review his situation?"

Jesse laughed heartily. "Come on, Jaylene. You know better than that. It's all resolved. Mr. Matthews is going to work for Jerry Dentman in PR. He's going to be a senior community relations specialist."

"That's nice."

"Yeah, it's a new position. Dentman's been given extra headcount for it." Jesse paused and then continued dryly, "The word's going out that it's something that Malcolm has wanted to establish for a long time. He was just looking for the right person. Anyway, what are you going to do about the other two hundred and ninety-nine minnows being thrown into the sea?"

"Nothing," Jaylene answered. "I got involved in that individual situation and I resolved it to a proper conclusion."

"That seems to be a feminine blind spot," Jesse said. "You get involved with one person and completely miss the big picture."

Jaylene chuckled. "I consider that a compliment, Mr. Whitmore. A male blind spot seems to be to forget the individuals who make up a whole organization."

Jesse was silent a moment and then he burst out with, "I have some news for you."

"What's that?" She straightened up in her chair.

"Margolis is resigning. Officially, it's going to be to pursue his own business interests. Actually, it'll be because we're booting him out. He had a kickback scheme going with our suppliers to our Far East plants and was netting a good piece of change for accepting substandard material."

"That's why he wanted the presidency of the new consolidated foreign subsidiary," Jaylene mused. "His kickback income would have tripled."

"At least," Jesse said. "Anyway, little girl, here's the new lineup. Burnbridge is retiring and we're bringing Kareau into a corporate marketing post, where he belongs anyway. That gives you a clear shot at the brass ring. There are a few good folks up here who are behind you."

Jaylene knew exactly whom he meant. She took a deep breath and slowly let it out. Jesse had always been straight with her, and now was not the time for her to sneak a card off the deck.

"I have some news for you, too, Jesse. I'm going to be a mother."

There was a very long silence before Jesse spoke. "Sometimes this modern world moves a little fast for an old country boy from Texas. You want to explain that to me?" His voice was quiet and controlled, a sure sign he was about to explode.

Jaylene wasn't worried though; she was sure about what she was doing. If he wanted to know how it happened, she'd tell him. "A man made love to me. One of his sperm got past my device and fertilized an egg inside of me. In about seven months I expect to give birth. That's all."

"That's all?" he snapped. "It sure in hell isn't all. Goddamn it, Jaylene. I want some details."

Her hand clutched the phone tightly but her voice stayed calm. "As in who, what, where, when, and why?"

"I mean, like what the hell are you thinking about, getting pregnant? I've invested a lot of time and effort in your career. I think I have a right to know what's going on."

She took a deep breath. "It was an accident. I never planned it."

"Accidents can be corrected."

"I don't want it corrected."

"What about the father?" Jesse asked. "Any chance he'll be a nice house-hubby? Or are you planning on doing the whole wife and mother bit?"

Jaylene pursed her lips tightly. "I'm not marrying the father."

There was a long tense silence on both ends of the line. Finally Jesse spoke. "My God, Jaylene. I can't believe you've thought this all through. Do you know what you're doing? What you're throwing away? The board of directors will have a fit when they find this out. Folks in Arp, Texas didn't like it much when an unmarried girl got pregnant, but their reaction is going to seem downright friendly compared to that of the board."

"I expect that," she said quietly.

Jesse sighed and his anger seemed to disappear. "Why don't you take some time off and go away to think this all over?"

"It won't change my mind."

There was another long silence, and when Jesse spoke again, she sensed he was starting to accept her decision. "Have you really given this serious thought, Jaylene?"

"Yes."

"You were really close to a big brass ring. I mean, based on annual sales, our new foreign sub itself would rank up among the top fifty corporations of the world."

She couldn't reply. She knew what she was giving up. But she also knew how much she was looking forward to the future with her child.

"The fast track is a merry-go-round that doesn't stop. You jump off, it's real hard to get back on."

"I know all that, Jesse. But this is right for me. I really have thought it all out, and I don't want the same things anymore that I used to want. I don't think I have for a while now."

"Yeah," Jesse replied as if he knew what she was talking about. "I thought you were a bit distracted the last few months. I was afraid that fire in your belly was going out."

"It's life in the belly now."

Jesse chuckled sadly. "You're so damn good at your job that I usually forgot you were a woman."

A lump came to Jaylene's throat. She knew that Jesse meant that as a compliment. He had judged her on her capability. The lump stayed and she could not reply.

"Well, you tell me how you want to handle this. We'll take care of it."

"Thank you, Jesse," she replied quietly.

"It's going to be tough to replace you. You were a tiger who played team ball. You're smarter than any two people I know, but the way you handled it, it didn't bother anybody." He paused a moment and then when he spoke again his voice seemed a little husky. "Good luck, honey."

The phone went dead before she regained her voice. She just hung it up slowly, then laid her head on her arms and cried. She wanted the baby more than she wanted TIE, but it was hard to give it up; hard, and frightening. It was also time to move on.

Ray could hear Jaylene calling for help. She was in trouble. He tried to run, but his feet felt like lead weights. He had been running along a river but mud was holding him back. Each step grew heavier. Jaylene's cries were getting fainter. His lungs were on fire and he was feeling light-headed. Oh, God. He was going to pass out.

Ray tried to make his eyes focus. He was looking up at a large white cloud, a large white sky?

Once his eyes worked, he still could not orient himself. He was lying on a cold floor and staring up at a dirty white ceiling. He turned his head slightly and looked around him. He was in an old bathroom. The fixtures were chipped and the pipes exposed. Where was he?

He slowly pushed himself into a sitting position and found that his feet were manacled and his left wrist was chained to a long water pipe near the bathtub. What the hell was going on?

His head ached, his eyes burned slightly, and the skin around his nose felt sensitive. He got to his feet, clinging to the sink to fight the dizziness, and looked in the cracked mirror. There was a redness around his nose and eyes. Otherwise he still seemed in one piece.

He looked around, but could not figure out where he was. The door to the bathroom had been removed, and he could see it leaning against the wall in the hallway outside the bathroom. He heard some muffled voices but saw no one. Where the hell was he, and why?

His mind was foggy and uncooperative. It was Valentine's Day and he was supposed to be seeing Jaylene. He had flown in from the Far East earlier that day. Or was it yesterday? And then he had come on to Miami where he had been met at the airport by two TIE employees. Two strange TIE employees. Why hadn't he asked for any identification?

He felt stiff and tried to stretch his cramped muscles, but the manacles restricted his movements and the chains rattled against the fixtures. A blond youth in his late teens suddenly came to the door and looked in on him, then left without saying a word.

Ray sat down on the edge of the bowl and fought off a wave of dizziness.

"Welcome to the Ritz Swampy, professor."

Ray looked up. It was the chauffeur. He had shed his coat, cap, and tie. His light tan shirt was open at the neck and the sleeves were rolled up halfway.

"What am I doing here?" Ray demanded.

"Right now you're sitting on the edge of your ass looking stupid," the man sneered. "But the folks who run things here are going to use you to make themselves a little change."

Ray stared at him. This was a kidnapping plot? "Are you sure you know who I am?" he asked slowly. "I'm just a professor at the Harvard Business School. And they won't pay any kind of ransom. I'm not that important."

"You're rat shit to me, professor," the man jeered. "But you're going to help us get Janie."

Ray shook his head. "I'm afraid you've got the wrong man," he pointed out. "I don't know any Janie."

The man's sneer turned to a mean scowl. "She calls herself Jaylene now, but her real name is Janie Switek and she's my wife."

Jaylene? Ray felt as if he had been kicked in the stomach. What could this foulmouthed creature have to do with his Jaylene? She would never have married a worm like this. Why, he wasn't even fit to be in the same room with her, the same city even. "She never said anything about a husband," Ray said defiantly.

The man's left cheek started to twitch. "That's 'cause she's a lying, two-timing slut. When this little job is over, I'm gonna make her sorry she was ever born."

The man's hatred worried him. Not for himself, but for Jaylene. She seemed so alone, so vulnerable. He remembered her reluctance to talk about her life before college and could understand it if Switek was part of it. Had she been as alone then, so that marriage to this lunatic was the only way open to her?

His heart bled for her, and he felt even worse for all the hurt he had caused her. Why had he been so wrapped up in his own fears that he couldn't see her needs? She had reached out to him so many times in the past, and he had backed away selfishly. How could he make up for it now? What could he do to keep her safe from this madman?

"Whatever happened between you and Jaylene is in the past," Ray said coldly, his fear for himself forgotten. "She probably divorced you years ago."

Switek's eyes went wild; his breath started coming in quick gasps as he advanced into the room. "We're still married and she's been cheating on me with you. She lay with you and now is with child," he said, his voice quivering with rage.

Switek's archaic language suddenly frightened Ray. And the more frightened he grew for Jaylene, the angrier he became, both with himself and with the situation. If only he hadn't been so selfish and fearful of involvement, she would have opened herself up to him more. Maybe she would have told him about Switek, and somehow this situation could have been avoided.

If only his hands were free, he'd fight Switek right now. He'd make sure Jaylene was safe, no matter what the cost. "Why don't you take these chains off?" Ray taunted. "Let's see how big you talk when my hands are free, too."

"I'm going to teach you not to touch another man's wife," Switek hissed. "I'm going to take care of you and then her."

Another man, a tall Latin, came into the room and

pulled Switek back just before he reached Ray. "Señor Switek," he said sharply. "We have a task to do."

They gazed at each other steadily for a moment and then Switek backed down. The Latino walked back out into the hall. When Switek looked again at Ray, his face was composed, although his eyes still had a wild glint in them.

"Okay, professor," Switek said. "We have a job for you."

Ray just stared at him, not saying a word or moving a muscle.

Switek pulled a paper from his shirt pocket and shoved it in Ray's face. "Here. We're going to put you on the phone to that little slut and you're going to read this."

"No," Ray said simply without looking at the paper. He had hurt Jaylene enough already; he would not hurt her any more.

Ray's resistance only inflamed Switek's anger. "You're gonna do what I tell you," he shouted, his face twisted with rage.

"No way, José," Ray repeated.

"You bastard," Switek screamed. "I ain't no damn spic." He pulled a gun from behind him and came closer. "You're going to do exactly what I say," he snarled.

Ray looked into the crazed eyes and figured that his end was near. He clenched his teeth and shook his head. There was no way he was going to cooperate in a scheme against Jaylene. Maybe it was best that she didn't know how he felt about her. Maybe this way their plan would fail.

Switek raised the hand with the gun and Ray tried to ward off the blow with his hand. The manacle pulled his hand up short, though, and he saw the pistol coming slowly toward his head. Then there was an explosion of color and pain.

Jaylene massaged her temples with the fingers of each hand. Telling Jesse hadn't been easy. She had expected he would be angry and he probably had a right to be. Over the years, she had always wanted what he wanted. TIE had always come first. She smiled grimly to herself. TIE had come first, last, and in between, because it was the only thing she'd had.

There was a light rap on her door and Nancy stepped in. "Sorry to bother you," she said, "but you wouldn't happen to know where Dr. Carroll is, would you?"

Jaylene glanced at her in surprise. "I thought he was in the Far East someplace as part of his study. Doesn't Rita have his schedule?"

"Yeah, she does."

"Then why ask me?"

Nancy looked uncomfortable. "Well, I just thought you might have heard from him. You know, you and he—" She stopped and shrugged slightly.

"We haven't done anything on a personal basis for a long time, Nancy."

"Oh, I'm sorry," Nancy replied. She turned to leave.

"Is he supposed to be back?"

Nancy nodded.

"It's a long trip," Jaylene said. "He's probably taking the day off."

Nancy shook her head slowly. "He arrived on an American Airlines flight from L.A. at seven this morning. A limo was supposed to meet him, but it had a minor traffic accident on the way to the airport. By the time it got there, he was nowhere to be found."

Josef raised his arm and struck the smirking face again and again as the professor went down. The bastard had laid with his wife and deserved to die. Janie had sinned, too, and would pay the price. But all in due time. Right now, it was the professor's turn.

Josef raised his foot to kick at the fallen man, but was suddenly jerked off his feet from behind. The pistol was snatched from his hand and he was thrown across the hallway and up against the wall.

"You relax, señor, or you die."

Josef stared into the huge barrel of the forty-five-caliber pistol. At the other end of the gun, he saw the hard, unemotional black eyes. His anger drained from him.

"I'm okay, Sandor."

The dark eyes did not even blink. He spoke in Spanish from the side of his mouth to the kid in the room, JC, who went into the bathroom and slapped the professor lightly on the face.

"He ain't coming around, Sandor."

"Get Lucia," Sandor said, this time in English.

"Hey, Sandor," Joseph wheedled. "Why don't we all sit down and relax?"

Sandor's face showed no emotion. "You move an eyelash and you are dead."

JC came hurrying back with a tall, slender woman. She went quickly over to the professor and put a hand to his neck. "He lives," she said quietly, and waved a bottle of ammonia under his nose. He still didn't move.

Goddamn sissy, Josef thought. How many times had he been hit a lot harder than that and hadn't gone out? How the hell was he supposed to know the guy was a weakling?

After trying several more times with the ammonia, the woman looked at Sandor. She shook her head and said something in Spanish.

Sandor merely grunted. Then he turned to JC. "You watch the crazy one. I must call Raoul."

JC nodded and came over toward Josef, waving his gun at him slightly. "Sit down, Joey. And spread your legs out in front of you."

Josef slid down the wall and did as he was told. He listened to Sandor's rapid-fire conversation on the telephone in the next room. "What's going on, JC? I ain't got the hang of the lingo yet."

"You're in deep shit and sinking," JC told him without blinking an eye.

He leaned against the wall and gazed in on the professor. Josef mentally measured the distance from where he sat to the door, but he quickly abandoned all thought of running. He had seen JC pop rats with his revolver and knew that he was fast and deadly.

Sandor returned to the hallway. "Raoul comes and so will Brewster."

"Brewster ain't planning to get involved at this level," Josef corrected him.

Sandor smirked. "He is involved from the very top to the very bottom."

Josef just shrugged as he leaned his head against the wall and closed his eyes. He had done what he had to do. He didn't care if Raoul or Brewster understood. A man had to punish those who brought shame to his family name.

The time dragged and Josef grew bored. Lucia checked on the professor several times, but he still had not come around. What difference did it make anyway? They had him, and that was enough to make Janie do what they wanted.

He sensed some movement and saw two men, cradling shotguns in their arms, go to the windows. They relaxed and spoke to Sandor in Spanish.

"Raoul's here along with your partner," JC told him.

Raoul and Brewster came in, followed by three other men. Raoul's face was set hard and Brewster was awash in sweat. His eyes lit on Josef and he moved quickly to his side. "You stupid bastard," he squeaked, and kicked him in the ribs.

"He deserves to die," Josef stated.

Brewster was about to deliver another kick when Raoul barked a command in Spanish. One of the men roughly removed Brewster and escorted him into the other room. Josef could hear the murmur of voices, but couldn't tell what they were saying.

"Say, JC," Josef said. "I'm a little dry. How about if you got up and got me a little water?"

JC shook his head. "They just about got your case taken care of. You're either going to be able to get your own drink or they're gonna slit your throat and it'll all spill out anyway."

Josef's face twitched angrily as JC chuckled.

Suddenly the murmuring stopped and the men trooped back. "You explain things to your friend," Raoul said to Brewster.

Brewster remained while the rest of them, including JC, went back to the kitchen. Laughter and the sound of beer bottles opening came from the back of the house.

Brewster glanced over at the still prone professor. "You are one stupid son of a bitch, Joey."

"He's been humping my wife," Josef protested in an aggrieved tone.

"She ain't been your wife for twenty years," Brewster said, his voice sounding strained. "Now listen and listen good." Then he went on. "This is our last chance. You blow this and we die."

Josef just stared at him coldly as he went on. "Since the professor isn't in speaking condition, you're gonna have to call your Janie. She's leaving for Colombia tomorrow. If she wants her professor back, she just brings the package that's delivered to her hotel back with her and leaves it on the plane. Got that?"

Josef nodded, not caring if Brewster's stupid plan worked. He had a score to settle with Janie and her professor, but he'd play along with the little game for now. More than the professor, he wanted his chance at Janie, and when he got that chance, nobody or nothing would stop him.

Jaylene's direct line rang shrilly.

"Jaylene Sable speaking."

"Hello, Janie."

The voice was all too familiar. Memories of terror and pain washed over her as her hand tightened on the telephone. "How did you get my private number?"

Josef laughed harshly. "Just shut up and listen to me. We've got your boyfriend. If you want him back, you're gonna have to do me and some friends a little favor. If you don't, that little bastard you're carrying will never know its daddy."

Her head spun with fear and her hands trembled slightly. "I don't believe you," she said. "You're lying like you always did."

"You damn slut," he screamed over the phone. "We've got him, and if you want to see him again you'd better play ball."

Jaylene willed herself to stay calm. She had to think straight. "I don't do anything unless I see Dr. Carroll. You tell that to your boss."

"I ain't got no boss," Josef shouted. "I got partners."

She fought not to get into an argument with him. He had always been irrational, but she could count on his hatred of her. And that's what was threatening Ray the most. "I have to see Ray alive and well before I'll do anything," she told him, her heart pounding madly.

"You better do what we say," he threatened.

"I have to see him first," she repeated. "No pictures or phone calls. I want to see him in person."

Josef laughed bitterly. "Any special piece of his person you prefer?" He slammed the phone down hard.

Jaylene hung up the phone and took a deep breath. She was trembling and felt as if she were going to be sick. My God! That maniac had Ray. All the careful barriers she had erected started to fall. The fact that Ray had rejected her and the baby didn't matter. She still loved him and was frightened for him.

She rose to her feet and pushed the button on her intercom. "Nancy, get in here," she barked.

The door popped open in a matter of seconds, but before Nancy could ask any questions, the words spilled out of Jaylene's mouth. "They've kidnapped Ray. My ex-husband, Josef, and some partners are holding him. They want me to do something in return for his life. I demanded to see Ray first."

Nancy was staring hard at her, but Jaylene couldn't hold on anymore. Her hands were already shaking and a cold sweat was breaking out over her body. Nancy's face swam before her eyes.

Chapter Twenty-seven

"Are you sure you're all right, Jaylene?"

Jaylene looked up into Nancy's worried face. "Yes, I'm fine. I just slipped. I tried to move too fast and I caught my heel."

She was still feeling queasy, but she was not about to tell anyone that. Nancy had spent enough time hanging over her anyway. Someone had to rescue Ray. Josef was a vicious and dangerous man. Ray could be killed.

Somewhere amid all the confusion, Lou Hawks, the corporate director of security, had come in and was deep in conversation with Lennie Carragio, their local director of security. Jaylene got up and moved purposefully to where they were standing.

"What's your plan, Mr. Hawks?" Jaylene demanded.

"We have it under control, Miss Sable," he replied shortly.

"You're not answering my question, Mr. Hawks," she snapped impatiently. "And I don't plan to ask it again."

His smile was not reassuring. "I've already executed my plan. I called the local authorities and it will be in their hands."

"Is that all?" She couldn't believe it.

"Miss Sable." His voice was just a bit too patient. "It's their responsibility. We don't even know if Carroll has been kidnapped, and if he has, it's not in our charter of responsibility to do anything."

What was wrong with him? Why couldn't he see that

Ray was in danger? "It's connected with TIE. They want some—"

"Look, ma'am," Hawks said smoothly, "I know that Dr. Carroll is a friend of yours and that he has a working relationship with TIE, but the local authorities are really prepared to handle this sort of thing."

It was time to use some ammunition. She was not leaving it to any local authorities who didn't know or care about Ray. TIE was going to do something. "Dr. Carroll is also Malcolm Cabot's godson," Jaylene said quietly.

Lou Hawks blinked at her, but covered his astonishment quickly.

"That's the Malcolm Cabot we all know as our CEO," she said, still in a very quiet voice.

"I gathered that, Miss Sable," Hawks replied dryly. "That is an interesting fact and certainly does put a new light on the proceedings." For the first time since Jaylene had met Hawks, his cynical smile turned up both sides of his mouth. "Could I use your phone, please?"

She nodded and he moved quickly to it. She heard him place an emergency call to Stuart Cavendish in their corporate office, but she was feeling light-headed again and sat down on the sofa. From there she could only hear snatches of Hawks's conversation and gathered he was asking Cavendish to contact the FBI in Washington, mentioning something about not wanting to step on the local authorities' toes.

What would she do if something happened to Ray? Not having him herself was one thing; knowing he might be killed because of his involvement with her, something else entirely. She felt warm and accepted a handkerchief to dab at her forehead.

Nancy came over to her. "I called Rose," she said.

Jaylene looked up, somewhat startled.

"I'd like her here, Jaylene. She's a real solid citizen."

Jaylene smiled and nodded. "I'd like her here, too." Then she quickly added, "And you, too."

Nancy squeezed her shoulder, and Jaylene felt a lump in her throat.

Another man entered her office and Hawks immediately

went to him. She could hear Hawks explaining that New York had just called and that the FBI had been alerted. It wasn't his fault, he assured the man. Corporate headquarters had done it. Jaylene smiled cynically. Everyone seemed so worried about protecting his own skin. Was anyone worried about Ray's?

Hawks brought the new man over to her. "This is Detective Kedvale, Miss Sable. He'll want to ask you a few questions."

"Fine." Jaylene smiled.

"Mind if I sit in?" Hawks asked.

Both Jaylene and the detective shook their heads. Then she repeated her story. The detective nodded from time to time and took notes.

Hawks frowned at her. "Did you say someone was going to pick Dr. Carroll up at the airport?"

"Yes," Jaylene said. "They had an accident on the way there. Nancy could tell you more about that."

They called Nancy over and plied her with questions about the travel arrangements for today and the regular procedures. Hawks was silent for several minutes, then spoke briskly. "Get everyone connected with the travel operation on this floor and lock them up someplace," he ordered Len Carragio. "I want them out of the flow of this operation."

Carragio nodded and went out.

The Miami detective got a puzzled expression on his face. "Aren't you violating somebody's constitutional rights? None of those people have been charged with anything."

Hawks stretched his thin lips across his teeth. "We're not arresting them. We're just changing their work area temporarily." He turned to Jaylene and coughed out a few chuckles. "We're just redecorating the office area. Right, Miss Sable?"

Jaylene just nodded. Did he suspect that someone here at TIE was involved? She ran quickly through the people up here. Who would want to endanger Ray's life?

"I would like just two things, Mr. Hawks," Jaylene said suddenly. "That my office be the situation command post

and that Nancy stay with me." She had to stay in touch
with what they were doing. Not knowing anything was by
far the worst.

Hawks hesitated.

"I know that she was aware of Ray's travel plans, but I
trust her, and I'd be more comfortable with her by me,"
Jaylene went on.

Hawks studied Nancy's expression, then looked back at
Jaylene and shrugged.

Ray was staring down at the worn linoleum. Had he
dozed off again? But then the dull, horrible ache in his
head answered his question. Oh, God, it worse than any
hangover he could remember. A slight moan escaped his
lips.

A female voice called out in Spanish, but Ray did not
have any idea what she was saying. His command of Spanish was only fair, and he was not fit to concentrate right
now. He tried to sit up, but the world tilted and he fell back
to the floor.

"Easy there, my friend, easy."

Ray looked up. A gray-haired man with calm blue eyes
stood near him. A black-haired woman with a hard face
stood behind the man. They helped him into a sitting position against the bathtub.

"Who are you?" Ray asked.

"A doctor," the man said. "A medical doctor."

"Doctor who?"

The man just smiled. "You are not in any position to
check credentials, my friend. Let's just say that I am the
best available."

The world was beginning to tilt again, so Ray closed his
eyes. Replying was just too much of a bother right now. His
head hurt so. He brushed at his forehead and was surprised to find it was bandaged.

"When you are able to stand I'll show you my work," the
doctor told him. "You will find it to be very professional."

He turned and said something to the woman. She returned in a moment with some water and the man's black

bag. She gave Ray the glass while the doctor took a couple of tablets out of a bottle.

Ray shook his head when the doctor tried to hand them to him. He didn't trust these people. Those pills could contain anything. But just the act of protesting made the pain double and triple.

"These will relieve the pain in your head. I would advise you to take them. It will make the next few hours bearable."

After a moment's hesitation, Ray took the pills and swallowed them. Right now he didn't care if the pills were a narcotic or a poison. The pain was so bad that he was willing to take the risk.

After Ray had swallowed the pills, the doctor checked his eyes and listened to his heart. "Without X rays I can't really be sure," he said as he replaced the instruments in his bag and closed it. "But you appear to be handling the trauma to your head reasonably well."

"Good," Ray replied sarcastically. "I'm sure they would prefer to shoot a healthy man."

"I didn't understand that to be in their plans," the doctor said quietly.

"Just what the hell are—"

"How is he, doc?" the Latin man from the airport asked.

"He's coming around." The two men went out into the hall for a whispered conversation.

Ray wondered where the other one from the airport was. Switek. The one who said he was married to Jaylene. Could she really have been married to that swine?

A nagging memory awoke more worries. How did Switek know Jaylene was pregnant? Ray doubted that she had announced it over the six o'clock news. So had Jaylene told him? Had she seen him recently? Did she see him regularly? Ray's head began to ache even more. The damn medicine wasn't doing a thing.

A little while after the doctor left, the Latin man returned with a very fat, profusely sweating man. "You talk to him," the Latino commanded, then left.

The fat man stepped over Ray and sat on the edge of the

bowl, balancing uncomfortably on the rim. He looked vaguely familiar.

"Damn heat," the man muttered, wiping his face with a dirty-looking handkerchief. "It really gets to me."

Ray didn't think it was hot at all, but he chose not to reply.

The man stared at the floor for a long time, then finally looked up and said, "We were all worried about you."

"I'll gladly go and relieve you of that responsibility."

The man tried to smile, but it just came out looking sick. "It ain't that simple, professor."

"Why are you holding me?" Ray asked. "No one will pay any ransom for me."

"Your girlfriend's real interested," he pointed out. "We're working out a little deal with her right now."

Jaylene? The mood she was in the last time he saw her, she'd probably laugh if they threatened to kill him.

"My memory isn't doing too well right now," Ray stated. "Which girlfriend are you referring to?"

"Cute, professor. Real cute. That Sable broad at TIE. The one that's carrying your kid."

How did they all know about the baby? If they all knew about that, why didn't they know that she had thrown him out of her life? Did he have any chance of convincing them that they'd made a mistake so they'd leave Jaylene out of all this? "You people obviously have some problems with your network," Ray said. "Jaylene and I are finished. That's not my child she's carrying."

"Come off it, professor," the man said wearily. "We both know that ain't true. If it wasn't your bastard, why would you have offered to marry her?"

Ray tried not to show his surprise. "If you know that much, you ought to know she refused me."

The man shrugged. "She may have refused you, but she sure was worried when Joey talked to her."

Damn. He hoped she had the sense not to get involved. Ray looked over at the fat man. "Who's Joey? The one who says he was married to her?"

"They were married all right, professor," the man snapped. "Right after she got thrown out of school for carrying dope for him, but they were divorced more than twenty years ago."

He really knew nothing about her life, Ray realized sadly. He knew nothing about any troubles she might have gone through; all he knew were the problems he had given her. And now it might be too late. He might never see her again, never be able to take her in his arms and tell her he was sorry.

"Anyway, professor," the man interrupted, "I ain't here to tell stories. We just need your girlfriend to do one little job for us. She does that and you're home free."

"What's this little job?" he asked suspiciously.

"She's taking a trip to Colombia tomorrow. While she's there, a package gets delivered to her room. All she has to do is bring it home and leave it on the plane. We'll take it from there."

They wanted her to smuggle in drugs in exchange for his life! He hoped she had called the police right after Switek called her. These guys were into the big time and he hoped Jaylene would stay far away. His head began to throb again.

"Anyway, she wants to see you," the fat man went on. "You know, see you sing and dance. You just tell her to follow instructions and everything will be fine."

Like hell he would!

Some of his anger must have shown on his face, for the other man quickly shook his head. "Look, professor, I ain't got nothing against either of you personally, so just follow along and you'll all stay healthy. But if you try any funny stuff, I'll be right with my partners in putting you away. The way I figure, you owe me one for putting the skids to Margolis."

"Margolis! How the hell do you know him?"

The man's face twisted in a semblance of a smile. "You might say that him and me were partners. We did some nice business together and were going to do even better in the future, but you put the kibosh to that."

"You didn't hitch your wagon to a very good star," Ray pointed out.

The fat man shrugged and then stood up. "They say

hindsight is twenty-twenty. Anyway, remember what I
said. When you see your girlfriend, just tell her to follow
orders and don't think."

"When am I—"

The man held up his hand, but before he could speak
Switek came to the door. "Hey, Brewster. I can't reach
that Kastle dame."

The fat man's face twisted angrily and he pushed Switek
from the room, berating him for his stupidity.

Ray just hung his head down between his knees. The
pain was dull and steady and at times a few spots would
dance before his eyes, but it was bearable. The realization
of just how much danger Jaylene was in, was not.

"You stupid asshole," Brewster hissed at Josef. "Where
do you carry your brains? Up your ass?"

"What's the matter now?"

"What's the matter? Hell, you call me by name, and talk
about that Kastle broad, and then ask me what's the matter?" Brewster spat angrily on the floor.

"It don't matter what the pretty boy knows. He ain't
gonna make it past sundown today," Josef stated coldly.

"You'd better check with Raoul about that," Brewster
warned. "He might have something to say."

"I don't give a damn what some fucking spic wants."

"Will you shut up?" Brewster hissed in his face. He
looked around, but the Latinos were lounging some distance from them. With luck, no one had heard Joey's stupid remark. "So, anyway, you can't get ahold of Kastle."

"No," Josef replied. "I called three, maybe four times.
She ain't at her desk. Some other broad wants me to leave
a message, but I didn't."

"Good," Brewster remarked.

"Hey, I wasn't born yesterday."

Brewster gazed at the pale, strained face in front of him.
The eyes were cold and expressionless.

He sighed. "Did you manage to find out when the Sable
broad leaves for Colombia?"

"Yeah, the dame at Kastle's desk says she's leaving between seven and seven-thirty this evening."

"Damn," Brewster muttered. "They moved it up. That means the meet has to be this afternoon." He started toward the front of the house.

Josef put up a hand to stop him. "I want my piece back."

Christ, that was all he needed. "Now, Joey," he said soothingly. "You got in trouble with that thing before."

"If I don't get my piece back," Josef threatened, "I'm taking all these spics out with my bare hands."

"I'll look into it," Brewster assured him, and went down the hall.

Damn. Everything was turning to shit. Margolis had wimped out and Joey was freaking out. If he got out of this in one piece, he'd be damn lucky.

Raoul's face split into a thin smile as Brewster approached him. "You are starting to stink like a herd of pigs, my friend. Are you nervous about something?"

Brewster clenched his teeth for a moment but decided to ignore the question. "The meet's gotta be around six."

"I understand that," Raoul said.

Brewster nodded his head. "Ah, Joey wants his piece back."

Raoul looked at him, his smile erased. "That man is crazy. Have you looked in his eyes? I wouldn't give him a plastic fork."

"Look, if we don't give him his piece, he's going to raise a ruckus."

Raoul just shrugged.

"We might need him," Brewster persisted. "The professor is real scared of him. He'll do anything Joey says. Let's use him to hold the professor up at the meet."

"You think there will be trouble?" Raoul asked.

"I ain't got no crystal ball," Brewster grumbled.

Raoul just watched him.

"Fill his cylinder with empty rounds," Brewster suggested. "Pull the heads, dump the powder and put the heads back on. That way he won't be able to shoot any of us in the back."

"You are a very creative person at times, Mr. Merrill."

Brewster shrugged. "It's an old cop trick. We used to do it for a joke."

Raoul laughed and patted him on the cheek. "A comedian, too. A man of many talents."

Brewster said nothing as he watched Raoul walk toward one of his men. One of his talents was survival, he told the man silently. He knew he wasn't making any profit out of this operation, but he was going to get out with his skin intact.

The door to Jaylene's office burst open and a black policewoman rushed in. The group of police officers, FBI agents, and TIE security personnel stopped talking and looked up.

"Someone called to check when Miss Sable's flight to Colombia was leaving," the policewoman told them. "Claimed they were from the mail room and had a package that had to get on the flight."

"Was it an outside call?"

"Yes," she said, then left. Jaylene assumed she was returning to her post at Rita's desk.

"They were just checking to make sure," someone said.

"Yeah, this is going to force them to make their move today."

"Hope they bite all the way. It's really got to be before sundown. The sharpshooters don't like the sniper scopes." Jaylene walked to her window to stare out at the postcard-perfect Florida day. Sunshine and not a cloud in the sky.

Had she done the right thing? As soon as she had received Josef's first call, she had notified security. Should she have waited? Should she just have kept her mouth shut and gone along with what they wanted?

The FBI was sure that they wanted Jaylene to return with a large load of cocaine. According to the DEA, segments of the underworld were jockeying for territory. A new group had money and men, but no product. The old group had a tight hold on the supply lines. If the new group could bring in one big load, they felt they could become established.

A pained smile twisted Jaylene's face. It sounded like a good problem for a business school case study.

She leaned her head against the glass. Oh God, how had

Ray gotten involved in all this? She knew, but didn't want to admit it to herself. He had gotten caught because of his presumed relationship to her. If they hadn't been involved, he would be safe. Josef would never have noticed him. He was in it because of her, and somehow she had to get him out of it.

This time a tear almost flowed onto her cheek. The heroine was going to rescue the hero, even though he didn't want her. So even if the rescue was successful, she'd still have nothing.

There had been two more calls from Josef, but he wouldn't put Ray on the line. He wouldn't even discuss it. Now they were waiting for his final call. What instructions would he pass along? Would they just insist she do their job for them, or would they let her see Ray? Had she done the right thing in demanding that? Should she have just gone along with their plot? It had all happened so fast, she hadn't had time to think out all her options.

"You're doing the right thing, honey."

Startled, Jaylene jumped at the voice at her elbow. "Oh! Hi, Rose. I was just—" She shrugged her shoulders, unable to continue speaking.

"This way, at least he has a chance. Otherwise, once the stuff was on the plane, they would just kill him."

Jaylene turned back to the window. "Yes, I suppose."

"That's fact, Jaylene," Rose insisted. "That's how that scum operate. They don't want to risk being identified by Ray."

"Maybe they have him blindfolded."

Rose shook her head. "An experienced debriefer from the bureau would still get a lot out of him. Nicknames, special sounds, smells, a lot of stuff. And these guys know that." Rose put her arm around Jaylene's shoulders. "You're doing the right thing, honey. This is the only way the two of you have a chance."

Two tears finally escaped to flow down her cheeks and she wiped at them. Maybe this was the only chance for Ray's life, but it would not change things between them. They had no future, and only the child she carried within her would be proof that they once had a past.

The ringing of her direct line jerked her out of her reverie. The crowded room became deathly silent. She let the phone ring one more time and when Hawks nodded she picked it up. An agent picked up the extension and turned on a tape recorder at the same time.

"Yes?"

Josef's rasping voice came across the line. "Go to Flager and Southwest Twenty-second Road. Across the street from the Buy-Low Station. In the telephone booth there'll be further instructions. Stuck in the Yellow Pages."

"How is Ra—"

The line went dead. Jaylene took a deep breath to gain control and then replaced the receiver as the room burst into activity.

TIE's security people went off to check on the limo that was being specially fitted for the expedition. The FBI agents made final contact with the pilot who would fly the traffic helicopter they had rented from a local radio station. Local police went about getting trucks with range-finding equipment in place and ready to roll in a matter of minutes.

The door opened and Detective Kedvale came in with a woman dressed in a business suit. "This is the stand-in," he announced.

The FBI group leader nodded and joined Jaylene near the window. "Sorry to put this pressure on you, ma'am," the agent apologized as the woman walked toward them. "We would have liked to give you a little more time, but we had trouble finding an officer small enough. She'll need to get a crash course in you."

"What?" Jaylene had no idea what he was talking about.

"She's your stand-in, Jaylene," Nancy explained to her.

Jaylene shook her head slowly. "You can't use a stand-in." Couldn't they see what danger that would put Ray in?

The man's demeanor stayed calm, but he beckoned to Hawks. "The woman is a professional, Miss Sable. This is the way we always execute such operations."

"We can't let you take a risk," Hawks added.

"I know you're just doing your job, Mr. Hawks," Jaylene said. "But I'm a very temporary asset for TIE."

A number of faces stared at her, blinking. "I am leaving TIE in a few weeks." After a moment's hesitation, she added, "For personal reasons."

Hawks quietly excused himself and walked out of her office. To make a quick call to New York no doubt, Jaylene thought. A statement like that would need verifying from his standpoint.

The other man remained professionally calm and, in a soothing voice, he went on, "I'm sorry, Miss Sable. Whatever your personal or business relationships are, we can't allow you to go through with this. We need a professional who will know how to react in this type of situation."

Why were they worrying about her when Ray was the one in real danger? "She doesn't look like me," Jaylene argued.

He smiled. "She's not a twin, but she is close. Now all you have to do is demonstrate some of your personal mannerisms, just in case they have someone who is familiar with you."

"My ex-husband is working with them," Jaylene said quietly. "He knows me quite well." Then anticipating his question, she added, "He's seen me, up close, as recently as a few weeks ago."

There was absolute silence in the office as she pressed on. "They would kill Dr. Carroll and your policewoman in a matter of a few seconds. That's how long it would take Josef to see that this woman was not I."

"Those are some new facts that we should review," the agent said in a careful manner.

"If you remember, sir," Jaylene said quietly as she looked at her watch, "we now have just under thirty-five minutes to pick up our instructions. You have no time to argue. I'm going."

Hawks returned to the room to hear the end of her statement. "It's her decision," he said curtly.

The agent took a deep breath to hide his irritation, then very firmly said, "Let's roll. No stand-in."

Everyone seemed to move at once.

Nancy and Rose went out of the office with Jaylene. The stand-in came with them, carrying her uniform, and she began changing back into it in the elevator. She gave her business suit to Jaylene.

"The jacket's been fitted with kevlar panels," Nancy told her as she and Rose helped Jaylene change her skirt. "Bulletproof panels," she explained.

Jaylene finished dressing in the limo. The bulletproof panels in the jacket only came to her waist.

As Rose was helping her with it, she whispered, "This will only protect your heart. If we had known you were going to do the meet, we would have gotten a longer jacket."

Jaylene looked at her in surprise. "How long have you known?"

Rose just hugged her. "Maybe a week or so, honey."

They clung to each other for a moment.

Chapter Twenty-eight

"Eat this," Nancy ordered.

Jaylene looked at the box of Chicken McNuggets that Nancy was handing her from the front seat.

"I'm not hungry," she responded wearily.

"You are going to eat those things by yourself," Rose threatened. "Or I will shove them down your throat, without any kind of sauce."

Jaylene shook her head, close to tears. "They're playing games with us, Rose. They've probably killed him already."

They had been driving for hours, circling, twisting, and turning, picking up instructions which led them to further instructions. They had just finished refueling for the second time.

"This is big business, Jaylene," Rose said. "They wouldn't waste their time playing games for nothing."

"You don't know Josef," she said. "He's sick."

"He isn't running this," Rose pointed out. "With the amount of money involved, the investors aren't going to leave any part of this operation in the hands of a nut."

The three of them were sitting in the car while Tom was off near an unmarked vehicle reviewing the latest set of instructions with Hawks, the detectives, and the FBI agents.

Nancy shot them a quick glance and turned back to Jaylene. "Eat, Momma," she ordered quietly.

Jaylene looked from Rose back to Nancy. "Have I been carrying a sign around my neck or what?"

They both just smiled mysteriously, then Rose tapped

the box in Jaylene's hands. With a sigh, Jaylene opened it and took one.

"They're cold," she grumbled.

"That's what you get for arguing," Rose said gruffly. "I always told my kids that God made the food cold if you argued with your mother."

Jaylene smiled wanly as she forced herself to continue eating. Even just the few minutes of joking had helped. It gave her a chance to stoke the flame of hope a bit. She put another piece in her mouth and sighed when she saw there were two more pieces left.

"Something's up," Nancy said.

Jaylene's head popped up and she saw Tom hurrying toward the car. She started to put the box aside, but Rose stopped her.

"I thought you were Italian," Jaylene grumbled. "You're acting more like a Jewish mother."

"I'm a grandmother," Rose said. "That's a nondenominational profession. Hurry up and finish those things."

Jaylene put another piece in her mouth and then put the box under the seat as Tom leaned in the window.

"This looks like it," he announced. "Rose, go with that agent." He indicated a blue Plymouth with his head. "They just want the three of us in the limo, Miss Sable."

Rose gave Jaylene a hug, and left as Tom climbed quickly into the driver's seat. He handed Nancy a map, then pulled the car into the traffic.

"They're directing us into that area with the red X," he said. "We talked to a sergeant familiar with that sector. He said that it was mostly open area with some old barns."

"This lake very big?" Nancy asked.

Jaylene moved forward onto the jump seat behind Nancy so that she could see and hear what they were discussing. She wasn't familiar with the area but she just felt better being part of the action.

"Four, five acres," Tom said. "There's a big swampy area behind it. They're having us come in from this side."

Nancy looked at the map and then out the window. "Smart," she muttered. "They're bringing us in from the east. By the time we get there, we'll be looking right into the sun."

"Will that be a problem?" Jaylene asked quietly.

Nancy didn't answer immediately, but looked at Tom. "Is it a big open space?"

"The sergeant said three, four hundred yards across."

Then Nancy turned to Jaylene. "At that distance, the sharpshooters will have to use scopes. The glare from the sun in their faces will be a little bit of a problem, but their biggest concern is that the sun will reflect off the scopes. These guys will be looking for that, and if they see too many flashes, who knows what they'll do."

Jaylene's stomach quivered in fear. She knew what they would do: they would kill Ray for sure.

"Move back, Jaylene," Nancy ordered as she came scrambling over the front seat into the back of the limo. She spread the map out before them. "Okay, let's go over the whole thing. These little boxes are where the barns are. They'll probably bring Ray out of one of them. They'll most likely have us stop the car out away from the barns. You'll have to walk to them."

Nancy stopped and looked into her face. "The stand-in is trailing us. You can still change your mind."

Jaylene just shook her head numbly. Her voice was petrified with fear, but she would not back out.

Nancy continued. "The range-finder trucks will be here and here." She pointed to spots on the map. "They'll home in on your bug."

Jaylene checked for the little device that was disguised as a button on her jacket, then silently nodded.

Nancy smiled encouragement. "Walk until you're about ten feet from whoever is there. Then stop. The range finders'll triangulate on your position. Talk. Say anything to anybody, but talk. They need at least fifteen seconds to locate your coordinates and feed them to the sharpshooters. At the end of about fifteen seconds, you hit the ground and hug it. I'll give them the signal and all hell will break loose."

Jaylene nodded.

"You can still call for the stand-in."

She shook her head. Nancy hugged her, then, without a word, crawled back into the front seat. Jaylene heard Nancy and Tom review the special changes that had been made to the limo. She heard the murmur of their voices but did not connect any words to them.

Ray could die today; she could die. All three of them could die today. She knew she was risking their child's life, but she loved its father, too. She couldn't stand by and not help. Maybe somehow they would all be fine. They had to be.

Ray was blindfolded but the dots still danced in front of his eyes. Either the medicine was wearing off or it hadn't been strong enough in the first place. His head was really starting to pound again. That rap he took when Josef had shoved him into the car hadn't helped, either.

They had left the house he had been held in about a half hour ago, he guessed. He had been blindfolded and couldn't see where they were or where they went, but from the sounds and smells he knew that they had left the city. The road they had been on last was gravel in parts, dirt in others, with lots of ruts and potholes. He could be wrong, but he suspected that now they were in a barn. It might not have been used for the last several years, but the smell of moldy hay and animals was still strong.

"They should be here in about twenty minutes." He recognized the voice of the blond man they called JC. "I'm going to go out and wait for them."

"Where's the crazy one?"

That sounded like their leader. Ray thought he was called Raoul. He was trying to remember these details so that he could help the authorities when he escaped. If he escaped.

He tried to force his pained mind to think. He had to escape. That would be the only way to keep Jaylene out of the trouble that she was being dragged into. The only question was, how? He had already tested the manacles and they were tight on both his wrists and ankles. The damn blindfold didn't help any, either.

"Do you think the woman will really come?"

"I don't know," the voice that he knew as Brewster responded. "Most of the time the cops will go with a stand-in, you know, a police officer that's built pretty close to the mark. But I don't think that will happen here. That's a tough lady that does what she wants and this meet was her idea."

"That is true."

Damn. He hoped it wasn't true. He was smart enough to play along with whomever they sent. Jaylene did not need to come herself.

"The chances are good that she just wants to see if her lover boy is alive. He is the father of her kid. If he's okay, she'll go ahead and pick up the merchandise."

"If you have a god, Mr. Merrill, you had best make some offerings to him."

"No sweat, man."

Merrill. Brewster. His voice had a definite quiver to it. Mr. Brewster Merrill was very much afraid.

Hope and fear raced through Ray's mind. He certainly hoped that he would get out of this alive, but he was more worried that Jaylene was going to show up. He kept telling himself that she wouldn't be that foolish, but he just didn't know. Maybe she felt she owed him something. She owed her baby life, that's who she owed something to. He hoped she had sense enough to see that. He stopped and swallowed hard. Their baby; he corrected himself mentally. She owed their baby life. Lord, he'd give anything to be around to see their child.

"Limo coming up the road," JC announced.

"It is time for Mr. Merrill and me to leave, Sandor. You take care of things here."

"Yes, sir."

"Blackie will come with me and Spider and Reyes will go with Mr. Merrill."

"I don't—"

"Our sponsors insist, Mr. Merrill. The roads twist and turn like a snake. Also, some very bad people tend to congregate in this area. We want to keep you safe and sound."

The threat in the voice was obvious, and there was no other sound from Brewster.

"JC and Smokey stopped the limo."

"We are going now. Spider, take him." There were some shuffling steps. "Sandor, I leave you six men, plus the two out front. If things don't go well, kill the professor, then make your way to the boat."

There was silence, and then Ray heard a boot scrape near the door. He tensed himself for the unseen enemy.

Tom turned the limousine off the county road onto a muddy track. Thick vegetation surrounded them. Jaylene clenched her hands nervously. She felt more at home amid steel and concrete. Even the trees here seemed threatening.

"Open the hatch and then yank on that little yellow wire hanging down under the dash," Tom told Nancy.

Jaylene saw her push a button on the dashboard, then heard the quiet hum of a motor opening the sun roof above her. Hot, humid air came in. As Nancy bent low, Jaylene moved forward to the jump seat.

"Hatch motor all dead," Nancy announced as she sat up, flashing a brief smile at Jaylene.

She tried to smile back but her stomach was a mass of bouncing butterflies. She dearly wished that they could stop at a bathroom right now.

"Got the second set of keys?" Nancy asked Tom.

"Yeah, in my sock."

"That's good." She smiled. "They'll find them, but it's not too obvious."

"You want them to find the keys?" Jaylene asked, puzzled.

"We're guessing that they're going to stop the car a good distance from where you'll meet Ray and make you walk the rest of the way. And just to keep us from driving in after you, they'll take our keys."

"So why do you want them to find the extra set?" she asked.

Tom laughed grimly. "Because we don't want them to check the car out too closely."

She looked at him but he kept on driving. Nancy saw her puzzled look and explained. "We had our mechanics do a little adjusting. They'll probably take both sets of keys, so there's a little ignition button under the dash that'll work just as well."

"And there's another button on this side that'll open up a little hiding place we had made," Tom told her, glancing at her in the rearview mirror.

"What's in there?" Jaylene asked.

Nancy gave Tom an irritated look.

"Is it something that you don't want me to know about?"

"We just don't want to distract you," Nancy replied.

Tom glanced quickly at Nancy, then turned slightly to see Jaylene. "There's an Uzi in there for me. A machine gun," he added. "We aren't letting you go in there without some protection behind you."

"Oh." She suspected that was meant to reassure her, but it didn't. They were playing games with Ray's life. What if his captors found the ignition button? Or the machine gun? They'd probably all be killed.

Nancy seemed to read her mind and tried to explain the operation more fully. "When the sharpshooters start firing, Tom and I are just going to lay down a little covering fire. That's why we left the hatch open. I'm going to drive, and he's going to stand on the seat and spray lead with that little Uzi."

She took Jaylene's hand in her own and gave it a comforting squeeze. "You walk to about ten feet in front of Ray. Then hit the dirt. Hug the ground no matter what you hear. Tom will keep his fire high, but the sharpshooters will be going for the bull's-eye."

Jaylene nodded, trying to keep herself from trembling. She could do it; she just had to hold herself together a little bit longer.

"They'll probably have some guys in the barn," Tom added. "So there could be a lot of lead flying around. Plus there'll be a heap of noise. Sirens. Gunfire. Maybe some screaming, but you just stay down."

She could do that. Walking was going to be the problem. How could she walk when her legs felt like rubber?

"Play like you're a little mole, Jaylene."

There was so much to remember. So much that could go wrong.

"And don't forget," Tom reminded her, "you have to make them come out into the open. Stay out in the clearing and make them come out. The sharpshooters need a clear line of fire."

"If they argue," Nancy added, "just tell them you're not falling for any of their crap. Tell them you know if you go near any building, they'll capture you, too. You may have to bluff them."

Jaylene just nodded, looking from Tom to Nancy and back again. But weren't they leaving something out? She wasn't going to be the only good guy there.

"What's going to happen to Ray?" she asked. "Will the sharpshooters know what he looks like?"

"He's a smart guy," Nancy assured her. "He'll get out of the way."

What if he couldn't? What if something happened? What if he's confused? Or surrounded by his captors? Oh, God, anything could happen.

She glanced out the window, hoping to distract her thoughts. The trees had thinned out somewhat and she caught glimpses of the lake far off to their left.

"Jaylene," Nancy said quickly. "If you have any doubt whatsoever—"

"There's the welcome wagon, ladies," Tom interrupted.

"It's gonna go, babe." Nancy's voice was hard and jarring. "It's gonna go. You gotta believe."

Jaylene nodded as she stared out the front window. Two men were standing off to the side of the road, waving them down. Beyond them was a open space with only weeds and tall grass growing. An old barn was in the distance.

"They have Uzis too," Nancy remarked under her breath.

"Quality people use quality equipment," Tom said.

Jaylene made herself smile at the rough humor as Tom pulled to a stop beside the men. One was a thin blond and the other a tall, heavy black man.

"They look like an equal opportunity employer," Jaylene said, forcing herself to match their humor. Nancy patted her hand.

The blond man waved them out of the car with his gun. They stood on the muddy track as he searched them. Tom first. They laughed when JC found the extra keys and put them into his pocket. Then he searched Nancy and Jaylene.

After finishing Jaylene, he snickered. "How was that, ladies? Slow enough for you?"

Jaylene felt unclean after the man's pawing, but she remained silent.

"Those kevlar panels look real tough," he remarked, then laughed. "What're you gonna do if we shoot you in the head?"

Nancy took control. "We didn't come here for a church social, fella. Let's get on to business."

The blond man smirked and walked back to pick up his gun, while the black man spoke into his walkie-talkie unit. "We're sending the lady up." He pointed toward the dilapidated barn partially visible in the distance.

"Wait a minute," Nancy said, putting a hand out to stop Jaylene. "I don't see anybody there."

"He's in the barn, sweetie," the blond told her.

Nancy shook her head. "No dice."

Jaylene put her hands behind her. She didn't like this kind of bargaining. Ray's life was at stake. But she had to trust Nancy, she reminded herself. She had to trust Nancy.

"The name's JC," the blond snarled.

"Bring the merchandise out, JC," Nancy said quietly, staring at him without blinking. "Or we all go home and you explain to your boss why this whole operation went down the toilet bowl."

JC glared at Nancy, then he turned to the black man. "Smokey, tell 'em to bring the professor out."

The man called Smokey mumbled into his unit. There was some sputtering and static.

"They don't like it, JC. They don't want the professor out alone and no one wants to come out with him."

Jaylene could hardly breathe. Now if this whole insane plan would just work.

"Tell 'em to send the crazy out."

Smokey put the unit to his mouth, but before he could speak, JC snatched it from him. "Let me talk. That nut's probably hanging around." He spoke into the unit in Spanish.

Then he turned to Nancy. "They'll bring him out. Then you can put the glasses on him and see he's okay." He handed Jaylene a pair of binoculars.

Nancy shook her head. "We'll put the glasses on him just to make sure it could be him, but the lady sees him up close."

"Who the fuck you trying to bluff, blondie?" JC snarled. "You aint' got no chips to bet."

"My boss lady has the plane, junior."

"I told you the name is JC, bitch."

Jaylene could scarcely breath as he spoke into the walkie-talkie in Spanish again. Along with having to go to the bathroom desperately, she now felt like she was going to throw up. They wouldn't hurt either her or Ray, she tried to convince herself. They needed them both. Her for the airplane, Ray for insurance that she'd obey. Neither JC nor Smokey suspected anything else might happen. She quickly pushed the thought of the rescue plan from her mind, for fear one of them might read it on her face.

JC stopped talking into the walkie-talkie and listened for a moment. The answer came back as affirmative and they all turned to look toward the barn. Two figures came out a door and moved over to the near side of the building. Jaylene started to raise the binoculars to her eyes.

Nancy snatched them. "Let me take a look, Miss Sable."

A tremor of irritation went through Jaylene. Why was Nancy pushing in like that? She raised the glasses to her eyes and then quickly looked at Jaylene. "He looks something like Dr. Carroll, boss lady. You can go up for a closer look."

Jaylene just nodded and started to move forward. Nancy tossed the binoculars to JC and then took Jaylene by the shoulders. "Just walk slow and steady. We have some excitable folks around. Make sure it's Ray and then do what we told you." She stared hard at her and Jaylene nodded her head. "Just turn around and come back," Nancy added quietly. Then she gently pushed Jaylene off.

Jaylene took a few steps through the tall grass. Turn around and come back? Was Nancy changing the plans? Had she seen something amiss? If she did, why were they sending her out? Was it really Ray?

Jaylene took a deep breath to steady herself. More than likely Nancy's last bit of advice was to throw the two men off. If they had even the slightest suspicion that something was wrong, she was sure they would kill Ray.

The ground was rough, so even without Nancy's advice, Jaylene would have had to walk slowly. She stepped in a hidden puddle and her foot sank up to her ankle. She was glad she hadn't worn a favorite pair of shoes to work today, she thought, fighting back the urge to giggle. Something snagged her stockings and she felt them tear. TIE's PR department better not have scheduled a meeting with the press when this was all over. She wiped her sweating hands on her skirt.

She could see the two figures near the barn more clearly now and she felt her heart skip a beat. One of the men was Josef. The other looked like Ray, but his head was bandaged. Oh, dear God, was he hurt?

When she was about three tennis court lengths away from them, she stopped. She had to get them out in the open somehow. The whole rescue depended on it. She thought quickly.

"Come away from the barn, please," she called out, trying to control the tremble in her voice.

"You're not giving orders here, Janie," Josef shouted back. "Now get over here like a good little girl."

She took a deep breath. It was her wits against Josef's. Surely that was a battle she could win. After all these years, here was her chance to come out on top.

"The sun's in my eyes, Josef. I can't see."

"Shade them with your hand and get over here, stupid."

"They said I wasn't suppose to."

"I said come here," he almost screamed.

Jaylene bit her lip. Some of her old fears trembled at the edge of her will, but she refused to recognize them. She was stronger now, tougher. She wouldn't fold under his hatred as she used to. Ray's life, and possibly her own, hung in the balance.

She took a deep breath. If she could outwit all of TIE so that Dick Matthews kept his job, she could outwit Josef.

"I can't, Josef. They won't let me." She didn't have to fake the tremor in her voice.

"Damn," Josef swore. "How did someone as dumb as you ever get a supervisor's job?" He yanked at the other man. "Come on, professor. Move your ass out here."

They were coming toward her and Jaylene felt her body start quivering. It was Ray and he was hurt. He was moving in a very strange, slow manner, and his head was bandaged. What had they done to him?

She wanted to run to him, hold him in her arms and protect him, but Josef's hatred came across the clearing as strongly as any words. If she couldn't protect him, at least they would die together. She clenched her teeth and forced herself not to move. Pull them out as far as she could was the order.

Josef stopped about a hundred feet from her. "I ain't walking another step, Janie. If you want to see your boyfriend, get your ass over here."

Jaylene started walking again. They were well away from the shadow of the barn and from any trees that might block the sharpshooters' vision. Now she was supposed to hit the dirt. Except she wasn't going down alone, leaving Ray to figure out what was going on by himself.

She flashed Ray an encouraging smile when she had crossed about half the distance. It's all going to be okay, she tried to tell him, but his answering glare was anything but friendly.

"Jaylene," he shouted. "What the hell are you doing here? Get out. For God's sake get out of here."

He tried to wave his hands, but they were manacled. The sight of the chains nearly tore her heart out. Then he tried to move toward her, but Josef grabbed him by the arm.

"Go back," Ray yelled at her. "Will you get the hell out of here?"

"Easy, lover boy," Josef sneered.

Seeing that his attention was on Ray, Jaylene began running forward, but uneven ground slowed her progress. Another thirty feet at least before she could get him down. Would Josef stop her?

"Ray, darling," Jaylene cried and ran toward him, her arms spread wide as if she couldn't bear to be apart from him.

"Ain't that cute?" Josef sneered. "Old Janie's running straight to hell."

Ray jerked loose from Josef. "Jaylene, stay away from me," he screamed.

He threw his weight at Josef and knocked him off balance just as she was flying over the last few yards. She threw her arms around Ray and knocked him to the ground. They would be safe now, she prayed. They had to be safe.

Ray pushed her off of him. "Jaylene, get yourself away," he insisted and tried to struggle to his feet. "I'll take care of Josef."

Tears of panic flooded her eyes as she scrambled toward him. "No, Ray. Stay down. You've got to stay down." She grabbed his leg and tugged at his arm, keeping him from rising.

"You goddamn slut. You're going to hell."

Josef's twisted and contorted face was before them. His pistol was pointed at her. She couldn't breathe. She couldn't even move. Josef's mouth moved as hatred and venom poured forth, but she couldn't even hear the words. All she saw was the gun pointed at her.

Suddenly Ray threw her to the ground and flung himself on top of her. She could hear him shrieking obscenities at Josef, but nothing seemed real except that gun and Josef's face.

The gun moved closer and closer, then made a sound like a muffled cap pistol. She and Ray were both going to die. Their child would never be born. Her hands clung to his body, and tears blurred her vision. The gun made another muffled pop and she realized someone was screaming. It was her own voice.

Then there was a loud crackling sound and Josef's head

exploded. Her screaming changed into wild sobs and she closed her eyes, burying her face in Ray's shoulder. His arms stayed around her as the world exploded into a torrent of sound that seemed to go on forever.

Screams and explosions split the air. Gunfire seemed to be all around them. How could they possibly not be hit? Ray's arms tightened around her as another burst of gunfire broke out to her right. Then there was a moment of silence before she heard shots off to her left.

Suddenly the noise of a siren grew louder than the sound of the guns. Jaylene opened her eyes cautiously, blinking in bewilderment. "We're not dead?"

"Not yet," Ray grunted.

From where she lay under Ray, she saw the TIE limousine swing around close to them. The next thing she saw was Nancy running toward them, grinning.

"You guys don't waste any time, do you?"

Jaylene just stared at her as Ray released his hold, then she sat up, wondering if she'd ever stop shaking. Her suit was splattered with mud and blood. She looked up to see Josef's body lying near her. Her stomach turned and she looked away, watching Ray get unsteadily to his feet. He didn't seem to be too worried about what they had just gone through. In fact, he looked furious.

"Did she tell you?" he demanded of Nancy. "Did she tell you she's going to be a mother?"

Jaylene stared at him. What was he ranting for now? Had they bumped him on the head one too many times? Didn't he notice he had been rescued? Largely through her efforts, she might add.

She turned away as multiple sirens converged on them. From where she sat, she could see police cars and unmarked vehicles coming into the clearing, lights flashing.

"Keep them down, Nancy," Tom shouted sharply. "Stray rounds in the area."

Nancy knelt down and pulled Ray along with her. "Get down, doc. It's a little dangerous to stick your head up yet."

"I know it's dangerous," he snapped. "So why the hell did you allow her here?"

Jaylene was getting a little annoyed. He was talking about her as if she weren't here. Or else didn't have brains enough to speak for herself.

"Hey, it wasn't my decision," Nancy said, absolving herself of all responsibility. "The lady decides those things for herself."

Ray turned toward Jaylene, his eyes still burning. "What in heaven's name ever possessed you to put yourself in this situation?"

"You were in trouble," she pointed out sharply. Whatever they had done to him must have rattled his brains.

"I was in a tight situation. I was not in trouble. There was no reason to risk your life and the life of your child—our child—in such a stupid way."

"Would you have rather been killed?"

"I would rather have not been responsible for your risking your life."

Jaylene just stared at him for a moment. Anger had stopped her trembling and she was starting to feel more like herself. After the way he had treated her in the past, he was going to berate her for saving his life? If that wasn't just like him!

"Believe me, there was absolutely nothing personal in my actions," she informed him. "You were involved in this solely because of your relationship to me and to TIE. I would have felt honor bound to do the same for anyone in this situation."

"Oh, would you? That shows how little sense you have," he snapped.

Jaylene refused to engage in such a stupid argument, noticing suddenly that the gunfire had stopped. There were just flashing lights and policemen milling about. With the noise of the attack quieted, Ray's strident voice was more noticeable and they were becoming the center of attention. It was about time she showed that she, at least, had some control and put an end to his little tantrum.

She got to her feet and turned to Nancy. "Are the paramedics around?" she asked. "I think one should check Ray's head. The wound could be serious."

Ray got to his feet also. "The paramedics are needed all

right, but not for me. You're the one they should be checking."

"Me?" she cried angrily, all her good intentions forgotten. "I may have been insane for caring what happened to you, but I don't need the paramedics."

Two men in uniform came hurrying toward them with medical bags. She spoke before Ray had the chance. "Please check this man over carefully. He has a head wound which seems to be rather severe. And getting worse by the moment."

"I'm fine," Ray insisted, glaring at her. "You need attention more than I do. I'm not a pregnant older woman."

"I'm not all that old."

"Old enough to know better than to throw yourself into the middle of a gun battle when you're pregnant."

"Hold it, people," one of the paramedics interrupted them sharply. "We have enough room in the ambulance for both of you. So why don't you save your energy for something else?"

"Fine," Jaylene agreed, not bothering to look at Ray. An ambulance was driving slowly toward them over the rough field. It stopped alongside them, and one of the paramedics pulled open the door. Both she and Ray glared at each other. Neither of them moved. "Ladies first," he said with wave of his hand.

"Thank you," she said coldly.

She climbed in and sat on the jump seat, leaving the stretcher for him. Her lips were tight as she cast him an occasional angry glare. Was it just that morning that Nancy had thought her Valentine's Day lacked excitement and romance? Somehow she preferred her schedule as it had been.

"Sounds like a heap a excitement back there, Reyes."

The man called Spider had stopped the car and was listening through the open window. Brewster heard the crackle of rifle fire in the background and then the whine of many sirens.

That bitch. It sounded like she had gone ahead with a

rescue operation. Just went to show that you couldn't trust anyone these days.

The cops were probably operating under radio silence but Brewster knew that it would end soon. Then the news of the rescue would come over the scanner they had in the car. He really didn't care to hear it. The professor was dead or snatched back. Either way, it was over. It was time to run.

"I hope you like boats, Señor Brewster," a quiet voice spoke from in back of him.

Sweat was starting to pour out of him. Brewster just stared straight ahead of him. He didn't want to excite Reyes. Brewster knew that he was the dangerous one.

"Sure, Reyes," Brewster replied. "I like boats. Why?"

Spider snickered. "Raoul's gone to his boat. He said if anything goes wrong to bring you over."

"Who says anything's gone wrong?" Brewster demanded.

"This is a very quiet area, señor," Reyes's voice purred from behind. "To have so much noise is most unusual."

"Damn it," Brewster burst out. "It could be just a big car accident on the interstate."

"It's too far away for the noise to be this loud," Spider said. "Plus that sure sounds like a deer rifle to me."

"You guys are just—" The crackling of the scanner and Reyes tapping him on the shoulder seemed to hit him at the same time and he froze.

"Operation Harvard successfully complete. Mop-up in progress. All perimeter units be on the lookout for fleeing perpetrators. Will be on foot and by auto."

"That's it, Brew." Spider's smile was hard and Brewster swallowed painfully. "We're going for a little boat ride."

"Let's pull over and talk about this," Brewster whispered hoarsely.

"Can't do that, Brew."

Brewster groaned and closed his eyes. His stomach was churning and he needed a bathroom. "Pull over, Spider, will you? I need to take a leak."

Spider laughed as he halted the car for a stop sign at the two-lane county road. "Maybe the lady there has a handkerchief you can use."

Brewster's eyes rolled open and he looked straight at a short woman with dark hair. She was leaning on the car door and talking to a man near the front of the car. Stupid bastards. Didn't they even recognize an unmarked car when they saw it? The damn broad was probably a detective.

Suddenly the woman turned toward him and their eyes met. It was instant recognition. What the hell was Rose Locollini doing here? A spasm of pain shook him and Brewster bit his lip and closed his eyes again.

"I think we'd better cross this road and continue on the gravel one," he said softly. "It wouldn't be wise to bother the police."

They slowly crossed and bumped onto the gravel road on the other side.

Reyes spoke softly from the back seat. "The woman, Spider. She is jumping into the car."

"What the hell did you do, Brew? Make a face at her?"

Brewster opened his eyes. "Goose this thing, Spider. She made me. We worked on the force together a long time ago."

"You a cop?" Spider asked in shock.

Strong fingers grasped the hair on the back of his head. "Ex-cop," Brewster screamed. "Ex—"

He caught the flash out of the corner of his eye and then felt a gentle brush across his throat.

Chapter Twenty-nine

Rita smiled tightly at the security guard in the lobby. "Good morning, Al," she said, feigning a bright demeanor.

The man merely nodded as Rita replaced her badge in her purse. What the hell was wrong with him?

She thought he'd reached for the telephone as soon as she passed, but she told herself to relax. No one knew anything about her. The kidnapping and subsequent rescue had been on the news several times last night, but that didn't mean anyone suspected her. No one knew that she had been involved. All they could think about was wonderful Miss Sable who had come out smelling like a rose again. Every anchor in the city, plus those on the national networks, was painting her a heroine.

The elevator came and she stepped in, shivering slightly when the door closed. She had nothing to worry about. Brewster was the only one she had had any contact with, and he was dead. The whole affair was dead and buried. They couldn't pin anything on her.

She was worried somewhat when they were all kept after work yesterday, but it was just as well that she wasn't at her desk. Those damn losers would probably have tried to call her and someone might have been listening in. Now there was no way she could be connected with last night's farce.

The door opened and she stepped out. Was she wearing a sign "Losers Wanted" around her neck? Lowell, her two husbands, Margolis, and finally Brewster. Didn't this world have any men left?

Rita stopped and her heart skipped a beat. Lennie Carragio was sitting at her desk. She resolutely moved forward again.

"Good morning, Mr. Carragio," she said brightly.

"Mr. Hawks is waiting for you," he said, indicating Miss Sable's office with his head.

A coldness gripped her insides. "Sure," she said. "Let me put my purse down at my desk."

"Go right in, please."

She normally settled herself down at her desk and then made a quick trip to the ladies' room, but something in Carragio's voice put habit out of her mind. She moved to the door and stopped to knock.

"Go right in," Carragio ordered. "He knows you're here."

She opened the door. Hawks was at Miss Sable's desk signing some papers. "Come in and sit down, Miss Kastle," he said without stopping his work.

When she was seated, he looked at her. "I'll get right to the point, Miss Kastle. We know that you were involved in that episode with Dr. Carroll yesterday, and—"

"How dare you!" she exclaimed. "I've a good mind to speak to my lawyers."

He held his hand up and went on. "We also feel that you were involved with the epidemic of security leaks that have plagued this subsidiary for the past few months. An operative of ours saw you copying an unusually large amount of data after hours." He paused. "We have the dates and times if you'd like me to review them with you."

She stared at him for a moment and then shook her head. That jerk Margolis. He wanted everything. No screening.

"So we have some options that we'd like you to consider, Miss Kastle," he said. "You can contact legal counsel and we will enter into criminal proceedings against you. Or you can accept a mutual termination with a year's severance pay."

She stared at him. That couldn't happen to her. These fools! Didn't they know she had protection?

"I want to talk to Mr. Cabot," she insisted.

"This has all been cleared with him, Miss Kastle."

Like hell it had been! She wasn't any stupid fool who would believe anything. "I want to talk to him," she said stiffly. "Damn you. I'm not letting you throw me out with nothing."

"I think a year's severance is rather generous," he replied quietly.

"I've given my life to this company." Her voice quivered. She was close to tears. "Almost thirty years of service, and now I'll have nothing."

He stared at her and did not reply.

Chapter Thirty

"Are you sure you're ready to go back to work?" Nancy asked, opening the door of the limousine.

"I'm fine." Jaylene hurried into the building.

Nancy caught up with her at the elevators. "You know, you were in the hospital."

"I was only in overnight as a precaution, and that was three days ago. I had the whole weekend to recover." And to think. By Saturday morning, she had decided she had misjudged Ray. Surely he wouldn't have been that angry with her if he didn't care.

The elevator doors closed. "You just seem kind of pale, that's all," Nancy pointed out.

"I'm fine." Her anger with him had seemed petty and childish. She had been embarrassed by her actions and had tried to call him, but he hadn't been in his hospital room.

"How's Dr. Carroll coming along?" Nancy asked.

"Just fine, I guess." The doors opened and Jaylene marched down the hall to her office. Judy was sitting at Rita's desk.

"Good morning, Miss Sable," she said brightly, and jumped to her feet. "I hope you're feeling better."

"I'm just fine."

Judy followed her into her office. "I wasn't sure if you'd be back today, so I didn't let you get too booked up. And all those people know they're just tentative."

Jaylene glanced at the paper and put it on her desk. "It looks fine. Thank you, Judy." Actually, she had hoped to be kept too busy to think.

Once Judy left, Nancy looked over the schedule. "At least this will give you time to run over to the hospital and visit the doc."

Jaylene sat down and unloaded her briefcase. "If you mean Dr. Carroll, that would be hard to do. He was released from the hospital yesterday."

"Oh?"

Jaylene looked up at her. "And checked out of his hotel. No doubt to return to Boston."

"Oh."

That was similiar to her own feelings when she had found out. She had been all ready to try to start over, to assume that his anger at her had been a reaction to the stress of the situation, as her anger had been. She had never expected him to leave without a word.

"Hey, I'm real sorry, Jaylene," Nancy said.

Jaylene just shrugged. "It doesn't matter." It wasn't any big deal. She had only been in love with him, that's all. She picked up some papers and paged through them. "On your way out, would you ask Judy to send Neal in? With that light schedule, we can get a lot accomplished today."

"Sure thing." Nancy gave her a strange look, but did as she asked.

Once the door closed behind Nancy, Jaylene did not know whether she was glad to be alone. She hated having to pretend that she hadn't been hurt by Ray's actions, but she also hated being alone with her thoughts.

She had tried to tell herself for the past twenty-four hours that there could be lots of reasons why Ray had left without saying good-bye. Maybe he was anxious to get to New York to see Malcolm and turn in his report. Maybe he was more seriously injured than she knew and wanted to get to his own doctor. Maybe he didn't like feeling beholden to her and wanted to get away.

She stood up and walked to the window. Rose was leaving at the end of the week. She and an old friend named Ben were going to go visit grandchildren together. Then, if they could still stand each other, they would settle down someplace. Sounded like a nice plan. Jaylene wished she had one just as nice.

There was a knock on the door and Neal came in. "You okay, Jaylene?" he asked.

"I'm fine," she snapped, then shook her head as she sat back down. It wasn't his fault she hurt so much. "Really, I'm fine," she said more softly.

Without any appointments to interrupt them, they worked through the morning. Jaylene felt tired but was fairly pleased with their progress. She was not interested in lunch, however, even though Neal kept dropping broad hints. She was about to suggest they cover one more report when Judy buzzed her on the intercom.

"Miss Sable, Dr. Carroll is here to see you."

Jaylene first reaction was shock. She had not expected to see him, certainly not today.

Neal got to his feet. "I'll just go have my lunch now," he said.

"Fine." Jaylene got to her feet, too. What did Ray want? Was it just some final report on the consolidation?

Neal let himself out and Ray in at the same time.

"Hello, Ray," she said. Her voice sounded annoyingly weak.

"Hi."

He looked rather pale and unsure of himself. She indicated the sitting area off to the side. "How are you feeling?"

"Pretty good."

He followed her over to the chairs and waited for her to sit down. She couldn't decided between the sofa or a chair, but finally chose the chair.

"I've got a bit of a headache, but the doctor said it's to be expected."

She nodded, her hands clenched tightly in her lap. "I don't suppose he'd approve of all this traveling, either."

He looked surprised and she felt a blush creep over her cheeks. "I called your hotel yesterday and they told me you had left. I didn't expect you back in town this soon." She hadn't expected him back at all, actually.

"I never left Miami," he said. "Just the hotel. The reporters were getting a little pesty."

"Oh." There was a long silence that made Jaylene nervous. "So how's the report going? Do you have it finished?"

He shrugged. "Pretty much so. I'm scheduled to present it to Malcolm early next week."

"Oh." She frowned. Creative conversation wasn't her strong point today. She cleared her throat. "I heard about Margolis."

He nodded. "One of his pals was behind that whole episode last week."

"Margolis?"

"Oh, I don't think Margolis had anything to do with it personally. He just had this private investigator that he used for some dirty work, and he was the one who wanted to expand his income through the use of TIE's corporate jets."

"You mean Merrill?" she asked. "Yes, Rose told me all about him. Seems she knew him from her former days on the force." She paused. "They found his body on the outskirts of the city."

"Oh?"

"His throat was slit."

Another silence descended on them, and Jaylene was delighted when a knock sounded at the door. Nancy came in.

"Can I get you guys some coffee? Some lunch?"

Jaylene looked over at Ray and he shrugged his shoulders. "Some lunch would be fine. Maybe a sandwich and coffee."

Jaylene shook her head. "Just coffee for me."

Ray frowned at her. "Just coffee? What kind of lunch is that?"

"I'm not very hungry," she told him. "Besides, I had a big breakfast."

"And what was that? A piece of toast with your coffee?"

What had gotten into him? Had he suddenly turned into a dietitian?

He turned to Nancy. "Bring up two lunches. And no coffee for her. Milk."

"Milk?" Jaylene cried, and rose to her feet as she glared at him.

"Sounds like time for me to disappear." Nancy laughed as she left. "See you later, guys."

"Just who the hell do you think you are, coming in here and ordering me around? I can eat what I damn well please."

He got to his feet, also. "Proper nutrition is extremely important for pregnant women, especially high-risk mothers."

"If you're thinking of making another crack about my age, forget it," she warned. "Your doctorate is in economics, not obstetrics."

"You don't need a doctorate in anything to realize you have to eat properly when you're pregnant," he snapped. "Just some common sense."

"So we're back to that subject, are we?"

"It's not my fault you aren't taking proper care of yourself."

"I'll have you know I'm taking excellent care of myself," she informed him. "If this is why you came to see me, to present a lecture on nutrition, you could have saved yourself a trip."

"Well, I didn't, damn it, I came to give you this." He pulled a small box out of his pocket and shoved it into her hand. "I had bought you a box of candy for Valentine's Day, but it got lost along the way. I thought this might be a better idea."

Surprise knocked the anger out of her for a moment as she slowly opened the box. There was a ring inside that looked suspiciously like an engagement ring. She looked up at him, not sure what to say.

Ray looked sheepish. His anger appeared to have disappeared, also. "I was a fool, Jaylene," he said quietly. "Deep down, I'm not really the playboy of the western world. I guess I was just scared by my feelings for you."

She felt behind her for her chair, and slowly sat down again. She put the ring and the box on the table in front of her. She wanted to make sure she understood all of this completely.

"I thought we went through this before," she pointed out.

"No," he corrected and sat down, also. "I acted like an

ass and offered you the protection of my name before. I was not exactly suggesting a real marriage."

Jaylene's hands were tightly clutching the arms of the chair. She loved him; she wanted to marry him. But she wanted her idea of marriage, not his semipermanent, non-restrictive kind.

She needed to get everything out in the open. "I know that I may seem like the perfect liberated woman of the eighties, great career and really in charge of my life. But, actually, I'm just an old-fashioned girl at heart. My idea of marriage is love and trust and faithfulness."

He nodded. "That's mine, too. You might not believe it from some of the things I've said, but I've been running from commitment for so many years now that it was hard to shake the habit." He grimaced slightly. "I've been told recently that it's because my mother died when I was three. Maybe it's true. I don't know. All I know is that no matter how much I ran, I couldn't get away from you."

She frowned at him. "That's terribly romantic."

"Hell." He rubbed his forehead with his hand. "I'm doing this all wrong, aren't I?"

He got to his feet and came over to her, then knelt down on one knee. "Jaylene, I love you very much. Will you marry me?"

She bit her lip and looked at him for a long moment. "Are you sure, Ray?" she whispered. "You're not just doing this because you feel like you have to, are you?"

"No, I'm not doing it for any reason other than that I want to marry you," he said impatiently. "Now, will you answer the question before my leg goes to sleep? You may be a very young mother-to-be, but the father-to-be is rather elderly."

She laughed and cried at the same time as she threw her arms around him. "We can't have that, can we?" she said. "In spite of your old age, I love you, too, and would be delighted to marry you."

She felt Ray's arms encircle her. "Your injury hasn't hurt your arms any."

"I've kept some other parts safe, too," he whispered.

There was a rap on the door and they drew slightly away

from each other. Nancy stepped in with a tray of food. "Uh, hi, guys." She looked from Jaylene to Ray and uncertainty seemed to cloud her face. "You guys want me to guard the door for a while?"

"No, that's okay," Jaylene said. Then, indicating Ray still on his bended knee, she said, "Ray's just asked me to marry him."

Nancy looked down at Ray and her smile brightened again. "Oh, yeah, that's the way guys used to do it," she said. "That's kind of cute."

"Many men still do it this way," Ray grumbled, and got stiffly to his feet.

"Oh yeah?" Nancy turned to Jaylene. "So what'd you say?"

"She said yes," Ray answered.

Jaylene nodded her agreement. Nancy squealed in delight, put down the tray, and rushed over to hug Jaylene. "I guess it was safe to bring you milk then," she said.

Jaylene glared at Ray. "This once, yes. But I do not intend to be bossed around for the rest of my life."

"Oops, sounds like time to leave again," Nancy said, grinning. "Don't worry about the food. I just got cold sandwiches, so there's no hurry getting to them."

When she was gone, Ray pulled Jaylene up to her feet. "What do you say we move over to the sofa where we'll be more comfortable?"

"If that's a request and not an order, I'd be happy to," she said.

They fell into each other's arms before they made it to the sofa, but somehow they found their way there. It was wonderful to be in his embrace again. They had been apart for so long, she just couldn't get close enough.

His mouth came down on hers and she lost herself in sweet surrender to her love. Her hands moved over his back, feeling the muscles that held her so tightly. She wished they were back at her place so that they could welcome each other home properly.

Ray pulled back slightly. "Do you have any idea how terrified I was when you showed up in that field? I kept imagining them killing you and knew that it would be all my fault."

"Your fault?" she asked. "You were kidnapped because of your relationship to me, remember?"

"But I didn't have to be. I thought those two guys at the airport were strange, but I didn't want to say anything. I thought they weren't quite up to TIE standards, but instead of rocking the boat, I just went along with them."

"That hardly makes you responsible," she argued. "Besides, knowing Josef, he probably just would have panicked and taken you at gunpoint or even shot you there." She buried her head into his shoulder.

"Well, I have to admit the guy did give me hope, though," Ray admitted and grinned at her astonished look. "I hoped that your aversion to marriage was because of your experiences with him, not your feelings for me."

She laughed and kissed him gently. His lips wanted to linger on hers, but she pulled away. "Actually, I'm not averse to marriage. Just marriage without love. And I was pretty sure that was what you were offering."

"I don't think I knew what I was offering," he said. "But I couldn't believe it when you refused me. Lucky thing I phrased it better this time."

"Somewhat better, but not a great deal," she told him.

"My greatness lies in other areas," he teased, and proceeded to arouse her passionate longings with just the placement of his lips on her neck. "How well do you think Nancy is guarding that door?"

The ringing of her phone answered for her. "Not well enough," she sighed, knowing she had to answer it but not wanting to move.

"Let it ring." His hands unbuttoned the top few buttons of her blouse and his lips explored the new territory.

"I can't," she argued weakly, and sat up. "I think it's my direct line. I have some ideas to use on Jesse, and refusing to answer his calls might definitely hamper their effectiveness."

His hands did not want to release her. "My ideas will simplify a lot of our location problems," she added. He released her reluctantly and she got the phone.

"Where the devil were you?" Jesse asked. "I thought you'd had a relapse or something."

"There wasn't ever anything the matter with me to have a relapse of," she pointed out. "But I'm glad you called. Did you read Hawks's full report on last week's incident?"

"Yes, of course I did, and that was a damn-fool stunt you pulled. If you have such liking for danger, maybe you ought to join the police force when you leave TIE."

She smiled over at Ray as she spoke into the phone. "Actually, that's one of the things I wanted to talk to you about."

"Oh?"

"Did you read the part of the report about Rita?"

"Yes, and that was—"

She interrupted him. "You remember her, the one I wanted to get rid of but wasn't allowed to and who, because of her trusted position by other TIE officers, was in a position to provide the kidnappers with necessary information. And, if rumor is correct, only facing dismissal with a year's pay."

"Get to the point," Jesse said sharply.

Her smile increased. "I just think you owe me one."

"Yes," he agreed cautiously.

Ray got up and went over to the lunch tray. It was good to have him back, she thought, but turned her mind back to Jesse. "I was also giving our relationship a great deal of thought. Now, I'll admit that I couldn't have gotten where I am without your help, but I also helped you get where you are."

"I never said you didn't." Jesse's voice was suspicious.

"But I know you haven't quite reached your goal yet. You want Malcolm's chair when he retires."

"I've made no secret of that."

"Yes, but to get it, you're going to need the best financial person behind you."

"Don't tell me who that is, I can guess." Jesse had a laugh in his voice.

"After working with me all these years, you shouldn't have to guess," Jaylene pointed out. "I'm the best and you know it. I want to stay on with TIE as a part-time financial

consultant with a computer terminal so I can work out of
my home."

Ray suddenly was over at the desk with a glass of milk.
He put it down in front of her with a smile. She glared at
him.

"Damn it, Jaylene, there are other problems that we discussed," he pointed out. "If it was just my decision, I'd hire
you in a minute. I know it's going to be damn hard to get to
be CEO without your expertise, but what the hell do you
expect me to do? My balls are between a rock and a hard
place. If I back you, I could be putting my own career at
risk."

"Why? I've got great credentials, and with you and Malcolm behind me—"

"Hold it right there," Jesse said. "Malcolm's an original
Puritan father. Your little trek into motherhood is not
going to sit well with him."

"Would he rather have it known that his brother's
former mistress was involved in a kidnapping plot? That
she was kept on at TIE in spite of the objections of the people who had to deal with her? And that she was just losing
her job instead of facing criminal charges?"

There was a long silence at the other end of the phone,
and Jaylene worried that perhaps she had gone a bit too
far. Everything she said was true, but Jesse knew her well
enough to know that she wouldn't leak anything to the
press about Rita. Suddenly, she heard a low, deep chuckle
at the other end, building slowly into real laughter.

"Damn it, Jaylene. I'm lucky you're not a man or you'd
be giving me a run for the money for that CEO spot."

"No, you're lucky I don't want it yet," she pointed out
with a smile.

"Okay, kid, you've got the consultant position. I'm not
sure how I'll pull it off, but I will."

"It won't be that hard," she assured him. "I'm damn
good at my job."

"That you are, kid, that you are."

"Oh, and Jesse?"

"Yeah?" He sounded suspicious.

"Is it okay if I take a few weeks off for a honeymoon at the end of the month?"

"A honeymoon?" He was definitely in shock, and she smiled.

"Thanks a lot. Talk to you soon." She hung up her phone. Ray was sitting on the edge of her desk and reached for her hand to pull her close to him.

"So we're getting married at the end of the month, are we?" he asked, enclosing her in his embrace for a kiss. "Maybe you'd better be my nurse this afternoon, then."

"Your nurse?"

He grinned. "Well, the doctor told me to get plenty of bed rest, and the early afternoon is the traditional nap-time . . ."

She laughed and reached over for her intercom button. "Judy, Dr. Carroll and I are having lunch out. Will that pose a problem with my schedule?"

"No, Miss Sable. Mr. Fielding's scheduled for one-thirty, but I'll call and tell him he's been moved to four. You'll be free until three, if that's all right."

"Perfect." She released the button and looked at Ray. "Well, doctor, shall we go?"

He shook his head. "Not until you finish your milk."

"Ray!" she protested.

He handed her the glass. "I thought all you little kids liked milk."

She made a face, but drained the glass. "I'll get you for this."

He took the empty glass from her and kissed her milky lips quickly. "I love you."

**Now an Operation Prime Time
Television mini series starring
Deborah Kerr and Jenny Seagrove**

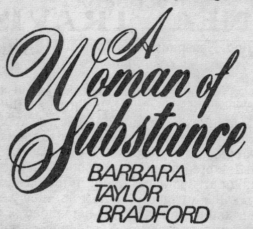

A
Woman of
Substance

BARBARA
TAYLOR
BRADFORD

THE IRRESISTIBLE NATIONWIDE BESTSELLER.
Set against the sweep of 20th-century history, it
tells the compelling story of Emma Harte, who rises
from servant girl to become an international corporate
power and one of the richest women in the world.

"A long, satisfying novel of money and power,
passion and revenge." *Los Angeles Times*

"A wonderfully entertaining novel."
The Denver Post

49163-X/$3.95

An **AVON** Paperback

A FAREWELL TO FRANCE
Noel Barber

"Exciting...suspenseful...Masterful Storytelling"
Washington Post

As war gathered to destroy their world, they
promised to love each other forever, though
their families were forced to become enemies.
He was the French-American heir to the famous
champagne vineyards of Chateau Douzy. She
was the breathtakingly sensuous daughter of
Italian aristocracy. Caught in the onslaught
of war's intrigues and horrors, they were
separated by the sacrifices demanded of them
by family and nation. Yet they were bound
across time and tragedy by a pledge sworn in
the passion of young love, when a beautiful
world seemed theirs forever.

"Involving and realistic...A journey to which
it's hard to say farewell...The backdrop of
World War II adds excitement and suspense."
Detroit News

An **AVON** Paperback   68064-5/$3.95